Family

Connections

Sequel to Connecting Hearts

by Val Brown and M.J. Walker

ISBN   0-9744121-4-7
First Printing 2003
Cover art and design by Anne M. Clarkson

Published by:
Dare 2 Dream Publishing
A Division of Limitless Corporation
Lexington, South Carolina 29073

Find us on the World Wide Web
http://www.limitlessd2d.net

Printed in the United States of America

Acknowledgements

We would like to thank Jane Wageman for her expertise in Neurology and knowledge of ALS and Monica Croatti for her insights and information. We also want to tell Di Bauden how much we appreciate her writing the foreword for the book.

No thank you would be complete without mentioning the team at Limitless. You've done much more than transfer our words to the printed page and we are grateful.

Special Notation

Please note that our authors are international. You may see spellings and some words that are unfamiliar to you. These words are not spelled incorrectly but, rather, represent the national spelling of the writer. We at **D2D** encourage international authors to submit their manuscripts to us and have elected to leave them in their original format so that you may enjoy the international flavor as much as we do.

<u>Foreword</u>

ALS, Amyotrophic Lateral Sclerosis, Lou Gehrig's Disease, or Motor Neuron Disease; depending on where you live the terminology will change describing this fatal neuromuscular disease. No matter which label or name it falls under, the properties of this illness are all the same and hit home all too hard. ALS has affected my family three times in my 35 years. Once, with my grandmother, once with my aunt, and finally again with my mother. More times than any one family should ever experience. What is ALS? It is a silent predator that slowly steals its victim's abilities to walk, talk, move, eat and eventually breathe. No known cure has been found to treat ALS as of today. Researchers are testing many new trials to find and stop this horrific illness. Stem cell research is one of the more promising possibilities for ALS patients. Stem cells could very well develop into new nerve cells, which would replace or restore the damaged neurons in afflicted ALS victims. Many tests still have to be done before this treatment can be performed on those with ALS, but it is one of the more hopeful research developments to date. Until successful treatments can be found, my family will hold tight and pray that ALS doesn't affect any more of us. One thing that I have learned with this disease is that it absolutely doesn't care who it affects. It used to be Lou Gehrig's disease, but in all actuality, it's anyone's disease.

For more information or to make a donation to help the researchers along, please go to www.projectals.org.

--Diane S. Bauden

Love, Unscheduled

One day you're standing, alone in the rain;
A feeling you've learned to accept.
Then you hear somebody whisper your name:
A stranger you're heart swears you've met.
It's not in your date book.
You know it's not wise.
But you feel yourself falling,
Right into those eyes.
Before your heart
Can tuck and roll,
You're face to face -
With the rest of your soul.
"Where in the world do we go from here?"
The brain kicks in again.
But, soulmates will know that wherever it is,
It's better than where they have been.
So, next time you're standing out there in the rain,
It will be in the arms of your love.
Enjoying the warmth, two halves of a soul,
Eternal, like heavens above.

Sam Ruskin

Chapter 1

Mid-June in northern California was spectacular this time of year. The days were hot but hadn't yet reached into the blistering 100's that were known to show up frequently in the town of Silver Valley. Later than normal spring storms had kept the snowpack intact longer in the Sierra Nevada Mountains and the great valley of California had not yet changed from green to summer brown. The golden poppies had bloomed exactly as Randa Martin had hoped when she scattered the seeds on the hill in back of her farmhouse a little over two months earlier. Now the landscape was a riot of color showing off the California state flower in all its beauty.

The petite blonde wandered out her back door and stood on the porch looking around her with satisfaction. Attractive camellia bushes were rife with blossoms and newly planted pines were thriving. The small vegetable and herb garden was already providing fresh produce for her table and the yard was neatly manicured. The crowning glory to the scene though was a single perfect English rose.

An English rose by the name of Denise Jennings Randa thought. As if on cue a tanned arm showed itself from the depths of a large freestanding hammock, situated under the shade of a statuesque oak tree, in her backyard. An equally tanned hand curled palm upward and the index finger moved rhythmically in a beckoning manner.

Randa laughed and walked to the hammock where a very contented Denise Jennings swayed in the light summer breeze. Randa was struck yet again at the sheer loveliness of her lover and partner. The tall firm body, black hair and magnificent blue eyes were a combination that would always cause the blonde's heart to beat just a little faster.

"Nurse Martin! Nurse Martin!" Denise's voice cut through Randa's assessment and she locked gazes with the woman who had come to be her whole world in the space of less than a year. Denise made her voice faint and pitiful. "Nurse Martin, I believe I have become frightfully dehydrated in your absence. I thought you were just going inside to get some water."

Randa rolled her eyes and chuckled, "Oh, brother! That's laying it on a bit thick don't you think?" She held up one of the bottles of water, she had been carrying, and announced to an imaginary crowd, "And the award for best performance by a poet in a hammock goes to…Denise Jennings!" She reached out to award the bottle to Denise and shrieked as she found her arm grabbed and her body hauled into the hammock where she ended up nose to nose with the dark haired beauty.

Denise smiled into Randa's eyes and said, "I'd like to thank all the little people who made this award possible." Tilting her head slightly she was able to bring her lips to the waiting ones of the nurse. Both women sighed as their soft exchange ended. "Thank you, little person," Denise murmured.

Randa smiled. "You'll pay for that 'little' remark later; remind me in case I forget." Now it was Denise's turn to laugh as she wrapped her arm around the blonde and drew her closer.

"Do I still have to pay if I tell you I wasn't thirsty for water but for your company? There is nothing lonelier than a two-person hammock with only one person in it. What kept you anyway?"

"I got the water and put on a little extra sun block because some of us don't tan up to the color of an English walnut," she grinned, "but on the way back I had to stop and look around here for a minute. This place is gorgeous and most of it's because of you. You really have a green thumb you know."

"Yeah, it was one of the things I got from Sara." Both women were silent for a moment as they were caught up in individual memories of Denise's wonderful aunt who had passed away in March from Amyotrophic Lateral Sclerosis. Her illness had brought Randa and Denise together and her death had nearly split them apart. Their love had survived the storm though and they had ended up together just as Sara had hoped.

"I still miss her," Randa said quietly.

"Me, too," returned the poet. "It gets easier all the time though to think of her and only remember the good and happy times. You've helped me do that, helped me to keep her memory alive without all the pain I had after she died." Denise deposited a warm kiss on Randa's forehead and looked lovingly into her bright green eyes.

"It's my distinct pleasure, Ms. Jennings"

"Not yet but definitely later, Ms. Martin." A small gust blew up and rocked the hammock gently and the women relished the feeling of gentle movement and holding on to one another. They had only been living together a little over two months and things had progressed relatively smoothly. There were the usual adjustments to be made when any two people started sharing the same living space. Denise was a 'roll the tube of toothpaste up from the bottom' kind of person and Randa preferred to squeeze it in the middle.

Randa wasn't sure what made living with Denise the relatively easy thing it had been. That they were deeply and totally in love wasn't even a question. The nurse thought it was more likely the fact they were friends before the romance happened and nothing that had happened since then had changed that fact. *We have so much more between us than just sex,* the nurse thought. *Not that the sex isn't great, mind you.*

Randa snuggled deeper into DJ's embrace as the flower scented breeze moved the hammock gently again. The contentment that welled up in her soul was spoiled only by a thought that had been plaguing her for weeks. Her brows scrunched together in irritation.

"Stop it," Denise said. Her voice caused a pleasant burr in the chest Randa had her head on.

"Stop what?" Randa returned.

"You know what. You're thinking about it again."

"Was not."

"Yes, you were. I can always tell. First your eyebrows scrunch up, then your whole body becomes tense and finally you get a death grip on me if I'm anywhere in your general vicinity," Denise explained. She looked down meaningfully at the nurse's arm that had been casually draped across her middle and was now doing a pretty good imitation of a vise-grip.

"Sorry," Randa squeaked and loosened her hold on the taller woman. "I'm not sure why this is bugging me so much. It didn't bug you, did it?"

"Nope. It was just another day. Maybe you should stop thinking of it as June 29th, another day that will live in infamy."

"Maybe," Randa said but sounded doubtful.

"Maybe you should think about something else entirely," the poet purred.

"Any suggestions?"

"Plenty," Denise mumbled as she moved her head to begin a delicious nibbling of the nurse's earlobe. Randa gave herself over to the wonderful sensations created by her partner and resolved to not think about it for the rest of the afternoon. *Not going to think about it at all, not a single thought.*

"You're doing it again," Denise laughed and soon had the nurse laughing with her. Then the poet returned her attention to the neglected earlobe and Randa was able to forget, at least for a little while, that she was about to turn thirty.

****

It was a little later in the afternoon that Denise found herself once again alone in the comfortable hammock. Lying with legs crossed at the ankles and hands behind her head she looked up into the low branches of the large oak tree. The blinding rays of the sun shone down through littered gaps in the trees branches. She moved her head

4

from side to side, watching as the sun would disappear from one breach only to appear from behind the thick wooden stem of another. The sheer brightness of the glowing orb made her wish she had remembered to bring her sunglasses out with her. Closing her eyes, DJ settled herself further into the gentle swing of the hammock.

Thinking back over the past couple of months DJ couldn't believe the changes that had occurred. Everything, she once held a great importance in remaining constant in her life, had changed. Sara was gone, she was presently living in the United States and what was more – she was soon to lose the anonymity she had held sacred for most of her life. Denise thought she should feel a certain amount of apprehension at the notion but surprisingly enough there was none. For the first time the possibilities of the future didn't seem so daunting and the poet thought she knew the reasons why. Maybe it was Sara's words that she still kept folded in her wallet or maybe it was Randa but the fact remained that for the first time she actually looked forward to her future – to their future.

At the beginning of July her new anthology of poetry was to finally be released. That meant she would be travelling back to England. The date had been pushed back so it would coincide with the announcement of the pending release of DJ's first novel under her full name. Carl had planned it so she could make the announcement at the first publicity gathering. Denise planned to leave for England the day after Randa's birthday. She couldn't help but be slightly amused by Randa's reactions to the fast approaching day. She seemed to regard her thirtieth as her own inevitable apocalypse. *Still* the poet thought, *lets hope the day I have planned for her will make her wonder what all the fuss was about.* Denise smiled because she knew Randa had no idea about her plans; she wanted them to be a surprise.

Opening cerulean eyes DJ squinted as the sun's light assaulted her sight. A tickling built within her nose before she sneezed violently causing the hammock to sway perilously side to side. When the movement eased Denise held one hand in front of her eyes as she swung her body around and placed her bare feet upon the grassy earth. Pushing to her full height the poet adjusted her shorts and tee shirt before moving back towards the house. Randa had disappeared some time ago and she was beginning to wonder what her lover was up to.

Living with Randa had proved to be an experience in itself. She soon discovered that the blonde had been on her best behaviour while staying with the Jennings women. It wasn't until she arrived in the US that Randa's little idiosyncrasies and bad habits began to show through. Denise thought she should be annoyed by Randa's continuous ability to squeeze toothpaste from the middle of the tube. She thought she would be horrified by Randa's consistency in disposing of her day's clothing upon the floor and not to do the laundry until the basket was literally begging for reprieve. In any other case she would have been shaking her head in disapproval at Randa's bulk buying of 'Dr Pepper' and trying to load the shopping trolley with convenience foods. But with Randa she found all these traits endearing. They made up the woman she was happy to spend the rest of her life with and she loved it. She loved following the blonde through their bedroom picking up her clothing and thought it was fun to remove and put back the convenience foods Randa often attempted to hide in their shopping trolley.

Stepping up onto the back porch, Denise walked into an open plan kitchen. The cool linoleum floor was a welcome relief from the sun-heated ground. With furrowed brows Denise padded through the kitchen, dining room and on into the living room looking for Randa. Nothing. Then from the corner of her eye she spotted a single tennis shoe lying upon the floor. Searching further she noticed a second shoe by the entrance to their bedroom. With a smirk DJ bent down and picked up the navy shoe as she headed towards the bedroom. Her smirk turned into a full-fledged grin as she detected a trail of clothing heading towards the en-suite bathroom. The sound of the shower reverberated around the room and her grin turned into a chuckle as she heard Randa's happy singing voice suddenly echo over the noise of the shower. Picking up the rest of the clothing and

6

depositing them in the laundry basket, Denise trotted over to the bathroom and peeked around the door. She saw Randa through the clear glass of the cubical, her head thrown back under the spray of hot water and singing a non-descript tune that DJ was sure she was making up as she went along.

Amused as each flat, out of tune lyric passed the nurse's lips, DJ felt her evil streak come into play – again! She had caught Randa in the shower only last week and had played another trick on the unsuspecting blonde. Thanks to her height and long reach she had stood next to the wall by the shower with an extra bottle of shampoo in her grasp. She had reached over the cubical door and poured a steady stream of the bright blue liquid upon the nurse's head. DJ remembered how long it had taken before Randa realised she was having difficulty washing the suds from her hair and then the delight she took in pretending to get caught just so the miffed nurse would pull her into the shower!

With a snigger, Denise slid through the door deciding, this time, to go for the oldest trick in the book. Reaching out towards a white porcelain sink she wrapped her hand around the hot tap before swiftly turning it on. Bracing herself, Denise didn't have to wait long before Randa shrieked and backed away from the spray of now freezing water, staring accusingly at Denise.

"Jeez… oh my god!" Randa exclaimed.

DJ smiled innocently as she said, "I think your shrieking is more in tune than your singing! Was that soprano?"

Randa narrowed her eyes as she turned off the water. Denise picked up a large white towel and handed it to the nurse as she stepped out of the shower. Randa remained quiet and the poet began to get a little nervous. *So much for me thinking we would get a repeat performance of last week's shower scene!*

"Randa?"

The nurse blinked.

"Umm…" Denise recognised her lover's 'look' and instantly got the feeling Randa was planning her vengeance. "Sorry?" she said weakly knowing she had just backed herself into a corner with 'she of infinite patience'.

"Please just get it over with now. I don't think I can stand the waiting."

Securing the bath towel around her body, Randa arched her eyebrows. "But that's the best part. Don't worry... when you least expect it... you'll get what's coming to you."

"Oh! Well... can I get what's coming to me now?" Denise asked lasciviously.

"Now?" Randa repeated as she loosened the towel and let it drop to the floor. Stepping forward she sidled her body towards DJ and took the poet's hands, placing them upon her hips.

"Hmm," the dark haired woman purred, "this is more like it."

"Oh yeah!" Randa hummed as she brought her lips to DJ's neck placing teasing kisses along the poet's flesh. All the while her left hand discreetly reached out until she located the cold-water tap. With practised skill and precision she turned on the water then placed her hand directly under the stream causing the cold water to spurt through the air and drench the poet's head and shoulders.

With a shocked splutter DJ backed away surprised. "Hey!"

Randa shrugged. "I thought you needed to cool down a little," she laughed.

"Oh funny!" DJ whined, shaking out her wet tresses.

"So..." Denise frowned, "why are you having a shower at this time of the day anyway?"

"Derek called and asked me to cover a shift on the site in about half an hour so I thought I would freshen up a little." Randa ran a hand through her saturated locks and shivered as droplets of cool water ran down her neck.

"Cold? Want some warming up?"

"I don't think we have time for the kind of warming up you have in mind!"

The poet pouted as she said, "I can do quick!"

Randa's expression changed to a look of disbelief. "Says she who takes her time to even unwrap a chocolate!"

"That's only because I have to savour every single moment of it. My supply is running low again and if I ring Carl to send me some more he'll start whingeing about wanting me to go back to England sooner. He can wait until the beginning of July like everybody else. I am taking a long overdue holiday. Besides it's not like I haven't been working while I've been here."

That fact was certainly true. For the poet – what had started out as a simple jot down of ideas for her new novel had turned into the desire to bring that tale to life. She had spent between five and six hours a day writing and because she didn't have her own computer, nor did she remember to bring her lap-top she had to find time to write when Randa wasn't herself working on the Brightwood information site.

"Well I can't stand around here all day. I now only have twenty minutes until I need to log on." Passing Denise, Randa slapped the poet's behind. "Are you making dinner tonight?"

"Whatever you desire," DJ paused a beat, "as long as I don't have to pull it out of the freezer."

Randa rolled her eyes as she stepped into the bedroom. Looking around she held out her arms in confusion. "Where are my clothes?"

"How about some good old traditional home cooking?"

Heading towards the laundry basket Randa looked back at her lover briefly, "Sounds okay by me." She lifted its lid and found her discarded clothes in the bottom of the basket. With a shake of her head Randa replaced the lid and crossed over to the chest of drawers. She pulled out a clean pair of white shorts and a green crop top.

"How about stew and dumplings?" Denise headed for the bedroom door, her eyes fixed upon Randa's naked form. "Yummy!"

"Well it seems as though you like the idea," replied the nurse as she slipped into her shorts.

"Oh I don't know," DJ leered, "Who said I was referring to the dinner?" Meeting Randa's gaze she winked before darting out of the bedroom.

****

9

It was past midnight and, with the absence of sun, the land was cast in total darkness. The distant nocturnal sounds of evening predators echoed over the hills. Sitting upon the top step of the back porch, DJ looked out ahead. With the only source of light coming from the kitchen behind her Denise was only able to see a mere couple of feet ahead. Resting one arm upon her knees she held a chilled can of Randa's much loved 'Diet Dr Pepper' in her free hand.

The air changed as a cool, gentle breeze caressed her flesh and DJ heard more than saw the rustle of the oak and peach trees. She acknowledged this was her favourite time of the evening. When the shroud of darkness enveloped the land and its calming influence seeped into her soul, clearing her mind of all doubt and worry.

Behind her DJ heard the recognisable sound of soft approaching footsteps. She smiled in the semi darkness of the porch and waited for her lover to approach. Randa always knew where to find her at this time of the night.

The footsteps drew closer.

"Hey."

Denise instinctively opened her legs as Randa stepped around her and took a seat on the lower step between the poet's limbs.

"How was it?" she asked.

"Ugh…" Randa let her head fall back against Denise's chest. "Busy. Lots of genuine people plus one guy who decided to make a pain of himself. Seems he thought it would be funny to log on just to ask what colour 'scrubs' I was wearing."

DJ chucked, forcing the blonde to lightly slap her thigh. "It's not funny, Miss Jennings. God I need a drink."

As if on cue Denise brought the can of Dr Pepper into Randa's line of sight. "Here you go."

"You're drinking this now?"

"No." Denise smiled. "I brought it out for you. I knew you would want one when you finished your shift."

Randa twisted her body and looked up at DJ. "More like you swiped if from the fridge so you could roll it over

10

your forehead and cool your heated brow."

DJ stared down at her lover's dimly lit features trying to maintain an expression of annoyance. "Damn it, will you stop reading my mind?"

The nurse smirked as she turned back and settled into Denise's embrace. Placing her finger under the tab Randa opened the can. She jumped unexpectedly as a spurt of the fizzy soft drink speckled her neck, chin and shoulders. "What the…!"

Wiping a single droplet of Dr Pepper from her cheek, Denise blinked and tried valiantly to keep her composure but her body shook with silent laughter.

"You did that!"

"I would never," she chuckled

"Why don't I believe you?" Randa questioned as she took a leisurely drink, trying to maintain her dignity. She began wiping the stray droplets from her cheek.

Denise smiled. "Actually I didn't… but I wish I did because that was funny. Of course there is also a plus side to this."

"And that would be?"

"This." DJ bent her head and moved her lips over Randa's shoulders. They parted as her tongue reached out and swept across the sweet droplets, removing them from her lover's flesh."

"Oh yeah," Randa hummed, "works every time."

"What does?" Denise mumbled as her soft licks travelled up the nurse's neck.

"Well if you didn't shake the can then who did?"

Denise paused.

"Just a little discreet shake… a little squirt … and hmmm heaven!"

The poet reached forward placing her fingertips upon the side of Randa's chin and re-directing her gaze. "You sneaky little bugger!"

The nurse waggled her brows and laughed as she turned back and once again settled herself into DJ's embrace.

A comfortable silence flowed over them and Denise tightened her arms around Randa. She closed her eyes and buried her nose into the blonde's fragrant locks. DJ realised she was wrong before; **this** was her favourite time. Dwelling in the ebony veil of tranquillity with Randa securely wrapped within her embrace.

Randa's voice broke the calm. "How are you feeling about the book launch when you go back to England? Was Carl kidding when he said the press was going to be there?"

"No, he wasn't kidding," Denise sighed. "As for how I feel... I'm not sure. I feel a little ambivalent."

"Yeah?"

"Hmm. I'm a little nervous as to what will happen, how it will be received and the reaction to my... dedication. But at the same time, I can't wait."

Placing her can down upon the wooden steps Randa wrapped her arms across DJ's, hooking their fingers together. "I know what you mean. I get these flutters of nervousness in my stomach every time I think about it and about people's reactions to you and me. I'm scared for you, Denise. In this world I am one of the nobodies; the nameless face in the crowd. But you... you're the face they've all been waiting to see. You're the one behind the words, the thoughts and the emotions. I don't want them to judge you for anything other than the soul I fell in love with."

DJ frowned as she placed a kiss upon Randa's head. "First of all you are not one of the nameless faces in the crowd, Randa. You are everything. You are **my** everything and you make all of this possible. You make me possible." Denise looked up into the star specked sky. "Look up there. Look at all the stars and pick just one."

Randa did as bade. "Okay?"

"That single star that you have chosen... that is me... but all of those other stars in the sky Randa are you. You are my world, my existence. You give everything around me the beauty, grandeur and completeness of unity that makes up the universe. Do you understand?" At Randa's silent nod Denise continued. "As for everything else... we will just have to wait and see. I'm not afraid of what people think of me any more, Randa. All that matters to me is you."

12

The body in front of her shuffled and then Randa turned around, balancing on her knees as she stared at the poet with a smile. "How do you always know what to say to make me feel better?"

DJ shrugged shyly. "I just tell you how I feel."

"Well please don't ever stop!"

"Never." Denise replied as she bent forwards, sealing her lips with Randa's. Pushing to her feet, the blonde nurse still within her grasp, DJ moved from the back porch carrying Randa into the house. As the back door clicked shut and the kitchen light was extinguished they rendered the night to its comforting darkness and nocturnal predators.

Chapter 2

Just another half an hour and Randa had a date with an English poet, a cold Corona and a hammock. The nurse sat back from the computer and contemplated exactly what form of reward her cooperation with Derek should take. The Webmaster of the Brightwood Information Network had called early in the morning begging Randa to take the eight-hour day shift scheduled to begin in less than an hour. The nurse had just finished her own shift at eleven o'clock the previous night and doubling back was something she hadn't had to do since she quit working in the hospital, but she knew how Derek had juggled schedules when she needed time off so she acquiesced. She acquiesced, but not without the promise of a reward. *I'm thinking San Francisco Ballet tickets here* she mused during a lull on an otherwise fairly busy Friday afternoon.

Derek wouldn't mind the request for ballet tickets and in reality he would probably get them for her for nothing if she asked. He had always been Randa's best friend though now he and Denise had become thick as thieves. Randa smiled at the memory of the day she told him about Denise; who she was and who she would be in her life. Derek had arrived unannounced, as usual, at Randa's house only three days after Denise's arrival in the States. The two women had been in the living room enjoying each other's company- a lot. Derek had breezed right in through the front door, went wide eyed and breezed right back out. After hastily re-arranging her clothing Randa found him on the front porch grinning like an idiot.

"Wow, Randa, I didn't know there was local talent like that. Maybe I should move out of the big city and start checking out the small towns. And here I was thinking you were going to save yourself for that poet you had the hots for."

Randa opened her mouth to speak as Denise pushed open the screen door and joined her. "I wouldn't exactly say I'm local talent," said Denise, her English accent flowing over the words like honey. "More like a souvenir she picked up in her travels."

Randa laughed as the poet stood beside her and wrapped a loving arm around her shoulder. "Derek, this is Denise Jennings. You know, D Jennings, the poet?" Derek's jaw dropped and he was unable to summon a sensible word to his lips. "Denise, this rather mute person is Derek, my best friend and sometime boss. Enjoy the silence, it won't last long."

Derek recovered enough then to demand the whole story from Randa. By the end of his visit he had extracted the tale from them and they had extracted the promise of a warning phone call on future visits in return. As Randa walked Derek to his car he turned to her and a serious look crossed his face.

"So you're sure about this? You're really happy?"

"Derek, do you remember last year when I told you that when I found the right person for me it would be happily ever after?" At his nod she continued, "This is happily ever after."

"If that's how you feel then I suppose I could learn to love tall, dark and literate too. I guess there's only one question left to ask."

"And that would be?"

He sighed dreamily and asked, "Does she have a brother?"

Randa was roused from the memory as the object of her thoughts wandered through the living room just then and stopped behind the nurse. The poet leaned over, placed a soft kiss to the blonde's neck and said "Mail," before heading out the front door. The old gray mailbox stood at the end of the dirt driveway to Randa's property and the two women split the chore of picking up the day's offerings from the post office. The nurse's attention was drawn back

15

to the computer screen and away from the front window where she had been admiring the way Denise's long legs looked as she sauntered to the mailbox in denim cutoffs. The computer voice announced "one in from the waiting room," which was the way a nurse knew she had a consultation pending.

Randa saw the username Megan appear on the chat room screen. **Welcome to the Brightwood Information Network. I'm Miranda Martin, RN. How can I help you Megan?**

Hi.

Hello, Megan, what can I do for you? Randa was accustomed to new users of the network needing some assistance in getting their questions asked as well as answered.

My name isn't really Megan but my Mom said I should never tell anyone my real name on the computer. Megan is my sister's name. Is that okay?

Randa had to smile. **That's very okay. How old are you Megan?**

10 and a half. How old are you?

Randa laughed softly. *Boy, kids sure are direct.* For a moment she considered shaving a few years off her age but decided she could be truthful with a ten year old. **Almost thirty** she typed.

Are you really a nurse?

I sure am, Megan. Did you want to ask me a question? Randa's curiosity was getting the best of her now.

What happened was the other day my Mom and Dad were fighting and I was listening to them but they didn't know it and I heard them talking about Uncle Danny and they said he was sick.

Randa read the sentence and pieced together the scenario. **Your Uncle Danny is sick? Did they say what the problem is?**

They said he had HIV. Is that bad sick? My Dad said he doesn't want Uncle Danny to come over anymore. I want Uncle Danny to come over. He takes me and Megan to get ice cream and he lets us pick which kind.

He knows magic and could pull a quarter out of your ear.
He does that all the time and he lets us play with his
Nintendo and Roscoe who is his dog. I don't want Uncle
Danny to be sick.

Randa's heart broke as she realized just how cruel the
world could be in allowing a ten year old to deal with a
problem as big as this. She thought about it for a moment
and decided to continue being honest with the child.

Do you know what HIV is?

Sort of.

Megan, your Uncle Danny has a pretty tough
problem. He has a disease that makes it hard for him
not to get sick. Have you ever had an earache or a sore
throat?

Yeah.

Well those kinds of things are called infections and
your Uncle Danny would have a difficult time fighting
them because of this disease, but there are medicines
that can help him not be so sick. He can feel good and
be around for a long time so he can keep taking you and
your sister out for ice cream.

What about what my Dad said? I told my sister what
Dad said last night and she cried. Why can't Uncle
Danny come over?

Fear? Prejudice? Ignorance? Randa thought one of
those was the answer but also knew she couldn't hurt this
young girl or confuse her anymore by saying so. **I don't**
know, honey. Sometimes even older people have a hard
time when someone is sick. Maybe your Dad will change
his mind.

I hope so. Okay I have to go now because I have to
set the table for supper. That's my job.

All right Megan, you take care now and if you have
any more questions you just ask me or any of the other
nurses here, okay?

Okay. Thank you. You're nice. The girl typed. *My*
real name is Amy.

Randa smiled at the simple trust of a child. **Nice to**
meet you Amy and I'll keep your real name our secret.
Bye.

17

Bye.

Randa closed the chat room and logged off the network. She couldn't get Amy out of her mind and wondered if she had said too much, too little or the wrong thing. She needed to talk it over with Denise the way she always did when there had been a particularly frustrating or emotional shift on the network. *Speaking of Denise, where is she? She went to the mailbox over 20 minutes ago.*

Randa went to the picture window and saw Denise still down at the mailbox. She wasn't alone there, however, two middle-aged women had joined her. Randa squinted, thinking she knew the women from somewhere. Then it hit her and she moved quickly out the front door. By now, she knew the women from the Church of the Righteous Gospel, would have taxed Denise's patience. They had come to the door of the farmhouse once or twice in the past, irritating Randa with their ultra-conservative viewpoints. The nurse had tried to politely tell them she wasn't interested, but this had only seemed to spur them on rather than discourage them. Finally, after the women had condemned just about everything the nurse believed in, Randa had asked them to leave and not return to her property.

Now they're down there talking to Denise. She's probably crazy by now. Randa hurried down the driveway intending to make her feelings clear in a very forceful way, but as she reached the mailbox she was surprised to find the churchwomen smiling up at the poet.

"I certainly do agree with you that a woman's place is in the home, living in a monogamous, loving marriage for as long as you both shall live," Denise was saying. "There's nothing more fulfilling than that." As Randa approached she opened her arms and drew the nurse in close for a warm hug. "And here is the woman I intend on doing that very thing with." The smiles dropped like rocks from the faces of the two women as Denise gave a little wave and said, "Well, we must be going now. We have a few pentangles to draw before the full moon. Have a nice day!"

Randa and the poet walked slowly back up the driveway but not before Randa looked back at the still gaping women and stuck her tongue out while pointedly putting her hand on Denise's butt.

Denise snorted, "Oh, very mature, Randa."

The nurse replied with a brilliant smile and said "Dignity, always dignity." They both broke out into laughter as they climbed the porch stairs together.

"Those people are everywhere, Randa. Usually I ignore them but today I just felt in the mood to tease them a little."

"Oh yeah, and you did an excellent job, too! That bit about 'marriage for as long as we both shall live' was priceless!"

Bright blue eyes held green ones in a look of complete devotion. Denise leaned in and gave the nurse a quick kiss on the lips. "Why, Ms. Martin, you should have known that's the one thing I said that wasn't a tease."

Denise broke the gaze and moved through the doorway, starting to open the mail. Randa could only stand there as stunned as the two women who were only just now walking away from the mailbox.

Marriage?

****

The day after found Denise lying out upon a large tartan picnic blanket, writing in the garden. The hot sun shone down upon her meagrely dressed form causing beads of sweat to tickle her flesh. She had spent the early morning watering blooming flowers before the sun had risen. Then she had pruned the bushes, cut the grass and removed some of the low hanging branches from the oak trees. Through all of this Randa had slept on unaware. DJ knew she needed time to recuperate after working two long shifts mere hours apart.

Pushing back the silver framed glasses that had slipped slowly down her nose Denise tapped the end of her pencil upon a white writing pad. She had been writing for the past three hours accompanied by a steady flow of small bottles of cider. Four empty, clear glass bottles stood in a row by the edge of the red and green blanket. She was beginning to feel the effects of the fifth bottle. *Maybe I started drinking too early,* the poet thought, realizing that a quarter past one in the afternoon may indeed be a little early.

Suddenly a dark shadow passed over her causing Denise to look up and find Randa's smiling face staring back.

"You're awake," the poet said as she noticed Randa was still dressed in the blue and white gingham shorts and tee shirt had adorned for bed. "Just!" she added.

With a yawn Randa collapsed into a cross-legged sitting position. She nodded groggily. "Uh huh."

"Still tired?"

"Not really... just immensely relaxed!" The nurse looked around Denise as she said, "As it seems are you!" She picked up DJ's arm and studied the time on her wristwatch. "It's a bit early in the day for drinking isn't it?"

Denise pushed herself to sit beside Randa, facing her. "Yes I suppose so but I was in a mood. I felt this ostentatiousness take over me, and suddenly the guise of a tortured, alcoholic bard took possession of my soul. I was powerless to resist."

Randa rolled her eyes as she lay upon her side and picked up Denise's pad. "So, have you been writing some poetry?"

"Yes!" The taller woman pulled the pad from Randa's hand, "and you are not allowed to read until I have finished."

Randa poked out her lower lip and fluttered her eyelashes.

"And that wont work either!" DJ placed the pad back down on the blanket and took a drink from her fifth bottle. She offered the cider to Randa who refused it with an expression of revulsion.

"Ugh, no thanks, it's a bit too early for me. I had a glass of milk and a cookie before I came out here." Randa looked down at DJ's pad, suddenly changing the subject as she said, "I've always wondered how you managed to write with such beautiful handwriting. Mine is so scruffy that when I worked at the hospital my co-workers voted me 'Nurse most likely to have been a doctor in a previous life'."

20

Denise laughed as she moved down onto her back and looked up at the sky. "I love your handwriting... it's... unique!"

"Uh huh!"

"As for me, I suppose I take after my mother. She always took pride in presentation." Denise put her hands behind her head as Randa rolled onto her back and shuffled towards the poet, placing her head upon DJ's shoulder. The feel of the sun-bleached tresses tickled the side of Denise's chin.

"You never really talk about your parents. Can you tell me something about them?"

Denise felt Randa shift and she cast her gaze down to be greeted by clear green eyes close to her own. "Sure." She ducked down and kissed Randa softly before turning back and looking into the deep blue sky.

"Well... for as long as I can remember both my mother and father worked. We didn't have a great deal of money. We lived on the ground floor of a high-rise block of flats on the outskirts of the city. It wasn't one of the most desirable places to live but there were worse, believe me! My mum worked three jobs, five days a week and one on a Saturday afternoon. In the mornings she would clean offices at a large law firm in the city centre. Then at lunchtime she worked as a dinner lady at my school. She would serve the food and or supervise the children on the playground. I used to get free school dinners for the low-income families. In the afternoon she worked three hours at a florist making those baskets arrangements of flowers for special occasions."

"So you got your green thumb from Sara **and** your mother!" Randa said.

Denise shrugged. "I suppose so. Anyway... my dad was an architect. He worked for a small company where he really didn't get much appreciation for his obvious talent. Apparently he was good; mum often said so. Then when I was nine, dad got a new job working for a bigger firm earning a lot more money. Mum was able to quit two of her jobs and we were finally able to move out of the flat. My dad bought a nice house. It was an old Tudor dwelling but needed a lot of work doing to it. Dad called it a 'fixer upper' and said he would be able to do the work himself. So we moved into our new home and I got a nice big bedroom complete with light pink walls and a 'Muppets' frieze."

Randa chuckled.

Denise smiled but it quickly faded. "We were in the house for no less than two months before the fire." Her voice lowered, "before they died." Denise shifted her body indicating that she wanted to move. Randa rose to sit and DJ followed, facing her lover.

The air seemed to cool around her as Denise took a deep breath.

Randa frowned, noticing the distant look in DJ's eyes. "Denise?"

"I've never told **anybody** this before. Not even Sara."

"What?"

"Afterwards, I heard the fire chief say the fire was caused by faulty wiring. He said the house was old and needed re-wiring and it was more than likely a dodgy connection at one of the plug sockets in the living room that started the fire. It originated in that specific location."

"I guess that sounds logical," Randa said with a frown.

"Yes." Denise looked down and traced her finger over the blanket following a long red line. "Randa... the socket didn't work when we first moved into the house and for the following few weeks after. Then my dad got his hands on one of those Betamax players, which meant we needed another socket. He thought those things were really great and I suppose at the time they were. So that Saturday Dad decided to fix the socket... and that night..." DJ looked meaningfully into Randa's eyes.

The nurse's expression fell as a look of horror overtook her features. "That night the fire started." It wasn't a question.

Denise nodded. "I mean... I was never completely sure but at the same time... I was. I still didn't say anything. How could I? What was I supposed to say? I certainly couldn't tell Sara that I was sure Dad caused the fire. Randa, my dad was a brilliant architect, a great carpenter and passable plumber but he was no electrician. He just wanted the pride of being able to say he fixed the house up himself."

"Oh, Denise!" Randa whispered.

The poet took a shuddering breath. "I've never told anybody that before."

Randa reached out and took DJ's hand. "I'm glad you told me."

"Me too." DJ pulled Randa towards her and into a strong embrace. Randa climbed into her lap and wrapped her legs around Denise's waist, laying her head upon the taller woman's shoulder.

"I hate that you had to carry that around with you for so long. Did you ever have to go through any form of therapy for what happened?"

Denise nodded as she moved her hands over Randa's back. "I did for a while but I didn't like it. I started to rebel because I disliked going. Sara helped me more. You know us Jennings women like to keep things to ourselves!"

A peaceful quiet settled between the women, broken only by the distant sound of a highflying aircraft. Denise looked up into the sky and watched the airplane's white vapour trail expand and disperse in the flawless blue sky. She bit her trembling lip as salty tears clouded her vision.

"For so long I wanted to hate him, Randa. I really tried. I wanted to hate him for taking himself and my mum away from me but I couldn't." Denise turned her glazed eyes back to Randa and tears rolled lazily down her cheeks. "He was my dad, you know."

Randa cupped Denise's face as she leaned forwards and kissed away her tears. "What was his name? You've never told me that."

The poet smiled. "Daniel. Another DJ!"

"And your mother's name was Lina?"

"Short for Angelina, yes."

The women relaxed into each other's embrace, once again, as Denise took comfort in the woman within her arms. After a while Randa asked, "Do you have any pictures of them?"

DJ thought for a moment. "Yes I do actually, back at home. When I go to England for the launch I'll bring some back with me, okay?"

"That would be great." Randa ran her hands over Denise's shoulders. "Thank you for trusting me enough to tell me, Denise."

"Trust isn't an issue, Randa. I love you." DJ grinned. "You get to know all of my deep, dark and dirty little secrets!"

Randa extricated herself from DJ's lap and rose to her feet. "Really? All of your deep, dark and dirty secrets huh?" She folded her arms and looked down at the poet. "Like for instance you'll tell me what your middle name is?"

"What makes you think I have one?"

"You said you did!"

Did I? Denise thought for a moment. "Oh yes... so I did!" *Damn her and what she can wheedle out of me with those talented fingers of hers!* She smiled inside.

"So?" Randa unfolded her arms and placed them upon her hips, she quirked an eyebrow in expectation.

DJ fell silent as she pondered her answer. As what she hoped was a charming smile graced her lips, Denise stood up beside Randa. "Have I told you how much I love you today?"

"Yep."

"Oh... um," She lowered her voice, "have I showed you?"

The nurse seemed to momentarily waver. "I um... um... well... well no but don't go changing the subject."

"I wasn't, I..." Denise paused as the distant sound of a ringing telephone drifted to her ears. *Saved by the bell.* "Oh hey that's the phone!" Planting a brief kiss upon Randa's lips DJ ran off back towards the house. Jogging into the living room she picked up the shrilling handset. "Hello?"

"Well if it isn't the silky tones of the tall, dark and literate one."

"Hi, Derek, what can I do for you?" DJ sat down upon the edge of Randa's desk.

"This is my warning call to say I'm on my way over for some lunch. Is the coast clear? You know I still haven't been able to wipe from my mind the image of you and my best friend 'in-flagrant-e'!"

The poet laughed. "The coast is very clear, Derek. Well Randa has yet to get dressed but that is only because you have been working her ragged the past day or two. How long will you be?"

"I'm sitting outside the house right now."

Slipping off the desk Denise approached the window and looked out onto the driveway. She spotted Derek's little red car as the man waved from inside the vehicle. She waved back.

"Who are you waving to?" Randa asked as she entered the house.

"Derek is in the driveway."

"Well duh!"

DJ sniggered. "I was talking to Randa, Derek!"

"Oh."

"Don't just sit there then. Get your arse inside the house!" *And save me from the 'Randa Inquisition',* she added in thought.

"Oh I do love it when you get all macho on me!" Derek hung up and exited his car.

"Okay," DJ stated as she trotted towards Randa. "I'm going to start some lunch. Are you going to get dressed?"

"Sounds like a plan."

Randa headed towards the bedroom and DJ watched her disappear with an affectionate smile. She needed this time alone with Derek so they could finalise the plans she had been making for Randa's birthday and knew this would be her perfect opportunity.

Chapter 3

The curtains were closed, in the large master bedroom, leaving the bright new day unable to penetrate the darkened room. From the tousled double bed in the centre of the room light snores sounded from underneath jumbled covers as its single occupant slept on unaware of the dawning day.

Denise entered the room already showered and dressed in her khaki cropped trousers and navy tank top. With a happy smile she walked bare foot through the bedroom carrying an assortment of objects on a wide wooden tray. A single red rose, a sheet of paper, a small pot of jam with several slices of toast. A pile of cards, small presents, a camera, one glass of orange juice and a bottle of her favourite mineral water.

Placing the heavily loaded tray upon the bedside cabinet DJ looked down at the slumbering form hidden under the covers. The night before Randa had retired to bed as late as possible stating that she wanted to delay the inevitable for as long as she could. She had disappeared into the shower only to emerge fifteen minutes later looking like, as Denise had called her, 'a miserable drowned rat' and had fallen into bed asking not to be woken until DJ flew back to the States in July. Denise humoured her and agreed knowing she would not be keeping her word. She did understand how the blonde felt, as she too was not looking forward to their time apart.

Climbing upon the bed on her knees, the poet straddled Randa's huddled form and slowly shuffled up her cocooned body. When she was sure she reached the edge of the covers she bent down and slowly pulled at the thin quilt.

"Randa?" Denise sang, spying a crown of blonde hair.

The nurse groaned unintelligibly as she tried to burrow herself further into the covers.

"Randa… come on it's time to get up."

"What time is it?" Came the muffled response.

"Half nine." Denise paused as she smiled and said, "On the twenty-ninth of June."

It seemed to take a moment for DJ's words to compute in her sleep-muddled brain. "Ugh… noooooo… go away. This is a bad dream!"

Denise laughed and placed light kisses upon Randa's barely revealed shoulder. "No it isn't," Kiss, "come on," Kiss, "Wakey wakey, birthday girl."

With a dramatic sigh Randa rolled onto her back and sleepy green eyes greeted the new day. "Good Morning world; Hello oblivion. Are vultures circling around the yard yet?"

DJ rolled her eyes as she straightened her posture. She sat upon Randa's stomach but held most of her weight on the backs of her legs. "Come on, Randa. It is a beautiful day." The poet gesticulated as she spoke, "The sun is shining; there is not a cloud in the sky. The garden's sweet floral scent is seeping into the house and the birds in the trees are chirping 'Happy Birthday' tunes just for you."

Randa looked at Denise skeptically.

"Well okay, maybe not the last one but it is a beautiful day. I refuse to let you lie here and mope in bed when I have such a wonderful day planned for you!"

"What? What do you mean 'planned'? What plans?" This seemed to spark Randa's interest and she pushed herself into a sitting position looking at Denise inquisitively. "Denise, I don't want anything today. I just want to lie in bed and hide until you get back from England." She fell back down into the covers and draped one arm over her eyes.

"Oh come on, please remember that it is only for a week and I will hate it as much as you while I'm away." DJ leaned forward and placed a soft kiss upon Randa's lips.

She removed the arm and looked deep into glazed green eyes. "I refuse to let you lie here and wallow all day. Turning thirty is not the end of the world and as soon as you realise that the better. Now I have breakfast for you."

"Yippee."

"A pile of cards and gifts?"

Randa's eyes shifted to the right and looked towards the tray upon the cabinet.

"You know I never felt any different when I reached my thirtieth." Denise knew that statement was 'almost' true. She had initially felt a slight feeling of doom as the day approached but when it finally arrived DJ realised she had no idea what all of her brooding had been about.

"So… how about we start this beautiful day hmm?"

"Ugh, okay I suppose if I have no choice." Randa moved once again to a sitting position and picked up a slice of toast. She eyed the assortment of items with a frown and reached out, picking up the folded sheet of paper.

"Ah ah ah," Denise snatched the paper from Randa's hands. "This is mine."

Randa narrowed her eyes as she asked, "What is it?"

With a smirk, Denise climbed off the bed and stood tall. "This is my um… it's a little something I wrote for you."

"A poem?"

"Nope." DJ opened the sheet of paper and looked briefly at the precise handwriting. "Being as though you seem to envision being thirty as the beginning of the end I plan on showing you that 'thirty' is not that bad. So anyway, last night while you tried to drown yourself in the shower I wrote you a little something. Would you like to hear it?"

Randa nodded eagerly, the slice of toast all but forgotten in her hand.

Clearing her throat, Denise straightened her back and looked down at the 'essay'. "Okay… Thirty Reasons Why I love Randa Martin, by Denise Jennings." DJ looked quickly to see Randa smile at the title.

Taking a deep breath she began. "Number one, I love your smile that brings sunshine to each new day. Two, I love your cute button nose. Three, I love your hands; so skilled and yet so gentle. Four, I love your voice, especially its passionate timbres." She looked up quickly and winked. "Five, I love the way you always seem to know what to say. Number six, I love your cute little toes and seven I love your caring heart. Eight, I love that you can make people feel so comfortable around you and you draw them in so easily. Nine, I love the pink tints of your blushes and number ten; I love your ticklish feet. Eleven, I love the way the sun shines golden in your hair, and twelve how you can make even the scruffiest of clothes look damn sexy on you. Thirteen, I love the way you make me laugh so easily and fourteen I love the way you make up songs in the shower. Fifteen, I love your taste, sixteen your scent and seventeen, your talented tongue." Again Denise looked up and waggled her eyebrows; she noticed Randa had discarded her breakfast and seemed to be hanging intently on every word.

"Eighteen, I love that sleepy look on your face when you wake up and nineteen, I love how you watch me while I work. Twenty, I loved how you kissed away my tears when I was sad, and twenty-one…" DJ smiled, "I love it when you pretend to pick your nose when you think little children are looking at you in the street. Twenty-two, I love the feel of your hands on the back of my head," again DJ smiled, "And twenty-three, I love your sea green eyes. Twenty-four, I love the way you kiss and twenty-five, the way we can sit talking for hours. Twenty-six, I love the way you dance with the broom when you sweep the porch and twenty-seven the way you suck strawberry jam off my fingers. Twenty-eight, I love the way you turn eating Mexican food into a religious experience. Twenty-nine, I love the way you hold me when you sleep and thirty… I love you because you are you…" DJ looked back up to find Randa sitting on the edge of the bed. She stepped forward and bent down onto her knees, "…and you make it so damn easy to feel this way." Placing the sheet of paper upon the floor DJ reached out and cupped Randa's cheek. She tried to gage the unreadable expression upon Randa's face.

"Hey it wasn't **that** bad was it?"

"I loved it," Randa said as she pulled DJ towards her and took possession of her lips. Denise let her hands fall to Randa's bare thighs and moved them up to cup her behind and pull her to the edge of the bed. Their lips parted as the kiss deepened and DJ groaned as she felt Randa's fingers sink into her hair and her lower body grind against her.

With effort Denise pulled away. "We have to stop. We don't have time for this."

Randa pouted. "What? But it's my birthday. I thought I get whatever I want on my birthday. If I recall correctly, somebody, no more than an inch away, said to me that she likes the feel of my hands on the back of her head." she grinned sexily as she slowly spread her thighs.

Oh God help me..."I... I know but we have to eat breakfast and you have to open them," Denise nodded towards the pile of presents by her bed. "You have to get showered and um... dressed because we will be going out at about half eleven."

"Going out? Where are we going?"

DJ prodded Randa's nose. "It's a secret." Climbing to her feet, she grabbed the camera and sat beside Randa. "Right, family photo." Putting her arm around the bewildered blonde, Denise brought their heads together and held the camera in front of them as she placed her finger on its button. "Say... 'It's great to be thirty'!"

The camera flashed and DJ turned to Randa "You didn't smile."

"You didn't give me much of a warning."

"Want to go again?" Denise held up the small camera but Randa dived from the bed, pulling the sheet with her.

"No! Let me at least get myself looking a bit more presentable first." Holding the sheet against her naked form, Randa disappeared into the bathroom leaving a smiling Denise looking at the en-suite's closed door. Shaking her head DJ looked at the tray and grinned.

"Oh hey, Randa." She grabbed another of its items and approached the bathroom door, knocking lightly on the white barrier.

The door slid open and Randa peeked out of its narrow gap. "Can't I even have one minute of time to brood over this day?"

"Nope." DJ stuck two fingers into the pot of strawberry jam she was holding and held the mixture to Randa's lips. "Taste this."

Randa did as asked and wrapped her lips around the poet's fingers; her eyes grew wide in surprise. "That's Sara's jam."

"Yep." Denise dug her fingers back into the pot and pulled out another scoop of the soft red mixture. "I gave your mum the recipe the other day and she made this for us." She sucked the jam from her fingers, closing her eyes in delight. "Hmmm."

Randa pulled the fingers from DJ's mouth and placed them in her own. Denise could feel her insides melt as she felt the blonde's tongue wrap around her digits. *Oh god... we don't have time... we don't have time... we don't have time* she chanted. The poet felt her skin flush with heat as arousal flowed throughout her veins. She looked down at the half revealed form of her naked lover.

Pulling Denise's fingers from her mouth Randa said, "I really did love your essay."

"Yeah? Um..." Denise cleared her throat, "Well wait until you reach sixty!" Keeping her eyes focused on any area of Randa's body above her shoulders, DJ backed away from the door. "Okay, I better go and... and... get some," she poked her thumb over her shoulder, "get some thing done." With an affirmed nod Denise turned and headed swiftly out of the bedroom door.

****

Denise stood on the front porch, hands on hips as she looked out over the front lawn. With dark shades upon her nose, to shield her eyes from the glare of the mid morning sun, she tapped her foot impatiently – waiting. Randa seemed to be taking her time in getting ready but as long as they left the house at half past eleven DJ didn't mind.

Pulling a set of keys from her pocket the poet twirled them around her index finger. When she discovered Randa drove a truck she was adamant that she never travel inside the 'contraption' and had leased a new Lexus a few days later! Denise was very particular about her cars and always opted for the luxury business or sporty models, preferably either a Lexus or an Alfa Romeo.

Oh come on Randa, she thought. There were two stops Denise had to make before they reached her planned destination. Denise had booked them all into an exclusive resort that Randa had often stated she wanted to visit but thought it would be too expensive. The poet had a schedule and she intended on keeping it.

Looking down at her watch, DJ shook her head. Moving towards the front door she poked her head into the house. "Come on, Birthday Girl. I want to get there while it's still daylight out here."

"All right, all right I'm coming." Randa emerged from their bedroom dressed and ready to go. She picked up her bag from the corner of the sofa and headed towards Denise. "Come on then, Miss Impatient, let's get going to this clandestine destination."

"Well it's about time."

Randa rolled her eyes as she closed and locked the front door. "Do I look okay? I have no idea where we're going so I don't know how to dress." She looked down at her simple white top and light blue jeans.

"You look beautiful." Denise leaned forward and kissed Randa briefly before taking her hand and leading her away from the house. "And you still had two and a half minutes to spare... congratulations!"

"Thanks... I do try."

They climbed into the Lexus and DJ pushed her key into the ignition. Instantly, a loud jingle from the radio filled the car as the engine roared into life. "Are we ready?" she asked, turning down the music.

"Sure are."

"Then lets go." DJ eased the car onto the road and headed off down the street.

They had been driving in a comfortable silence for no more than five minutes and during that time Denise had been aware of Randa's continual stare. She had discovered that it was the patented 'Martin stare' as she had seen Janice

Martin use the very same one while talking with her daughter on several occasions.

With an amused sigh Denise turned briefly towards Randa. "Okay... what?"

"Aren't you even going to give me even a little hint about where we're going?"

Denise was certain she detected a slight whine in her partner's voice. "No and you know I wont either so you'll just have to be patient. We will be there soon enough." Denise took a left at the next junction and just ahead she spotted a familiar figure standing on the corner. She smiled as she approached Randa's best friend.

"Hey, there's Derek!" Randa said surprised.

"Yep." Denise slowed down the car and pulled in by the roadside. Derek's smiling face greeted them as he opened the back passenger side door and climbed into the vehicle.

Randa turned in her seat to address her friend as DJ commenced their journey. "Derek... not that I'm unhappy to see you, but what are you doing here?"

"I'm part of the afternoon birthday entourage." He leaned forward and kissed Randa's cheek. "Happy Birthday, sweet thing. How does it feel to reach the big three zero?"

Randa groaned as Denise chuckled. "I wouldn't push it Derek. It took me long enough to even convince her to get out of bed this morning."

"So that's why I've been waiting on that street corner for the past ten minutes. You know I was beginning to get a little worried. A good-looking guy like me standing on a street corner... I don't need to tell you about the looks I got. If I had been there any longer I'm sure I would have gotten a few monetary offers for this body of mine!"

Randa grinned as she said, "Yeah maybe to get you to go away!"

Derek's jaw dropped as he glared at his best friend. "Oh... I'm hurt! And here was me breaking all my plans today just so I could spend the afternoon with my friend on her birthday. I had to beat the admirers down with a stick just so I could leave my front door this morning and that's

33

all the thanks I get?"

"Derek you really do have a flair for the dramatic!"

"Just making my point, babe. Now..." Derek looked out of the window, "are we nearly there yet?"

Randa switched her gaze from Denise back to Derek. "You know where we are going?"

"Of course I do!"

Randa looked back at DJ. "How come he knows?"

"Because it's not his birthday..."

"...Yet!" Derek added hopefully.

"So he is allowed to know," the poet finished.

A few minutes later Denise took another left onto a familiar street and Randa looked in surprise at her.

"I know this area. A friend of my mom lives here."

"Uh huh." Denise stopped her car by a driveway and sounded the horn. A moment passed before Janice Martin emerged from her friend's house and made her way towards the car. She got into the back seat and sat beside Derek.

"Mom? Okay now I really am confused."

"Happy birthday, honey." Janice smiled brightly.

Denise looked over at the older woman and winked. She had discussed her planned afternoon with Janice and Derek and they were both more than willing to participate. Derek because DJ had stated that she was 'footing the bill' and Janice because she had always wanted to visit the place Denise was proposing. The four of them would spend the day together but Denise planned the evening for just Randa and herself. If she was to leave for England the very next day she intended on making the best of the time they had before she left.

****

Forest Springs Resort was embedded in a valley between two tree-covered hills. It was an exclusive establishment of health and relaxation. A narrow stream ran to the left of the large complex; its crystal waters so clear that much of the underwater life was visible to the naked eye. The centre itself was a wide three-story building and painted a bright white. It's beauty and unique design stood out against the backdrop of the emerald green hills.

Denise took the long narrow road that led towards the complex and looked over at Randa. The blonde's eyes widened as she realised where they were heading.

"Forest Springs? We're going to Forest Springs?" Randa asked incredulously. She wound down the window and stuck her head out into the sizzling air. The heat was a stark contrast to the air-conditioned interior of Denise's leased Lexus.

"Hey Randa, get your head back in babe. You look like one of those inquisitive shaggy dogs!"

Janice laughed at Derek's statement and the nurse pulled her head back inside the car. She looked towards a grinning Denise and said, "This is your surprise?"

"Half of it." DJ replied, "Tonight I have a little something extra planed for just you and me." Denise followed the signs that led to the front entrance of the complex. She pulled up beside a young man dressed in a matching green shorts and tee shirt. "I hate valet parking," the poet groused, "if this were my car nobody would drive it but me. It's a good job this one is leased I suppose."

"If you don't mind me saying, DJ, I think you have an unhealthy obsession with cars," Janice said teasingly as she stepped out into the rising midday heat. "Have you noticed this, Randa?"

"She's just particular about her cars," Randa defended as she followed her mother around to the building's entrance. "I can't believe we're here. I've always wanted to come here for a little 'R and R'. Did you know they have hotel rooms where you can spend up to a week here? Make a vacation out of it and everything!"

"Oh that sounds good to me," Derek said joining Randa and Janice, "A week of lying on my back while all my whims are catered to."

Janice smiled. "I'm sure they encourage some forms of exercise also, Derek."

"Well as long as it's not mandatory."

Denise approached the waiting man with caution. "Okay…" she held out her keys but didn't hand them over. "I would appreciate it if you took extra special care of this car, mate. No speeding, no going over speed bumps at more than 5 miles per hour. You handle this car like it is your pride and joy. Like your very life may very well depend on the way you treat it, okay?"

Randa shook her head as she approached Denise. "I'm sure he gets the message," she smiled at the nervous young man.

"Just making sure." DJ narrowed her eyes as she handed over her keys.

As they were accepted, Randa pulled DJ away. "I think you scared him!"

"Hey I have to be sure. That isn't my car." She watched as the Lexus pulled away from the curb. "Though I am thinking about upgrading. This new model is such a superb drive."

The four entered the complex through electronic front doors and stepped into a wide foyer. The floor was covered in black marble and along white walls were tall plants in terracotta pots. Denise spotted a middle-aged woman standing behind the wide front desk wearing much the same clothes as the parking attendant. The woman was currently assisting a couple wearing matching purple and green sweat suits. DJ grimaced at the colour co-ordination.

Derek looked around their surroundings. "Oh you know... I'm going to get me one of those exfoliation scrubs for my face. Do they do those things for the whole body?"

The three women turned towards Derek with amused expressions.

"Oh and do they have those Swedish, blonde, overly muscular masseuses? I sure as hell have to get me one of those too. And what do those mud baths do? Also... I have to try the seaweed wraps and... and oh I know what I really, really want to try..."

"Colonic irrigation?" Denise asked, stone-faced.

Randa snorted but held her tongue.

Derek's features dropped as he shuddered visibly. "Not on your life. Damn, that makes me want to clench just thinking about it!"

Mother and daughter laughed at Derek's expression as Denise approached the front desk.

36

****

Emerging from a single, private shower cubicle, Denise wrapped a green complimentary towel around her naked body and approached Randa. The nurse and her mother had just re-showered after visiting the mud baths while the poet had managed to talk Derek into a game of racquetball. The match between poet and Webmaster had been a serious battle in which Derek emerged the victor. Denise had been a good sport and accepted the defeat gracefully. That was until the younger man had insisted on doing a victory lap around the court ... several times. After the fifth circuit DJ had threatened to launch the Webmaster out of the court with her racquet if he didn't stop.

"Where's your mum?"

Randa looked around briefly and re-hooked the edge of her towel around her body. "I think she went to ask about the times for lunch. We're all supposed to fit in a massage before we eat. Then after that it's facial time!"

"Yep." Denise sat beside Randa on the low wooden bench and looked around the shower room. Along the edges were rows of private cubical showers with a square bench in the centre of the room. She realised they were it's only occupants.

"So how on earth did you manage to talk Derek into physical activity?"

"I told him I had a long lost brother who was dying to meet him!"

"Really?" Randa asked with amusement.

"No." Denise laughed. "I actually insulted his macho pride by telling him there was no way he would be able to beat me as I was a racquet sports champion at school. That sure brought out his competitive nature."

"Were you a racquet sports champion?"

"No," Denise replied.

Randa smiled as she asked, "Who won?"

"He did. He then proceeded to do a victory lap around the court singing 'We Are The Champions'. He only stopped after I threatened 'GBH' on his arse!"

"What's that?"

"That's what he said." She chuckled as she continued, "it means Grievous Bodily Harm; it's a police terminology in the UK. He soon quieted down."

"That sounds about right." The nurse shook her head and looked up at DJ. "Did I tell you that I'm having a wonderful time? I've always wanted to come here."

"Well just remember that this is only the beginning. Tonight I have a more private celebration planned for just you and me." DJ wiggled her eyebrows for effect.

"And you're not going to give me any clue?"

"Not a one."

Randa arched a single eyebrow as she rose to her feet and turned to look down at Denise, their knees touching. "Oh?" Looking around briefly to reaffirm that they were indeed still the only two occupants in the shower room, Randa leaned forward and braced her hands upon the poet's knees. "Ever made out in a health club?"

Denise gulped visibly. "Pardon?"

A slow smile spread across Randa's lips as she took DJ's hands and pulled her to her feet. Without saying a word she began pulling Denise towards the nearest corner shower cubical, making sure it was away from prying eyes.

"Randa, what are you up to?"

"This." Randa pulled Denise into the cubical and closed the thick frosted glass door. Pushing DJ up against the moist, white tiled wall she pressed her own body into the poet. "Just thanking you; in the most appealing way I can at this moment in time." Randa lowered her lips to DJ's chest.

"Um... Randa?" Denise felt the nurses hands glide along her sides. "Should we be doing this here? We might get chucked out!" Inquisitive hands tugged at the edge of her towel. *Oh god.*

"Hell yeah!" Randa whispered as Denise's body was revealed.

Capturing the searing gaze in her lover's eyes, Denise felt her resistance slipping – fast. "Oh what the bloody hell." Spinning around she changed their positions and thrust Randa against the wall. Gathering the nurse's hands and holding them above her head, DJ wasted no time in claiming the nurse's lips in a deep passionate kiss. Denise took control as she caressed Randa's tongue with her own, feeling a deep groan rumble within the blonde's chest.

Pulling back, Denise looked into heavy lidded green eyes. "We'll get our memberships revoked!"

"What memberships?" Randa breathed.

"That was half of your birthday present."

"Oh wow, Denise, that's… OH!" Randa gasped as DJ thrust against her and re-claimed her lips. Their kiss continued until an unexpected sound broke through their passionate haze.

"Hello?"

Both women froze.

"Randa? DJ?"

"Mom!" Randa whispered, wide eyed.

"Oh bugger!" Denise quickly reclaimed her towel from the floor and hastily wrapped it around her rapidly cooling body. "Well get back out there then!"

"No… you first." Randa replied.

"You first."

"Girls?" Janice enquired.

"GO!" DJ whispered harshly.

"You go." Randa countered.

"It's **your** mother, Randa."

Both women grabbed their partner, insisting that the other should go first and as DJ pushed open the cubical door they jumbled out of the shower together. Denise felt her cheeks flush as she came face to face with Randa's curious mother.

"Hi mom," Randa squeaked, "I was just showing Denise the…"

"Tiles/shower head," the women said in unison. They looked at each other accusingly.

"I was just showing Denise the tiles in the shower because we were thinking about getting the guest bathroom done," Randa said timidly.

Janice nodded.

"Yes and I was showing Randa the shower head. I was thinking of getting a shower massage..." DJ's eyes widened, "for um... therapeutic reasons of course..."

"Of course." Janice echoed.

Denise nodded. "So..." she looked down at a cringing Randa. "We should go and get ready for the next... thing... we are booked in for!" Receiving a nod from the blushing blonde both women headed back towards the changing rooms leaving one very amused older woman watching them leave with a restrained smirk.

****

Janice, Randa and Denise all opted for a body massage while Derek had proclaimed that he had wanted to 'see what wonderful things they did with seaweed'. They then met up an hour later for a lunch that Derek had deemed 'way too healthy for his manly body' but had eaten with gusto all the same. The final treatment of the day was full facials and manicures, which they had booked earlier that morning.

Seated in a row, the four sat side by side. Their heads were relaxed back with colourful skin treatments covering their faces and white robes adorning their bodies. A light music played in the background breaking the silence of the large room. Denise sat in the first chair, next to her was Janice next to her was Derek and on the far end of the row sat Randa. This was their last therapy session of the day.

"What colour's your face gloop, Denise?" Randa asked.

DJ reached up and swiped the edge of her chin with her middle finger. She then lifted the corner piece of cucumber, which was covering her eye, and studied her digit. "Ugh... it's pink!"

Randa laughed. "Mine's blue."

"Why couldn't I get blue too?" the poet whined.

"Because you have combination skin like me and this was the appropriate mask for our skin types." Janice replied.

"Mines green." Derek piped in and then proceeded to lick his finger. "Hmm, it tasted pretty good too. Kind of like apples and pears."

"You're not supposed to eat it, Derek." Randa pulled the cucumbers from her eyes and glared at her friend.

"Well it tastes nice!" Derek swiped another portion of the green mask from his face and offered his finger to Randa. "Trust me... try some."

With caution Randa leaned over her chair and tasted the mixture from Derek's finger. "Wow, you're right!"

Pulling both pieces of cucumber from her eyes Denise turned to the pair and said, "If they intended on us eating this stuff they would have put face mask on the menu at lunch today!"

Randa and Derek twisted in their seats to look at the poet and they both broke out in a fit of giggles.

"What?" DJ asked

Derek took a deep breath. "Oh... you look funny with your wet hair slicked back and that pink stuff all over your face." Derek chucked again as he continued, "Hey try yours it might taste like strawberries!"

Shaking her head DJ leaned in her chair and placed the cucumber slices back over her eyes. "No thanks... I had enough to eat at lunch."

"So..." Janice started, "Did you enjoy your time with the seaweed, Derek?"

"Sure did, Mrs. M."

"And you didn't go getting yourself into any trouble?"

"I would never!" the Webmaster stated seriously and Randa rolled her eyes.

Janice smiled. Though she herself was unable to see due to the cucumber slices covering her own eyes she could read their expressions just by the inflections in their voices. "That's good to know. At least you weren't getting yourself into any mischief!"

"What does that mean?" Derek then asked, as DJ felt herself shrink into her black leather seat.

"Oh just that these two were up to no good when I found them earlier today."

"Mom! We were not!" Randa protested.

Janice lifted the slices from her eyes and gazed at her daughter. "Oh, Miranda please. I've known you for thirty

41

years now. I know that guilty expression like the back of my hand and don't you think I don't. It's the same look I remember right back to the time I told you that you couldn't leave the table until you had finished all of your vegetables. Then I caught you scraping them off your plate behind the dining room curtains half an hour later!"

Denise burst into laughter.

"Mother!" Randa whined, "I was seven years old!"

"And your point is? Remember honey… every look!"

Randa turned her glare to the laughing poet. "And you can shut up too! She was talking about both of us you know."

Denise tried to lessen her mirth as she said, "I know but that is funny. Even now you try to sneak your broccoli on my plate when you think I'm not looking!" She started to laugh again.

"Denise, if you don't stop laughing I might very well have to tell mom and Derek about the times you used to put on shows in the back yard of your apartment block for your parents and Sara!" Denise quieted considerably. "Remember… Sara and I spent many hours alone together and she had an awful lot of stories she used to tell me while you were locked away in your study… working!" A mischievous grin spread across Randa's features.

The poet sobered as she said, "Deal!" Her eyes met Randa's in a silent duel until both women grinned and chuckled at their behaviour. Shaking her head, DJ sat back into her chair and replaced the cucumber slices upon her eyes. She knew that even if Randa had have told them about the little 'plays' she used to stage, it wouldn't have made any difference to her. DJ wondered if there was anything Randa could ever say or do that would cause a true anger inside of her. *Probably not,* she realised.

Peeking at the clock on the wall Denise realised it was almost half past five in the afternoon. They still had enough time to drop Derek back at his car and Janice back at her friend's house. They decided DJ would pick them up on the way to the spa, as she wanted to add to the mystery of where they were going. Denise knew, that for Randa, having her mother and best friend there would add to her

42

enjoyment of the day and hopefully help her to realise that – as the cliché states – 'age is just a number'. *Still*, the poet smiled, *the day isn't over yet.*

****

It was late in the evening. The sky was littered with a million stars and a shimmering fragment of the moon hung low in the dark sky. With no presence of a cool wind or drop in temperature the night was warm and comfortable. From a distance the escalating sound of a car engine approached the darkened ranch style home and pulled into the long driveway. The temporary light that lit up the front porch, as the Lexus approached, disappeared when the engine died and the night once again surrendered to a familiar silence.

Denise swung open her door and jumped out of the car. She jogged around to the other side and opened Randa's door. "Ma'am!"

"Thank you, Jeeves." Randa joked as she stepped out of the car and DJ shut the door with a soft 'click'.

"My pleasure." Together they made their way to the front porch arm in arm.

"So how did you like dinner?" Denise took Randa's hand and led her up the steps.

"It was wonderful," replied Randa as she pushed her key into the lock, opening the front door. Both women stepped into the house and Denise turned on the lights. She looked around the open plan room lost in thought. Sighing, DJ turned back towards Randa.

"God I wish you were able to come with me tomorrow. I've got to go through that whole caboodle with the press in a couple of days and I have no idea what will happen. Then I have all of those interviews and book signings and that could very well be swayed by the response of the press. Carl said he would be there to hold my hand but... well I could think of somebody else I would rather do that with." She smiled lasciviously.

"I can do more than just hold your hand." Moving closer to DJ, Randa placed her hands upon the poet's and

43

slowly slid them up her arms. "A week just feels like a **long** time to be apart from you. Remember what happened last time we parted? I don't want anything like that to happen again."

"It won't." DJ assured her as she wrapped her arms around Randa. "The launch is in Manchester and you have my number for the hotel I'll be staying at. Then I'll go back to Derbyshire for the first book signing so I'll be at my house. I promise I'll fill you in every step of the way." Leaning closer DJ planted a kiss upon Randa's nose. "I also promise there will be no more uncertainties, doubts and silences while I am away from you."

Randa pursed her lips before saying. "You never know what might happen."

"I'm sure a lot will happen but as long as I have you beside me, physically or spiritually I know I can handle whatever will eventuate." Denise combed her fingers through Randa's soft tresses and cupped the back of her head. "So how about we make the most of this night?"

"You know… you've been full of good ideas today."

Lips slowly inching closer both women paused just short of touching. Denise let her hands fall to cup the shorter woman's behind and pulled their bodies tighter together. "You still have the other half of your birthday present to open." DJ by-passed Randa's lips and lowered her head to the nurse's neck. Moving her lips teasingly over Randa's warm skin she caressed the soft flesh with her tongue.

"More."

"Uh huh… I did say that the membership was only half of the present." Denise mumbled.

"No," Randa grinned as she clasped the back of DJ's head. "I mean '**more**'. If I remember right we still have an encounter in a shower to finish!"

"Hmm." DJ followed the graceful curve of Randa's neck and returned to waiting lips. Her tongue snaked out slowly and traced over Randa's bottom lip before she sucked the succulent flesh into her mouth. The feel of the nurse's body pressed tight against her own and her unique scent was rapidly fuelling her desire. "So you don't want the other half of your present?"

"Sure I do," Randa replied with a smirk. "Where is it?"

DJ's eyes slid across the layout of the open plan house. "It's in the bedroom."

"Oh sounds like my kind of present."

"I definitely think you will like this," the poet said, a confident glint shining in her eyes. Her voice lowered as she said, "Do you want it?"

"You know I do."

"Ah well then... follow me." Denise released Randa and slowly led her into the bedroom.

Chapter 4

Hand in hand, Denise pulled Randa along to the bedroom. Once there, Randa took over and feverishly began removing clothes from the poet.

Under the assault of passionate kisses and seeking touches, Denise panted, "What are you doing?"

"If you don't know I must be doing it wrong," chuckled Randa. "What does it look like I'm doing? I'm opening the other half of my birthday present. Oh, and just look at the wonderful wrapping!" Randa murmured as she pulled DJ's shirt over her head.

"No, Randa!" the poet said removing herself from the nurse's reach. "Well, not no but just not yet. Don't you want the rest of your present?"

Randa was confused. "You mean there actually is a present? You're not the present?" She stood with brows scrunched, hands on hips.

Denise smiled and with her finger to indicate the dresser said, "Over there."

Randa allowed a slightly sinister grin to pass over her face. Bending over and giving a good imitation of a woman carrying a rifle, Randa skulked toward the dresser. "Here is Randa 'Bring 'em back Alive' Martin hunting for the last…" she looked over at Denise who nodded. "Last of the birthday presents," she continued. "After this hunt, Ms. Martin has indicated she will be going after bigger game in the form of the rarely sighted species Derbyshire Poet. The Poet is a crafty animal hunted mainly for its delectable flesh. It's said the Crocodile Hunter coined the phrase 'Isn't she a beauty?' after a brief sighting!"

DJ laughed as she shook her head and said, "Life is never dull with you, oh Great Blonde Hunter."

Randa extended an index finger toward the top drawer and raised two eyebrows in question.

"You're ice cold, nurse," the poet responded. Randa dropped the index finger to the second drawer.

"Warmer, but only slightly," was the next reply. The third drawer yielded "Now you're getting hot." The fourth and final drawer was greeted with a "Blazing hot!"

Randa laughed as she opened the drawer. On top of Denise's cable knit sweaters and winter turtlenecks was a tiny box wrapped in gold foil paper. She sobered immediately as she removed the tiny box from its hiding place. Making eye contact with the poet she felt a shiver pass down her spine. "Denise…"she began but felt unable to complete the sentence.

Denise quickly moved to Randa's side and guided her to the bed. Sitting down side by side, the poet urged "Open it, love."

Randa's hands shook a little as she peeled the gold paper away to reveal the white leather ring box underneath. Swallowing an audible gulp, Randa tipped open the lid and drew in a sharp breath. Shining brightly in the box was a silver band with inlaid Blue John; the same stone as in the necklace Denise had given her for Christmas. The stone was flanked with engravings of the Celtic symbol for eternity as well, matching the necklace that rarely left Randa's neck.

Randa was quiet for so long that Denise dipped her head to look into the blonde's eyes. "Don't you like it?" DJ asked nervously. Green eyes looked up to hers awash in tears.

"Oh God, Denise, I love it. I just…I guess I didn't expect it." The poet smiled at the reassurances and said, "Well go on; try it on." Randa removed the ring from the cushion holding it in the box. As she did she noticed engraving on the inside as well as the outside. Tilting the ring she was able to read the words placed there. *Eternity will not be enough.*

This time tears overflowed Randa's eyes and spilled unashamedly down her cheeks. Knowing what had prompted the fresh tears, Denise pulled the nurse into her arms and quietly said, "It won't be, you know. It won't be nearly long enough for us. As long as there will be a you or a me, there will be a we." Denise kissed the golden hair gently as she felt Randa's tears on her skin.

Taking the ring from Randa's hand, Denise asked, "Allow me?" Randa nodded consent, not yet trusting her voice. Denise slid from the bed and kneeled in front of the nurse.

"I love you, Miranda Martin. Nothing and no one will ever be able to change that. You hold my heart, my soul and my future. This ring is the symbol of all that. Will you continue to make me the happiest woman alive by wearing it?"

Randa looked into earnest blue eyes and smiled through her tears. Taking a steadying breath, she found the heart to smile and say clearly, "I would be proud and honored." Denise smiled back and slipped the ring on the third finger of Randa's left hand. Raising up she met the lean of her partner and the sweet kiss they shared sealed the moment in their hearts and their memories.

Randa broke the kiss feeling more composed. "I do love you, Denise Jennings. It seems like I always have and I know I always will. You've changed my whole outlook on turning thirty."

"I did?" questioned the poet giving Randa a surprised look.

"Yep, if I had to live to be thirty to be as happy as I am right now, I only wish the years would have passed quicker. Numbers like that aren't going to mean anything to me anymore except to mark the years we're together." She brought Denise back into her embrace and kissed her with the all the love present in her very full heart. They held each other tightly for a while, reveling in the closeness.

Denise moved back slightly but stayed within the nurse's arms. "Well, it seems you've successfully captured the Derbyshire Poet. What do you intend on doing with her,

Bwana?"

"The same thing I'd do if I caught a tiger by the tail. I'm going to hang on and enjoy the ride!" With that Randa pulled the poet up onto the bed and her body. Wrapping her legs around DJ, Randa did as promised and held on. The ride lasted long into the night.

****

The security checkpoint for the British Airway gate was crowded. Randa stood in the embrace of the poet, knowing new regulations would permit her to go no further with Denise. As the mass of humanity in San Francisco International Airport moved forward through the scanners, Randa felt the uncertainty in her heart again. She clung tightly to Denise who had her arms wrapped just as tightly around the nurse.

"I suppose I should get on to my gate," she whispered into golden hair. "You've got the number for the hotel and if there are any changes in plans, I'll call you straight away." Randa nodded and continued to hold tight. This parting at the airport in San Francisco felt achingly familiar to the painful one in London earlier in the year.

"Except this time I will be staying in touch, I won't be afraid to say 'I love you' and I will be coming back." Denise smiled at the shocked look on the nurse's face. "You must have known it would be on my mind as well." Eyes held as Denise reached up to softly cup the blonde's cheek. "I love you, Randa Martin."

Randa's eyes misted as she replied, "I love you too, Denise Jennings. Finish up this book business and hurry back to me. I'm going to miss you every second you're gone."

The kiss was long and slow before Denise reluctantly pulled away and moved through the security checkpoint. Randa watched as she picked up her carry-on bag from the x-ray scanner. For a second it seemed the poet would continue her walk to her gate but instead she turned to look back at the nurse. Randa's heart ached at the look of hesitation on Denise's face. Randa knew only she could give the poet the freedom she needed to make this trip and endure the separation. The nurse raised her left hand and pointed to the ring situated there. Gazes locked as Randa mouthed, "I love you" and nodded. Denise seemed to receive her message of support and love because she smiled and with a small wave, moved toward the gate and out of Randa's line of sight.

The nurse turned to leave the departure area, wiping away a small tear that had slipped down her cheek. *It's only a week* she thought. *Only a week, then she'll be back. What could possibly happen in a week?*

Chapter 5

Manchester's Belmont Hotel stood out as the most prestigious and exclusive hotel in the city. Primary consideration for all international visitors, those of high social standing and even premier league soccer teams, the five-star establishment was not only a first class lodging but also a venue for conference and social gatherings. It was the largest building in the city and its rectangular structure stood on forty-five levels, not including the vast underground parking facility. On the roof a large helipad was situated in its centre, which was used by many well-known figures in both the financial and entertainment business.

Denise stood by the side of the curb, black carryon upon one shoulder and matching suitcase situated by her feet. She looked up at the tall, dark brick, ominous structure with disdain. Never having been a fan of multi-story buildings she hoped Carl had been able to book her into one of its lower floors. The slightly nauseous feeling DJ got whenever she rode the elevators of a tall building she presumed stemmed from her childhood and the fear she experienced as she tried to escape her burning home. It was the feeling of being trapped on any floor above the ground, which still managed to unsettle her somewhat. The closer to the ground and the least amount of stairs to get there, the better as far as DJ was concerned.

Narrowing her eyes Denise moved them over the large bold lettering on the front of the building. Its name stood out on the charcoal brick background with eye catching gold letters. Taking a deep breath as she prepared to enter the hotel and face the oncoming events, DJ picked up her suitcase and made her way towards the double doors. An elegantly dressed gentleman wearing a maroon and black three-piece suit opened the brass door and DJ nodded her thanks as she stepped into the lobby. Its size surprised her, having expected something much larger due to the visual grandeur of the building. Denise approached the wood panelled front desk listening to her footsteps echo upon the pristine white floor.

Standing behind the desk was a young man wearing a navy suit. He smiled politely as DJ approached. "Welcome to the Belmont Hotel, Madam, how can I help you?"

Denise smiled politely. "Hi, I have a reservation under I presume the name of Denise Jennings. It would have been booked by either a Carl or Christine Lloyd."

The sandy-haired man looked down at the computer's screen as his fingers flew efficiently over a black keyboard. His brows furrowed together as he said, "I have a booking for a D. Jennings but it wasn't booked under either name you mentioned."

Hmm, DJ thought for a moment. "Okay then, I presume it was booked under 'Lloyd and Windsor Publishers'."

The clerk looked again. "That's right." His eyes scanned over the visual display unit. "A double room, non smoking, full facilities for three nights?"

"Yes."

"Excellent. If you would just sign here?" He handed DJ a computerized log, "And provide one form of identification which is just standard procedure; preferably something with both a picture and signature upon it."

Denise signed into the hotel and handed over her driver's license. Once all procedures were completed she was given her key for the sixth floor and turned to follow an elderly porter who had appeared out of nowhere and had picked up her case, ready to escort her to her destined floor. She followed him through a small archway and entered a much larger foyer that was literally buzzing with life. Ahead of her stood a double set of brass elevators with a uniformed man standing beside them. *They have somebody*

52

to press a button? She thought with a wry grin. Around her were a wide variety of shops, a well-known eating establishment, and dotted throughout the area were small groups of people or solitary individuals going about their everyday business. Denise ran her tongue over her front teeth as her eyes moved back to the restaurant. She was hungry and hadn't eaten anything on the plane. Although food in First Class was superior to economy she hadn't had much of an appetite and had spent her time either trying to sleep or watching the in-flight movie. Her journey had taken eleven hours straight from San Francisco to Manchester and she had been more than a little relieved to finally alight from the aircraft. Denise looked down at her watch and decided to get settled into her room first. She looked back towards the porter and found him waiting for her by the elevators. With a sheepish smile she jogged towards the waiting man and together they entered the lift. As the doors mechanically glided shut and the small compartment started its short journey to the sixth floor DJ counted each numbered light as it indicated the passing of another floor. She barely acknowledged the man standing beside her holding her suitcase, her mind being otherwise engaged on how long it would take before she could exit the enclosed space. Then with a jolt the compartment ground to a halt and the door slid open.

"Sixth floor," the porter said with a smile as he led Denise out into the hallway. She looked down at the plush pale cream carpeting upon the floor, feeling its deep pile beneath her feet and wondered how much the hotel charged for a single night. It seemed no expense was spared in creating a luxurious environment for its guests. *Hell, they have a guy to press the button on the lift; I wonder whether they have somebody to turn the shower on for you?* DJ chuckled to herself and received an amused look from her porter.

"Room six fourteen," he said, stopping by a large white door.

Denise slid the key into the lock and easily opened the door. Stepping into her room she took a moment to inspect her surroundings. By the middle of the far wall stood a large king-size bed and she gazed longingly at its comfortable appearance. To the left of the bed stood a double wardrobe and a door leading into an en-suite bathroom and to the right a dressing table and supposedly well stocked fridge. Opposite the bed was a large satellite television.

Hearing a thud DJ turned around to see the porter place her suitcase by the wall. "Is there anything else I can get you, Madam?"

Denise shook her head as she pushed her hand into the back pocket of her jeans and pulled out a small pile of notes. Extracting a five-pound note from the fold she handed it to the older man with a smile. "No thanks, mate, that will be all."

With a nod the porter left her room.

Taking a deep breath Denise turned back into the room. Pulling her arms out of her light black jacket she let it drop onto the corner of the bed as she herself fell into the soft fragrant sheets. The time difference was beginning to catch up with her and all thoughts of food left her mind as she instead decided sleep would be a welcome relief. As she closed her eyes her last thoughts were of Randa and the last morning they had shared together before she slipped into a dreamless sleep.

****

The loud ringing of the suite's telephone was what had pulled Denise from a deep slumber. Lifting her heavy head from the bottom of the bed the poet adjusted her position and snatched the receiver from its base. Her head fell down onto the pillows as she answered the call.

"Yes?"

"Hey, DJ, I see you made it back safely."

"Carl..." looking down at her watch DJ regarded the time with confusion. "God it feels like midnight... I can't believe it's only five o'clock in the evening." She yawned quietly, covering her mouth with her free hand.

"Well make sure you judge your sleep right for tomorrow. The launch begins at three o'clock in the afternoon and we have a lot to get through before then."

"Great."

"Listen DJ, we have to talk… can you meet me tonight? We can catch up and talk about the itinerary for tomorrow, etcetera. There are some things I need to discuss with you."

Swinging her legs over the edge, DJ sat upon the corner of the bed. "Sure, where are you?"

"In the hotel; room fifteen oh seven. How about you meet me for dinner in the tenth floor restaurant in one hour? I really do need to talk to you. I don't want to concern you but this is important stuff."

"Concern me?"

"Oh no, nothing to fret about. So can we meet?"

"Okay." Denise looked back at her watch. "How about half six?" She realized she needed to call Randa and let her know she had arrived back in England safely.

"Fine by me."

"Right, see you then Carl."

"Later, DJ."

Falling back upon the bed's surface Denise stared at the rotating ceiling fan. She knew Randa would still be sleeping after having pulled an all night shift on the Brightwood site last night so decided to leave a message on the answer phone. Looking at the telephone handset still within her hand she followed the guidelines for making an outside call. Randa always turned the telephone off when she was sleeping during the day so DJ knew she wouldn't have to risk the chance of waking her lover. After the recorded message finished Denise waited for the beep.

"Hi, it's me. Just want you to know that I got here okay. God…I think I miss you already. I have this great king-size bed and you are not here to share it with me. Anyway I am in room six fourteen; call me reversed charges to this room whenever you can okay. I love you. Bye."

Disconnecting the call, Denise forced a weary sigh through pursed lips. She decided a shower might help to clear her mind and lying doing nothing just reminded her of how much she was beginning to miss Randa. Decision made, the poet headed towards the shower.

55

****

The Belmont Hotel boasted three exclusive restaurants and each one offered a high-quality variety of world cuisines. From Eastern dishes to European mixtures the three restaurants combined to offer a first class selection of tempting delights.

Denise Jennings walked into the large tenth floor restaurant, scanning the wide semi circled room. In the centre stood a grey stone waterfall in the shape of an open oyster shell. A gentle trickle of water flowed out from the top of the stone shell and cascaded in rivulets down into the circular pool underneath. The rest of the floor space was covered in tables and as DJ's eyes searched out her friend a smartly dressed man in a black tuxedo and strong oriental features suddenly appeared by her side.

"Ma'am, do you have a reservation?"

Denise looked down at the slight man and then once again out over the patrons in the restaurant. She wondered whether she had dressed smartly enough in her simple black trousers and tight red sleeveless top. "Yes I'm here to meet a Mr. Lloyd. I don't seem to be able to spot him."

"Ah yes… follow me please."

With a shrug Denise followed the small man to the far side of the room. She weaved her way around the maze of neatly dressed tables making a mental note of some of the dishes available. Ahead of her she soon recognised a familiar crop of dark blonde hair.

"Table seventeen," said the waiter.

Denise nodded her appreciation. "Thanks, could you bring a jug of water to the table please?"

"Certainly, madam, I'll just be one moment."

The waiter headed towards the kitchen as Denise approached her friend. She sidled up behind Carl stealthily and placed her lips beside his ear. In as husky a voice as she could muster Denise said, "Been waiting long, honey?"

The editor's frame literally jumped as he spun around in his chair. His eyes relaxed as he spotted Denise, then lit up as he studied the poet. "DJ! Wow what the hell

56

happened to you?" he sprung from his chair and regarded Denise closely casting an appreciative eye from head to toe. "Is this what a couple of months in the States does to you?" He stepped closer. "Nice tan!"

Denise smirked, "If you study me any closer, Carl, you might just discover the absence of tan lines!" She rolled her eyes and hugged her friend. "So how are you?"

"Excited DJ, very excited!" Carl retook his seat and Denise sat opposite him. "Tomorrow's the big day!"

"Yes." Denise looked down at her empty wine glass and circled her finger over the rim.

Carl frowned as he asked, "Nervous?"

"Just a little."

"Hmm." Carl nodded his head and decided to momentarily change the subject. "So... how is Randa?"

Denise smiled immediately. "She's great."

"I wish I'd had time to talk to her at the funeral," Carl paused hoping he hadn't just brought to surface any painful memories for the poet but at her simple nod he continued. "I only know her as the nurse who looked after Sara and the woman who remained by your side that entire day."

"She would like to have spoken to you too." The poet chuckled as she said, "She doesn't understand how I always seem to answer the telephone whenever you call and she never gets to say hello."

The waiter interrupted their conversations as he brought a jug of iced water to the table. He handed them both a menu before disappearing to another table.

"So," Carl opened his maroon, leather-bound menu as he continued. "No tan lines you say? Please tell me you haven't turned into one of those beach babes who spends her entire time catching rays and drinking cocktails down by the surf?"

"The beach?" Denise stated, "I haven't set one foot on a beach since I have been there. This is just from the garden. Believe me... I did have a few tan lines to begin with but decided I didn't like them! Fortunately Randa's property provided plenty of seclusion for that not to be a problem!"

Denise thought back to the first time she had decided to lay out under the hot June sun, "'o' natural" as she had called it. Randa had been sleeping after working all night and had wandered into the garden mid-afternoon to find one very naked poet lying peacefully under the sweltering heat of the sun. DJ vividly remembered being pulled out of her state of relaxation by soft lips slowly working their way up her calves and inner thighs. She had soon abandoned her pursuit of the perfect tan for much more pleasurable activities.

Maybe it was her self imposed sheltered upbringing or maybe it was simply her reserved British nature but the poet did remember having slight reservations about such an intimate act in a rather open place – however brief it had been. It was Randa who had brought out Denise's exhibitionist side in the first place, giving her the confidence, for instance, to sun bathe sans clothes. However her feelings for Randa and the desire to express them whenever or wherever was never something she felt she needed to hide.

Carl began fanning his face with the leather bound menu. "Gosh, DJ, no more talking about naked tanning sessions, I'm only human for crying out loud! Lets move the subject away from bare bodies okay?" Studying Denise his features suddenly sobered. "There is something I need to discuss with you. Now this may be nothing and I may well be jumping in the deep end here but I need to tell you this."

Denise sat forward in her chair as she said, "You're not exactly calming my already edgy nerves here, Carl. You better elaborate before I start expecting the worst."

Nodding, the editor pushed his glass of wine to the corner of the table and placed down his menu. "Okay. Well as you know we've sent copies of the new anthology out to a selected group of media representatives who will be present at the launch tomorrow. We sent advance copies to two broadsheet newspapers, a couple of literary magazines and the book review programme 'The Open Book'." Carl frowned and placed his folded hands upon the table. "It seems to have sparked a lot of rumours and while none pertain to surmising your actual identity, probably because they will discover this, a lot has still been said. The trouble is that I think somebody from our firm might have actually leaked a few extra details that we were leaving for the launch."

"What details?" DJ asked confused and feeling slightly alarmed.

"Pertaining to the fact that you will be announcing the forthcoming release of a novel dedicated and based upon the life of your aunt, Sara Jennings."

Denise frowned. "But it isn't. It's just a fictionalised light hearted story based on aspects of her life with a parody of Sara as the main character."

"I know, but you know how rumours are, DJ."

"Okay." Licking her index finger Denise placed it back upon the rim of the empty glass and started moving it around the fine edge. "So what's the problem? I mean all of this will be sorted out tomorrow. What is concerning you so?" The poet was beginning to think that maybe Carl was overreacting.

"The trouble is this." Carl pulled two sheets of cream paper out of his black suit jacket's inside pocket. "These are two anonymous letters both I believe written by the same person who seems to think that you shouldn't release a book based upon the life of Sara Jennings when you don't know the full story. And if you do then you will omit it from this book to make her appear better!"

Denise expression twisted to one of confusion. "What?"

Carl handed DJ the letters. "We haven't taken any action yet but whoever this person is seems to think you are under a misconception about Sara and you wouldn't dare release the truth in this book." As Denise started to protest Carl continued, "Yes I know it isn't a true story of her life but that is what the rumours have stated. Look, I don't really understand what is going on here, DJ. I was hoping you might have some clue as to what this person is talking about and know how to handle it."

Denise looked away, her eyes scanning the assortment of customers sitting in groups around a multitude of tables.

In her own mind DJ was very positive she knew everything there was to know about Sara's life. She thought maybe this unknown person might have known about Sara's romantic history but that in no way led her to believe she was making the wrong choice in releasing her novel. After all this was **just** a fictionalised account of her life.

"As far as I am concerned or am aware, there is absolutely nothing I don't know of Sara's life. I think maybe this is just a case of somebody with nothing better to do. Maybe an ex-pupil who never got over Sara giving him or her a bad grade." She smiled as she opened up her menu and looked down at the first page.

Carl leaned forward in his chair and asked, "DJ, are you sure about this?"

The poet shrugged. "Yes. What else can we do? Believe me this is nothing." Denise looked back at the listings and ran her finger down the list. "How about a good old traditional curry?"

The editor's eyes lit up. "A vinderloo?"

Denise grimaced. "Well not for me. I'm afraid my stomach isn't quite made of cast iron like I assume yours is."

"Well I vote we order a wide variety of different dishes and just dig into them all. You know they do a famous appetizer selection. Maybe we can start with that?"

DJ nodded. "Sounds okay to me... go for it." Leaning back in her chair the poet looked down at the letters still laying upon the table. She picked up the top sheet of expensive looking paper and glanced over the bold script. Her brows wrinkled together as she wondered how the rumours had started and progressed the way they had. Well this certainly isn't what I was expecting. I suppose there had to be a little excitement this week otherwise I would have nothing interesting to tell Randa!

Not fully understanding the impact of the letters, Denise dropped them back down upon the table and resumed her perusal of the menu.

****

60

Randa opened her eyes to the afternoon sun and reached for the warmth of Denise's body. It wasn't until her hand had fumbled around the other side of the bed for a moment or two that she recalled it had been almost twenty-four hours since she had taken Denise to the airport. Even a busy night on the Brightwood Network hadn't helped her fall asleep that morning. She had missed the poet and the comfort she felt in the mornings when she would climb into the queen sized bed and snuggle up to the brunette. It didn't matter what kind of night she had, in Denise's arms she was safe and loved.

The nurse crawled reluctantly from the bed and headed off to the bathroom. The house seemed so empty. It hadn't seemed that way for the year she had lived there before meeting DJ, but it sure did now. Everything reminded her of the poet, the dresser with the neatly folded clothing and a bottle of the poet's favourite perfume on top. The shower, where they had some of their most interesting encounters, especially when Denise was in one of her playful moods. The mug in the kitchen with the picture of the man in a dress with the logo "God save the Queen." The last had been a present from Randa to DJ on their first foray into the City by the Bay together.

Randa wandered aimlessly around the house having no plans other than missing Denise when she noticed the red light blinking on the answering machine. Two rapid blinks followed by a pause indicated two messages waited to be heard. One of these better be Denise; I really need to hear her voice. The nurse depressed the Play button and listened as the first message started.

"Hey Randa, it's Tyler. Long time no hear, huh? Listen, Danielle and I broke up so I've moved back here. I'm staying with Rod and Sue until I find a nice condo or something. How about lunch for old time's sake? Give me a call; you have their number. I'm free tomorrow but the day after I start back in the ER."

Randa hit the Stop button a little surprised by the first message. Tyler was a nurse she had dated for a while when she was still working in the hospital. His intense love of the Emergency Room and his gregarious sense of humour

61

initially attracted Randa, but she soon found him to be a self-absorbed adrenaline junkie. He continually belittled her choice of the busy but less critical Cardiology floor. She could still see him, dark blue scrubs showing off his blond good looks as he regaled the small crowd of nurses with his exploits at the local omelette place after work.

"I mean this guy was a total mess! What can I say, when it's car versus 18 wheeler, the guy in the car loses every time!" Tyler was practically holding court. Randa found the whole thing obnoxious and from that point declined any further dates. Still, Danielle was a friend of hers, a co-worker on the Cardiology floor. Everyone, including Randa, had been surprised when Danielle had announced she and Tyler were going to San Diego to live together and work at a Level I Trauma Center. Though he was an annoying ass, Randa was curious about what had happened with Danielle. After consulting the personal phone book in her desk drawer, the nurse picked up the cordless phone and dialed the number.

"Hello?"

"Tyler? Hi, it's Randa."

"Randa! Hey babe, glad you called me back. How the heck are you?"

Randa cringed, remembering Tyler's frequent use of "babe", "honey", and "sweetie".

"I'm good Tyler, very happy. When did you get back?"

"Just got back yesterday," he said. *"Couldn't wait to get in touch with all my old friends again."*

You always were a fast worker Randa thought. She shuddered when she thought of how Tyler had pushed her for sex, starting with their very first date. She had managed to avoid his advances, but he hadn't made it easy. "Well, speaking of keeping in touch, we really didn't hear from you or Danielle after you left."

"Yeah, I know. We were kind of busy down in San Diego."

Randa was curious now. "So, did Danielle move back to Silver Valley, too?"

There was a pause on the line, then Tyler said, *"Uh, no. Actually she got hired as the Cardiology Unit supervisor."*

There it is! Thought Randa. *The truth is your big old ego balloon burst.*

Tyler's voice resumed its usual cocky tone. *"So, I thought that maybe now that I'm a free agent again, we could pick up where we sort of left off."*

Randa laughed. "Tyler, we didn't leave off anywhere. We stopped dating months before you and Danielle left. Besides, I'm involved with someone and that's involved with a capital I."

"Oh come on, babe. I heard about you and that English woman. You can't be serious about that. I know you and I know you're no dyke."

The nurse quashed an initial impulse to call the man an ignorant bonehead and hang up the phone. Instead she settled for a stony tone of voice.

"I really try to avoid labels, Tyler, so why don't we just say I'm a person who happens to be very much in love with a warm, caring, sensitive and incredibly gorgeous other person. The fact that she's a woman is just a bonus." Suddenly the second message on the answering machine popped into her mind.

"Speaking of her, I have to go because if it's a competition between talking to you and talking to her, you're not even in the running. Bye, Tyler." She hung up to spluttering on the other end of the line.

Moving back to the answering machine, Randa pushed the Play button and Denise's voice came on giving the nurse her room number in the hotel she was staying at. Glancing at the clock and adding eight hours to the time, the blonde figured the poet would definitely be in bed then.

Randa stopped by the kitchen and pulled a bottle of water out of the refrigerator. *Need to keep my fluids up* she thought. Still carrying the phone with her, she returned to the bedroom and settled back under the covers. She picked up the slip of paper Denise had written the name and number of the hotel on. She dialed the international number then the city code and phone number.

63

"Belmont Hotel. How may I direct your call?"

"Room six fourteen, please," the nurse requested.

"One moment please," the voice replied and shortly the phone was ringing again.

"Hello?" a somewhat sleepy Denise answered. Randa smiled as she heard the voice of her partner.

"What are you wearing?" the nurse breathed.

"Randa! God, I've missed you." Denise's voice had brightened considerably. "I'm still knackered but I don't seem to sleep as well here as I do in our bed."

Our bed, the thought that the poet felt so much at home with her was enough to cause the nurse to let slip a small sigh. "Denise, I miss you so much. How is it going? Have you seen Carl?"

"Yes, we had dinner tonight. Everything is set up for tomorrow as we planned. I don't mind confessing I'm a little nervous to be facing the press and then there's this other business."

"What other business?" the nurse asked. "What's happened, Denise?"

"Oh, it's probably nothing. Carl said the premise of the novel was leaked which wouldn't be a problem except he received two letters that in essence said if we knew the whole truth about Sara we wouldn't be publishing a book in her honor."

Randa sat up in the bed. "What do they mean 'the whole truth'?"

"I don't have the foggiest notion, but it's more than likely just some crackpot. This is the first time I've had to deal with this part of the business and this kind of thing probably happens all the time. I was just never exposed to it before. I wish you were here to hold on to as I go through this; we make quite the team you know."

"That we do, my friend. Tell you what, how about if we talk for a while until you feel like you can rest?" Randa said as she settled back down.

"Mmm, that sounds nice. What do you want to talk about?" Denise asked.

Randa gave a soft laugh as she snuggled deeper into the comfortable bed. "Well, you can answer my original question. What are you wearing?"

A rustling of bedclothes was heard on the line and the poet replied, "My tartan boxers and that comfortable red tee shirt I love. Very sexy, eh? You tell me now, what are you wearing?"

"A sheet," Randa said, her voice dropping a little as her hand slid over her breasts on its way south.

A short silence came from the hotel room followed by more rustling of bedclothes. Denise's voice came slow and sexy over the line. "I have a feeling I'm going to sleep very well after this conversation."

Chapter 6

It seemed the sun had risen way too early for the day of the book launch. Its blinding rays woke Denise as they beamed directly onto her face. Instantly she cursed the fact that she'd forgotten to close the curtains the night before. She also cursed the room's eastern facing window and the fact that the day had even arrived. It had taken her much longer to get to sleep the night before as the couple in the room beside hers had decided to keep her awake with their heated arguing. Yawning, Denise rolled onto her side and pulled her watch from the nightstand.

"Half six!" she exclaimed with a feeling of shock. She hadn't wanted to greet the land of the living until at least nine o'clock.

With a groan of annoyance she fell back down onto the pillow, once again cursing the occupants of the room next door whom she was sure were still sleeping away, blissfully unaware a new day had even begun. Letting her mind wander, Denise thought back to the night before and the conversation she and Randa had shared. A smile spread across her lips as she recalled Randa's words, the sound of her voice and the way she breathed down the phone. *That certainly was a new experience,* she thought and sighed as she recalled the sensations the blonde had managed to instil within her from so far away. *She doesn't even have to touch me anymore; I feel so stimulated just thinking about her!*

Realising her line of thought was leading towards dangerous territory DJ decided a change of mood was in order. Looking back at the nightstand, her left arm ventured out from under the warmth of her covers and reached for the television remote control lying beside her watch. Denise retrieved the black plastic gadget and snuggled back into the covers while turning on the television. Placing one hand behind her head she commenced flicking though the varied offering of channels.

After monotonous minutes of aimless switching DJ dropped her remote control with a sigh of boredom. She looked at the TV with a frown as an overgrown brown bear pranced around a colourful studio set. *God if this doesn't lull me back to a state of comatose I don't know what will!* As the bear started singing an inane song about the importance of brushing ones teeth, Denise rolled over and buried her head under her pillow and thought about the coming day.

Today she had the launch, which started early afternoon. It was being held on the second floor of the Belmont in a stylish function room. Carl had taken her down to look over the room the night before and she had been surprised by its elegance. They had even ordered a buffet style lunch to be served after the initial conference and general socialising. Unfortunately the thought of food did nothing to ease DJ's nerves and she seriously hoped she would be able to make it through the event without tripping or spilling her wine!

****

As the day progressed through the early morning the clear sky had darkened with heavy storm clouds. By midday the heavens had opened and showered the city streets with a heavy downpour of rain. That in itself was not unexpected, as Manchester was well known as being one of the wettest cities in England. Thankfully as midday gave way to early afternoon the sun resumed its dominance in the sky and as the last of the light rains lifted a rainbow arched its way over the land.

Standing at her hotel window, dressed in simple black trousers and a blue silk blouse, Denise looked out across the city. Below her window an assortment of cars and buses passed by, constantly disturbing the shallow puddles upon the well-driven roads. They sporadically launched great splashes of rainwater onto the pathways, occasionally hitting unfortunate pedestrians.

Resting her head upon the windowpane Denise looked down and watched the metropolis of life below. It was a far cry from the peace and tranquillity of the rural surroundings of Randa's property. DJ remembered one day in particular in which the distant rumble of a highflying airplane had been the only sound she had heard all day. *Bliss.*

Drumming her fingers upon the windowsill Denise took one more look at the rainbow in the sky before turning towards her room. Sitting upon the edge of her bed with elbows resting upon his knees Carl Lloyd closely inspected a document detailing Denise's schedule for the following days. He frowned, rubbing his cleanly shaven chin as he placed the document beside him on the bed.

"You have one interview tonight, one tomorrow morning and then two in the afternoon all before you leave to go back to Derbyshire. Then you have three book signings one near your home town, one in Birmingham and one in London."

DJ grimaced as she pushed herself away from the window. "Can we not talk about that now? I would like to get today over with first if you don't mind."

Carl held up his hands as he said, "Point taken. Okay let's just deal with today." He leaned back, bracing his weight upon his hands and slightly bounced upon the bed's surface. "I think yours is more comfortable than mine. They gave Chris and I a water bed and those things make me sea sick."

"Chris?" Denise questioned, "When did Chris get here? I thought she wasn't able to make the launch."

"She arrived late last night after my mum and dad agreed to look after the kids... god help them! She really didn't want to miss this and besides... you know how good she is at mingling. She is down there right now keeping all the guests and press happy until you arrive." Carl arched his eyebrows and looked at Denise expectantly.

"I know, I know." DJ hesitated as her eyes flitted around the hotel room. "I'll just be one moment." Heading towards the far end of the room she disappeared inside the bathroom and closed the door behind her.

The steady drip of a leaking tap broke the silence of the smaller room. Facing the sink Denise placed both hands upon its rim and looked into the mirror. Uncertain eyes stared back and she closed them, taking a deep breath.

"This is it... there's no turning back now, DJ." Looking back at her reflection she combed long fingers through her hair wishing she hadn't decided against putting it up in a smarter style.

"It's almost half past two, DJ," shouted Carl from the bedroom.

"Okay, okay." Taking one final breath of courage Denise turned from the mirror and walked back out into the bedroom.

Carl smiled. "All ready?"

"I wish Randa could have been here too...god I feel like I'm going to throw up!"

"Once you get down there you will be fine... I know you, DJ."

Quickly swiping an abandoned bottle of mineral water from the wooden dresser, Denise took a drink of the warm liquid. "Right... let's go."

****

From her vantage point the poet had a perfect view of the function room as she peered covertly through the small window of its doorway. Blue eyes scanning the layout, DJ spotted the wide table at the far end of the room. In front of that table stood a line of chairs reaching five rows back. She presumed that would be where the conference would take place. Those chairs had not been there when she and Carl inspected the room the night before.

69

Standing around the room, various sized groups of people stood in conversation. Some of them held small note pads and Dictaphones while others held the advanced copies of her new book. DJ even spotted two men holding rather expensive looking cameras.

From behind the poet Carl peered over her shoulder. "Ready?"

"I suppose it's too late to change my mind?"

"You started the ball rolling, DJ. You have a room full of people all waiting to see whether D. Jennings really is a travelling gypsy with a tormented mind!"

Denise laughed. "Well for that purpose alone I might just want to get out there and quash all of those blasted rumours."

"That's my DJ." Carl tapped on the small, square window and Denise watched as Christine Lloyd turned at the sound and approached the door. She slipped outside leaving one foot against the frame to keep the door ajar.

"Ready?" she asked sweeping her long red hair over her shoulders. "The buzz in this room is alive with speculation and expectation. It is quite exciting."

Denise felt her heart rate increase with anticipation. Rubbing sweaty palms upon the cotton material of her trousers she looked once again through the window. "Okay… lets get this started."

With a nod Christine looked back into the room. "I will do a short introduction. I'm sure you will know when it is your cue to enter." Placing one hand briefly upon Denise's arm for reassurance the auburn haired woman nodded quickly – then she was gone.

The poet watched her leave with a wry expression. Between Carl and his wife he was definitely the warmer natured of the pair. DJ had always found she was able to relate better with the editor than his wife even though Christine was the co-owner of the publishing firm and had offered Denise her original contract.

"Here we go," the editor said as his wife stood at the head of the large room and called for silence.

As a hush floated over the room Carl and Denise were able to hear Christine as she began her introduction.

"Well ladies and gentlemen… as you know we are here today for the launch of the fourth anthology of poetry by D. Jennings. Being as though this is the first of such promotions, as Miss Jennings has previously preferred to remain away from the public eye, I am sure you can imagine what an exclusive event this is. Now before the general socialising, one on one conversations and dinner… we will be holding a press conference in which Miss Jennings will be answering a selection of your questions."

Denise took a deep breath of warm air and placed her hand upon the gold door handle. Her sweaty palm slipped over the smooth, cold surface. *God I hope I don't have to shake any hands.*

"And so ladies and gentlemen it is my great pleasure to introduce to you the country's most respected and read author and most successful poet… still living," Christine stated pointedly causing murmurs of humoured acknowledgement to ripple through the gathering. "Miss Denise Jennings…"

An eruption of rapturous applause rose from the crowd and Denise swallowed back a feeling of nausea as she pushed open the door and walked into the room.

The loud echo of rapid clapping suddenly slowed as the gathering received their first glimpse of D. Jennings. Feeling a wave of self-consciousness wash over her, Denise smiled shyly as she made her way through the function room to the once again rising applause. With a nod of acknowledgement Denise took her place behind the table and stood in front of the centre seat. She looked out among the crowd of smiling faces and began to feel a little more at ease. Denise wasn't prepared for the looks of appreciation and respect she saw shining back at her but that in itself helped to calm her nerves and give her the self-assurance she needed. From several positions the flash of cameras sparkled around the room.

As the applause gradually ended, Denise realised she would now have to speak. Keeping her standing position she fought the urge to fold her arms as she began.

"Well as I am sure you can imagine this is all rather overwhelming for me," she smiled, "However I would like to thank everybody for attending this afternoon. I hope we all have a pleasant time... enjoy the meal... but for now I believe you have some questions so why don't we start with them?" As another light applause rose from the gathering Denise took her seat in between Christine and Carl. The editor had discreetly made his way to the front of the room while DJ was talking. Pulling her chair into position, Denise turned to Carl and received a wink of support. She smiled and turned back ready to face the questions.

Hands started to rise and Denise nodded to a middle aged man with a receding hairline.

"Miss Jennings," he began, "Rupert Green, The Times Literary review. I would first like to ask what I am sure we are all most eager to know. Why did you keep your identity so closely guarded and why do you now feel the need to come out into the open?"

Denise entwined her fingers together and placed her hands upon the table. "Well... basically I suppose I was and still am to a point... a little shy. At the time I was comfortable remaining out of the public eye. I was young and had no idea my work would be so positively acknowledged. I've always been a relatively private person."

"So why now?"

"Lots of changes occurred in my life," Denise blinked as another camera flashed in her face. "I realised I could no longer continue to live my life in the rut it was becoming. I had to move on and accept the changes... so I did. Besides I felt it was about time I quashed those rumours about me... and I assure you that I do not possess the tackle of a man!"

Amused chuckles rose from the crowd before hands lifted once again and DJ nodded for another person to speak.

"Miss Jennings, your poetry has recently been included in the high school syllabus. How do you feel about having your work put under the microscope in such a way?"

Denise grinned. "I am very flattered. It was certainly something I never expected but I was pleased nonetheless. I

72

always hoped in some way I would be able to touch somebody with my words. I in no way claim to possess a greater knowledge or desire to hold a status of high regard. They are just my thoughts and feelings. If I am able to touch somebody... in some way and make a positive difference in his or her life then I feel that I have achieved my goal. It is all I have ever wanted."

"Miss Jennings?" A female voice said. "Is one of the changes in your life that you mentioned the death of your aunt, Sara Jennings?"

"Yes it was." Denise answered simply.

"And why did you live with your aunt and not your own parents?"

DJ shuffled uncomfortably in her chair. "My parents died in a house fire when I was ten years old. I lived with Sara... my father's sister from then on."

A chorus of hands rose once again and Denise pointed towards a smartly dressed woman in a navy suit.

"Hello, Miss Jennings. Julia Ford, assistant editor for Passions of Prose Magazine. Is it true you are planning to release your first novel based upon your aunt's life?"

Denise internally rolled her eyes as she answered the woman's question. She had hoped this question would arise though so she could put a stop to the rumours that were travelling around.

A young man quickly raised his hand and asked his question. "After writing just poetry what makes you think you can successfully make the transition into fiction, Miss Jennings?"

"Well... all I can say is that this certainly isn't the first work of fiction I have written. The only difference is that this book will be published under my own name."

"Are you saying you have written under a pen name?" He pushed.

"I'm afraid I am not allowed to answer that question under the restraints of the contract it was written under."

"You've written for somebody else?"

"I'm sorry I am unable to answer that."

Another question arose. "Miss Jennings, in your dedication you included a very personal message to a

Miranda Martin."

"Yes?" Denise said simply.

"Are we to believe this was a declaration of your sexual preference?"

Here we go, the poet thought. She had wondered how long it would take before this line of questioning commenced. "It wasn't so much a declaration of that as it was quite simply a affirmation of my feelings for Randa."

"So you are in a relationship with this woman?"

Denise felt her hackles rise at the way the reporter described Randa. "Yes, I am in a relationship with **Randa**. Very happily so."

From beneath the table Denise felt Carl squeeze her knee in a show of support. "There has to be at least one!" He muttered, lowering his head. The brunette refrained from smirking as another body rose from the crowd.

"Miss Jennings, what would you say to those who state that revealing your sexuality along with your identity was nothing more than a publicity stunt?"

Fighting the urge to pound her head upon the table, Denise leaned forward. "I would say they are wrong. My reasons were purely personal and simply part of a transition within my life."

"And you are not afraid this will alienate your fans… the people who admire you and your work… and who gave you this success?"

DJ looked around the room before answering. "I suppose that if they really are fans then it shouldn't make any difference. My writing is all they knew of me. I will never claim to be anything I am not. The fact that I fell in love with a woman was due to the wonderful person that she is… it had little to do with her gender."

"Is she here today?" A voice called out.

"No, Randa had to work," Denise said.

A young woman sitting in the front row raised her hand. "Miss Jennings, I work for the Daily Edition." Denise instantly recognised the name of her local Derbyshire newspaper. "We recently received an anonymous letter stating your rumoured forthcoming book based upon your aunt's life…"

"Though it is not," Denise interrupted feeling suddenly concerned.

"Well yes... but the letter stated that some facts you include in this book will be fabricated or will only tell half of the truth about Sara Jennings. The letter leads us to believe that either you are hiding certain facts or you are ignorant of them."

With a frown Denise turned towards Carl who looked back with an expression of concerned confusion. Biting the corner of her lower lip DJ looked back to the assembly of expectant faces. "I don't see any relevance this will hold to the book as it is **just** fiction. As for my aunt... well apart from the fact that I assure you that I do know all aspects of her life... I don't necessarily think they are other people's concern. My aunt passed away after falling victim to a terrible disease and I would like to pay her the respect she is due by not bringing her personal life under scrutiny." Denise paused as she felt a tight ball of emotion swell within her. She took a deep steadying breath before continuing. "I hope you will understand how tough this was for us all and show Sara the respect she deserves by letting her rest in peace."

As a quiet applause ascended from the crowd of guests, Denise let a small smile of thanks past her lips. *Please change the subject,* she thought as the sound died.

"Miss Jennings?" A young man with ash blonde hair emerged from the gathering. "First of all I would just like to say that I am a fan of your work and I would very much like to know where do you gain your inspiration?"

DJ sighed internally as she delivered a winning smile and answered the man's question.

The conference progressed smoothly from then on but from within the crowd cold, blue eyes stared penetratingly into Denise disguising the hurt and animosity that was bubbling so heatedly within.

Chapter 7

Five thousand miles away, Randa was finding it difficult to concentrate on the myriad of tasks she had assigned herself for the day. The tasks were designed to keep her mind anyplace but on Denise in her first public appearance and press conference. The herb garden was weeded, the cracked mopboard in the living room was replaced and small cucumbers were soaking in brine well on their way to becoming pickles. During all the tasks though, the nurse's mind returned time and time again to Denise.

Randa knew why Denise had emerged from the shadows. The poet's dedication in *Connecting Hearts* showed the nurse the depth of DJ's love and the strength of her commitment. The decision to continue into the light was part and parcel of that action. Now Randa felt a huge responsibility to make Denise's transition to being a public figure as painless as possible. To that end she tried to give the poet all the love and support she would need in the changes about to happen to her.

Randa looked at her watch for the thousandth time, realizing Denise was still in the middle of the publicity activities in Manchester. She knew it would be some time before she would be able to call the poet and find out how the day had gone. *I feel so damn helpless sitting on the porch steps in Silver Valley when I know Denise is putting herself and her work out on the line.*

Randa thought about the conversation she had with Denise yesterday. At least she thought about the part of the conversation they had before Randa's libido had sat up and clambered for attention. *God, I've never done that before. I'm glad Denise just went with me on it. Phone sex, one more thing off life's little to-do list!* The nurse smiled to herself at the memory.

Randa was a little bothered by something that Denise had mentioned. *Why would someone write to say if they knew the whole truth about Sara they wouldn't want to publish the book?* The blonde knew Denise had fictionalised Sara's life, the story was to be light-hearted and inspirational, not a biography. If you discarded the way the book was written you still had the glaring fact that someone was trying to blacken Sara's name. Randa felt her protective nature rise; Sara had been a good friend to her as well as Denise's aunt and mentor.

Standing from the back porch steps and brushing off her denim shorts, Randa moved through the screen door into the house lost in thought. It wasn't until she stopped at her desk and spied the phone that Randa had an idea. *Maybe there's someone who can shed a little light on this whole thing.* Finding the number, the nurse dialed then listened as the connection was made.

"Hello?

"Diane, hi. It's Randa."

"Randa! It's always lovely to hear from you. How are you, dear?"

"Fine, Diane. Denise and I are both fine. I know she'll tell you herself when she comes up to Derbyshire for the book signing. She said she definitely wanted to have a good visit with you."

"I'll be looking forward to that, it's been a while since we've had the chance to just sit and chat. We did quite a bit of that when Sara was still alive."

Diane had been Sara's best friend and, as Randa had learned after the older Jennings' death, much more important to Sara than that. Sara had been in love with Diane though circumstances that Randa wasn't sure of had

77

kept them apart.

"I envy you those times, Diane. It seemed like I just got to know Sara when she lost her ability to speak and then died. I wish I'd known her better." Randa wasn't sure what she was fishing for but if anyone knew something about Sara that Denise didn't, it would be Diane.

"What was Sara like when she was younger? You two met in college didn't you?"

"Oh, yes!" Diane chuckled. "I haven't thought about those days in such a long time. I had just moved to London which in the late 1950's was a very exciting place…"

****

London 1958

Sara Jennings folded the piece of paper yet again after scratching through another entry on it. This would be the seventh flat for let she'd seen that day. The list of possible rentals was dwindling rapidly. *It never fails; either the flat is nice and the flatmate is strange or the person is fine but the flat is a disaster* she thought.

Sara's patience was wearing thin. It was Wednesday and she needed to get her living arrangements settled before classes started on the next Monday. Staying with Geoff and Alice Spicer, friends of her brother, was only a temporary solution. The Spicer's were a lovely couple but spending the next few terms with them in their tiny extra bedroom wasn't the university experience she had been hoping for.

The young woman looked around as she walked down the street toward the next address on the list gleaned from the bulletin boards around the campus. The neighborhood was older but seemed well cared for. There were pensioners as well as young mothers pushing apple-cheeked infants in their prams. The brilliant blue of Sara's eyes observed all this as she stopped briefly to straighten her scarf around her dark brunette hair. Checking her look in the reflection of the chemist's shop window, she was satisfied with her appearance. Her coat was clean though slightly worn, a testament to her working class background.

Her father had been a tailor before being killed on the beaches of Normandy in 1944 when Sara had been just eight years old. Her mother used the training from her wartime job as a military camp cook to earn a job as a cook at the university in Birmingham. Sara and her brother Daniel who was four years her elder, grew up on the campus. It was there she discovered a love of books and learning, eventually deciding to pursue the dream of becoming a teacher. Daniel had decided on a career in

79

architecture and had just returned to Birmingham after completing his final term at college in Manchester. He had recently become engaged to a lovely young woman by the name of Angelina and they planned to marry in a few months after he became established with the local company that had hired him.

Sara was glad her brother was so happy with his life but in her heart she knew that his kind of life was not for her. She wanted to see more of England and the world than the city she grew up in. After long discussions with her mother it was decided Sara would attend the university in London to work toward her teaching degree. Daniel had contacted a school friend and Sara was given a part-time job in the law office Geoff Spicer worked in.

That brought her to this day and the thus far futile hunt for a suitable flat. Drawing herself up to her full five foot nine height, she moved along the sidewalk when a small sign in a downstairs window caught her eye. **Flatmate wanted, third floor** it said simply.

Deciding she had nothing to lose, Sara went up three steps into the building and from there up the stairs to the only flat on the third floor. Taking a deep breath and sending a little prayer skyward, the brunette knocked on the door. There was a short interval and the door swung open allowing the sound of Doris Day's "Secret Love" to filter out into the hallway. Friendly brown eyes peered up at Sara from behind small wire framed glasses. A bob of light brown hair topped a five foot four frame.

"Yes?"

"Good afternoon. I've come about the sign in the window downstairs."

"Right. Well, I'm Diane Chamberlain and I'm the one looking for a flatmate. Sorry the sign downstairs didn't say any more but with Mrs. O'Neal as the resident on that floor I was lucky to get anything posted at all. Actually, I was going to post a notice at the university this afternoon. Are you attending there?"

"I start on Monday," Sara nodded. "I'm Sara Jennings, by the way. Can I take a look at the place? If it's convenient, of course."

"Oh, certainly. Please come in. It's a little small but there are two bedrooms. The bathroom is shared. The place isn't new but everything seems to work just fine. I've only been here two weeks myself."

"Really?" asked Sara. "Where are you from?"

"Derbyshire, a little town you wouldn't have heard of. How about you?"

"Birmingham." Sara noted a little record player with a stack of 45's next to it. On a large chair next to the record player a book was propped open, obviously in the process of being read.

"*Peyton Place*? I wonder if the required reading list will include that book?"

Diane blushed prettily. "If it doesn't, it should!"

Sara laughed with Diane. She glanced around the flat and was charmed by it and the cute woman who would be her flatmate. "Listen, Diane, I suppose I should do this the correct way. I should go home and think it over, haggle on the rent a little and get back to you in a day or two, but I have a good feeling about this. If you don't have any objection, I'd like to move in and share this place with you."

Diane cocked her head a little to the side, looked up at the taller woman then broke into a small grin. "It might be nice to have someone around who could reach the top shelves at that." She extended her hand to Sara who took the warm appendage in hers and shook it.

"Welcome home, Sara."

****

Randa hung up after talking with Diane. Glancing at her watch, the nurse thought it was probably late enough that Denise would be finished with the press conference and other publicity obligations. She reached for the phone again to call the poet and find out how her day had gone. Though she hadn't learned anything dark or scandalous about Sara, Randa felt she was right. If there was something in Sara's past that Denise didn't know about, Diane did.

****

The busy days that followed for Denise passed surprisingly quickly. It was only when she sat listening to the rapid chug of the train she acknowledged that very fact. The sound of heavy metal moving along robust, steel tracks sounded so distant from inside the train's carriage. Sitting with a seat to herself, Denise nursed a cup of pungent black coffee, holding the polystyrene container against the imitation wood table. With both hands wrapped around the warmth of the cup the poet looked out of the window, watching the rapidly passing scenery. Rich green fields were filled with herds of large cows and flocks of lazy sheep. It had been a very long time since DJ had last boarded a train, much preferring the luxury of her own car but she had to admit, being able to relax as she travelled the long journey from Manchester to Matlock was a welcome relief. Sometimes sitting behind the wheel of a car in heavy traffic was incredibly frustrating.

Moving her gaze back inside the carriage, Denise looked around the sparsely populated compartment. Apart from a harried looking elderly gentlemen with three children, a woman surrounded by shopping bags and a smartly dressed businessman reading the daily broadsheets, the carriage was otherwise empty. Many of its yellow, green and red patterned seats were left unused. The poet thought that it must have been the slowest part of the day – transportation wise. She grimaced as she studied the appalling pattern upon the seats, glad that in her black jacket she didn't clash with the mix of colours.

Taking a drink of the overly strong coffee, Denise reflected back over the last two days. The initial book launch had progressed incredibly well. She had spoken to many people who had seemed genuinely interested in wanting to talk to her and ask about her writing. Denise had decided that being the centre of attention wasn't nearly as ominous as she had considered it to be. So much so that Denise had agreed with the producer of a famous literary program on channel-two television to appear as a guest.

The Open Book was a Monday evening programme that discussed forthcoming publications, reviewed new books and interviewed guest authors. DJ had been aware that they had discussed her on several editions of the show and the producer was thrilled that she agreed to an interview. The only trouble was the scheduling and date of her appearance and Denise acknowledged that she might have to return back to England at a later date. She hoped Randa would be able to accompany her for that as she was positive Randa would have a wonderful time; plus there was the fact that Randa's presence always increased the poet's own confidence.

Staring down at the black sludge the rail company called 'coffee', DJ sighed and pushed the white container away. However much she had enjoyed the interviews and mixing with a variety of people, she was happy to be returning home to Derbyshire. A part of her had missed the place she had lived all of her life and spent so many happy years. Of course the house did, towards the end, hold much less happy memories but Denise experienced a feeling of closure the nearer home she travelled.

The train arrived at Matlock station just before two o'clock in the afternoon, one hour behind schedule. Lugging her suitcase and carryon, DJ strolled through the station's terminal and out into the main street. Approaching the curb she spotted a row of waiting taxicabs and headed in their direction. Reaching the nearest one Denise climbed into the back and soon found herself on the long car journey home.

An hour later the car's brakes screeched to a halt outside the ex-miners cottage. The building looked very much the same as how she had left it over two months before except for an overgrowth of untamed weeds. However, the rose bush in the centre of the small lawn was in full bloom and deep red flowers stood out boldly against the dark brick house.

Paying the driver, DJ lugged her cases out of the car and headed towards the front door. Taking keys from her jacket pocket she unlatched the lock and walked into the house. DJ had expected the alarm to chime out its warning but only silence greeted her. With a curious frown DJ placed her luggage by the far wall and walked into the living room. The curtains were wide open and a fresh yet artificial scent clung to the surprisingly warm air. Instantly having an inkling as to the reason behind this, Denise listened carefully. The sound of a door closing closely followed by the tinkering of metal against porcelain drew her further into the house.

Not wanting to scare the person she now knew was in the kitchen, Denise called out softly, "Hello?"

"DJ?" A recognisable voice called back.

With a smile of acknowledgement Denise stepped into the kitchen to find Diane in the middle of preliminary preparations for a dinner. "This is a surprise," she said.

Diane smiled as she dropped her knife and moved to engulf Denise in a welcoming hug. "I thought I would just come over here... air out the house and prepare you something to eat ready for your return home." Diane pulled back and looked up at the poet, holding her at arms length. "Well look at you! I think the American climate agrees with you. You are looking well."

"Thank you." DJ studied the older woman closer wishing she could say the same but Diane was looking undoubtedly frail. "How are you feeling?" The poet asked, concerned as she took notice of the smaller woman's pale skin and withered features. It was obvious the slight woman had lost weight.

"Oh you know... I can't complain."

DJ nodded as she asked, "And how is Shell?"

"Stationed in Germany at the moment. I get regular calls from her. When I told her you were coming back from the U.S. for a while she told me to give you her best." Diane moved back over to the work surface and continued preparing her vegetables.

Shrugging out of her jacket, Denise hung it upon the back of one of the kitchen's pine chairs. "You don't have to do this, Di. I very much appreciate you preparing the house for me and looking after it while I was away but you really don't have to make any food. I was just going to call one of the local takeaway restaurants."

"And you wonder why I do this!" Diane shook her head with a smile. "Humour an old woman, DJ." She handed the poet a large knife and said, "How about you help slice those potatoes?"

"No problem." Accepting the black handled knife, Denise commenced her slicing.

"So how was the press conference? I haven't had time to read about it yet but I presume there will be a feature in the Daily Edition."

DJ sighed as she placed her sliced potatoes into a large saucepan of cold water. "It was mad! I don't mind admitting that I was terrified. My palms had sprung a leak and my stomach was doing the tango." Denise chucked to herself as she continued. "But it was alright. I had a couple of difficult questions but I think everything went very well. Even the one on one interviews were okay. Anyway it was a hectic couple of days but I am glad to be back in Derbyshire. I now have three book signings over the next three days. I'll stay here but travel down to London for the signing tomorrow. Then come back in the evening for the second signing in Derby the day after."

"And you have time to eat... when?"

DJ rolled here eyes. "I'll fit it in. Maybe we should make extra, put it in containers and store them in the freezer!"

With a smirk Diane lifted a small collection of Tupperware lunch boxes. "I spoke to Randa on the telephone yesterday. She told me you had a busy schedule so I thought I would make sure you were taking care of yourself... besides, Randa asked whether I would mind doing so."

Placing her hands upon slim hips Denise pretended affront saying, "Is there a conspiracy going on behind my back? She never told me that when we spoke yesterday."

"Must have slipped her mind."

The poet narrowed her eyes. "Hmm!" Looking back down at the selection of vegetables upon the work surface Denise opened a bag of runner beans. "Okay... let's carry on preparing the food. You will join me for dinner won't you?"

"I would love to. You can tell me all about the press conference while we eat."

"Deal." DJ replied as she began preparing the beans.

In a moment of companionable silence, DJ's mind wandered back to the book launch. The questions asked by the reporter who worked for the Daily Edition had remained in the forefront of her mind. It wasn't so much the fact that she believed Sara did have a shady past, as it was that somebody had taken time to write the letters. If there was a feeling that unsettled her it was the notion some unknown person seemed to have grievances against Sara and herself – and she had no idea why.

Lifting a large saucepan Denise placed it upon the gas stove. She looked back at Diane and wondered whether she should tell the older woman about the letters. Shaking her head DJ picked up a box of matches from a side shelf and pulled one of the small sticks from the box. Lighting the match she turned on the appropriate knob and lit the ring, blowing out the matchstick's flame once done. Denise knew she couldn't tell Diane about the letters. Not wanting to worry or upset her aunt's friend she considered it the best move to make

"So," Diane said, interrupting DJ's chain of thoughts. "Tell me all about America. Randa tells me you turned into a bit of a sun worshiper." Diane looked the poet up and down. "I see she wasn't kidding," Diane teased causing DJ to laugh and temporarily pull her mind from the concerns that were plaguing her consciousness.

****

The next day found Denise in the heart of London, standing in one of the United Kingdom's largest chain of bookstores. Situated in one of the staff's private rooms on the fourth floor, Denise looked out of the window to the street below. Stretching from the side entrance of the bookstore and flowing way past the shop and around the corner a long queue of waiting people patiently stood. *Unbelievable,* the poet thought, *so many people!*

Today was the nationwide release of her new anthology and she was in London to mark the occasion by signing copies in the country's capital. Pushing her hands into the dark blue denim of her jeans DJ observed the waiting line of people, unseen. She could identify copies of her previous two books held by certain people in the queue.

From behind, Denise heard a door open and she turned to see Carl strolling into the staff office. A wide smile lit up his sparkling eyes and Denise groaned, wondering what had excited the editor this time. Folding her arms, DJ sucked her front tooth as she arched her eyebrows – waiting.

"Do you have any idea how far that queue reaches?" Carl exclaimed.

"Around the corner?"

"Around the corner! Are you kidding? Around the corner, across the road, down the jetty and all the way to Timbuktu!" Carl sat down upon a large brown leather couch against the wall. He placed one arm over the back of the couch as he said, "I went out and wandered among the waiting people. I tell you, DJ that article about you in the Times was one hell of a write up. I think the fact that they included a picture of D. Jennings may have slightly increased your popularity!"

"Ugh," Denise groaned and let her body fall onto the couch beside Carl. "I didn't know they were including a picture although I suppose they would."

Carl wiggled his eyebrows. "It was a great article, DJ. I'm not surprised there are so many people out there. I would be if I didn't have your signature on a million and one documents back at the office."

Denise chuckled.

"So how are you feeling? You don't seem as nervous as you did a couple of days ago."

With a shrug the poet rose from the couch and walked back to the window. "Taking it all in my stride. It's all I can do. You were right, Carl. I did start the ball rolling so I suppose I have to go with the flow."

"Hmm." Carl followed Denise to the window as he adjusted his navy tie. "Did you sign all the advanced ordered copies?"

"Yes… it warmed up my wrist for the scribbling marathon I am about to partake in. Randa would have loved this. I wish she could have seen the crowd! Plus I bet she would have loved shopping in the capital. We could have visited Harrods!"

"Oh I'm not too sure about that," Carl replied.

"Why not?"

The editor sniggered. "Well it's just that I overheard a group of women out there who were not only commenting on your literary mind but also your physical attributes. Randa doesn't suffer from a bout of the green-eyed monster does she?"

"Umm… well not that I am aware." Denise looked at Carl dubiously. "Really? They were saying that?"

"Yep," Carl answered, simply deciding not to tell DJ that he had also overheard the women daring each other as to who would have the courage to ask the poet for a kiss. He had to move away from the group after that, finding himself unable to hold back his amusement.

An expected knock drew both editor and author away from their personal musings. Carl nodded as a tall thin woman entered the staff room. Her head of short brown hair was peppered with grey and she wore a pair of spectacles around her neck suspended by a silver chain. She smiled warmly as she said, "Everything is ready… if you are, Miss Jennings?"

Carl looked at Denise expectantly. "DJ?"

"As I'll ever be," the poet replied before following Carl and the bookstore manager to the staff's elevator.

Stepping inside the wide compartment Carl looked at Denise with an amused smile. "Did I tell you that since the article in the Times we've had orders for your books from certain…" he held up his hands and made little quotation marks with his fingers, as he said, "…Women's book shops." DJ frowned causing Carl to sigh exasperatedly. "You know…'women's books shops'. Don't make me have to spell it out for you, DJ." At the poets still confused look Carl shook his head. "Ugh god! You know… women… shops just for women… aimed at your specific

88

gender. Umm… for women who like um… women."

Unable to hold her stoic confusion Denise grinned inanely.

"You are an evil woman, Denise Jennings," Carl growled but chuckled at the poet's behaviour. "You just love to make me squirm," he said as the bookstore manager laughed at the pair's behaviour.

"Not really, you are just too easy to tease sometimes," DJ replied. The elevator doors opened to the bookstore's ground floor and they walked out into the main shop.

****

Two hours had passed since the signing had begun and Denise presumed she had to have been about half way through the queue of waiting people. Looking up briefly as another small group was ushered over to her table, Denise reflected over the past hours. She had been surprised by the diverse mix and varied age group of people. She was most impressed by the younger age group; teenagers who were studying her works at school. Denise hadn't been able to spend much time talking with people. The store manager had explained that due to the large number of people waiting it would take far too much time if she insisted on talking to them all. Denise understood this but in an effort not to appear ignorant, she willingly answered questions when she thought she was able.

Casting a swift glance to the corner of the store, DJ briefly observed Carl. The editor had kept his position out of the lime light but had eagerly watched the events with an enthusiastic smile. Her brows furrowed together as she noticed an almost evil smirk etch its way onto Carl's features. Wrinkling her brow further DJ followed Carl's line of sight to where the next group of people were approaching her table. She looked back at Carl to see the editors smile widen. When he noticed Denise watching him he looked away quickly – the picture of innocence. *Okay... what is he up to?*

Turning back to a group of women approaching the table Denise delivered a friendly smile. "Hi," she said as four women reached her.

They seemed to smile nervously before the first woman; a tall brunette with large brown eyes placed her copy of her book onto the table. "I adore your writing," she said, "I wrote a paper in College on your poem 'Untitled too'. I received an A for it."

Denise chuckled as she pulled the book towards her and opened the cover. "That was quite a long one."

"Yes and fascinating... very fantastical. I always wanted to know what you were thinking when you wrote that."

Restraining laughter as she signed her name DJ said, "Probably not a lot... alcohol can do that to you!"

"Ah," the brunette smiled, "Well that explains it." Leaning forward she placed a small slip of paper upon the table.

Denise looked down at the note curiously and just suppressed an exclamation of surprise as the young woman kissed her cheek. As soft lips drew away from her, DJ looked back at the brunette to see her wink before picking up her book and strolling away. She noticed the woman give her friends a 'thumbs up' and felt a blush tint her cheeks. Looking back at Carl she noticed the man laughing in the corner.

With an indignant glare she mouthed, "You wait."

Carl grinned as he beckoned the poet with wiggling fingers and burst into laughter once again.

Rubbing the side of her nose to hide her embarrassed smile, Denise looked back at the waiting line. She ignored the slip of paper that held the brunettes name and telephone number. *Okay... Now I wonder what Randa will say to that.*

Chapter 8

"Put your lips on Denise again and somebody is going to get slapped!" Randa yelled at the television set.

The nurse was no longer sure that the satellite system she'd had installed earlier that morning was quite the good thing she expected it was going to be. Instead of being a surprise way of letting Denise keep up with what was happening in England, it had been Randa on the end of the news.

In checking out the British television channels to see which ones would be accessible to the poet, Randa had been interrupted in her channel surfing by the sudden appearance of the startling blue eyes of Denise herself. The news program that was on apparently had a report on the world of the arts. The announcer was talking about the successful book signing earlier in the day that the poet D. Jennings had done in London. A line of people waiting to meet Denise was shown, and then came the infamous shot of a fan kissing Denise on the cheek. The sharp eyes of the nurse did not miss the slip of paper placed in front of DJ before the kiss occurred.

As the report ended, Randa used the remote to shut the system down. A quick glance at the clock showed the nurse she had just enough time to set up the other surprise she had for Denise. *No rush. What is it that they say? Revenge is a dish best served cold.*

The nurse flipped her computer on and when it had booted, she ran the disk for the new hardware. Once the hardware was installed she restarted her computer, connected to the Internet and waited. She didn't have to wait long.

Within five minutes, a rapping noise let Randa know that Denise was online also. As prearranged, they had both

91

downloaded the same Instant Messenger program to use while the poet was in Derbyshire. To chat in real time on the computer would save them money as well as allowing Randa to chat while on the job if she wasn't busy.

The IM box popped up.

Hi love, how was your day? Came the message from Denise.

Very enlightening. Randa typed. **How was yours? How did the book signing go?**

It was very busy... lots of interesting people out there buying the book... nothing special though.

Must have been boring for you. Wasn't there anything to break up the monotony?

No, not really. You know me, nothing but work, work, and more work.

Randa had to laugh. She wasn't really upset at the events at the book signing. She knew that loving someone who looked like Denise Jennings was going to have its tough moments, but the hell they'd walked through together made her confident of their love. It was adorable that the poet would try and shield her from the actions of that one fan but it wasn't necessary. *I'm a big girl, Denise. It's time to show you how adult I am.*

Denise, do you have your computers speakers on? The nurse typed

After a moment, DJ replied "*Yes, why?*

Click on the button above the chat screen marked webcam. Randa booted the webcam and put the image of herself up into one corner of the computer screen.

Wow! Typed DJ. Randa noted there was one viewer of her webcam. *When did you get this?*

"This morning, do you like it?" Randa said into the webcam's microphone.

That's amazing! I've got to get one for here so we can chat face to face!

"Now, Denise, as I assume I have your complete attention I'd like to ask you about a little incident that happened at the book signing. Did you honestly think I wouldn't find out about that woman kissing you? I'm assuming her phone number was on that piece of paper she slipped you," Randa teased.

Randa, I didn't encourage her or anything! Was her swift reply.

"I know that, love," Randa stated smoothly. "Why would you want her when this is waiting at home for you?" Randa checked the camera angle with a quick glance to the screen and slowly began unbuttoning the cotton shirt she had on.

Randa, don't! Flashed on the IM screen.

"Why not? If British womanhood is giving all for their poets the least this American can do is give my all as well." Randa slipped the shirt from her shoulder revealing a black lacy bra that enhanced her attributes nicely.

Randa, stop! How do you turn this thing off?

"Why would I want you to turn it off when I'm just getting started turning you on?" Randa opened the top hook on the front closing bra and smiled saucily into the camera.

Randa, Diane is here. She says to say hello and she loves the IM feature I brought her up to the study to see.

The smile froze on Randa's face as she quickly shut down the webcam. Dropping her head to the keyboard she flushed a fire engine red in embarrassment. *Why does nothing like this ever work out for me? First it was Sara, now its Diane. Why don't I just see if I can get on British TV and humiliate myself in front of the whole nation instead of one person at a time?*

Randa? Randa, are you still there? The nurse read the line as she lifted her head.

Nope, I'm not here. I've expired from mortification! She typed back.

Randa, Diane's not here. I was just teasing you because you were teasing me. I liked it when you do that. Will you tease me a little more? With the camera on of course... I rather like it!

For an instant Randa was poised to fire off an irritated response to Denise's last note, but then a small smile crept over her features. She remembered how hard it had been for DJ to loosen up in the first place and how she loved it when the poet showed her sense of humor. She wasn't going to have her change now. Randa reached for the mouse and reactivated the webcam. *So, Ms. Jennings, you want teasing? I can most definitely do that!*

****

For a short while after Denise had logged off her computer, Randa remained online. Might as well check the e-mail before I get some rest before my shift on the Network tonight.

Opening the Inbox revealed several forwarded jokes from her mother, a little spam and a newsletter dealing with Amyotrophic Lateral Sclerosis. Since the time Sara had been afflicted and died from the dreaded disease, Randa had tried to learn as much about it as possible. Keeping up with newsletters and information sites helped her understand a little better what Sara had faced.

This particular newsletter talked about grants being given and the research being done in the field. At the very end of the e-mail though was a small section entitled "Incidence". The nurse read on and discovered some very disturbing facts that sent a chill through to her bones. The information was about the incidence of ALS in America, but Randa thought the incidence of MND, as it was known in Europe, would probably be the same. It seemed each year over five thousand new cases of ALS were diagnosed in the U.S. Of those, approximately ninety to ninety-five percent were "sporadic", but five to ten percent were "familial". That was the word that chilled the nurse. In cases where the disease was familial, where one or more family members had the disease, there was a fifty percent chance that children would inherit the mutated gene and develop the disease.

Randa knew Denise's parents had been killed in the house fire and her grandfather had been killed in action in World War Two. She desperately needed more information on the poet's family.

God, please don't let me have to tell Denise she faces the risk of going through the same thing that Sara did. After all she went through, that would be too cruel. The nurse closed her e-mail and sat numbly before the computer, trembling a little at the possibility.

****

Being away from the country's capital Denise never expected there to be as many people at her second book signing. She was half right. Although there weren't as many as in London, the poet realised that it would still take her several hours to get through the sitting. The signing in London had taken a total of just over five hours. By the time she had finished, Denise joked that she was positive she would soon develop a case of 'repetitive strain injury' in her left wrist.

Being a Saturday morning, the city of Derby was alive with activity. Every store was open and the streets were bursting with shoppers and groups of children passing the time. People whisked through the city centre immersed in their own worlds and offered no form of apology if they should collide with others. The smell of numerous fast food restaurants and the familiar sound of voices and transportation engines filled the atmosphere. The only sight that strayed from the norm was the large queue forming out of the city's major bookstore.

Hidden in an enclosed corner of the department and looking through a tinted glass window, Denise watched the line of waiting people. Standing with an arm resting upon Carl's shoulder she shook her head.

"I had no idea."

"What?" Carl asked as he re-buttoned his suit jacket. "That you would make this kind of impact? That so many people would want to meet you?"

Denise moved her arm as the editor adjusted his clothing. "Hmm." She looked her friend up and down. "I don't think I have ever seen you without a suit or at least a tie. Do you even own a pair of jeans, Carl?"

"Of course I do," Carl defended. "What about you? Do you own a dress at all?"

The poet frowned in thought. "You know... I have absolutely no idea. I can't even remember." She laughed and looked out of the window. "It's a Saturday morning,

Carl. You really don't have to be here today. Not that I don't appreciate your support but I am aware you have a wife and brood of offspring at home. I don't want to dominate your time now do I?"

"I want to be here," Carl insisted. "I have been waiting on this day for years. Besides, who else is going to keep an eye on you for Randa? What if in a moment of weakness and due to the fact that you miss her you might..."

"Never..." DJ interrupted, "it will never happen, Carl."

"Yes, well... it was worth it just to see you blush. I have never seen that before. You should have seen your face when that brunette kissed you. I wish I had a camera."

Covering her eyes, Denise groaned. "Ugh, give it a rest, Carl. At least I didn't pocket her phone number." She cast a suspicious glare towards the editor.

"Oh go on will you... I was just removing the note so nobody else would take advantage of it. Anyway what possible use would I have for those digits? I got the distinct impression that I was not her... flavour... if you know what I mean!"

"Flavour?" Denise asked confused.

Carl sighed. "Oh come on, DJ. I am a bloke you know. I don't have an aversion to watching those late night porn..."

"Hold it... okay I get you, Carl." Denise smiled with a touch of malice. "If I were you I would quit before others feel the need to change their opinions of you."

"Like you don't..."

"Carl!" Denise lowered her head and stared at the editor through long lashes. She poked his chest with her index finger and said, "Your arse is this close to receiving a personal visitation from my foot."

The blonde man held up his hands. "Okay, okay... point taken." Grinning, he looked down at his watch. "It's almost half nine. Are you ready to get out there?"

"Bring it on," Denise exclaimed and together with Carl she walked out onto the main shop floor.

The store was not yet open. It had been agreed with the manager that the shop would open half an hour later in preparation for DJ's signing and the amount of people believed to be turning up. In that point they were not disappointed. Denise looked around at her surroundings. The store held many alcoves, each dedicated to a specific genre of literature. The ground floor held the majority of the fiction titles. In the centre of the wide area a large staircase and elevator were situated that led to the second and third floor. The poet had been captured by their design when she first entered the building. The staircase spiralled up and around the elevator casing and in itself stood as a feature of the bookstore.

Moving her gaze along the numerous rows of books Denise looked to the far end of the shop floor. Reminiscent of the day before, a large table had been set up for her signing. To the right was a display area holding many copies of her latest anthology. She looked back at Carl who was busy searching through a large table entitled 'Bargain Books.'

"By the way," Denise said as she peered over his shoulder, "Randa knew about that woman anyway."

"Really?" Carl looked up surprised. "You told her?"

Shaking her head Denise pulled Carl away from the table and continued her approach to the signing area. "Nope, she's only gone and installed satellite television so I can get Brit shows in the US. She saw it on a news item."

"Unlucky!" Carl laughed. "Was she pissed?"

"She was actually okay about it." Smiling in memory, DJ thought back to the conversation she'd had with Randa the night before. It had been the nurse's idea to communicate through their computers even though Denise had assured her that she would pay any long distance telephone costs. She even tried to encourage Randa to call her reversed charges but Randa still insisted on other less expensive means. Besides, using Randa's new toy had turned out to be an amusing event and she had never been able to resist teasing the blonde.

Positioning herself upon the corner of the table DJ glanced at Carl. The editor had taken a detour from the signing area. He was now heading back towards her accompanied by a smartly dressed woman in a pinstriped suit with long blonde hair.

"DJ, this is Kay Blackwood; the store manager."

Oops! Rising from the table sheepishly Denise held out her hand. "Hi."

"Miss Jennings, it's an honour to have you here today."

"No problem." Denise smiled politely. "So I take it we are ready to get under way?" The poet made a show of flexing her hand, causing the other two to smile. "I'm ready and raring to go."

The manager looked around the store. "I presume I shouldn't leave the queue waiting any longer... so yes, I do believe we are ready." With a polite nod Kay Blackwood walked off in the direction of the main doors.

Carl watched her leave with a grin. Letting his head fall to the side his eyes rested upon the woman's retreating behind. Denise caught his line of sight and rolled her eyes. Reaching out she grabbed the blonde man's ear and pulled him around to the back of the desk.

"Ouch, Ouch, Ouch! Bloody hell! DJ, are you trying to pull it off?" He rubbed his ear with a low hanging lip.

"No, I was just going to remind you about that gold band around your finger!" DJ lifted his left hand and tapped his wedding ring.

"Nothing wrong with looking." Carl straightened his blue, two-toned checked tie. "I would never be unfaithful to Chris. 'I' wouldn't even allow another woman to kiss me."

DJ sat down behind the desk and let her feet rest upon the wooden surface. "Jealous?"

"Yes!" Carl smiled as he said, "Anyway... no matter what I say I know that woman would still of had more chance with me than you!"

Understanding his meaning Denise nodded. "You are bloody right there, Carl. There is only one person for me!"

"Lucky sod."

Denise frowned. "Who?"

"Randa... you... the both of you. You know that I..." Carl paused as he caught movement in the corner of his eye. He looked across the shop floor. "Looks like you are in business!"

Eyes wide, Denise pulled her feet from the table and sat up straight. A flood of people began to filter into the shop. "Let the madness begin!"

****

Feeling a slight cramp settle into her left wrist, Denise dropped her pen and looked up at the middle aged man standing by her table. With an expression of thanks the greying man walked away and DJ took a moment to massage her stiff hand. Nimble fingers manipulating her left palm, she glanced over at the last of the waiting queue. Denise figured she had to have signed over two hundred copies of her book. By the look of the remaining line she presumed she now only had two or three people left. An internal flood of relief washed over her. The poet hadn't moved from her chair in almost three hours and the desire to stretch her legs and ingest something other than mineral water was becoming a high priority in her mind. She looked across the shop floor to where Carl stood. He was busy tucking into a sausage roll that he'd just brought from the bakery across the street. He had slipped past her earlier stating that the bakery also sold éclairs and that thought alone had fuelled her desire to continue.

Draining the remaining water from her bottle Denise looked over to the queue. Two of the remaining three walked over and she smiled wondering how they would act. Denise had found she was able to put them into a number of categories. There were the shy people who blushed more than spoke. The stunned people who seemed more surprised to see her than anything. The exuberant people who talked non-stop and felt the need to ask her as many questions as they could, and of course the small group of opportunists who flirted with Denise and even propositioned her for a night out. Though the poet did admit that they were *mostly* women she wondered whether any of them had actually taken her dedication to Randa seriously!

A mother and young daughter stopped by DJ's table and the poet looked up expectantly.

"Umm." The woman placed her copy of the book down and froze.

Denise opened the front cover as she looked back and forth between the mother and daughter. "What would you like me to write?"

Seeing no response from her mother the young girl said, "You can write 'to mum and your name'."

Denise smiled as she leaned forward in her chair. "I don't think I can call your mum... 'Mum'!" She smiled at the mother politely, noticing she was still rather quiet. DJ looked back at the girl, "You will have to tell me her name."

The young girl giggled. "It's Clair."

"Okay." Denise said as she signed her book. "Nice pigtails, by the way."

"My mum did them." The little girl smiled and looked up at her mother.

DJ nodded as she handed her book back to the woman with a smile.

"Thank you," she said. "Sorry."

"No problem." Denise winked at the young girl. "Have a good day."

The girl waved as her mother led her away and Denise chuckled as another book was placed in front of her. Still smiling she looked up into light blue eyes framed by red wavy hair. "Hi."

"Maggie." The woman said simply.

"Umm... okay." Furrowing her brow, Denise opened the book and signed her name. She looked back at the redhead and pushed her anthology over the surface of the table. A silence stretched out between them as Denise waited for her to either speak or take the book and leave. When the woman did neither the poet's expression changed to one of confusion. She didn't want to appear impolite but the way in which the woman was looking at her was beginning to feel disconcerting.

"Is there something...?"

"You think you know everything about her?" Maggie interrupted, "But do you know who I am?"

"I um..." as what the woman was saying sunk into her mind, clarity hit DJ and she realised she was facing the writer of the anonymous letters. Denise rose to her feet. "You," she said, "You wrote the letters?"

"You don't know who I am... why would you?" Maggie continued.

Denise studied the redhead carefully. She didn't understand what Maggie was saying. "Look, I think you may have your wires crossed here. I have no idea what you are trying to imply and for that matter what you are even talking about. I really don't appreciate..."

"Oh, you don't appreciate?" Maggie interrupted again, "I bet it has always been about you and what you want, hasn't it?"

Confused, Denise asked, "What?"

"Why would she want you and not me?" Maggie leaned closer to the poet. "What is so special about you?"

Confusion clouding her mind, Denise sighed in frustration. "Look, why don't you just explain yourself or leave? I really don't have time to stand here and play mind games with you. What do you want?" DJ thought back to the words in the letters. "What do you mean about Sara? What truth?"

Maggie looked at the poet in surprise. "You really don't have any idea, do you?"

"What?" DJ growled in frustration.

Looking at the poet evenly the redhead said, "I'm Sara's daughter."

DJ blinked as Maggie's words filtered into her mind. She snorted and shook her head. "I was told to expect this kind of thing but that was low."

"You think I am lying?"

"You really don't want to know what I think." Turning away sharply Denise picked up her pen and pulled her black jacket from the back of the chair. Folding the garment over her arm she turned to walk away but found her elbow caught in a strong grip. The poet's angry blue eyes turned to look back at Maggie. "Let go of my arm."

"No, not until you listen to what I have to say. Believe me this was just as much a surprise to me as it is to you.

How do you think I feel knowing that that woman abandoned me? Now I see she lied to you too."

With a growl Denise pulled her arm out of Maggie's grasp. "Don't ever refer to Sara as 'that woman'. In fact, don't refer to her at all. I can't believe this." Denise attempted to walk away but the taller woman blocked her path.

"You can't walk away from this, Denise. I'm not going to fade away."

"You can do whatever the hell you want," Denise seethed. "Just as long as you get the hell away from me."

From the other side of the store, Carl was watching the scene unfold. At first he believed Maggie to be nothing more than a talkative fan but by the expression on DJ's face he knew that was not he case. Placing the remains of his lunch in his side pocket Carl approached his friend.

"You're crazy," Denise said as she took another step away from the pushy redhead.

"I just think you need to know the truth about her."

DJ glared at Maggie as Carl appeared by her side. "And what is that truth? What is it exactly that you want from me?"

Maggie paused then said, "Well... I want..." She frowned, shaking her head.

Carl placed his hand upon Denise's tense shoulder. "Is everything okay, DJ?"

"Yes... everything is fine." Issuing one final glare at the redhead Denise turned and walked away. She heard heavy footsteps approach as Carl fell into stride beside her.

"What the hell was all that about?"

Denise looked at Carl briefly before gazing back at the signing table. Maggie was gone. She turned back to Carl. "I believe that was our anonymous letter writer."

"Yeah?" Carl looked back surprised. "What did she want?"

The poet scowled. "To tell me she was Sara's daughter."

"Bollocks!" Carl stopped and held Denise's arm, forcing her to do the same. "Are you kidding me?"

DJ shook her head.

"What did you say to that?" Carl asked incredulously.

"I told her she was crazy," Denise replied and looked once again to the empty signing area. The whole encounter had left her feeling angry and disoriented. The conviction shining in Maggie's eyes had confused her. The woman clearly did believe what she was saying and that in turn concerned Denise. A niggling feeling in the back of her mind refused to quiet and although her heart told her not to believe Maggie's words, she found herself questioning her resolve. *It was the eyes*, Denise thought, *they were so familiar.*

Suddenly realising she was being spoken to, Denise turned back to Carl. "Pardon?"

Carl's brow creased in concern. "I was just asking whether you are alright. You look a little peaky."

"Umm," rubbing her forehead as if to clear her confused mind, DJ nodded. "Sure." Taking a deep breath she scanned the shop floor. "Are we ready to go?"

"Yes... I just need to talk a moment with Mrs. Blackwood," Carl paused, "Will you be okay?"

Denise nodded reassuringly and watched Carl head off. She then looked back around the shop floor knowing who she was looking for but saw no sign of Maggie. Leaning back against a row of shelves Denise closed her eyes. She felt angry and confused. How could that woman say such hurtful words? She didn't understand and for the first time since DJ came out into the public eye, she firmly wished she had not.

Chapter 9

London, April 1961.

The whimpering sound from the other bedroom was what caused Sara to wake. This was not the first time Sara had heard this particular tone of whimper and she knew what it meant. The whimper was Diane and it happened after every visit to her home. The petite brunette had returned two days prior from spending Easter with her parents in Derbyshire and, like clockwork, the restless nights had returned.

Between work and her studies, Sara never had the time or money to return home on the short breaks at school and managed to go home for Christmas and a short time in the summer only. Diane's family was moderately well off and she was therefore expected to return to the bosom of her family at every opportunity. The whimpering had started sometime during their second year at the University.

Sara had questioned Diane about the restless nights she experienced after returning to London, but each time she had been assured it was the strain of travel and homesickness after coming back. Initially those explanations had seemed reasonable, but as time had gone by and the students were in their third year at college, those reasons now appeared less plausible. Sara wished she could get Diane to confide in her as she confided in her about everything else, but in this matter she remained silent.

Now Sara lay in her bed staring through her bedroom window at the crescent moon on its downward path in the night sky. The moon and Sara were old friends and on the many nights she could not sleep she would listen to the radio playing softly and weave stories in her mind about the moon and its magic. It was during one of those times she had first heard Diane's distress and this was such a night as well. From the other bedroom in the small flat Sara could hear Diane turn over restlessly.

Maybe she'll soon quiet thought Sara, but knew in her heart that it would not be so. The demons in Diane's sleep would remain for several days yet and both flat-mates would suffer because one did. Soon the thrashing in the other room became more pronounced and Diane no longer whimpered, but cried out. Sara could take it no longer and rose from her bed. Pausing only to slip in quickly to a pair of house slippers, she made her way to Diane's bedroom. The sight of her best friend in such agony tore at her heart.

Moving to Diane's bed, Sara decided this night she would press for the truth. She couldn't let Diane suffer like this anymore, not if there was anything she could do about it. They had been through so much and trusted each other so deeply that this needed to come out between them. Sara sat on the edge of the bed and gently touched the other woman's arm.

"Diane? Diane, wake up. You're having a bad dream, dear. Come on now; wake up. That's a good girl." Diane slowly came to full consciousness and fixed watery brown eyes on Sara. With a small cry, Diane reached for Sara and held on tight as she sobbed.

"I'm not stupid, Sara, I'm not! He's so wrong about me, they all are. I am smart and I can be a teacher if I want to!" Sara placed one arm around Diane's shoulders as she stroked her friend's bobbed hair and murmured words of comfort until Diane's tears subsided and the sobs were reduced to the occasional hiccoughed breath. Feeling Diane was at last calm enough to talk, Sara reached over to the small lamp on the bedside stand and turned the light on. Her friend's eyes remained red rimmed and she protested the brightness.

"Turn it back off, Sara! I don't want you to see me like this." Sara complied and the two sat together on the bed quietly. Sara pressed for the truth.

"Diane, you're my best friend. You know I've never had a sister and even if I had one I couldn't love her anymore than you. Please, you have to tell me what the matter is. I can't stand to see you suffer like this." Diane sniffed a little then reached for her friend's hand and held on tight. Sara returned the grip, hoping to give strength to her friend to reveal what had been troubling her.

"Oh, Sara, it's such a mess. It's my father of course. I told you he disapproved of women attending University and he only let me come because Mum thought some education would make me a more desirable catch, marriage wise. Marriage and babies! You would think Victoria was still on the throne!" Sara gave a small smile as Diane used this phrase frequently when observing some part of society that had not advanced as quickly as others. Previously it had been used to describe social progress, Parliament and London public transportation. Sara's smile disappeared with Diane's next statement though.

"Dad is going to make me leave University at the end of the term, Sara. He says it is time for me to get married, settle down and start producing grandchildren. I know he's said that in the past, but now Mum agrees with him and Roger as well." Roger Barlow was a young man that Diane had been seeing since they were children practically and there was always supposed to have been "an understanding" between them. Diane had never said she was in love with Roger and Sara thought Diane secretly felt it was more of a friendship than anything else.

"They all want me to leave school. They want a summer wedding and an end to all this 'nonsense' about me wanting to get my 'B-Ed'. It's not nonsense, Sara! I love attending the University and I so very much want to teach. I love our little flat; it's almost more of a home than Derbyshire is to me. I'm not ready to lose all this but what can I do? Dad controls the money and he'll cut it off if I don't do as he wishes. It's hopeless!"

Sara felt a sharp stab of pain near the area of her heart as she realized what this would mean. Diane would leave school, leave London and leave her. Sara was not one to be bothered with self-delusions. She knew she had harbored more than friendly feelings toward Diane for some time. She also felt by looks and intuition that Diane had those feelings for her also, but an unspoken agreement left those publicly unacceptable feelings buried. Now faced with the loss of Diane, those feelings yearned for acknowledgement.

"Do you need their money, Diane?" Sara asked. "We could find you a job; maybe the Spicers could help you as they've helped me. You don't need to give up your dream if you don't want to. I could help a little and we could economize more. You don't have to go." Diane moved a little back from Sara and looked up into blue eyes that looked a dark shade of gray in the muted light of the bedroom.

"You're the strong one here, Sara. You work and attend classes. You more than do your share around the flat and help me when I'm in danger of falling behind in my coursework. I admire you so much and I can admit I'm not that strong. I love the thought of teaching, but it doesn't come as quickly or as naturally to me as it does you. I've never met anyone who was meant to teach and work with children as much as you. I'm afraid I couldn't carry all you do and hope to be a success."

The friends looked at each other silently. It was on the tip of Sara's tongue to admit her feelings for Diane, to hold her and give her comfort and let her love have expression. As much as she wanted to, she knew she would never give voice to those emotions. The silence grew somewhat uncomfortable and Sara lowered her gaze to their still entwined hands. *There's nothing to admire about me, Diane. I'll never be able to say how much I love you. I'm such a coward.* Cowardice was overcome, however, by a petite brunette who claimed to have no strength at all.

"Sara?" The taller woman's eyes returned to those of her friend. "Sara, I don't want to leave here, but more importantly I don't want to leave you." Diane blushed furiously but continued. "I know you're too honorable to ever speak on this subject so I must. Sara, I'm in love with you. I have been for some time now, but I think it may have been from the moment I opened the door on the day you came to look at the flat. I think you feel the same way as I do, at least I hope you do because if you don't I'm going to feel very embarrassed for doing this." Diane leaned forward and quickly and gently brushed her lips against Sara's.

Sara was stunned for a moment before a radiant smile broke across her features. "Of course I love you, who else could I love? You're the dearest person to me; you're my best friend and confidante. Don't worry about this problem with your family. We have the rest of the term to figure something out and we'll do it together." Diane returned Sara's smile and for the first time that evening appeared to have a modicum of hope about the future.

"And Diane? Please don't ever feel embarrassed about doing this." Sara leaned forward and returned the sweet kiss she had been given moments earlier. Diane moved over a little in the bed and Sara turned to sit with her back against the headboard. Diane snuggled close and the two women sat quietly in each other's arms until sometime near sunrise when they fell into an exhausted but quite happy sleep.

****

Randa closed the e-mail from Diane. She was learning so much about Sara's past and was glad Diane had reached the point in her life where she could talk about what had happened so long ago. Diane had said with her message, "There's no one to hurt now. Sara is gone and I'm tired of living a half-truth. It will be nice for someone else to know what happened back then, especially someone like you and Denise who can understand the feelings we had."

The nurse was very honored by those words and knew she would share the story with Denise as soon as she knew the rest of it. Right now she didn't know enough to shed light on Denise's family history or the problem with the anonymous letter writer. *I'll find out, Denise. I'll find out for us then nothing will get in the way of our happy ending.* As she closed down her computer, Randa wished for the millionth time for the strong arms of the poet and the reassurance of her presence. *Be patient, Randa, you'll be with her soon.* The blonde made her way to the bedroom and slipped into bed. Holding Denise's pillow to her, she finally fell asleep with thoughts, then dreams, of her love.

****

To Denise's surprise the day had been incredibly fine. Like the previous morning, she'd had another early signing that started at nine o'clock. Three hours later she had finished and after politely declining a Sunday lunch with the store's manager, a Mr. Evans, she left for home. Carl had decided to stay at home with his family and so DJ had spent her free time conversing with Mr. Evans. She had found the store's manager highly entertaining as he regaled her with amusing tales of strange customers, but when the signing had finished the poet just wanted to go home. Memories of the day before persisted to besiege her mind. She was unable to banish thoughts of Maggie from her head. The slight feeling of paranoia pertaining to the notion that the redhead might actually show again succeeded in driving her away from Birmingham as expeditiously as possible.

Steering her Lexus into the driveway, Denise turned off the engine and climbed out of the vehicle. Looking up into the flawless blue sky, DJ closed her eyes. She could hear a light wind rustle around the blossoming hedges and an excited dog barking in the distance. The warmth of the early July day had surprised her. Although it didn't compare to the luxurious American heat, it was comfortable. So much so that DJ had discarded her jacket for the short sleeved black tee shirt and blue jeans she was wearing.

Denise reopened her eyes and looked down at her keys. Singling out the appropriate key for the front door she headed across the driveway and let herself into the house. A light aroma of potpourri clung to the air and DJ smiled. The fragrance was Sara's favourite and even after all this time she could still detect its scent. Dropping her jacket upon the stairs, DJ headed to the upper level of the house.

Her flight back to America was early the next morning and she was more than a little anxious to return to Randa. Although she still had many publicity duties to uphold and a photo shoot as well because Carl had persuaded her to agree to a picture of herself on the back cover of her new novel, she still wanted to return home. The poet didn't realise how much she would miss Randa. Denise had to admit she did find that acknowledgement slightly perplexing. Not so much the fact that she missed Randa as the realisation that the blonde created a balance and harmony within herself that she believed calmed her soul. In the presence of the nurse, Denise felt complete. It was something that had never concerned her before, but suddenly she knew Randa was the most important person in her life.

Reaching the top of the stairs, DJ headed towards her bedroom. Kicking off her black and white training shoes she picked up her suitcase from the corner of the room and placed it upon her bed. She flipped open the lid and stared down into the empty container. Denise realised it wouldn't take her long to repack her assortment of clothing. Prodding her bottom lip, DJ's mind wandered in thought as she tried to remember what she had to take back with her to the States. *Chocolate,* Denise thought with a grin, *of course! Let's see, what else?* Denise frowned in thought. "Pictures!" she said suddenly and headed back out of her bedroom. She had promised Randa she would bring back some pictures of her parents and they were all stored in the attic. Standing on the tips of her toes, Denise reached up to the loft hatch and pulled it away from the ceiling. Taking a secure hold of the cord to the aluminium-framed ladder, Denise pulled the steps from the loft. As she readied herself to enter the attic the ringing of the telephone sounded through the otherwise quiet house. Mumbling about the irony of timing, the poet jogged back down the stairs and answered the phone.

"Hello," she said, internally hoping she would hear Randa's voice.

"Hello... Denise Jennings?"

The poet frowned at the unrecognisable voice. "That's me."

"Ah, hello again, this is Maggie. I am sure you remember me from your book signing yesterday."

"What?" Denise felt a sudden mix of anger and confusion. "What do you want? And more importantly, how did you get this number?"

"I understand you may be slightly alarmed," Maggie started, *"But you know why I am calling. As to how I obtained your number… well, my parents gave it to me. A little overdue as I am sure you can imagine, but…"*

"Hold it," Denise commanded. Rubbing her brow in disbelief, DJ looked down at the cream coloured base of the telephone. "Your parents gave you this number?"

"Yes."

"Your parents!"

"Yes… well like I have recently discovered, not my biological parents." The tone of Maggie's voice held a clear hint of resentment. *"But yes it was them all the same".*

A swift cramp of anxiety twisted Denise's insides. "Look, I don't know who you are or what you think you will achieve from this stunt, but if you think for one moment that I believe you… you're wrong." The poet started pacing through the house. "Don't you think I would be aware of a rather large fact like that? Now if you don't stop hassling me I will…"

"Hassling you?" Maggie laughed abruptly. *"I just want you to know the truth. I see it was kept from the both of us. What I don't understand is what the hell is so special about you? Why would she choose you over me?"*

Feeling anger rise within her, Denise stopped her pacing in the centre of the living room. "You know, I have never heard anybody speak such a load of bollocks!"

"Oh, and this coming from the supposedly highly regarded literary mind!" Maggie said sarcastically.

Taking a deep breath, DJ said calmly, "I'm going to hang up now and I never want to hear from you again."

"I can prove it," Maggie said swiftly.

DJ looked out of the living room window and stared at the overgrown blades of grass shining under the warm sun.

111

They swayed gently, manipulated by a soft southerly breeze. "How?" she asked cautiously.

The poet was surprised as Maggie launched into a concise explanation without seemingly pausing for breath. *"Sara gave birth to me at the beginning of her teaching career. During that time it was obviously unacceptable for a single woman to conceive and so she gave me up for adoption. My adoptive parents were the couple that had taken Sara in when she first arrived in London... Geoff and Alice Spicer. Though she apparently kept in touch, once I was born Sara left London to travel, temping in schools around the country. That is all I know."*

When Maggie finally ceased talking Denise moved the phone away from her ear and looked down at the plastic device. Her turbulent flurry of feelings since their conversation began had all turned to one of complete uncertainty. DJ knew that Sara had resided with a couple in London that she called 'the Spicers'. She did leave London to start temping at schools around the county.

Blinking from her thoughts, Denise heard the distant sound of Maggie's voice calling for her. Feeling utterly disoriented, the poet hurriedly disconnected the line. The phone switched off with a light beeping tone. Scratching the back of her neck, DJ turned away from the window and leaned against its ledge, the phone hanging limply by her side. She didn't understand. It appeared that Maggie did seem to know an awful lot about Sara's past and she wondered how that was possible. Of course it was probable that somebody who did know of Sara's past was assisting Maggie, but whom? And why would anybody want to cause this kind of trouble? Finding herself unable to surmise any logical explanations, DJ thought of the one person whom she hoped would be able to shed some light on her dilemma. Crossing the room, Denise sat down upon the sofa and dialled a familiar number. She waited patiently for the line to answer, but after a minute of ringing Denise disconnected it. Unperturbed she dialled a second, longer number. After a short moment the mobile telephone was answered...

"Hello?"

"Hi, Di, it's me. I tried to call your house, but you were out."

"Yes, I am visiting a friend. I'm in Bournemouth at the moment, DJ. Just for a couple of days... I arrived early this morning."

"Oh... I'm sorry to disturb you..."

Diane interrupted quickly saying, *"No disruption, honey... you know that. What can I do for you?"*

"Well..." Denise paused and took a deep breath. "I've been approached by a woman claiming to be Sara's daughter." When she heard no reply, Denise asked, "Diane? Did you hear me?"

"Umm... yes I did... and?"

"And? And what?" DJ brushed her fingers roughly over the puckered material of her jeans, flattening the fabric around her knee. "She is just some crack pot, right? I mean she seemed to know some details but..." Denise waited for Diane to speak.

"What did she say?" the older woman asked. *"Did she give you her name?"*

The poet frowned at this. "She said her name was Maggie and she really seems quite hostile towards me. At first I thought she was just a loon, but she knows things, Di. I don't know what's going on."

An audible sigh echoed down the line. *"DJ, this is something I think we should discuss in person and not over the phone. My coach leaves here tomorrow afternoon. Can we meet and talk then?"*

"But I'm..." Denise paused, wondering why Diane thought it was best that they spoke in person. Surely Diane knew she was to leave for the States the next morning. "This **is** something we need to discuss in person, isn't it?"

"Yes," Diane answered. *"It seems we have a great deal to talk about."*

Denise nodded and rose to her feet. "Okay... I'll see you soon." Walking through the house the poet made her way into the kitchen. "Diane... is there an element of truth in her claims?"

The older woman hesitated. *"We'll discuss this when I get back... it is for the best, DJ."*

"Okay, see you then, Di."

"Goodbye, DJ."

Disconnecting the line once again, Denise pushed the phone into the back pocket of her jeans. Suddenly, trepidation as to what Diane wanted to discuss with her plagued DJ's mind. *Sara couldn't have a child... She just couldn't.* Turning towards the kettle, Denise picked it up and filled the electric container with water before returning it to its base. Switching the device on she then opened a wall cupboard and pulled out a large mug. Looking down at the multicoloured porcelain cup, she ran her fingers over the design. Denise had painted it herself, the mug and colours being an arts and crafts Christmas gift when she was eleven. Denise had designed the mug for Sara, writing her aunt's name in large blue letters encased in a wobbly pink heart. That had been so long ago. Her childlike writing and the faded paint a testament to the age of the mug.

Ignoring the boiling kettle and with the container still within her grasp, DJ wandered out into the back hallway and on into Sara's room. A cold chill of memories passed down her spine. It was the first time she had allowed herself to venture into the room. The hospital bed and medical equipment had all long since been returned, leaving the room feeling quite empty. The bed was bare and apart from a wooden chair, dressing table and wardrobe there was not much else to fill the bedroom. Unused floral curtains hung half open at the window and a box containing Sara's personal possessions stood in the corner. Hair accessories, a shawl, an assortment of ornaments and a multicoloured scarf filled the box. Upon its closed surface and keeping the flaps of its lid down, lay the last novel she and Randa had read to Sara, *Les Miserables*.

Pushing her free hand into her pocket dejectedly, DJ stepped into the room. Her socked feet almost shuffled upon the thick pile of the carpet. Confusion clouded her mind and the notion that Maggie may indeed be speaking some ounce of truth scared her. Leaning against a bare wall, Denise slid down to the floor and sat with her legs

114

crossed upon the beige carpet. Placing Sara's mug between her thighs she pulled the cordless phone out of her pocket.

DJ sighed as she let her head fall back against the wall. *I suppose whatever it is, I will find out soon enough.* Not knowing what Diane was going to say caused her heart to hammer with apprehension. Looking back at the phone resting in her right hand DJ hit the speed dial to connect with a certain long distance number.

After long moments a sleep filled voice answered the phone. *"Hello?"*

"Hey... Did I wake you?"

"Hmm... I wasn't working last night so yeah, I guess."

DJ smiled as she said, "Sorry." She could just imagine what her lover looked like at that precise moment. There was no doubt about it; the adorable expressions Randa pulled while waking up managed to warm more than just her heart!

"It's okay," Randa mumbled. *"I've just got to get in enough rest before you get back!"* she chucked evilly before adding, *"God I've missed you."*

DJ bit her lip nervously. "Me too, but..."

"But?" Randa asked.

"But I can't come back."

"What?" The blonde asked clearly alarmed. *"Ever?"*

"Of course not ever!" The poet chuckled despite the situation. "The thing is that I've discovered the identity of the mysterious letter writer."

"You have? Who is it?"

DJ wrinkled her forehead. "I'm not sure. Supposedly she is claiming to be Sara's daughter."

Randa was momentarily silent before saying, *"Daughter? Sara doesn't have a daughter... does she?"*

"No, not that I am aware of!"

"Oh! Denise... what the hell is going on?"

"I'll find out tomorrow when I meet with Diane. That is why I can't come back... she is in Bournemouth for the night. Gosh Randa, I am so confused I don't know what to think." Denise sighed as she said, "I'm not sure when I will be able to return at the moment."

"Oh!" Randa said dejectedly.

"The thing is…" DJ ran her fingers over the rim of the coffee mug. "Randa, I can't cope with all of this on my own. I need you here. I really want you to come over. I know Derek said that the company wouldn't allow you another paid leave so soon, but that isn't a problem is it? I mean… I am being paid the equivalent of a ten-year wage just for appearing as a guest on that bloody book programme and doing my first screen interview with them. We will always be more than comfortable in that department." A desperate tone edged its way into DJ's voice. "Please… I need you, Randa."

"Okay," Randa said simply.

"Okay?"

"Of course," Randa replied softly. *"If you need me nothing is more important than that, Denise. I want to be with you."*

Chin falling to her chest with relief, DJ closed her eyes. "Thank you… I want you with me too." Feeling a measure of confidence flow through her, Denise rose to her feet. "Okay, so how about you make the necessary calls on your end and sort things out? Then get back to me and I'll find the appropriate available flight for you and book you a seat."

"Sounds good to me. As soon as possible, right?"

"Yes… thank you, Randa."

"Nothing to thank… I love you, Denise."

The poet smiled. "I love you too. Talk to you in a while. Bye."

"Bye, love."

Denise closed the line happily. Though she was still greatly concerned with what Diane wanted to talk to her about she knew that with Randa's presence she could face what lay ahead. Suddenly that notion didn't seem so disconcerting. Acknowledging the sheer desire to be with Randa was all part of the many aspects to being in love. *What on earth could be wrong with that?* Happy with the knowledge that Randa would soon be with her, Denise headed off in search of the Yellow Pages.

116

Chapter 10

For the second time in the span of a year, Randa found herself on a plane in its final approach to England. There were differences between this time and the last to be sure. Last time Randa was heading to England unsure of what she would find and the greeting she would receive. Last time she hadn't yet seen the face of the person who would become her life. Last time Sara had been alive.

This time Randa was going to Britain secure in the knowledge she was heading to the person who was the greatest blessing in her life, a person who was the sweetest part of it. *There was so much I didn't know a year ago* the nurse thought. *I didn't know what it felt like to be in love, to put someone higher in importance than myself. I didn't know how truly loving someone could make you feel so worthwhile and how being truly loved in return could make you feel so cherished. I didn't know Denise Jennings.*

The nurse had heard the old tales of how soul mates were one half of a whole that had been split by some ancient god and how you weren't complete until you found that person. That story never rang true for Randa. She always felt saying another person completed you was tantamount to saying you were less of a person without them and she just didn't feel that way. Randa more felt that Denise was a special blessing in her life and the icing on an already very good cake

She fingered the silver ring on her left hand. She knew for certain she would never want her cake without the icing again. Denise had not only become part of her heart, she **was** her heart. That was why when Denise called and said she needed her, Randa hadn't questioned the why, just the when. It was Derek who had questioned everything else.

118

"Randa, you are my best friend and one of the best nurses I've had the pleasure to work with on the Brightwood Network, but you only just got back to working full-time two months ago. Brightwood is generous with their time off, but you barely have anything accrued to use. If you go this time, you have to go on a leave without pay," he had said. "You're sure you want to do that? I know you love DJ, but I also know you've got a lot of pride. You're going to be dependent on her if you don't have an income. Is that going to sit all right with you?"

Randa had thought about it for a minute. She had enough money back in the bank to cover a month or two of mortgage payments on the house, but after that she would be dependent on Denise totally if they had to stay in England longer. The nurse's pride was stung a little but overriding that sting was her love for Denise. There had been no choice.

"She needs me, Derek. It's as simple as that. If she needs me then I'm there. I don't have an option anymore; she'll always be the first choice for me. I know I'll be more vulnerable than I've ever been, but I trust and love Denise. We can take care of any problem as long as we do it together." She heard Derek sniff over the phone.

"Derek, what is it? What's wrong?"

"Not a damn thing, girlfriend, not a damn thing. I only hope to one day be a tiny percent as happy as you are. Look, I can't give you paid time, but I can hold your spot for you. The person taking your shifts will always be temporary until you say differently. Now, do you need a ride to the airport?"

So Randa had once again made arrangements for the care of her property as Denise made arrangements for her journey. *Note to self* she thought. *Give Denise an extra thank you for making those arrangements first class.* She returned her crystal juice glass to the flight attendant as she straightened the very comfortable seatback in preparation for landing at East Midlands airport. Denise felt flying directly into Derbyshire would eliminate a lot of the driving time and hassle of getting in and out of London.

119

After the plane landed and taxied to the gate, Randa thought she could make out Denise's tall form in the windows facing the plane. Gathering her single carry-on bag she left the plane quickly, thanking the flight attendant for the excellent service. Making her way up the ramp the nurse felt her pulse pick up in anticipation. It was all she could do not to break into a run at the sight of her dark haired lover inside the terminal. She knew the wide smile on Denise's face was reflected on her own and she walked into waiting arms.

"God, Randa, I've missed you," Denise husked. "Let's get your baggage quickly because I want to kiss you senseless and I don't want to do it in front of all these people."

The nurse smiled against Denise's denim jacket. She knew it would tax her last bit of restraint, but East Midlands probably wasn't San Francisco in its tolerance so she stepped back and took the poet's hand.

"Yeah, baggage first, kiss senseless after," she agreed. Denise shouldered the nurse's carry-on and they moved toward the baggage claim area.

Randa looked over briefly at Denise as they walked and said, "Jennifer? Justine?"

"Sorry?" her partner said as a look of bewilderment crossed her features.

"Your middle name. Is it Jennifer or Justine? You have a great technique for changing the subject, but don't think I've forgotten I asked you about it. You never did answer me either, you just changed the subject."

"I did? I don't recall that at all. No, it's not Jennifer or Justine. It's...baggage claim."

Now it was Randa's turn to be confused. "What did you say?"

"I said baggage claim. We're here; so let me have the claim checks so I can get yours. Did you bring the duffel again?" Denise inquired as she held her hand out.

"Two of them actually. I thought you might like a few more things from home if we needed to stay much longer and... Hey! You're doing it again. You're changing the subject." She handed the two small tickets to the poet.

"I'm not changing the subject, love," Denise whispered as she leaned in close. "I just don't want us to be late for that business appointment. I believe there is a bit of kissing we are scheduled for followed by a fast drive home and then I intend to be 'in conference' with you for the rest of the day and well into the evening."

The nurse shivered a little with anticipation as she spied her two duffel bags on the carousel. Grabbing one as Denise hefted the other, she let herself be led toward the parking facilities and Denise's sleek black car. Placing the bags in the trunk they hurried to climb inside where they clung together in a series of heated kisses.

Finally pulling back for some much needed air, Randa sighed in happiness. "Home, James, and don't spare the horses." Hesitating a moment, she said, "It isn't James, is it? You didn't get saddled with a man's name as your middle name, did you?"

Denise let out a short laugh and she managed a "No, love" as her mouth met Randa's once again and the play of tongues commenced. Both women were a little breathless as they broke apart again. Randa felt the flames of desire licking at her intensely.

"Just drive, Denise whatever-the-heck-your-middle-name-is, and make it fast."

"Yes, madam, whatever the madam desires," Denise teased as she turned the key and brought the engine to life.

"You're going to find out what the madam desires right here and now if you don't start driving immediately," the nurse returned.

Denise saw the hunger in the nurse's eyes and knew her hunger was a match for it.

Denise drove.

****

"So, do you believe her story?" Randa asked as they drove into Bakewell.

"A big part of me wants to say no, that Sara never could have kept a thing like that from me, but there's something about the woman and the way she talks that makes another part of me believe she's telling the truth."

"Did you ask Diane?"

"I did. She wouldn't tell me the story on the phone; she said she wanted to do it in person. That scared me a little, Randa. If Diane was going to deny it she could have done that over the telephone easily enough. Suddenly I knew whatever the truth was I didn't want to hear it without you at my side."

The nurse reached out and laid a comforting hand on Denise's arm. "I'm here and I'm going to stay with you as long as you need me."

Denise guided the car to a smooth stop in front of the Jennings home. Turning off the engine she glanced over at Randa. "Plan on staying with me forever then."

The blonde smiled at her partner. "When is Diane going to tell us the story?"

"I've asked her to come round in the morning. I wanted to give you enough time to recover from your jet lag and anything else that might cause you undue exhaustion." The poet punctuated the last statement with a wink.

"Tomorrow will be soon enough for me," Randa said as she left the car. She helped Denise with the bags and walked to the front door. "It's strange. I know I just left my home yet I feel like I've come home again too. I guess it could be the company."

The poet took Randa's hand and brought it to her lips. "It's the company most definitely for me. Shall we go in? I believe we spoke of a conference earlier?"

"After you, love," the blonde said with a small curtsy as Denise unlocked the door and stepped into the house that held so many memories for them both.

"Jacqueline? Jane?" the blonde asked as Denise gave an exasperated groan and closed the door behind them. Further conversation would wait until much later.

****

Standing in front of the large oak framed mirror in the bathroom Denise diligently brushed her teeth. *As diligently as one can brush them when one is using an electric toothbrush,* she thought. Letting the oscillating bristles glide over her teeth her free hand fingered a stray lock of hair that had fallen free from her loosely styled French roll. Feeling the exposed back of her neck DJ wondered what Randa would say if she were to consider cutting her hair. The poet had worn it long for many years now and wondered whether it was time for a change.

As the toothbrush signalled the end of her two minutes, Denise rinsed out her mouth then splashed her face with icy cold water; once done she dried her face with a green and white striped towel. It was still rather early but DJ had showered and dressed over an hour ago. Looking down at her appearance, Denise brushed her hands over the red crop top and faded jeans that hung low on her hips. She realised she was showing a fair amount of midriff but thought, *what the hell. You are never too old to follow fashion. Besides, it's going to be another warm day today.*

Just then a familiar knot of tension twisted her stomach. DJ looked down at her watch for the eighth time that morning. It had just passed seven o'clock and she still had another three and a half hours before Diane was to arrive. Randa had done a superb job the night before of taking her mind off today's events, but as time crept ever closer DJ grew more and more anxious. She didn't want to believe what Maggie had said was true. Denise presumed she and Sara had always told each other everything. She then thought back to the confession she had made to Randa concerning her father. *But there was an honest reason why I couldn't tell Sara that. It would have hurt and upset her too much and I didn't want to add to the pain she was already feeling.* The poet's brow wrinkled in thought. *What would Sara ever feel she needed to protect me from?* Shaking her head as if to clear her mind, Denise opened the bathroom door and walked onto the landing. She headed back towards their bedroom.

Though the curtains were closed, the brightness of the room proved the sun was already shining high in the early morning sky. A ray of light filtered through a slight gap between the drapes and rested upon the turbulent looking bed. Denise cast a speculative gaze over the wooden framed bed, knowing Randa had to be in there somewhere. *Why is it she seems to hide so efficiently in one of these things?* Suddenly a slight movement from under the quilt gave away Randa's deep somnolent breaths. DJ crept further into the room, expertly avoiding the creaky floorboards as she approached the foot of the bed. Denise pulled the cover from Randa's body gingerly and frowned at the sight. The blonde was on her stomach, both hands by her side, lying diagonally across the bed. The shaft of light that stretched through the curtains shone across Randa's behind. Suddenly all thoughts of conversation flew from the poet's mind. Denise's lips curled into a lascivious grin as she whispered, "An open invitation?"

Climbing onto the bed, Denise lowered her lips, trailing them over Randa's calves, the back of her thighs and over her back. Randa twitched and sighed but otherwise remained very much asleep.

Grinning mischievously, DJ kissed across Randa's shoulder blades where she slowed her progression and brought her hands into play. Straddling Randa's firm behind, Denise gently massaged her shoulders. It wasn't too long before Randa stirred and groaned, luxuriating in the soothing caresses.

"Morning," Denise whispered, her lips close to Randa's left ear.

"Hmm," Randa responded. "What time is it?"

Denise trailed her lips across Randa's neck. "Early. I couldn't sleep so I decided to get dressed." DJ moved her hands down Randa's sides. The pads of her fingertips teased Randa's breasts. She felt the body beneath her tremble as Randa's breathing increased. Denise smiled.

"What are you doing?" Randa asked in a breathless whisper. Her head rose off the bed as she tried to catch a glimpse of Denise who was working her lips and tongue across her neck. Randa shivered and moved up her hands to clutch the bed sheets tightly.

Allowing one of her hands to move further, Denise pushed it down and over Randa's hips. "What does if feel like I'm doing?" she husked. "Randa, you're the only person who can keep my mind off the more anxious issues. What could possibly be more distracting **and** rewarding than making love to the woman I adore?" Denise didn't give Randa a chance to respond as she leaned forward, capturing Randa's lips in an awkward yet deeply arousing kiss. Their tongues wrapped around each other in a worshiping caress as they both started an agonisingly slow grind. DJ could feel her flesh infuse with heat and lower parts of her anatomy throbbed for a more direct touch. Her nipples tightened and strained against the material of her bra and, in one swift movement, Denise pulled her both her top and bra off together, disconnecting briefly from Randa's lips. The clothing fell discarded down the side of the bed. Once freed from the restriction, DJ pressed her flesh against the smooth plane of Randa's back.

When their lips parted again, harsh breathing filled the air. Randa whimpered in frustration and Denise knew the reason why, understanding the blonde's dilemma. Randa was torn between wanting to push up against the brunette's centre and push her own down against the firm mattress of the bed.

"Denise..." Randa groaned, her forehead falling back down to the surface of the bed.

"Yes?" DJ answered with a husky voice. She pushed her hands against the mattress enabling her access under Randa's body. Swiftly she encased Randa's right nipple within her finger and thumb, squeezing rhythmically. Randa cried out helplessly under the onslaught as Denise's other hand slipped under her hips and against her centre. DJ groaned, feeling the abundance of moisture that seeped around her fingers. She swirled them around Randa's swollen desire.

"God, Denise," Randa groaned. She pushed herself harder against DJ's long fingers.

"Hmm?" Denise asked. Her lips latched upon Randa's shoulder, taking the smooth, succulent flesh into her mouth where she sucked hard. Her entire body ached with swelling desire.

Randa whimpered harshly. "I need..."

Denise released Randa's flesh. "What do you need?"

"More," Randa responded in a coarse tone. "I need more. I want you inside me."

At Randa's desperate plea, DJ's body flooded with arousal. Her insides liquefied and flowed freely from within causing her body to throb uncontrollably with a need for release. She ached through a lack of much desired contact. Moving so that she was straddling Randa's left leg Denise rose to a sitting position, encouraging Randa to do the same. She sat on her knees, thighs spread wide apart as Randa sat in between them.

"Is this what you need?" DJ asked as the fingers of her left hand hovered around the entrance to the nurse's centre. She moved around in slow teasing circles but refused to enter.

Randa groaned, trying to push herself forward as her head fell back against Denise's shoulder. "God yes... please... do it... I need you, Denise."

Needing no further encouragement, Denise plunged two fingers inside her lover. The inferno of tight, wet heat that greeted her digits caused her own centre to contract with need.

Freeing her hand from Randa's breast, she moved it around to her jeans and quickly unsnapped the row of metal buttons. Denise wasted no time in plunging her hand down into her own aching need. She groaned in relief as she matched the rhythm of her right hand to that of her left.

Obviously feeling the movement behind her, Randa said breathlessly, "What are you doing?"

Denise sucked in Randa's lobe briefly before saying, "It isn't obvious?" She made a point of pulling Randa back against herself harder so the blonde was left little doubt as to what DJ was doing.

"God!" Randa gasped. One hand reached up to grasp her neglected breast as the other fought to hold the back of DJ's head. Randa pulled Denise closer and joined their lips together for a short breathless kiss before saying, "I wish I could see."

"Yeah? You like watching... hmm?" Denise looked over Randa's shoulder, seeing the blonde caress her own breast. She smiled and then closed her eyes as the musky scent of Randa's desire embraced her senses.

Randa gasped as DJ's thumb teased the source of her desire in circular movements. "I like watching you," she said, moving herself against DJ.

"Next time," Denise replied. She bit her bottom lip roughly as she felt herself rapidly approaching the edge. Quickly she sped up her movements inside Randa, wanting them to cross over together. The nurse groaned, one hand clutching DJ's arm. Her movements increased frantically and Denise felt Randa tighten around her fingers.

Feeling her desire reach its pinnacle, Denise whimpered in release. Randa's thighs tightened around her wrist, her own orgasm crashing through her body. The blonde called out her lover's name, their bodies trembling violently against one another.

As their feelings gradually subsided, Denise opened her eyes and looked down over Randa's sweat glistened chest. Randa's thighs were still holding her hand in a tight grip. Her breasts rose and fell with laboured breath. Wanting to gain her lover's attention, Denise gently moved the fingers still deep within the blonde. Randa groaned and her body twitched as she loosened her thigh's hold and Denise gently pulled her hand away from Randa's body.

"Wake me like that every morning from now on!" Randa chuckled and fell onto her side, pulling Denise with her. She then rolled onto her back and looked up at DJ who was lying beside her. "Feel better?"

Denise nodded. "Yep... you?"

Randa looked down to see Denise's hand still tucked within her jeans. She pulled at the hand, guiding it out of her clothing and up towards her lips. "Couldn't be better," she replied, slipping DJ's fingers into her mouth.

Denise sighed and rolled on top of Randa. "God, you know what that does to me!"

Randa wiggled her eyebrows and slipped the fingers from her mouth. "I know. I'm hoping it's already 'next time' and I'll get that show you promised."

"Promised?"

"Well you know what I mean."

"Sure!" Denise moved to a sitting position. "Unfortunately we've got to get moving. I have a list of chores to get done. I have to ring Carl and let him know I will be staying in England longer. He is going on at me about getting an agent now that I have revealed myself. I suppose he has a point. I can't rely on him to deal with all business matters now. Anyway we have to get all of this done before Di arrives and you still have to get dressed."

Randa looked to her left at the radio alarm clock. "Denise we have plenty of time... almost two hours."

"Exactly!" DJ leaned forward and kissed Randa quickly before sliding to the bottom and off the bed, pulling Randa with her. The blonde slid towards DJ. "Ugh... not only am I still tired, but you're going to give me friction burns at this rate." Her feet landed upon the floor, her body still reclined over the surface of the bed.

"Friction burns!!" Denise grinned. "Anyway, are you complaining that you're still tired? I thought you liked my method of waking you up?" Denise looked down at the unclasped buttons of her jeans and realised she needed to take another shower.

"Oh I do... believe me. So... got to get back in the shower?" Randa's hopeful tone was not lost on DJ.

Denise grimaced. "Hmm, damn it. There I was running ahead of schedule." DJ pulled Randa to her feet, letting her eyes linger over the blonde's exposed form. "Why do I have to find you so bloody irresistible anyway?"

Randa grinned widely. "Innate charm." Taking Denise's hand, the blonde pulled her towards the bathroom.

****

Checking her watch once again, Denise strode through the ground floor of the house. By the time she and Randa had gotten dressed they only had forty-five minutes until Diane was due to arrive. DJ looked out of the living room window. Her eyes scanned the street, looking for the older woman. As of yet there was no sign.

From the kitchen, Denise heard Randa as the nurse put away cleaned dishes. While Randa had offered to unload the dishwasher, Denise had telephoned Carl knowing he always arrived in his office the same time every day. The editor was thrilled to hear DJ was staying longer in England and doubly so that Randa had arrived. He made the poet promise they would finally get to meet before heading back to the United States.

Fighting against the urge to look at her watch once again, Denise slipped her hands into her pockets and headed back towards the kitchen.

"I don't know how much longer I can stand this waiting." The brunette leaned against the doorframe and watched Randa stack a row of tall frosted glasses in a cupboard. "Why do I feel life as I knew it and facts I thought to be true are all about to change?"

"Because your overactive imagination... which in any other case is a **good** thing... is now running ahead of you."

"But you've got to admit..."

"Nothing," Randa insisted. "Lets wait and hear what Diane has to say first." Randa closed the cupboard door and approached DJ. She wrapped her arms around the brooding woman's waist. "I'd offer to take your mind off things again but I don't think we have the time."

Denise pouted. "Shame." Leaning forwards she kissed Randa and jumped as the sound of a chain of slow knocks tapped against the front door. "That'll be her," DJ said as she quickly headed towards the front of the house.

Stopping suddenly, Denise turned and poked her head back into the kitchen. "Hey?"

Randa turned. "Hmm?"

"I just wanted to say thank you... for coming all the way here. I've been feeling rather confused the past couple of days but you made me feel a hell of a lot better."

This time the doorbell chimed repeatedly.

Randa smiled as she kissed DJ. "Anything I can do to help you... I'm more than willing." She winked before slapping the poet's behind. "Now go answer the door before Diane leaves."

With a nod DJ jogged away from the kitchen swiftly.

****

A silent tension hung over the room. Sitting in a single chair, Denise looked over at a very quiet Diane who was closely inspecting a fragment of lint upon her pale green skirt. Occasionally she would look up at DJ to see the poet wringing her hands together, her knuckles white with tension. Apart from the simple hello's exchanged when Diane entered the house; no other words had been spoken. Both women sat at opposite sides of the room in a nervous silence.

The door slowly creaked open and DJ watched Randa enter the room, carrying two mugs. She smiled brightly at Diane and placed her cup upon a small side table.

"Diane, it's great to see you again. How are you?"

"Oh I'm fine, Randa. How are you, dear?"

Randa nodded. "Good." The blonde handed DJ her coffee and pulled a bottle of her favourite soda from her pocket. "How was your trip away?"

The older woman smiled brightly. "It was nice to see old friends again. We aren't able to get together that often."

Noticing that DJ was yet to speak, Randa continued their conversation asking, "How was the weather?"

"Cold!" Diane answered. "It was by the coast. The sea winds really did whip up a draft." Diane continued to chat away nervously. "The sky was lovely and blue yet the air was awfully chilly. I was so glad I had taken my warmest overcoat. These cold winds are no good for my arthritis."

Denise looked up at Randa who had perched herself upon the arm of her chair before turning towards Diane. "Look! ... " DJ cast her gaze once more between her lover and Diane. "Not that I want to interrupt your tête-à-tête on the state of British weather but I do believe we have things to discuss!"

Diane sobered rapidly and her sombre expression returned. "Yes... that is right."

"Well I don't want to push but I think I have a right in knowing what all of this is about." DJ paused, feeling Randa's hand move soothingly over her back. She took a breath, lowering the curt tone in her voice. "I'm sorry… I don't mean to sound angry, Di, but it is just that… well… I need to know. I have some crazy woman following me who seems to hate my very existence and now I realise there were parts of Sara's life that I was never aware of. And to top it all off, this Maggie claims to be a part of that."

Taking her cup from the small wooden table, Diane took a drink of her sweet tea. "I know. I'm sorry, DJ. It's just that this brings back a lot of bad memories for myself as well." Diane sighed lightly, composing her emotions as she began to recount one of the most heartbreaking periods of her and Sara's life.

Chapter 11

London, June 1961

The last of the boxes were being packed. Sara sat numbly in the slightly battered wingback chair and watched as Diane wrapped the few remaining items of hers left in the living area of the third floor flat. Soon the only thing left of Diane's would be the small record player that had been a shared source of joy for the young women. The record player belonged to Diane, but they had jointly saved their coins and always went together to select additions to their collection from the music shop on the next block.

The term at the university would be finished in a week and Diane's father had made good on his pledge to her. She had been allowed to finish her education but her absence from Derbyshire would no longer be tolerated or subsidized. After the commencement exercises in ten days, Diane would be accompanying her parents and Roger back north where their engagement would be announced and the wedding date would be set.

Sara sighed in exasperation as she recalled the last few weeks with Diane. When the barriers had come down between them that night in Diane's bedroom, Sara had become one of the happiest women in Britain. She had known from that moment that she had found the one great love of her life. Their physical and spiritual intimacy blossomed and that, added to the devotion between them as best friends, was a strong and beautiful thing. *But it's not*

132

strong enough Sara thought bitterly. Diane was going home.

Diane looked over at her best friend at the sound of the sigh and knew instinctively what the other woman had been thinking. She knew Sara was trying again to think of another way for their situation to have a different ending. Diane knew that was an impossibility. She looked at the face of the most important person in her life and saw a grim expression clouding the brilliant blue eyes. *Sara, you are the most wonderful person in the world. You've kept your marks high and you're going to graduate with honors all the while working and helping me with my schoolwork. You're my best friend and my love and it's killing me to cause you this pain.*

When Diane announced she was returning to Derbyshire with her parents after graduation she thought all hell would break loose, but Sara had surprised her yet again. She made tea and brought it into the living room where she soothed Diane and calmly set about to find a solution to the problem. Hour after hour had yielded little results. No matter how logical Sara's reasoning, no matter how persuasive her arguments and no matter how passionate her declarations of love, Diane remained firm in her decision to leave.

Diane placed the last newspaper wrapped item into the box and glanced around the flat in assessment. The small flat had become more of a home to her than the large house belonging to her parents and she knew no matter what happened in her life that she would consider the years she had spent here with Sara to be the happiest of her life. Diane's gaze fell to the picture hanging on the wall that separated the doors of their bedrooms. Diane's cousin Rodney was an amateur photographer who had been visiting London and dropped in to see his cousin briefly in between her classes at the university. He had been experimenting with trying to capture the stately architectural composition of the buildings when on a whim he had decided to highlight Diane in front of one of the ivy covered structures. She was a camera shy subject who fidgeted nervously until she called out to a strikingly good-looking young woman.

Diane introduced Rodney to Sara and he was immediately taken with the tall, dark haired woman. He abandoned plans to capture the image of his rather ordinary cousin in order to concentrate on getting her friend on film. As he focused his camera and made adjustments to the settings he wondered how he could get Diane to move away from her beautiful flat mate. As he peered through the lens though at the two women who appeared to be idly chatting, he saw something that both amused and astonished him.

Suddenly his ordinary cousin was changed. Instead of the girl he had known all his life there was a woman of confidence and serene beauty. He wondered what had effected the change only for as long as it took him to realize the same look was on her friend's face as well. *I'll be damned* he thought and snapped the picture before either woman realized it had been taken. Two weeks after Rodney's visit, a sturdy envelope was delivered to the third floor London flat. Inside the envelope was a note from Rodney.

Sometimes a photographer needs to use all his skill to bring out the emotion and beauty of his subject. Sometimes, though, the subject doesn't need his help at all. Love, Rodney

The accompanying photograph showed Diane and Sara on a sunny afternoon gazing at one another, lost in conversation. That they were deeply in love was very apparent. Both women were stunned, but it was Diane who spoke first.

"Do I...do I really look like that?"

"That's how I've seen you from almost the first time I met you. I'm glad Rodney captured it so you could see for yourself," Sara vowed and leaned over to place a light peck on Diane's lips. They had gone out then to a nearby second hand store and purchased a small oak frame for the picture. Now Sara followed Diane's line of sight and gazed at the photograph too. She decided then to try one last time.

"Diane, please reconsider. I love you and I know you love me and if that's true then everything else will work itself out. I'll go with you to talk to your family. We'll tell

134

them you don't need their money or their approval and that you're not going to go through with a sham of a marriage to Roger. We can teach just as we always planned to do... anything as long as we can be together, Diane. Please don't go, I beg you." Sara's voice broke and tears formed in the brilliant blue eyes.

Diane turned away, unable to meet the pleading gaze any longer. With her back turned, Diane found the strength to say the words she knew she had to.

"Sara, I know we've said some things to each other and I know at the time we both thought we meant them. I think, though, that we need to face facts and grow up now. We are about to graduate from the university and begin our adult lives. The fanciful notions we had while in college need to be put away. I won't say it wasn't pleasurable, but do you really think anyone would accept two women together? Especially two women together in the social circles I will be expected to be in when I return home?" She turned back to Sara, knowing she had to look the taller woman in the eye as she said what she must.

"I'm sorry if I led you to believe we could have a future, that was very wrong of me. My future lies in Derbyshire with Roger. I admit I was infatuated with you, Sara. It was all very exciting, but I regret so much of what has happened between us. It wasn't fair for you and it wasn't right of me to let it go on. I don't want to hurt you, but this is the way it must be."

Sara was stunned and the tears spilled over, gliding silently down her cheeks. Diane chewed her bottom lip for a moment before continuing.

"My father will be here shortly. I think it's best if I stay with my parents at their hotel for the rest of the week. We will be leaving London immediately after the commencement exercises. The removers will be here tomorrow to collect my things. From this point on, I don't think we should see each other anymore."

Sara rose from her chair and moved to Diane's side and spoke in a voice choked with emotion. "Diane, I don't understand what's made you change. Please don't do this. You love me, I know you do."

"You're wrong Sara, I never did. Let's just put this down as...an interesting experiment, an experiment that's over now. Do you understand me? It's over."

Unable to take the torment any longer, Sara turned away and grabbed almost blindly for her coat and pocketbook. Stumbling to the door with the pain all but crushing her, she paused with her hand on the doorknob. She did not turn back to Diane but straightened up and spoke quietly.

"I love you, Diane Chamberlain and I always will. There will never be another for me in this life." With those words she opened the door and walked out, never looking back.

If she had looked back she would have seen a copy of her agony written on Diane's face. A heartbeat after the door closed, Diane slid to the floor, her body wracked with heart wrenching sobs. This was where her father found her fifteen minutes later.

"Diane! Diane, get up at once! I knocked twice and yet here you sit. Get up, girl!" Diane complied meekly, wiping the tears from her face with the back of her hands. Standing, she faced Miles Chamberlain, a large man with a commanding presence and tyrannical nature.

"Did you do as I instructed? You've told that woman you're finished with her?"

"Yes, Father," Diane replied meekly.

"It had better be so, Diane. I meant every word of what I said in Derbyshire. I think you know me well enough to know I never issue idle threats. Now, get your things and let us leave. It sickens me to be in this place of perversion."

Diane did as she was told. Two weeks earlier her father had intercepted a letter from Sara while Diane had been home for a final visit before graduation. Diane had protested the opening of her mail but her father had shouted down her objections saying he had every right to know what was going on under his own roof. The letter he held was damning proof of the very loving relationship between the two women. Diane recalled the first words with great

136

clarity.

My darling Diane,

You've been gone for only a few days but already I miss holding you in my arms, watching you sleep and the taste of your lips on mine...

Her father didn't need to read anymore to her. He demanded an explanation and Diane gave the only one she had. She had told him that she and Sara were deeply in love. She said she would not be coming back to Derbyshire and no marriage to Roger would take place. Her father said nothing for a moment but his countenance darkened with barely suppressed rage. When he spoke it was in a quietly dangerous tone.

"Listen to me, Diane. You will break this abomination off immediately! You will never see that whore again! If you defy me in this I will see that woman broken. She will never teach and I will see her hounded out of every position she does obtain. I will have her up on charges. The laws may not be enforced so well these days but I assure you they are still on the books and I will not rest until I see her disgraced and ruined. Do I make myself entirely clear?"

Where Diane would have risked everything for Sara, she would not let Sara risk everything for her. Sara never wanted anything but to be a teacher and now all her hard work was in jeopardy. Diane knew her father perfectly capable of ruining the life of the woman she loved. She knew what she had to do; to save Sara, she would do as her father demanded.

Thus the most difficult two weeks of her life had begun and now it felt as if that life was over. She didn't understand how her heart could continue to beat or how she could continue to draw breath. All her senses were numb, but that at least was preferable to the unbearable hurt she knew was still to come.

Her father moved to the door and held it open for her, silently commanding her departure. Putting her coat on, she moved to the door slowly. She passed by the picture on the wall and her gaze was drawn to it once again.

I'll love you forever, Sara Jennings. Please find it in your heart to forgive me.

As she moved by her father and headed for the stairs a final thought passed through her mind.

I'll never see her again.

****

Diane stopped here, fresh tears flowing down her cheeks. She turned to Randa and Denise.

"When my father died many years later, my mother gave me the letter back. She didn't have the courage to defy him either until after he was gone, but by that time our lives had been decided for us. I was married and a mother and Sara was teaching and taking care of DJ. Our chance had passed."

Randa stood silently, tears gracing her cheeks. She gripped Denise's hand tightly, feeling an answering pressure from her partner.

"The bastard," Denise muttered.

"He was that," Diane agreed. "We were, however, a product of our times. It wasn't acceptable then and though I know Sara would have fought him, I couldn't let her. I loved her too much for that."

Diane removed a handkerchief from her pocketbook and stood up. "Let me have a moment and I'll finish the story. I'm afraid the rest is no happier." As she moved off, Denise called to her.

"Diane, can you wait just a moment?" At Diane's nod, the poet made her way up the stairs and into her study. Within a minute she returned carrying an old leather briefcase. She handed the case to Diane.

"I know Sara would want you to have these. I didn't know how important they were until now."

Opening the case, Diane removed several old vinyl records and recognized them by their titles as being ones that she and Sara had purchased together. Reaching in again she pulled out a small oak framed photograph. There in the picture were Sara and Diane as they had been so many years ago, standing in front of the ivy covered building in the sunshine.

Through fresh tears Diane gave a smile of profound gratitude to the two younger women who were living the dream she and Sara never could. "She kept it, all that time she kept it. I never knew." She left the room then, unable to speak further.

Diane continued on her way as Denise turned to Randa. The dark haired woman moved into the safety of her lover's arms and wept quietly. Randa felt her cheeks wet with tears as well.

"I love you, Denise Jennings. I love you so very much."

Chapter 12

Randa sat with DJ upon the single sofa. Wedged between the arms of the chair and Denise's thigh she laid her legs bent over Denise's lower body. Within her hands she held the photograph DJ had given Diane. Intently she gazed down at the beautifully captured image.

"You look so much like Sara when she was young!"

Denise took the corner of the picture frame, twisting the print to her line of sight. "Runs in the family," she answered numbly. "You should see my father. It's part of our Irish heritage... that part of the family all seemed to have the dark hair and blue eyes."

"Irish?" Randa asked.

"I never told you?" As Randa shook her head DJ said, "Yes, apparently Sara said it was always obvious in me. The way I brush my teeth before breakfast. The way I brush my hair before I take a shower and open the bedroom curtains before I get dressed." She smiled at Sara's long running joke. "It's those silly Englishman, Irishman, Scotsman jokes!"

Randa took DJ's hand and kissed her fingers. "I just thought those acts were all part of your quirky personality!" Looking back at the photograph she said, "They look so happy together. It's heartbreaking to think that two people who were really in love would never be able to have the happiness they wanted together. It seems that a domino effect of obstacles always prevented them from being together. It's just so sad."

"Hmm... but all of this still has yet to explain who this Maggie is and what part she seems to play in Sara's past."

140

"I will be getting to that," Diane said as she re-entered the living room.

Denise watched the older woman make her way back toward the sofa. She seemed more composed after taking the time to freshen a little. Randa climbed out of the chair and approached Diane. She sat down beside the frail looking woman, placing one hand upon her shoulder.

"Are you feeling okay? Would you like another drink?"

Diane shook her head. "No, thank you and yes I am feeling slightly better now." She looked down at the leather case, her eyes moving over the collection of long playing albums. "I need to tell you the rest of the story. What I tell you now is what Sara related to me herself when we finally met again and made our peace."

Denise leaned forward in her chair. "About this Maggie?"

"Yes." Diane nodded and began the second part of Sara's story.

****

London, September 1961

For a Saturday afternoon the pub was sparsely populated. It was an old building, situated on the outskirts of the city and more frequented by elderly gentlemen and ex-servicemen who still wore their medals with pride upon old navy blazers. In the far corner of the room sat an elderly man wearing an oversized tweed jacket and tattered flat cap. Between his teeth he held a well used pipe and its acrid smoke flowed over the room like a light mist. By the entrance to the pub sat a similar looking man nursing a pint of Guinness. By his feet sat a loyal Jack Russell terrier. The shabby canine looked up at his master hoping the man would drop another 'pork scratching' his way.

Situated by the far end of the bar, Sara Jennings looked at her surroundings. Once again she wondered why she had agreed to meet her friend in this run down, back street drinking hole. Sandy had also studied with Sara and they both received teaching positions in the same primary school. She and Sandra had been relatively close and had recently arranged to meet for shopping excursions. Mainly it was for the simple act of being seen around the well-known retail outlets and occasionally buying the latest fashions. Though she didn't earn an awful lot of money, periodically Sara was able to treat herself and today was one of those days. She was hoping to buy a new necklace. It seemed bells worn around the neck had become all the rage and far be it from her not to follow the latest trends.

It was during one of their trips around town that Sara had disclosed to Sandra the nature of her relationship with Diane. Of course that was now over, it had been for over three months and although Sara managed to continue on with her life, inside she still felt empty. Sandra had told her it would take time but she would get over the petite brunette. Sara, however, knew that even though that may be true, she would never love another the way she did Diane. She didn't think she was able. The tall woman missed her flat mate terribly. When Diane had left, Sara felt unable to remain in the flat, which had been such a place of happiness for the both of them. The young teacher had sought other living situations. She discovered a male friend from university was leasing out a room in his recently emigrated parent's home. Although the rent would stretch her to the limit, Sara was more than willing to pay if she was able to get out of her present dwellings and away from what had become hurtful memories. So she had left the little flat, leaving nothing but a lone forwarding telephone number with the landlady. Sara moved into a nice midtown house shared by Ron her landlord, his sister Dotty and a medical student Kenny, who was hardly ever there.

Sliding her finger over the rim of her pint glass, Sara looked again towards the door as it swung open. She sighed in disappointment to see a young man with strawberry blonde hair enter, and not her friend Sandy. Their eyes connected briefly before the man headed off towards the far wall. He stopped by a jukebox that seemed so out of place in the dingy pub. It was obviously the landlord's pride and joy. Sara watched him slip a silver coin into the machine and make his selection. A moment later the quiet of the room was broken by the popular Beatles tune, "Love me do". The brunette rolled her eyes. That particular band was very popular, but she seemed to be one of the fair few who didn't see the attraction.

Draining her glass once again, Sara signalled toward the heavyset bartender. She wasn't a heavy drinker in the least but brooding over the events of the past months had given her the need to drown her sorrows. One drink had turned into two and then three and by her fourth Sara felt the need for something a lot stronger.

When the balding landlord approached she said, "A double vodka with ice."

"Make that two," said a voice from behind her.

Sara turned to see the young man with strawberry blonde hair. He smiled and slid into the stool beside her as their drinks were placed upon the dented, scratched wood of the counter. "My treat," he said and placed a five pound note by their glasses.

"Thanks." Sara picked up her glass and drained it in one go. She placed the empty container back down upon the bar and looked at the landlord. "Same again; he's paying." She jerked her head to the side, indicating her new drinking friend.

The man nodded towards the barman then turned back to Sara. "A woman after my own heart." He held out his hand. "Johnny."

Sara shook it firmly. "Sara. So what's a smart looking guy like you doing in a place like this?"

Johnny laughed. "I was about to ask you the same question. It seems I am not the only person looking to drink away my troubles today."

"So you got dumped too?"

"More like I found her in bed with my ex-best friend." Johnny shot back his glass and signalled towards the landlord who was now drying glasses with a tatty white cloth. "Keep them coming," he said, and then addressed Sara once again.

"You?"

Sara gazed down into her glass, swirling the ice around her vodka. "She dumped me for marriage and money."

"She?"

Turning towards Johnny, Sara delivered a steely gaze. "You have a problem with that?"

Johnny held up his hands, unnerved by the icy glare. "No, man!"

Sara nodded and drained her glass. She was in no mood to defend her feelings but she was loath to lie about them either. Widening her eyes, Sara blinked repeatedly as she began to feel the effects of the alcohol take over her body. Rubbing her forehead she waited until the bartender refilled both glasses before turning back to Johnny.

The young man held up his glass. "To women... and the way they mess with our heads."

Sara tapped Johnny's glass with her own. "To women... god forbid I ever become one," she slurred.

Laughing, Johnny nodded. "I second that."

Once again draining their glasses they slammed them back down upon the bar together and simultaneously shouted, "Fill us up!" The laughed stupidly as their bodies began to surrender to the oncoming onslaught of alcohol.

****

A muffled thud accompanied by a sharp intake of breath and a muttered curse pulled Sara from a heavy, alcohol induced sleep. Unable to open blurry eyes to the moderately bright room it took long moments for the brunette to gain her bearings. She realised two things. Firstly being that she was in her own room, though she had no idea how in fact she got there and secondly, Sara quickly realised she wasn't alone.

Sitting up, Sara groaned as her head spun and her stomach lurched. Taking a short breath she opened her eyes and came face to face with nervous green orbs and rumpled strawberry blonde hair. As shock registered in her system, Sara realised she was naked. The sheets that pooled limply around her body exposed her uncomfortably. Swiftly she pulled them up to cover her bare chest.

"Oh God!"

"That's what I said."

Sara stared at Johnny. "Did we...?"

Johnny pulled on his paisley shirt and started connecting the buttons. "The evidence seems to state that we did." He tucked his shirt into his trousers. "Look..."

Sara held up her hand, stopping the man from continuing. The expression upon his face and the tone in his voice told the young teacher all she needed to hear and for that she was glad. "No need to say anything. We drank way too much yesterday. This shouldn't have happened but it did... it's..."

"One of those things," Johnny finished for her, rolling his eyes. "Yes... I'm glad you agree. I didn't want to be the bastard here, but I haven't gotten over my last girl yet. However if things ever change..."

Sara shook her head, an emptiness filling her senses.

Johnny nodded. "Yes... you're right." He pushed his feet into large shoes, bolstering his height by another three inches, and then looked around Sara's room awkwardly. "Well... I better be going... and find out where on earth I am."

"Right." Gathering the deep green covers around herself Sara climbed out of her bed. Opening the bedroom door she allowed Johnny to exit first and followed him down the stairs to the directly facing front door. As she pulled it open she was shocked to see Sandy standing on the doorstep – hand held up ready to knock on the door. The blonde's surprised eyes took in Sara's scantily clad form and the young man who was stepping past her.

Sara looked at Johnny nervously. He nodded, forcing a tense grimace past his lips before he disappeared down the side of the house.

Sara turned back to Sandy. "Bit late," she said hollowly.

Sandra stepped into the house. "I came around to apologise, Sara. I had a bit of a family emergency... I'll tell you later." She closed the door behind her. "Who was that?"

Wrapping one arm around her stomach, Sara frowned. "I can't remember. I met him at that pub I was supposed to be meeting you in. We were drinking... a lot."

Sandy studied Sara closely. "You didn't, did you?"

Sara stared at her friend blankly.

"Man, I thought you weren't into all this free love!"

Realising the impact of what Sandy was saying Sara choked back a wretched sob. "How could I have been so stupid?" Her eyes glazed with unshed tears. "I just started drinking... thinking and drinking. That's more or less all I can remember apart from gaining a drinking partner someway through the afternoon." Sara thought for a moment. "Johnny... that was his name." As dizziness overtook her, Sara turned towards the stairs and sat down heavily. "What have I done?"

Sandra sat down beside her friend, squeezing her body into the remaining space on the narrow step. She tucked a lock of light blonde hair behind her ear as her other arm wrapped around Sara's shoulder. "How do you feel?"

"Like I have just cheated on the woman I love."

"But she..."

"I know," Sara sighed despondently. "I can't help it. I still love her... I know I always will, Sandy." The brunette groaned as her stomach turned heavily. "Oh... God!"

Jumping from the step Sara clamped one hand over her mouth as she dashed back up the stairs and towards the communal bathroom.

From the kitchen Kenny emerged curiously.

Sandra looked up at the sporadically seen medical student who was wearing head to toe black apart from a large target design printed boldly upon the front of his tee shirt. "Hello, stranger."

Kenny looked at Sandra in question. "What's wrong with Sara?"

"Bit too much to drink last night," she lied.

"Say no more." Kenny disappeared back into the kitchen. "One thirst quenching sugary drink coming up!"

****

146

It was almost six weeks later when Sara discovered she was pregnant. She'd had a feeling only a few days after her drunken encounter that something was different but dismissed her instincts for fear of what they may mean. She put them down instead to simple guilt and disgust at herself concerning her actions. On discovering the truth of her condition the young teacher fell into a state of absolute shock. Suddenly discovering she had another life within her was a bewildering notion. Her mind ran the gauntlet of emotions. Shock. Anger. Confusion. Happiness. Sadness. Swiftly she realised she needed to make some major choices in her life. She was a young woman alone who was only just able to support herself on her minimal teaching wages. Also there was the fact that she would become a young, unmarried mother and that in itself was severely frowned upon. Sara decided to keep the news to herself and did so for several weeks as she tried to consider her options. Her first choice was abortion and although she desperately tried to convince herself that logically it would be the best step to take – she could not. Yet Sara knew that looking after a child at her time of life, with no financial stability, would be hard. She wouldn't be able to give the unborn child the start in life that she felt every child deserved. So Sara thought hard and came to the conclusion that the best move for the child would be to give it up for adoption. She hoped two loving parents could succeed where she knew she would fail and this way she knew the child would gain a stable family life. What surprised Sara the most was her feeling of indifference concerning her decision. *Aren't mothers supposed to feel a maternal instinct?* She had wondered, feeling confused by her lack thereof. On simply realising she would be unable to look after a child; the most logical option for her was to give it up. Her resolution seemed so clinical.

When that decision had been made Sara then told Sandra and the people with whom she was sharing the house. It would be obvious to them, but she needed to keep her pregnancy hidden from everyone else. Luckily fashion during this time consisted of garments such as tank dresses.

The brunette knew that clothes such as these would disguise her growing condition and so she brought herself a selection of these dresses in bright colours such as orange and lime green with polka dots. An added bonus for the tall teacher was that due to her firm physique, her progressively showing pregnancy never became overly apparent. She was easily able to cover up her stomach with the hideous sixties fashions. Sara was able to keep her teaching position right up until she was seven months pregnant, eventually leaving when she stated she was taking a break before starting a new position.

Once the added concern of her teaching duties lessened, Sara's thoughts began to reel. Though inside the notion of giving up her child was becoming increasingly hard to bear, her major concern became who would take the infant. Sara was overjoyed when she discovered that Geoff and Alice Spicer, the couple that had taken her in on first arriving in London, had wanted to adopt for a long time. The couple had been trying for a child for a while but were medically unable to conceive. Sara instinctively knew these two people would make an excellent choice for her child's parents. They were both only five years older than Sara. She also hoped it meant that she would be able to keep a certain amount of contact with them. Sara accepted the fact that if Geoff and Alice became her child's parents she hoped they would allow her to keep in touch and informed of its development. Eventually the adoption papers went through, Geoff and Alice were the lucky parents and they agreed to keep Sara up to date with the child's growth.

Through all of this Sara hadn't once tried to make contact with Diane. Leaving only a forwarding telephone number with her ex-landlady, she hadn't heard from the petite brunette either. Thinking that Diane didn't want to make contact with her, Sara tried to accept the fact that they would probably never see each other again. Diane had made her choice and had chosen the life her family had wanted for her. It never stopped hurting, drawing Sara to the brink of tears on several occasions, as she acknowledged how her life had changed and how different it would have been with Diane. It would be some years later before they saw each other again. All the hurt and long buried love would resurface then as confessions were made and truths were finally brought into the open.

****

London, June 1962

Though the day had begun, the cloudy late spring morning had remained oppressively dark. So much so that the hospital's maternity ward was lit with artificial lighting. The cries of babies echoed along the wide corridors of the hospital.   There were several wards on the third floor maternity unit of the Royal Infirmary. Each one was filled with twelve mothers accompanied by their newborn children in little translucent cots by the sides of their beds. Sara was situated in the back corner of maternity ward three. She almost felt like the outcast, the dirty secret... the unmarried mother. Although several women had attempted polite conversation, she had remained distant.

Looking down into the cot beside her bed, Sara knew why. Ever since her child had been born almost seven days ago she wondered whether giving the little girl away was indeed the right option.   Sara tried to remain detached, clinical even, only giving her little baby attention when it needed feeding or changing. Other mothers in the ward had looked down on her, disgusted at her seeming lack of care. The truth of the matter was that from the moment her little girl was born, Sara's maternal instincts had fully asserted themselves. It broke her heart a little more each day as the time approached when Geoff and Alice Spicer would come to take her home.

The couple had already visited Sara several times since the baby had been born. Together the three had chosen the child's name – Margaret Elizabeth.   Sara agreed to this name because she simply liked the name Maggie and Geoff and Alice because they were both proud Royalists.

It was Friday, mid-morning and although Sara had only been awake for two hours the young woman felt as though those few hours had never existed. Sitting on the edge of her hospital bed Sara looked down at Maggie sleeping peacefully in her bed. From behind her she could hear voices of other mothers and the odd gurgle of newborn children. For the first time that morning there was a gentle tranquillity to the air.

Keeping her hands upon her lap Sara looked over her shoulder, her eyes trained upon the wide double doors of the ward. Through the window she could see the back of Sandra's head as she stood in the corridor. Her friend was conversing with the Spicers and a representative of the Social Services. Today was the day Geoff and Alice would take Maggie home and Sara had requested one final moment alone with her child.

Turning back to the translucent cot, Sara leaned forwards and pulled back the white crocheted blanket from Maggie's body. Sleepy blue eyes opened and Maggie whimpered in protest as Sara lifted her from the warm cocoon of her little bed. She pulled the child into her arms. Cerulean blue eyes, very similar to her own, looked up at her and Sara smiled in absolute affection. She closed her eyes, bringing Maggie's head to her nose as she breathed in her scent.

"I have to say goodbye," she whispered against Maggie's head and reopened her eyes. Sara raised the pads of her fingers and smoothed them over the silky soft skin of Maggie's cheek then ran them through the light reddish fuzz upon her head. The soft texture caressed her fingertips and tickled her senses.

"I hope one day you will understand why I have to do this." Sara ran her index finger over the infant's lips and Maggie lightly sucked upon her fingertip. "But it doesn't mean that I don't love you. I tried not to, really I did, but you are my little miracle, the most precious thing in the world and I do love you." Feeling her emotions begin to surface, Sara pulled her finger from Maggie's lips and held the tiny child close. Squeezing her eyes shut she rested her chin lightly upon the baby's head and swallowed down a tight ball of despair that was rapidly working its way to the surface. "I wish I could give you the life you deserve. I want you to have the best of everything you can possibly have. Geoff and Alice are a nice couple."

Sara kissed Maggie's cherub-like nose. From the moment the infant was born she had counted the days until they would both leave the hospital. She knew it wouldn't be with the newborn child within her arms. Sara had closed herself off from that thought. Instead she concentrated on recovering from a stressful delivery and providing Maggie with the vital sustenance she needed from her mother before the Spicer's took her away.

Cuddling the bundle within her arms, Sara laid her cheek upon Maggie's soft, fuzzy head. From behind her she heard the ward doors swing open and turned to see Sandra and the Social Services representative, Mrs Barker, heading towards her.

Looking back at Maggie, Sara kissed her forehead softly. "I'm sorry," she muttered against the infant's fragrant skin. "God... don't ever hate me for this. I just want to do what is right for you... that's all."

The echoing footsteps that slowly approached Sara eventually stopped by the side of her bed. Casting her vision to the right Sara gazed briefly at her friend and the Social Worker. There was a cold air of detachment in Mrs Barker's eyes that told Sara this woman could not afford to be swayed by maternal sentiment. Sandra stepped forward, placing her hand upon Sara's shoulder, but refusing to acknowledge the moment was about to end; Sara ignored her. Turning back to the now sleeping child lying serenely in her arms Sara held her impossibly closer, careful not to hurt the small bundle within her embrace.

"I have to do this," she said, trying to convince herself as much as the oblivious child. "It's the right thing to do... it has to be."

Feeling an emptiness encompass her heart, Sara looked back at Mrs Barker. The Social Worker took a step forward portraying a sincere smile and Sandra squeezed her shoulder a little tighter.

Leaning down the brunette placed her last loving kiss upon Maggie's head and then held out the child. She kept her eyes trained upon her lap, unable to watch as the weight was lifted from her arms. Sara held back a distraught sob.

She closed her eyes, biting hard upon her bottom lip as the echoing sound of retreating footsteps increased in distance.

A lonely void of chilling despair filled Sara's heart. She felt the distance between Maggie and herself grow as each footstep took her child further from her life. It was like her very soul was fading and her spirit dying. When the ward doors swung open and shut a titanic sense of panic overtook Sara's being.

"No!" she cried. Heavy tears that she had tried so valiantly to hold back could no longer be contained. "I can't." Jumping from the bed Sara turned and started towards the double doors. "I can't," she sobbed. "She's my baby."

Sara changed her pace from a speedy walk to a frantic dash as she desperately tried to find Maggie. Pulling the doors open she ran out into the corridor and looked in both directions, anxious to find Mrs Barker. As she turned to run down the corridor a firm hand captured her arm, pulling her backwards.

"Sara," Sandra pleaded desperately. "You can't do this. You know this is the best thing you can do for her."

"But she is **my** baby," Sara cried openly, no longer caring as she stared at her friend through blurry eyes. Salty tears ran down her cheeks, streaking her distraught features.

Sandra took her friend by the shoulders. "You know this is for the best. You have to let her go. You will see her again I am sure. Think of Maggie."

Sara clasped her friend's hands that were tight around her shoulders. "But she's mine, Sandy. She grew inside of me." The brunette continued to cry, speaking through weighty tears. "She is a part of me... I gave her life," she sobbed. "I thought I had nothing to offer her but I was wrong... I have love. What else could there be?"

Feeling her knees buckle the young woman fell lifelessly to the floor. Sitting awkwardly upon her legs she sobbed helplessly. Sandra knelt down beside her, holding Sara close. She ignored the passing mothers who gave curious looks and the medical staff who hovered around as they wondered how to help. It was hurtful enough for Sara that she had already been shunned by those mothers who did know and didn't agree with her actions. Now Sara understood why.

As her tears gradually lessened, Sara looked up at Sandra. "She will hate me. If she ever finds out the truth she will hate me. I mean... the only thing I know about her father is his name." Sara took a ragged breath. "He has no idea of her existence, as I know nothing of him. What kind of person can do something so stupid? What kind of mother would give up her own child, Sandy?" Sara rubbed her moist cheeks, her breathing harsh and broken.

"The kind of mother who loves her child enough to want her to have the best, even if that means giving her up." Sandra's own eyes filled with tears, her heart breaking for her friend. "It doesn't mean you love her any less. Maybe more so."

"More?"

Sandra nodded. "Yes, more because you love her enough that you can let her go. Let her be cared for by people who can look after and provide for her. Give her a stable home life with two loving parents who are desperate to share that love with another." Sandra kissed Sara's lowered head. "I can't even begin to understand how you feel, Sara, but you knew beforehand that this was what you needed to do... for little Maggie."

Sara let her chin fall to her chest and placed her forehead in the palm of her hand. "I feel like my heart has been ripped from my chest," she whispered and trembled as though she physically felt the pain.

Not knowing what else she could say, Sandra held her friend in silence. The echoes of footsteps and hushed murmur of voices faded to a dull quiet all around them. She held Sara until her tears were spent and then escorted her lifeless friend back to bed. Although Sara accepted her actions and knew they were right for her child, it would take her a long time to come to terms with her loss.

Chapter 13

"So it's true then," Denise mumbled. It wasn't a question; it was a statement of fact. Her eyes moved around the living room in desolation until they landed on the portrait of herself and Sara that Sara had commissioned the previous Christmas, their last Christmas together. Denise saw herself again as the gangly ten year old she had been with the woman who had become her role model, her friend and her surrogate mother. A woman who was probably closer to her than her own mother, a woman who had kept the most important fact in her life from DJ.

"Yes, it's true, DJ," Diane continued. "Sara told me everything after you and she moved here. After the fire and you lost your parents, Sara wrote to me. We had been writing since the time of my father's death when I could finally be sure he could never hurt her. She wrote and told me that she was moving here with you."

"Did she also say that history had repeated itself and she was being shackled with another unwanted child?" Denise asked with bitterness thick in her voice. Randa reached over and laid a comforting hand on the poet's arm. The nurse saw pain filled blue eyes turn to hers. "She never told me, Randa. She never told me and that is as good as lying about it."

"No, love, it's not," Randa replied, slowly shaking her head. "Don't you see? She didn't tell you because she loved you. She loved you the same way she loved that other little girl. She was strong enough in her love to let Maggie go and she was strong enough in her love for you to let you stay." The nurse glanced over to Diane for the assurance that she was right in her assumption.

Diane nodded. "Sara told me about Maggie. How she survived giving that little baby to the Spicers I'll never know. As part of the agreement the Social Services demanded at the time, the birth mother could have no contact with the adopting family. Sara's case was slightly different because she knew Geoff and Alice, but the outcome had to be the same. She could know what was happening to Maggie because Sara knew whom she was with, maybe even occasionally see her, but she could never tell her who she was. Can you imagine the torment? Sara endured it though because she felt she deserved nothing better. After giving her child away she felt as if she deserved no happiness at all. Then your parents died."

Denise had been staring down at her hands during Diane's explanation but now her eyes had a puzzled expression in them as she raised them to soft brown ones.

Diane smiled gently. "She wrote to me because she was certain at first she couldn't possibly give you the home and love you needed. She met with the Social Service worker who was caring for you before she arrived back in Manchester. She was working at a very posh school in London at the time and they had practically talked her into staying there permanently with talk of her becoming the next headmistress. She told the Social Worker there wasn't any way she could care for a ten year old girl in her present situation, but the truth was she was afraid of letting another child down."

It was Randa's turn to be puzzled. "Sara was afraid? She always seemed so sure and so strong, it's hard to imagine."

Diane gave a rueful soft laugh. "You didn't know Sara before she was tempered by the pain of giving her daughter away. I'm afraid it's a rare one of us that starts out wise, it's only in the living of our lives that we see the mistakes we made and learn from them." There was silence in the room as the women absorbed that truth.

"If she was so afraid, why did she take me? Did they make her take me?" Denise asked, almost seeming to dread the answer.

"Heavens no, child, she took you because she loved you. The Social Worker brought Sara to the house where you were staying, do you remember that?"

"Vaguely. I remember I didn't recognize her at first, I hadn't seen much of her. She sent birthday and Christmas presents but rarely visited."

"Well, DJ, she took one look at you and saw blue eyes that so reminded her of her brother and she was lost. She told me later that if it hadn't been for the terrible deaths of your parents it almost might have seemed God was giving her a second chance, a second chance to love and cherish a child. She quit the job in London and bought this house with the insurance money from your parents. She wanted you to have all the love and stability in a home that she could provide. She knew my daughter was near in age to you and by then we had accepted our role as loving friends. From that point on, you were the only thing that mattered in her life. Sara Jennings loved you, DJ, and nothing that happened before or after you came along will ever change that."

The poet did not respond to that statement. Instead she asked, "If Maggie had no contact with Sara, how did she find out Sara was her mother?"

"That was one of the things I found out over the last two days. I called Geoff and Alice after Sara died. The small bequest of jewelry she made me in her will was to go to Maggie. I kept that from you, DJ, but I did it at Sara's request. She never wanted you to doubt you were the only one in her life, but those few items of jewelry belonged to your grandmother and Sara felt that even if Maggie were never to know where they came from, she should have something of her heritage also. I gave the jewelry to Geoff and Alice and they decided it was time to tell Maggie about the adoption."

Denise rose then, made her way to the door and opened it. "I'm sorry, Diane, I just need a little time to absorb all this. It's been a very difficult day." She stepped outside leaving Randa and Diane behind in the house.

156

"She's shaken," Diane observed.

"Who wouldn't be?" answered the blonde. "She's had a lot of information to take in within the space of a single morning. She found out that maybe the person she thought she knew best, she really didn't know at all."

"I disagree," Diane said firmly. "DJ knew everything that was important about Sara. She knew she was a woman of uncommon wisdom, a great sense of personal honor and a deep and abiding love for her. What could be more important than those things?"

Randa chewed her bottom lip slightly. "I suppose you're right. You know, I wonder if Sara hadn't had to give up her child if she would have been the very special person she was in Denise's life?"

"I don't know that and none of us ever could. Maybe DJ needs to think about that."

Randa furrowed her brow. "There's one thing in all this that I don't understand. Why didn't Sara go to her family for help? Surely her mother would have understood. Maybe her brother would have adopted the baby. I would have gone to my family first. Why didn't she?"

Diane was thoughtful. "I never asked her about that because I didn't feel she needed to second guess her actions, but I think it was probably a combination of reasons. I think she was somewhat ashamed. I know she never forgave herself for sleeping with Johnny and the subsequent pregnancy. Her mother was already having problems. In fact, she would be dead within two years of Maggie's birth. Why she never told her brother I don't know."

The nurse nodded. "I think I need to talk to Denise about all this. She asked me to come over here and I'll be damned if I'll let her go through this alone even if I have to scour this town for her," Randa vowed, then hesitated. "I'm not really surprised at how much this is bothering her. She's got such a sensitive soul that even small matters affect her deeply. You'd be amazed at how she can start brooding over the tiniest thing."

"Oh, no I wouldn't," laughed Diane. "She's done it all her life. Now, let me tell you where she does that brooding…"

****

Lost in thought, Denise had left the house entirely confounded. In doing so she left behind her jacket, phone and even keys, her mind too busy trying to come to terms with what Diane had told her. Pushing her hands into shallow pockets, DJ walked aimlessly down the streets. The rubber souls of her training shoes scraped along the gravelled pavement and her eyes remained fixed upon the ground. Small stones that she found along the path were kicked further down the street in abandon. Passing a small newsagents Denise checked her pockets for loose change before disappearing inside the small paper shop. She emerged with two small boxes that she pushed into opposite back pockets of her jeans and continued on her directionless amble.

No matter what both Diane and Randa said, Denise couldn't see past the fact that Sara had still kept this from her. She couldn't exactly call it a lie but *was it deceit?* She thought. The poet couldn't understand why Sara would refrain from telling her **because** she loved her. *Surely that wouldn't be enough of a reason to do so? Didn't she trust me?* Shaking her head Denise kicked another pebble across the ground and looked up. Taking in her surroundings Denise naturally found herself standing by the edge of the main road facing the park. She looked beyond the black railings bordering the expanse of greenery and spied the path leading to the far end of the large tree clustered field. Checking both sides of the road DJ waited until a single decked green bus passed her before jogging across the wide road. The shrill of children's voices drifted towards Denise's ears and she spotted a small group of boys playing with a football to her left. Entering the wrought iron gates, the black and white ball rolled towards her and DJ kicked it back – her intentions solely focused on retreating to her hidden place of contemplation. The one place she felt she was truly able to withdraw within herself and dwell on her thoughts.

Strolling aimlessly past rows of strategically planted flowers Denise didn't even acknowledge the variety of lavish colours as she made her way towards the sheltered area of the park. The warm summertime sun heated the earth creating soothing natural scents that seeped into her senses. The air was still, generating what was turning out to be the warmest day so far that year.

Taking a shortcut through a crop of trees Denise continued to think about Sara. The tranquil sounds of birds singing in the branches above her didn't seem to register in her ears. *Why wouldn't she have told me?* Denise pondered. *Even if I might not have understood when I was younger, I would have now.* Spying a fallen branch upon the ground, Denise picked it up and resumed her journey. She tapped the large stick into the soiled ground as she walked. *She didn't trust me. Maybe she didn't want to destroy my illusions that I was the only child she had ever wanted?*

Feeling even more confused, Denise stepped from the edge of the woods and frowned as she spotted an elderly couple seated upon 'her' bench. The man and woman sat together with a small brown paper bag between them. By their feet two squirrels lurked timidly, waiting as the couple occasionally scattered pieces of stale bread onto the ground. Sighing, Denise threw her stick back into the woods and turned instead towards the main area of the park. After a short walk she began to see a selection of multicoloured apparatus. Swings, a roundabout, a slide and climbing bars were among the wide variety of entertainment available. Although there were children in the play area, Denise noted that the roundabout wasn't in use. In a spark of childlike desire the poet made a beeline for the neglected ride. The roundabout was old. Orange paint on the metal bars had chipped away in certain places revealing an older green colour underneath. The wooden platform, painted deep blue, had worn away in patches where children's feet had constantly landed upon its base. Stepping onto the platform Denise moved to the middle of the roundabout and sat upon the large, circular, metal rod in the centre of the ride. Crossing her legs at the ankle she supported her precarious sitting position and folded her arms.

159

The sky was a wispy light blue and Denise looked up into its stillness watching a single white cloud hang limply in the atmosphere. Suddenly remembering her detour to the local newsagents, DJ pulled the two small boxes out of her back pockets. Removing the cellophane wrapper from the larger gold box she pulled out a single white stick from inside and placed it between her lips. Taking a match from the smaller box Denise struck the stick across the rough side of the box and lit her cigarette. Taking a deep breath she grimaced as the smoke filled her lungs. *Why do I feel like I am fifteen all over again?*

Hearing the rustle of footsteps, Denise looked to her side to see a familiar figure approaching. Suddenly feeling like a guilty teen caught in a rebellious act, DJ held her breath and hid the cigarette behind her back.

Randa smiled as she neared Denise. "You weren't on the bench."

Still holding her breath Denise nodded causing Randa to narrow her eyes.

"What are you up to?"

Feeling lungs burn through a lack of oxygen DJ exhaled. A cloud of grey smoke billowed passed her lips. She took another deep breath before saying, "Nothing much."

Eyes as wide as saucers, Randa stepped up onto the ride. "You are not smoking?" She pulled DJ's hand from behind her back and saw the fuming cigarette in her fingers. The blonde looked up at Denise in question.

"I um..." DJ shrugged. "I just felt like it." She moved to place the cigarette back between her lips when Randa pulled it from her fingers. Stubbing it out upon the handrail Randa threw it to the ground.

"Denise, this is not you. You don't smoke!"

Looking down at her empty hands Denise said, "I used to. It was all part of my teen rebel period. Then one day Sara caught me and practically pulled it from my lips. She said if she ever caught me smoking again or even smelled it on me she would make me eat it!" The poet snorted as Randa grimaced. "I just laughed and that made her all the more angry. I realised she wasn't joking."

"So why now?" Randa asked and pulled the packet from DJ's back pocket. "Apart from making sure I never want to kiss you again!"

Denise looked down guiltily. "I was angry."

"At Sara?"

"I suppose." DJ slipped from the centre mechanism of the roundabout and leaned against the handrail facing Randa. She looked down at her lover, the hurt shining in misty blue eyes. "Why didn't she tell me, Randa? I don't understand. How could she not have told me something like that?"

Randa faced DJ. "I'm sure she had her reasons, Denise, but I doubt she kept this from you because she wanted to hurt you." The nurse reached out and took DJ's hand. Their arms hung between them. "Imagine how hard it must have been for her. At first you would have been too young to understand then I guess as time moved on it became harder to say anything. If I were in her position I wouldn't want you to feel anything less than how I felt about you by making you think that maybe I didn't love you as much as I did." Lifting DJ's hand Randa kissed her fingers and asked, "If I ask you something will you answer me honestly?"

"Of course."

"First of all... do you think Sara's love for you was in any way false? Secondly... looking at if from Sara's point of view and taking everything into account... what would you have done in her situation... really? Not what you would have liked her to have done, but what you would have done."

Surprised by Randa's questions, Denise couldn't help but see the credibility in what she was asking. Sara had never made her feel anything less than special throughout their time together; even when she had slipped into a rather recalcitrant phase in her teens. As for seeing the issue from Sara's point of view, Denise again thought of the facts surrounding her parent's death. She had hidden them from Sara. She had done what she thought she had to in order to keep her aunt from hurting any more than she already had with the death of her brother. That was a hard decision to make for one so young. Suddenly DJ wondered whether the decision she made had been the right one.

Looking back at Randa Denise said, "Maybe we all make decisions in our lives and can only hope we are doing what is right. We do what we think is best at the time."

Randa nodded.

"But it still hurts."

"I know, love." Randa stepped forwards and pulled DJ into her arms. "But look at this from a different angle. You do have family after all."

Denise kissed the top of Randa's head. "You are my family, Randa. The only difference is that now I have a relative who seems to despise my very existence. I don't know what I should do."

Randa gazed up at DJ intently. "What **we** should do. We're in this together." She clasped the poet's hand. "Always!"

Grinning, DJ leaned down to kiss Randa but the blonde suddenly pulled away. Frowning, Denise looked at Randa in question. The blonde shrugged and motioned over DJ's shoulder. "We have an audience."

Gazing over her shoulder Denise spotted a group of children watching them from a colourful and intricately constructed climbing frame. "Oh them. They are just waiting for their turn on this thing." Denise patted the roundabout. "But they'll just have to wait." She stepped off the platform and took a firm hold of the orange bar with both hands. "It's the rules of the playground... wait your goddamn turn." Denise proceeded to push the roundabout. Once it was turning at an efficient pace, DJ jumped back onto the ride.

"Man, I can just tell you were the playground bully when you were younger! Look at this... thirty two years old and hogging the toys."

"What?" Denise asked, keeping Randa in view as the background spun past her. "Is there an age limit on this thing? Anyway... when was the last time you were on one of these?"

Randa sat down upon the wooden platform. "We didn't come here to play on the swings, Denise."

"I know but I needed some respite." Denise stepped off the slowing ride and increased the speed once again. She jumped back on the section beside Randa. "Here, copy me." Stretching out upon the platform, Denise lay back and looked up at the sky. "I used to love staring at the clouds while spinning around. We used to see how long it would take before we would feel nauseous!"

"Nice!" said Randa as she copied DJ's actions and re-positioned herself upon her back. The blonde looked up into the sky. "You realise you're going to have to talk to Maggie."

Denise let her head fall to the side, looking at Randa. "I know. I'm just trying to avoid thinking about it for a while."

Randa smiled. "Okay." Moving her arm through the bar Randa took DJ's hand once again. "So what did you do after you made yourself sick on the roundabout?"

The poet grinned. "When this finishes… I'll let you know. Meanwhile lets just see whether Miranda Leigh Martin can keep up with the big kids!"

"Speaking of that," Randa said, a sudden persistence ringing in her voice. "Is your middle name Julia?"

Denise rolled her eyes. "You are supposed to be looking up at the sky."

"Fine." Randa looked away. "But I am not giving up on this," she mumbled.

DJ sniggered. "Uh huh."

****

The sky was lit with orange and red hues as the sun sank lazily into the horizon. Out along village streets tall orange lamps illuminated the almost vacant roads. Shining bright in the growing darkness of the park, decorative lights twinkled along the main cobblestone path. From the centre of the children's play area a slow yet constant creaking echoed in the dusk.

Sitting upon a narrow plastic seat, Denise wrapped her hands tighter around long metal chains. Her feet remained planted upon the ground as she moved herself slowly back and forth. Beside her sat Randa. Her legs hung limply as she manoeuvred her swing a little more vigorously.

"I can't believe we're playing on the swings," the blonde said.

DJ chuckled. "Oh come on. Sometimes us adults spend so much time trying to be 'grown up' that we forget the little things in life. We are never too old to appreciate the simple things... after a certain age I think most of us forget what uncomplicated pleasure we can derive from the most mundane activities. It's an escape... a release." Denise slipped off her seat and stood behind Randa. Placing her hands on the blonde's shoulders, she pushed her gently. "You can't tell me you have not been having any fun."

Randa planted her feet upon the ground, effectively stopping Denise's actions. "Of course I had fun. I always have fun with you, Denise, but you can't escape from what is going on. Where's the kick ass D Jennings who turned up on my doorstep all those months ago? She would never have let this bother her."

"She's on vacation."

"You're not going to hide... escape... or go reclusive again, Denise. One of Sara's last requests to me was that I make sure you didn't revert back to how you used to be. I'll be damned if you do!"

"She asked that?"

Randa nodded and rose from her swing. She turned around and placed one knee upon the seat, looking at DJ in the semi darkness. An ornamental park light illuminated the side of Denise's face and Randa caressed her shadowed features. "Remember you are not alone in this, Denise."

The poet smiled, about to respond when an insistent chirping rung out from Randa's sweatshirt. Randa looked down surprised, then pulled DJ's mobile phone from her pocket.

"You left the house empty handed so I brought your phone and keys with me." She handed the ringing telephone over to Denise who answered it begrudgingly.

"Hello?"

"DJ... I've been trying to get in touch with you at the house all afternoon," Carl said. *"Been gallivanting?"*

"Something like that; what's up?"

"Well the producer of 'The Open Book' has been in touch with me. Their guest had to pull out so they were hoping you would go down to record your interview. I thought that since you were presently in the country you would be willing to do this now instead of further down the line."

Denise pursed her lips in thought. She looked at Randa who had wandered over to the climbing frame. "When is it?"

"This Friday. They record on Friday and edit over the weekend then air on the Monday. They have also requested footage from the launch and your book signing." Carl paused, *"So what do you think?"*

"I'll have to talk it over with Randa. There's a lot going on here at the moment, Carl. Can I get back to you?"

"Okay, DJ, just don't take too long."

"Tomorrow," Denise said and disconnected the line. She looked back over at Randa and her eyebrows drew together in confusion. With an amused smirk she began to make her way over to her lover, unable to withhold her chuckles as she took in the blonde's position. Letting her head fall to the side Denise asked, "What are you doing?"

Randa was hanging from the climbing frame – upside down. Her knees were bent over a metal bar and her ankles were crossed trying to keep her suspended form aloft. Randa's arms were folded over her chest keeping her sweatshirt from falling and revealing her upper torso.

"I'm reliving my youth... It was your suggestion!"

Denise chuckled.

"Anyway who was that?" Randa continued.

"Carl. The producers from that programme want me to go down and record my interview this Friday. I told him I would talk to you about it first. Right now though I think we have something more important to discuss."

"And that is?" Randa unfolded her arms and DJ's keys fell from her pocket.

Denise bent down to retrieve them. "Maggie. We have to talk to her."

Lifting her body, Randa grabbed the metal bar of the climbing frame and unhooked her legs. She dropped gracefully back down to the ground. "That's a good idea." The blonde suddenly paused in thought and a shadow of concern crossed her features. "There are a lot of things to discuss."

Not noticing the air of disquiet that rung through Randa's voice, DJ nodded. "Sure. So... do you want to get back home? It's getting late... we have yet to eat... and I am bloody cold!"

Randa wrapped her arms around Denise's waist as the women started towards the path. "You feel cold! Why didn't you say something sooner?"

"I was having too much fun."

"How about a nice hot bath when we get back?"

"Only if you join me."

"Like I would be stupid enough to refuse an offer like that."

Light chuckles rang out over the empty park as the women swiftly made their way back home.

****

Randa closed her eyes as she slid down the length of a very warm soapy body and into the hot water. The water level on the tub rose dangerously close to the edge but crested just below the rim as she settled back against Denise. A sigh escaped her lips as she revelled in the temperature and the company.

"Warming up now?" the poet asked, the words a hot breath at her ear.

"Mmm, very nicely, thanks," Randa murmured. "I'm not squishing you too much am I?"

"Nope, we've got plenty of room in here," Denise replied and feeling the nurse comfortably settled between her thighs, brought her legs up and wrapped them over the blonde's. "This large tub makes it just perfect for two."

"I was going to ask you about that when I first got here last year. It seemed unusual for the tub to be this big. Did you have it put in because of your height?"

"Actually, Sara is the one who had it installed. She wasn't a short person but she realized that I was going to be even taller than her and so she had the thing put in just for my comfort when she bought the house. I wouldn't need it for another few years but she thought about it far in advance. That was just the kind of thing she would do."

They relaxed together quietly a while when Randa remembered something from their time in the park earlier. "Denise? What did Carl want earlier on the phone that you needed to talk to me about?"

"Oh, he just wants me to go down to London this Friday and be interviewed for that television program 'The Open Book'. I'm not sure it's a good idea at the moment with the Maggie situation."

"Maybe not, but I tell you, my inclination would be for you to do the interview. We don't know how this whole thing will shake out so why change what you would have done normally? It might actually be a good forum for clearing the air about the new book and putting some misconceptions to rest."

Denise considered this. "You may be right. I'll think about it." Denise wrapped her arms around the smaller woman and gathered fragrant bubbles on her fingertips that she deposited on the chin of her lover.

Randa tilted her head back and gazed into the unbelievably blue eyes of the brunette. "How do I look in a goatee?"

Denise studied her seriously. "I don't know, I kind of like it. See what you can do about growing a real one, will you?" Their combined chuckles caused the water to slightly slosh over the edge.

"Now see what you did," Randa observed. "You're going to have a mess to clean up when we're done."

"Me? I see two in this tub, my dear. That should be two to clean up the water."

"Well, normally you would be correct," the blonde smirked, "But as I distinctly remember, you were the one who suggested going 'double in the bubbles' so the consequences are yours too."

"Hmm, if I'm to be the upstairs maid then I warn you, I will expect payment for my services," Denise whispered.

Randa reached a slick arm up and gently pulled Denise's head forward bringing their mouths together in a sweet kiss. After a few moments she broke the kiss. "Take that as a down payment and remind me to settle this account with you later, under the sheets." She waggled her eyebrows suggestively at her partner.

DJ quirked an eyebrow at the nurse. "My, you're awfully nice to the help. Maybe upstairs maid isn't as bad a job as I thought."

The smile slipped from Randa's face as she as she turned to face the front again, leaning her head back against the poet. "Speaking of jobs, Denise, I need to talk to you about mine. When I came over this time Derek let me know it was without pay. I just don't have any more time off coming to me. I couldn't suggest working out of the house here like I did before because I didn't know how long we would be here or even if we would be in one place. There's enough in my bank account to hold me for a month or so but after that things are going to be a little tight for me."

"Randa, why are you worrying? I have enough money for us to live on even if you never worked. I don't see the problem."

"That's your money and besides, I don't want you to have to support me. We're supposed to be partners here and I feel like I'm not holding up my end of the partnership."

The poet was silent a moment. Her hands moved gently up and down the arms of the woman seated between her legs. "I know you're used to being independent and taking care of yourself so I suppose I understand why the financial thing would be important to you. Maybe it's time we consider taking the next logical step and pool our resources. I don't want there to be a 'yours' or 'mine' when it comes to income or bills or property. Everything I have is yours and I know you feel that way as well. Let's just put it all together and stop worrying about where it comes from."

Randa felt incredibly loved at that minute, knowing this was a big step for the two of them. "I guess there's a lot more to this living together thing than I thought at first. It isn't going to bother you that you will always be the bigger wage earner?"

"Money isn't what counts with us and never will be. As for the partnership thing, when you got on that plane in San Francisco to fly across the ocean to be with me simply because I asked, you held up more than your end of the partnership, you held me up as well. I needed you here, love, and without question you came. What is ever going to be payment enough for that?"

Randa blinked back tears as she took one of Denise's hands and brought it to her lips. "I love you, Denise. How do you always know exactly what to say to me?"

'Turn around here and maybe I'll tell you." Randa slowly turned around as Denise slid her body down and underneath the blonde's.

"You sure you want to try this in here? The floor is going to get awfully wet," Randa said as she gently peppered Denise's face and neck with soft kisses.

"No worries, love. The maid can always clean up later," the poet chuckled. Her laughter was brief as an exploring hand made her forget about anything other than the blonde in the tub with her.

****

Denise and Randa sat at the kitchen table the next morning sharing an omelet and toast. The silence as they ate and read the morning newspaper was comfortable.

"I've thought about what you said. I'm going to do it," Denise said as she lowered the front page.

"The interview? Good. I think you should," replied the nurse as she folded her part of the paper. She picked up the dirty dishes and took them to the sink to rinse and place in the dishwasher. "How long will you be gone?"

"We will be gone for a few days. You don't seriously think I'm going to London for an interview on television

169

and not have you with me? Besides, we might find another large tub."

Randa blushed as she recalled the previous evening. "Maybe we wont make such a mess of the bathroom floor next time."

Denise rose and joined Randa at the sink. "I don't care if we do, it was worth it." She dropped a quick kiss on the blonde's lips, paused and went back for another.

"Mmm, first you make breakfast and now dessert, too," the nurse murmured. "I'm a lucky woman."

"You'll be luckier when we get to London. I plan to spend some time with you just letting you see the city."

"Oh, man, I've always wanted to see the Tower and Big Ben and Parliament! Then I want to see Buckingham Palace and have high tea at the Ritz. God, I love everything English!"

Denise laughed as she brought the nurse closer. "As long as you love this one English person, Miss Randa, the rest can sod off."

"You know, I haven't seen the inside of a real English bedroom for a good hour or so. Maybe we should start our tour there?" Randa whispered suggestively as DJ began nibbling her earlobe.

"What have you got against an English kitchen?" the poet returned, now kissing her way down the blonde's neck.

"Not a thing," Randa said. "As long as you're cooking."

"Oh I am," Denise chuckled. "I definitely am."

Chapter 14

Denise's shiny black Lexus cruised down the motorway at a steady rate of eighty miles per hour. It was Thursday afternoon and the women were travelling down the M1 on their way to London. The sky was grey and all morning a gentle rainfall had soaked the land. Through sporadic gaps in the clouds DJ could see the sun trying to break through. She had watched the television weather report that morning and was pleased to see the following days in the south of England were to be cool but sunny. The poet planned on taking Randa around the city to show her some of the sights.

Beside Denise sat Randa, nursing a bottle of mineral water. This was to be their first overnight trip away together and DJ couldn't believe how much Randa had tried to pack for the two-night visit. The blonde was adamant that she take a change of clothing to cover every occasion – just in case. Denise had to convince Randa that they would not need formal evening wear while they were in London. Everything she had planned would take place during the day, including a surprise DJ had devised with the help of Carl. Ever since Randa had read "Les Miserables" to Sara, the nurse had expressed a wish to be able to see the stage production. So when DJ had contacted Carl to tell him she was going to do the interview for 'The Open Book' she had asked him to see whether he could obtain tickets for the musical. She knew Carl had many contacts in that area. He had called back no less than half an hour later informing her that he was able to get her two tickets for the Saturday matinee performance. He also reminded her that he had

171

pulled a lot of strings to get them and she 'owed him big'! Denise didn't mind; she was thrilled and only just able to keep from telling Randa the news. It was supposed to be a surprise after all. She couldn't, however, remove the smirk from her lips and Randa had spent the remainder of the day looking at her with a suspicious eye.

It would not be the first time Denise had seen the musical. Sara had taken her to see it when she was twenty-four. She had remembered crying most of the way through it, even back then. Knowing Randa as she did, Denise knew she would be as emotionally affected by the musical as she was.

Feeling a gentle tap on her arm Denise blinked from her musings and turned to Randa. The blonde was holding out the bottle of half consumed mineral water. She accepted it with a smile of thanks and took a quick drink before handing it back. They had sat in an almost comfortable silence for the past half an hour; the quiet was only broken by the low melody of the radio. Randa would occasionally switch channels every time a song came on that she disliked but the music remained constant.

With an internal smile Denise thought back to her conversation with Randa while they had been packing their bag. The nurse had been talking excitedly about all the places she had wanted to visit and DJ hoped Randa wouldn't mind possibly forfeiting some of those plans for her surprise Saturday afternoon. She planned on leaving London after the show and travelling back to Derbyshire by Saturday night. The day after, Denise intended on ringing Diane to ask her for a contact number to get in touch with Maggie. Although Denise was putting off facing the woman who seemed so full of hatred towards her, DJ knew she needed to talk to her. She had to at least try to clear the air.

Recalling her banter with Randa as they packed, Denise recalled how Randa had searched the poet's wardrobe trying to find the appropriate outfit for DJ's television interview. Randa decided it was a choice between casual, smart, power, something that screamed intelligence or total femininity. She then set herself the impossible task of locating a dress in the poet's wardrobe. Denise chuckled as she remembered Randa asking, "Don't you own a single skirt or dress? What do you say to us going out shopping for one?"

To which Denise had replied, "I'll pretend I didn't hear that!"

Randa laughed. "Don't tell me your legs have an aversion to sunlight."

"No," Denise said. "I have an aversion to crotch-less garments."

The nurse flipped down the suitcase lid with a faux pout. "Well there goes the underwear idea I had for your birthday."

Denise laughed to herself causing Randa to further lower the volume of the music and look at her in question.

"You know... you've been smirking and chuckling to yourself since yesterday. What's going on in that devious mind of yours?"

"Nothing."

Randa tapped her fingers upon the side of her bottle. "Why don't I believe you?"

The poet shrugged.

"Did I ever..." Randa started, and then paused as the first notes of a familiar tune began to play on the radio. With an excited hoot that took DJ by surprise Randa increased the radio volume once again as her foot started tapping to the beat. DJ instantly recognised the familiar 'Blondie' hit. Keeping her eyes fixed upon DJ's curious blue, Randa brought the bottle to her lips and began to sing:

"Denise, Denise, Oh with your eyes so blue.

Denise, Denise, I have a crush on you,

Denise, Denise, I'm so in love with you, ohh."

A slow smile spread across DJ's lips as Randa fluttered her eyelashes.

"Oh when we walk it always feels so nice.

And when we talk, it seems like paradise.

Denise, Denise, I'm so in love with you, ohh."

The poet laughed as Randa started a semi jig upon her seat. She found it hard to concentrate on the road with the suddenly exuberant blonde beside her and had to turn down the radio.

"You are bloody insane. Remind me not to take you out in public too often!"

"Embarrassed?" Randa asked with a glint in her green eyes.

Keeping her gaze upon the motorway, Denise shook her head with complete sincerity. "No, I'm just worried about us sensitive Brit folk. I don't want them to be exposed to a crazy Yank."

Randa's mouth dropped. "I could make you pay for a remark like that."

"Oh, honey, you know I relish any punishment you are generous enough to dish!" Denise winked.

Green eyes narrowed with a playful menace. "I'll remember that."

"I'm counting on it," replied the brunette.

****

The next morning found Denise standing in front of the full-length mirror in their hotel room holding up the clothes she planned on wearing that day. With the black-cropped trousers in one hand and white top in the other she held the garments against her body. Cerulean eyes travelled up and down her frame in thought. *You can't really go wrong with simple black and white I suppose.*

A muted groan pulled Denise's attention from her scrutiny. She looked over her shoulder at the rumpled double bed to find sleepy green eyes watching her.

"Denise," Randa groaned. "It's five o'clock in the morning. What are you doing?"

"I can't sleep."

Her blonde head falling back down to the luxurious pillows, Randa sighed. "You don't have to be there until nine o'clock."

"We," DJ amended.

"**We** don't have to be there," Randa said. "Anyway, why can't you sleep? Either you're nervous about today or you're just out to see how many people you can wake up

174

this morning."

Denise hung her clothes upon the handle of the wardrobe and looked back at Randa guiltily. "Sorry. I would have left the room but that en-suite bathroom isn't really big enough to commence a decent pacing."

Randa sighed again. "Denise, come back to bed. We still have two more hours before we have to be getting up."

"Too late… I'm wide awake." Denise stepped towards the window and looked out over the hotel complex. Her fingertips drummed upon the windowsill in thought. "You know for an early, mid July morning it is quite nice out there."

Randa peeked out from beneath the covers. "I'll take your word for it."

"The sun is just beginning to rise."

"Uh huh."

Denise looked down over the hotel grounds. "And their outdoor swimming pool is heated."

"You are not serious…?" Randa studied DJ closely. "You are! You want to go swimming? Now?"

"Why not? It's exclusive to all guests… twenty-four hours, day and night. There is nobody else down there."

"Gee, I wonder why!"

"So… what do you say?"

"We don't have suits."

The poet thought quickly. "Well I have a tank top and some boxers. You have your shorts too and that sports bra. We can improvise. Come on what do you say?" Denise jiggled her eyebrows. "Just you and me."

Randa sighed as she looked at DJ's hopeful expression. "Damn it… How can I refuse?"

"Is that a yes?"

The blonde fell back to the bed. "Yes!" She rolled out from beneath the sheets and rose slowly to her feet. "Okay… lets go."

Denise kissed Randa with thanks, then the women picked out their makeshift swimming clothes before heading down to the hotel's outdoor pool.

It was still relatively dark outside but with the slow arrival of the gradually rising sun the eastern sky was a blend of shaded orange tints. That, added to the pool's water lights, created an almost striking contrast of light and darkness. There was a soothing stillness to the air. It seemed to settle over the dawning land like a blanket of serenity. In the distance the sound of early morning traffic just managed to penetrate the atmosphere.

Dressed in their impromptu swimwear and with the hotel's large bath towels wrapped tightly around them, Denise and Randa stepped out into the cool morning air. DJ noted the lingering scent of baked goods that hung in the air. She realised their hotel was situated close to a biscuit factory. The aroma of its tempting wares drifted out over the morning stillness.

Reaching the edge of the pool, Randa's eyes widened as a soft wind blew around them. "Jeez, that's cold." She groaned, pulling the luxuriously thick towel tight around her exposed body.

Denise let her towel fall to the edge of the pool. It landed upon the edging of aqua coloured tiles. "Well, the sooner we get in, the sooner we get warm." She too was feeling the frigidity of the cool morning air. Dressed in gingham boxers and a black tank top, DJ dived head first into the water. She touched the bottom before rising to the surface in the middle of the pool. The poet looked on amused as Randa, still wrapped within the embrace of her towel, tested the temperature of the water with her toes. "See, I told you it was warm."

Without saying a word, Randa shed her towel beside DJ's and jumped into the pool. A wave of water sprung out around her. She resurfaced beside Denise. "Hmm... this is heavenly."

"Yep." Denise's face took on a wry expression. "Just be careful how you dive!"

"Why?"

"Well... because if you happen to be wearing loose fitting boxers like mine... you could find them half way around your ankles due to the force!"

"No!" Randa's mouth dropped as her hands delved under the water to check the positioning of DJ's clothing.

"They are adjusted now," Denise said, batting away Randa's questing hands. "Anyway they only managed to slip to mid thigh before I caught them."

Green eyes narrowed with faux suspicion. "You didn't have a fleeting desire for skinny dipping, but changed your mind, did you?"

"I would never," said Denise sounding almost insulted. "Besides this is far too much of a public place for such acts. Now if we were in a more secluded area..." DJ winked before disappearing under the water's surface. The poet chuckled to herself as she circled Randa's legs, allowing one hand to slip up her thigh. She felt as much as saw Randa jump and bounce away from her wandering fingers. Unable to laugh underwater Denise emerged from its depths. She took a deep breath before delivering a rakish grin.

The blonde pointed at Denise. "Hey... no funny business. Public place remember?"

"What? They can't really see anything under the water but a flesh coloured blur."

"True," Randa conceded. "But that's not the point."

"Yes it is!" DJ swam closer to Randa. "So... want to wrestle under the water?"

The blonde looked at Denise with an absurd expression. "Denise, not only have I never wrestled... but I have never even considered it."

DJ loomed ever closer until she was almost breast to nose with Randa. She lowered her voice considerably "I never said what part of the body I was actually referring to."

"Ohh... you are an evil woman, Denise... 'Whatever your name is'... Jennings." Randa prodded DJ's chest. "But just remember, that makes two counts against you now that I intend on paying back!"

Really? DJ leaned forwards and kissed Randa softly. "I could make you forget," she said confidently.

"Umm... No you couldn't." Unexpectedly, Randa slipped beneath the water's surface and took a firm hold of DJ's shorts. A surprised shriek echoed around the complex as the poet's boxers were yanked from her body.

****

The television company had sent a car to pick up Denise at a quarter past eight. By a quarter to nine she and Randa had arrived at the studio and were sitting in the poet's allocated dressing room. Both women had been slightly awe struck as they were led through the building and saw many famous faces upon the walls. She was also certain she had spotted a couple of familiar personalities in one of the well-appointed dining areas.

Seated in front of a large mirror, DJ was silent as an extremely camp young man, called David, applied her make up. To her left sat Randa, her nose buried in a magazine that she had lifted from the reception area. From the corner of her eye Denise could see Randa flick through the pages of the colourful booklet and every so often look up at her with a smile.

Denise grinned internally as she recalled how Randa had managed to gain possession of her shorts earlier that morning. She then swam to the edge of the pool and climbed out onto the water's edge, still holding DJ's boxers. Randa had refused to hand them over until Denise promised her breakfast in bed **and** sexual favours for the next decade. The poet had agreed but afterwards declared Randa's actions too cruel and she had to devise her retribution. She however did admit she was considering accepting the decade of sexual favours and just retaliating against the breakfast in bed! *Then again one could consider them as one and the same.*

Denise's thoughts on retribution were interrupted by David, the make up artist, who was carefully lining the poet's lips, "I like to make a point of finding out about the people I am to work with. Although I am not an extremely literary person I did read about the dedication in your book and the press conference at your latest book launch." David turned to address the blonde. "Are you Randa?"

Randa rose with a smile. "Yes I am." She approached the desk where Denise was seated and leaned against the white, makeup-cluttered counter.

David looked back at Denise. "I kind of got that impression. I think what you said in your book, and at the conference were great… especially to all those reporters. My partner is in the unfortunate position where he feels he cannot tell people about himself."

"He works on the television?" Denise asked.

"Yes," David replied.

"But that doesn't make any difference anymore."

David shrugged and placed down his lip liner. He then chose the appropriate lipstick and returned to DJ's lips. "He seems to think it does… Anyway I just wanted to warn you about the presenter of the show, Andrew Miller. I have seen a slight bigoted side to him. I don't know how he is with guests but just watch out." David smiled. "He can be a little devious with his questions at times."

"Oh really?" An indignant tone sounded in Randa's voice.

Smiling Denise reached out taking the blonde's hand. "Don't worry… I can handle that guy."

Just then the door opened and a young brunette with large black headphones around her neck poked her head into the dressing room. "Are you all set?"

"We certainly are," David responded. He twisted DJ's chair around and the poet rose to her feet. She looked down at Randa to gauge her reaction.

The nurse hummed her appreciation. "Subtle but still more than I have ever seen you wear. I like it. Plus you wont need a chisel to remove it afterwards!"

"Funny!" Denise rolled her eyes as she followed the floor manager out onto the set.

Seeing the layout of the studio from an inside perspective, DJ was surprised by how small the set actually was. It was comprised of two extremely comfortable looking, black leather sofas placed diagonally in a 'V' shape. Between them stood a low coffee table upon which Denise could see a selection of her books. Around the outskirts stood three cameras and a row of black cables that lay upon the floor.

To her side Denise spotted the presenter of 'The Open Book' arriving on the set. She then spotted Randa, who was standing in the background, eying him warily. The poet felt the urge to go back over to her lover and reassure her that all would be okay, but at that moment Andrew Miller approached. He was a small, robustly built man who was very obviously wearing a hairpiece upon his head. Before he presented 'The Open Book' he had been a book critic for several national newspapers. Denise remembered him from that time, as he had been the first reviewer of her debut anthology of poems. He had been very positive in his acclaim. Denise hoped other matters would not sway him from the issue at hand. *I would hate to have to get contentious on TV!*

"Miss Jennings," Andrew Miller said, holding out his hand.

DJ shook it firmly. "Hello."

"It is a pleasure to meet you. I can't tell you how thrilled I was to hear you would be a guest on my programme. Personally I have been a fan of your writings for many years."

"Ah... well thank you." Denise said politely as Andrew Miller turned to answer, a cameraman's question. She looked over at Randa once again. The nurse was talking with David. Denise caught her eyes and smiled before turning back to the presenter.

"So are you ready to get started?"

"I am," Denise replied and followed Andrew Miller onto the set.

Chapter 15

"Well, that wasn't as bad as I thought it was going to be," Denise said with an astonished look on her face. "I expected something a little more like a cross examination."

Randa hooked her arm through Denise's as they walked out of the television studios. "You did just great in there. It seemed Andrew Miller was under your spell. I know the feeling."

This caused the poet to chuckle. "He might not have been such a big fan if he could have read my mind. It was that hairpiece! I kept looking at it trying to figure what animal it had come off. First I thought maybe it was a squirrel but then I discarded that and thought maybe it was some sort of dog hair. The debate raged through me the entire interview!"

"And what conclusion did you come to?"

Denise lowered her voice and whispered conspiratorially, "I decided that the hairpiece, combined with his atrocious cologne left no room for doubt. It was a musk-ox!"

Randa giggled but quelled her reaction when the subject of their conversation emerged from the double doors of the studio and headed for a car parked at the curb.

"Miss Jennings, Miss Martin, can I give you a lift somewhere?" Andrew Miller asked pleasantly.

"No thank you, Mr. Miller," Denise replied. "Randa and I are just going to have a pub lunch then take in some of the sights of London."

"Ah, well then if it's a pub lunch you're after you should try my favourite. It's just ahead and around the corner. You can't miss it. It's called the Dog and Ox." Giving the women a short wave, he slid behind the wheel of the car and smoothly made his way into traffic.

Randa looked at Denise. "He did not just say the Dog and Ox. Tell me he did not say Dog and Ox."

"He did, but at least he left out the squirrel!" Laughing, the women walked away from the studio and headed out for a day of sightseeing.

****

Denise opened the hotel room door and she, Randa and a mountain of bags and packages spilled into the room.

"Okay," Randa said as the last of their purchases was set on the table near the window, "Maybe you were right, that trip to Harrod's was possibly one stop too many on my tour."

"Hmm, let's see," the brunette said as she dropped onto the bed and began ticking off their stops on her fingers. "The Tower, the Crown Jewels, Parliament, Big Ben, Westminster Cathedral and Buckingham Palace. Not a bad day's work."

"Don't forget high tea at the Ritz. That was such a surprise. Thank you for arranging it." The nurse moved to the bed, put her knee on the mattress and leaned over to give Denise a slow, warm kiss. She then moved to the side of the poet and snuggled in against her. "As soon as I recover a bit I'll really show you some gratitude."

"I'm counting on it," Denise murmured as she placed a soft kiss on Randa's head. "So what would you like to do for supper?"

"Oh God!" Randa moaned. "I couldn't eat another bite! First steak and kidney pie at the pub, then all those wonderful things at tea. The pastry, the crustless cucumber sandwiches and those fabulous scones with the sweet clotted cream and jam. If I eat anything else tonight I'm going to explode!"

'That's good, then you won't be tempted by any of the chocolates I bought at Harrod's"

A blonde head snapped up. "Chocolate? You know there might just be a tiny bit of room left for a chocolate."

Denise laughed and moved from the bed. "I thought there might be so I had them wrap a few pieces separately from the rest for us to enjoy tonight." She rummaged through the packages until she found the one she was looking for. Holding the small green bag up in triumph she headed back to the bed, stopping only long enough to kick off her shoes and pull Randa's from her feet as well.

The poet settled against the headboard and Randa moved up to join her. They unwrapped the individual chocolates and sampled them with a sigh of contentment.

Randa reflected, "You know something? I really am a lucky person. I've got a bed, chocolates and a beautiful and wonderful woman to share them with." She tilted her head up to meet Denise in a lingering kiss.

"Guess that makes me lucky too because I've got the same thing," Denise noted as the kiss broke. "Mmm, raspberry cream, I like it."

Tell her now Randa thought *she deserves to know.*

The nurse turned to her partner. "I'm counting on you to stay lucky, love. We're going to need a little of that, I'm afraid." Denise's eyebrows moved together in a look of confusion. She tilted her head in a gesture indicating Randa should clarify what she meant.

"Denise, I know how your parents died and I know your grandfather was killed during the war. How did your grandmother die?"

"Sara said she had heart problems. Why? What's bothering you?"

"I was doing some reading and came across some disturbing information." Randa picked up the poet's hand and kissed across the knuckles. "You know ALS can strike anyone and anywhere. It's a pretty indiscriminate killer except in one incidence. It seems that in families where there is more than one case of ALS, there is a fifty percent chance of inheriting the disease."

Denise digested the information, realizing what Randa was saying to her. "My grandfather didn't live that long and neither did my parents. We can't know if they would have ever developed the disease. The only relatives I had that lived any length of time were my grandmother and Sara. One had it and one didn't." Denise rose from the bed and moved to look out the window.

Randa moved to join Denise. She wrapped her arms around the poet and laid her head on the strong back. "I've tried to find out more about your family, Denise, and I'll keep digging. Maybe we can find out about generations further back than your grandparents."

Denise turned slowly and gathered the nurse into her arms. "A fifty percent chance... one out of two, the same odds as the toss of a coin. Is that what my future will be? A coin toss?" Randa felt a fine tremor pass through Denise and she increased her hold on the brunette, yearning to provide her comfort and a safe haven.

"Randa, I don't want to end up as Sara did. I saw how she progressively lost everything that mattered to her until that damn disease took everything she had. It robbed her of her freedom, her dignity and her life. I'm not sure I could be as strong as Sara was, love. I know I couldn't deal with it with the grace she had and I couldn't bear to have you watch me go through it."

Denise moved back slightly from the embrace. "I just found you, Randa. I don't want to think about anything less than a long and full life with you." The poet's brilliant blue eyes brimmed with tears and a lone trickle made its way down one cheek.

"God, Denise, don't you know that every moment of my life is full just because you're in it? Listen, I almost didn't tell you about this but then a thought struck me and I knew I could tell you. All I had to do was think about us, about how we came to where we are now. In your wildest imagination you couldn't have come up with something less likely to happen than us ending up together. What are the odds that someone living a continent away and loving your poetry would meet you online go to another country and fall in love with you? A million to one? A billion to one? As a matter of fact that story isn't even plausible unless you believe in one thing and that thing is fate. We were fated to be together. Now I don't think that whatever power there is in the universe that worked so hard to get us together is going to tear us apart so easily. I love you Denise Jennings. No matter what happens in the future, that won't change. Whatever happens, we will deal with it."

Randa looked deeply into Denise's eyes and willed her to see the truth and conviction of her words. The sword of Damocles might be hanging over her head but she would never have to face it alone. Denise hesitated a moment then crushed the nurse to her in a fierce embrace.

"I love you too, Miranda Martin and I will deal with whatever my future holds as long as it holds you."

****

Denise and Randa rested on the bed wrapped in one another. No words were spoken, none was necessary. Randa broke the silence first.

"Denise, where is your cell phone?"

"In my jacket pocket. Who are you calling?"

"I just realized we need to call Diane and have her get some information for us."

"Randa, we can hire someone to dig into my family background. We don't need to ask Diane to do it. There are people trained to investigate families and previous generations."

"I wasn't thinking about previous generations of your family. I was thinking about this one."

Denise frowned a moment then understanding dawned on her. "Maggie...Sara's daughter...oh my God. She doesn't have a clue to the risk she faces." She brought up an arm and laid it across her eyes. "Welcome to the family, Maggie. I'm so sorry."

****

DJ awoke Saturday morning to find herself hanging precariously off the side of the hotel's double bed. Blinking unfocused eyes she saw as much as felt her right arm and leg hanging just above the carpeted floor. The cool room air touched her flesh causing an expanse of pimples to break out across her skin. Lifting her head the poet attempted to turn onto her back but found she was unable to move. Looking to her left she discovered the reason why. In her sleep Randa had managed to slowly push Denise further across the bed. The blonde was lying upon her back, right up against Denise. The rest of the bed was untouched.

Feeling the cool air send a shiver through her body, Denise retracted her limbs, pulling them back under the feeble amount of quilt she had. Gingerly turning she stretched one arm and leg over Randa. Her intention was to venture over to a more spacious part of the bed but as she crossed over Randa, two forest-green eyes captured her. Randa blinked and lifted one hand to rub her eyes. She looked back up at DJ who was frozen in place.

"Hi," Denise said sheepishly.

Randa delivered a sleepy smile. "Starting without me?"

"Huh?"

Randa made a point of looking the poet, who was still holding herself above her, up and down. The frown of confusion fell from Denise's features as realisation of what Randa was implying sunk into her mind.

"Hey! I would never! I was just climbing over the bed hog to more spacious parts." Denise inclined her head towards the three-inch gap she had been sleeping on. "Besides... **you** can talk." Denise rolled onto her side and placed her head in her hand.

"And what does that mean?"

The poet grinned. "Well not that I am complaining but I seem to be the one who is usually woken up by wandering hands and lips... I think I should start calling you 'Randy Randa'!"

Randa's jaw dropped as she pushed DJ backwards and rolled on top of her. "Excuse me!" With an impish tone she said, "I'm going to tell my mom you said that. It took her enough time to accept my request to call me Randa instead of Miranda."

Denise chuckled. "Oh please accept my deepest apologies." Looking up into Randa's eyes the brunette smiled. "Thank you for yesterday." She ran her fingers through light blonde hair. "I had been aware of the hereditary possibilities of ALS, but I suppose I just tried to blank them from my mind. It wasn't just the fact that I too could one day have this disease, as it was the point that if I did... I would be alone. That was an immensely unnerving notion. Up to a point though I am not nearly as worried about it as I used to be. That is all because of you." She pulled Randa down and hugged her.

During one of her and Sara's visits to the hospital, Doctor Macarthur had explained to them about the innate possibilities of the disease. Though that had initially been shocking to both woman Sara had helped to ease Denise's mind. It was only after Sara died and seeing how she had reached the final stages in her life that DJ again feared the disease. Though it had always been a bothersome feeling in the back of her mind, Denise tried to ignore it. She didn't want to broach the subject with Randa either, not knowing how the blonde would feel about it. Sometimes it was as though she almost forgot Randa was a nurse! Thankfully the blonde bringing it up in the reassuring way that she had, did help to ease the burden from her mind. *Besides,* she kept telling herself, *it's not a given certainty.* Denise clung to that one fact and knew that whatever happened, Randa would stand by her.

With the blonde head still tucked between her shoulder and neck, Denise reached out, pulling her watch from the nightstand. She studied its analogue face in surprise. "It's almost half nine!"

Randa raised her head and looked down at Denise. "So what do you want to do today? More sight seeing before we leave or stay in bed until we leave? Both options sound okay by me!"

Denise pondered Randa's suggestions for a short moment before saying, "There could be a third option."

"Really?"

"Yep."

"And that is?"

"I'm not telling."

"Why?"

A slow smile spread across DJ's lips. "Because it is a surprise."

"A good surprise?"

"I hope so."

Randa sighed. "Then can you tell me?"

"Nope... how can it be a surprise if I tell you beforehand? It kind of takes away that whole element of suspense, doesn't it?" Denise forced a steadfast expression upon her face. She arched her eyebrows and pursed her lips.

A far away look seeped into Randa's expression before she gazed back at DJ. With an almost nefarious smirk she asked, "What if I make you a deal?"

"And that would be?"

"I'll take back my decade of breakfast in bed and sexual favours if you tell me."

"Oh please!" Denise rolled over trapping Randa underneath herself. "That is **so** not a punishment for me. I am rather looking forward to a lifetime of servitude... under you... no pun intended!" Denise winked lasciviously.

The nurse's lips formed a pronounced pout. "Well, when do I find out what my surprise is?"

"Just be ready to leave the hotel today at one. Dress in the smartest clothes you brought down with you." Denise stopped to think. "In fact... wear what we bought while shopping yesterday. Just be ready to leave here at one o'clock and all will be revealed."

"You promise to tell me then?"

The poet shook her head. "Nope. I promise to take you there at that time and then all will be revealed."

"Okay." Randa gazed intently into DJ's eyes. "Are we going to the theatre?" She thought slowly, her logical mind working overtime. "A musical maybe? 'Les Miserables'?"

What? Denise starred at the nurse blankly. She ran her tongue over her front teeth before saying, "No."

188

Randa smirked as she looked up at Denise. "I'm right, aren't I?"

"Didn't I just say no?"

"Yes but I don't think I believe you." Randa suddenly wriggled excitedly underneath DJ. "I **am** right, aren't I? We're going to the West End?"

"No!"

"You can't lie, Denise."

"I'm not."

"Are too."

Damn it. Denise climbed off Randa and rose from the bed. Folding her arms she glared down at the blonde nurse who looked up at her with a smile. "You know it's a little disconcerting when you do that. How am I suppose to keep secrets when you seem so proficient at reading my mind?"

"You mean it really is true?" Randa asked surprised.

With a dumfounded expression Denise dumbly said, "Huh?"

"Well I was grasping at straws with a little bit of hope thrown in. I had no idea it really was that."

Rolling her eyes Denise scowled and attempted her most intimidating glare.

"You don't scare me, Denise Jennings."

"Oh? And why is that?"

"Well because it's hard to feel intimidated by somebody who is standing there as naked as the day she was born!" Randa laughed as Denise muttered unintelligibly and slid back under the bedcovers.

"So what do you think of my surprise?" Denise inquired, her hand idly tracing patterns upon Randa's stomach.

Randa smiled. "Come here and I'll show you exactly what I think of your surprise."

Denise edged closer until Randa captured her lips with her own. They kissed softly for several long moments until Randa stiffened and pulled away.

"Denise, … are you going to call Diane? We didn't do it yesterday and we need to get…" Two fingers placed upon her lips silenced Randa.

"Later," Denise replied. "I don't want to think about anything but right now." She moved again to kiss Randa, letting her lips roam across the blonde's jaw. With a light snort she mumbled, "Oh and by the way…"

"Hmm?

"I'm not as naked as the day I was born. I do have a little more covering upon my body since then, you know!" Denise smirked as Randa pulled back to look into her eyes. Suddenly understanding dawned her and she slapped DJ's behind playfully.

"Right… I don't know about you but I'm going to have a shower. We're going out soon, aren't we?"

"In about three hours!" Denise said incredulously as Randa dived out of bed and disappeared into the bathroom. *You've got to be kidding me!*

"I know." Randa poked her head back behind the doorframe. "That's why I better get ready." She jumped back into the bathroom and Denise heard the rapid spray of the shower.

****

The sound of soft snores filled the quiet Lexus. It was late in the evening. The sun had set, leaving the interior of the car cast in a heavy darkness. Only light from surrounding vehicles on the motorway cast sporadic shafts of illumination. Denise had been driving for almost three hours and knew they were almost home. Unfortunately Randa was aware of no such thing. The nurse had fallen asleep after only half an hour of travelling. Denise looked to her left, briefly studying her lover. Her leather jacket covered Randa's front torso and her head hung lightly to the side. The brunette smiled, her eyes turning back to the road. It seemed that having one's emotions put through the wringer had exhausted the nurse. Randa had thoroughly enjoyed the performance and DJ made sure she had packed enough Kleenex!

Before they had left for the theatre Denise had contacted Diane while Randa took her shower. The older woman had given DJ Maggie's parent's number and then DJ had rung them for her cousin's. The Spicer's had been more than willing to give her Maggie's number. It became apparent that Maggie had become increasingly distant from her family. Geoff and Alice hoped that Denise could get through to her. It was a hope the poet also held. Not only did DJ feel the need to close the chasm between Maggie and herself but she also knew there were other factors that needed to be discussed.

Turning from the motorway, Denise took dark, secluded, country roads until she reached home. Pulling into the driveway Denise switched off the car's engine and turned to Randa. The orange glow of the street lamps highlighted Randa's slumbering features. DJ regretted having to wake her.

Reaching over, Denise ran the pads of her fingertips over Randa's cheek. The smooth skin tickled her senses. "Hey," she whispered. Randa groaned and leaned into her gentle touch. "Time to wake up."

Green eyes fluttered open and stared at Denise in the semi darkness. "Are we home?" Randa yawned and rubbed her eyes. "I fell asleep!"

"Apparently!" Denise smirked wryly. "Come on sleepy head, time to get to bed. It's been one hell of a long day."

Opening her door DJ stepped out into the driveway. She looked over the roof of the Lexus as Randa emerged from the passenger side of the car. "You go into the house and I'll get the case and bags from the boot."

"The what?" Randa asked in a mischievous voice.

DJ grinned. "The boot."

"The what?" Randa slipped her key into the lock.

"The boot."

"Don't you mean the trunk?"

Denise pulled their cases and selection of colourful shopping bags from the car. She placed them on the ground to close the boot and lock the car before retrieving their bags and following Randa into the house. "Don't start that again."

Randa placed DJ's jacket upon the banister and then slipped off her own. "Well it's not my fault if you guys don't know how to speak properly."

"Oh you cheeky sod! I can't believe you just said that." Still holding their suitcase, Denise allowed Randa to take some of the shopping bags from her arms before following her up the stairs. "Of course I will assume that it was your sleep addled mind that has caused you to say such a thing."

Light chuckles filtered through the darkened house as Randa replied, "Of course."

"Good answer," Denise stated and entered the bedroom shutting the door behind them.

****

Mid-Sunday morning found DJ in the study sitting in front of her computer. Denise had woken up early that morning knowing she had a nerve-wracking task to perform. She had to ring Maggie. It was almost ten o'clock and as Denise sat writing, her eyes constantly shifted to the telephone by her side. Her mind was continually concocting reasons why she should not call. She might wake Randa. She may in fact wake Maggie or her family. DJ had been told that Maggie was married with two children. Turning blue eyes back to the computer screen, Denise continued writing. The sound of lightly falling rain hitting the windowpane accompanied the taps of her fingers upon the computer's keyboard. Time passed her by rapidly and before DJ realised it was eleven o'clock and a sleep rumpled Randa was shuffling into the study. Denise tipped her head back and looked up at Randa who loomed over her.

"Morning."

Randa leaned down and kissed the poet's head, careful of the delicate glasses that sat upon her nose. "Morning... how long have you been up?"

"Hours." Denise shrugged and looked back at the screen.

192

"I see you haven't called Maggie yet." Randa tapped the slip of paper holding Sara's daughter's telephone number.

"I will." Still holding her flow, Denise continued typing. She felt Randa's arms rest upon her shoulders and her chin upon her head.

"You missed a semicolon."

"Huh?" Denise looked up at Randa.

"There." Randa placed her finger upon the screen indicating the sentence in question. "You missed the semicolon... just there."

DJ studied her sentence again. She read the words through twice. *Well I never!* "That's rather astute of you, Miss Martin."

"What? You think I just fell into my love of literature. I did get my minor in English at college, you know. That started off the chain reaction that eventually led to reading you!"

"Awww!"

"And I never looked back!"

DJ chuckled as she inserted the semicolon.

"Okay. Well while you **make a phone call** I'm going to get some breakfast. Would you like something brought up?"

"No... I'll be down in a moment."

"Okay." Leaving one last kiss upon the poet's neck, Randa headed back out of the study. Denise watched her leave before turning back around. Her eyes slid back to the telephone and a strained sigh passed her lips. *Come on, DJ, what's the worst that could happen?* Denise pursed her lips. *Famous last words... I can just imagine!*

Taking a deep breath Denise lifted the telephone receiver and carefully dialled her cousin's number. Her fingers fidgeted nervously upon the desk as the line started to ring. Only brief seconds passed before the call was answered.

"*Hello*?"

DJ frowned at the male voice. *Must be her husband.* "Hi," Denise paused. "Um... could I speak to Maggie please?"

"Sure... who's calling please?"

"It's Denise Jennings."

"Oh!" The expression of surprise was evident in the mans voice. *"Well... yes... that would be good. Okay... um... hold on a moment please."*

Denise waited as she heard the sound of muffled voices.

"Hello?"

DJ recognised Maggie's hollow voice. "Hi, Maggie. I'm ringing because I think we need to talk. Um... if you are willing I would like us to meet and talk face to face."

There was a pregnant pause, as it seemed Maggie considered her request. *"So 'now' you believe me."*

"Lets just say I discovered a few truths from a certain person who was extremely close to Sara. There are things we need to discuss."

"Like what?" Maggie asked almost bitterly.

DJ pulled off her glasses and rubbed her temples with one hand. "Like the truth. Everything. You need to know what I have been told." When Maggie didn't reply, DJ continued. "I was wondering whether you would consider coming down here. We can talk. You can see the place Sara lived. I presume you don't even know what she looked like."

Maggie hesitated briefly. *"No, I don't."*

Hoping she had piqued her cousin's curiosity Denise asked, "Well? What do you say?"

"Fine." The begrudged response seemed a little forced. *"How does tomorrow evening sound?"*

"Great." Denise beamed. She felt a certain amount of relief as Maggie agreed to their conversation. After giving Maggie their address, Denise hung up and headed down to Randa. The blonde was rooting inside a cupboard and didn't hear DJ enter the kitchen.

Sneaking behind Randa, DJ placed her hands over the blonde's eyes. "Guess who has a visitor coming around tomorrow evening?"

Randa grinned. "You?"

DJ shook her head. "We!" She turned Randa around to face her. "Maggie agreed to talk and she will be here about six tomorrow."

"That's great. How do you feel?"

"Okay... at the moment." The poet's smile faded as a shadow of thought crossed Randa's brow. "What is it?"

"Well your interview on 'The Open Book' is being aired tomorrow evening."

Denise shrugged. "We'll have to tape it I suppose. As for right now..." Denise opened the fridge and scanned the empty shelves. "I think we need to get some food in. Fancy a trip to the supermarket?"

"Hey... yeah! I've been craving some chocolate chip cookies. Can we go to that place where you can use those devices and scan your own goods? I love those things!"

Shaking her head the poet chuckled, "Sure." She remembered how much fun Randa had playing with the hand held scanner the last time they shopped and how they ended up buying twice as much because of this.

"Great!" Randa winked. "Meet you in the shower?"

Lowering her voice, Denise enquired, "Why wait?" Taking Randa's hand she quickly led her back up the stairs and towards the bathroom.

Chapter 16

Monday morning was as beautiful as the postcards in the shops of Bakewell showed England to be. The sky was a deep blue with only a few puffy clouds floating across the wide expanse. The sun was shining brightly with the promise of another perfect day but in one house in Derbyshire there was a palpable aura of tension.

Randa predicted Denise would deal with that tension in one of three ways. She would make love, work in the garden or write. Denise surprised her by doing all three. Up far earlier than the nurse, Denise had worked in the garden from first light weeding the roses, pruning back the hedges and bringing fresh cut flowers into the house. Randa found her staring at the roses that had been placed in a porcelain vase and set on the kitchen table. The nurse stood next to Denise and wrapped an arm around her waist.

"That rose garden is a beautiful legacy from Sara," she said to the poet. Denise smiled and draped her arm over Randa's shoulders.

"It isn't the most beautiful part of her legacy, love. Our life is the best part of it. Every day that we are together, loving each other and living the life that she wanted for us, we honour that legacy."

Randa leaned her head on Denise and sighed. "You have such a way with words, my friend. You should really think about doing some writing professionally." Denise gave a soft laugh at that.

"You think I could be successful?"

"Well, I don't know," Randa teased, "But I would buy your book, if you autographed it of course."

"Mmm, an interesting demand," Denise murmured as she moved to nuzzle the neck of her partner. "Do you have any other requirements we should discuss?"

"Several," Randa returned as she moved her hands under the poet's shirt. "I have a whole list of them upstairs in the bedroom if you'd care to take a look."

Denise moved back and looked into the nurse's sparkling green eyes. "Let the negotiations begin." Breaking apart at the same time, they raced for the stairs.

****

It was later in the afternoon and Randa, fresh from the shower, caught up with Denise in the study. She was seated at the computer studying the monitor through her silver framed glasses. Randa recognized the look of concentration on Denise's face as the one she used when deeply involved in her writing. Not wanting to disturb the poet at work, the nurse kissed her on the cheek and turned to leave the room.

"Hey, English minor, come over here a second and take a look at this." Randa moved back to the poet's side and glanced at the screen then back at Denise.

"It's a poem."

"Brilliant deduction, Sherlock. Of course it's a poem. At least it will be when I get this problem fixed. I thought maybe you could take a look at it." Randa turned to the poem again and began reading.

"Well? What do you think?" Denise asked.

Randa studied her with uncertainty. "I'm not sure I understand what you think is wrong with it. From my perspective, it's perfect both from a grammatical and a literary standpoint."

A smile of triumph graced Denise's features. "I knew it! I knew it and I was right." The poet grabbed Randa and pulled her into her lap where she planted kisses across the nurse's face.

Randa reached her arms up and around Denise's neck and returned her kisses with enthusiasm. "I don't know what brought this on but you have one month to stop kissing me and explain yourself."

Denise laughed and hugged the blonde to her. "Ever since I started writing and had my first works published I have only ever hated one thing about the process. Once I've finished the writing it goes into the hands of an editor. From that point on it becomes frustration and agony for me. Carl has been wonderful as a publisher but he knows I hate having someone else second-guess and correct my work when they might not have the faintest idea of what I want to say or how I want to say it. So yesterday when you noticed the mistake in what I was working on, it gave me an idea."

"So...you tested me by having me read this poem?" Randa asked as she indicated the screen.

"Yep."

"But I didn't find anything wrong so how could I have passed the test?"

"That's just it, there wasn't anything wrong with it. You knew when to leave well enough alone and that's all I ask. I know you'll find any spelling or grammar mistakes I might make."

"Are you talking about me working for you?" the blonde asked.

"Well, I would never want you working 'for' me. How about if we say you are working 'with' me? There might be some nice financial rewards in being my editor."

"It's not the salary, it's the fringe benefits I think I'd really enjoy," Randa said as she deposited a brief peck to Denise's lips. "Let me think about it, okay?"

"Fair enough. Now, how about a little late lunch before Maggie gets here?"

"Good idea. I'd make it but I'd never want to cook 'for' you. Of course I'm perfectly willing to cook 'with' you."

Denise laughed at her partner. "How about neither of us cooks and we both pop round to the chip shop instead?"

"Why are we still sitting here? Lets go get those chips!"

****

At precisely six o'clock a small white car pulled up in front of the Jennings house. Maggie got out slowly and stared at the front door. From inside Denise and Randa watched the redhead look at the house.

"This is where she might have grown up if things had been different," Randa said in a hushed tone to the poet. "It's hard to imagine. She's the natural daughter of one of the finest women I ever had the honor to meet and love and she will never know her. That's got to be going through her head right about now. She had parents who loved her, a home and security but she never had this house or Sara or you."

Denise watched Maggie a moment longer then took Randa's hand. "Let's go try to give her some of those things." The couple went to the door where Denise paused to give Randa a quick kiss.

"For luck," she said and pulled open the door. Maggie watched somewhat warily as Randa and Denise came down the steps. Randa moved slightly ahead of Denise and reached a hand out to Maggie.

"Maggie, welcome to Derbyshire. I'm Randa Martin, Denise's partner and it's a pleasure to meet you." Maggie seemed a little hesitant but shook Randa's hand nonetheless. Denise moved behind Randa and placed her hands on the blonde's shoulders.

"Maggie, how are you?" the brunette asked.

"Surprised to be here, to be honest." Two sets of very similar blue eyes appraised each other with neither woman making any further comment.

Stubborn Jennings blood Randa thought. She turned to look up at the poet. "Denise, why don't you show Maggie the rose garden while I get us some tea?" She turned to the redhead. "It was Sara's pride and joy."

Maggie seemed to thaw at that news. "It was? I have a rose garden at home too. I love spending time there." She appeared to be touched by the connection with her biological mother.

Denise moved to show Maggie the way to the rose garden. "Sara loved her roses. She could spend hours out in that garden and I swear sometimes I think she even named those plants."

Maggie gave Denise a shy smile and the two of them moved around the side of the house.

199

Randa watched them go. *Thank you for that, Simon, and I hope our little conversation of this morning stays just between the two of us. I know you want what's left of this family to heal too.* The nurse went into the house continuing to think good thoughts of Maggie's husband.

****

Walking side by side with Maggie, Denise led her cousin around to the back of the house. Strolling hesitantly down the darkened entry they reached a high wooden gate and Denise reached over the barrier to release the lock. Once done she pushed the gate open and stood back with a nervous smile and let Maggie enter the garden. Following the redhead, DJ passed through the gate, closing and locking it behind them. She turned back and looked at a quiet Maggie. The woman stood at the edge of the grass looking around the spacious garden. DJ allowed a moment of silence to pass between them as they both gathered their thoughts. She was very glad she had taken the time to neaten the garden and bring it back to some semblance of the elegance it once held. It had taken a fair amount of work but Denise had laboured since the early hours of the morning. She cut the grass, neatened the edges. The poet was happy though she knew her green fingers could never rival her aunt's.

Sensing eyes upon her, Denise turned from her perusal of the garden. She looked at Maggie through hesitant eyes and smiled cautiously. "I'm um... glad you came."

"I think I am too." Maggie turned back to the garden and stepped onto the grass. "So this was her favourite place?"

"Yes. I'll admit that it's nothing compared to the beauty it held under Sara, but I'm trying. Sara had a knack... she knew the name of every plant, tree and flower there was. Sometimes I used to quiz her to test her knowledge." Realising she was rambling nervously, Denise quieted.

200

A gentle wind rustled through the garden and green stems swayed in the breeze. Denise turned her blue eyes from the daffodils to look at Maggie. The redhead had her back to Denise but she could feel a physical tension rise between them. Not knowing what to say, DJ waited for Maggie to speak. She looked down and moved her shoes through the short blades of the grass.

Maggie looked towards the far end of the garden, spotting the rose bushes. Denise watched as Maggie headed toward them and she followed silently behind.

"They are quite beautiful, aren't they?"

Maggie nodded silently as she held one of the half blossomed buds.

"I have no idea how she managed to grow them like that. How they wound themselves around the trellis in such a way. They are a unique flower." Denise hesitated before saying, "If you like you could take cuttings and grow some yourself."

"I would like that," Maggie answered quietly. She turned back to look at DJ. "I almost didn't come this evening."

Denise kept her gaze even. "What changed your mind?"

"I wanted to know."

"Know?"

Maggie's vision drifted. "The full story. I wanted to know why she gave me up. All I do know is that she gave me away to travel the country teaching. I was kind of hoping there was more to it than that. That is why I am here this evening."

"Yes... so much more." Denise turned to look back at the house. She saw Randa through the kitchen window. The blonde occasionally looked out, watching the scene with some degree of tension as she made their drinks. With a smile, DJ winked at Randa.

"How long have you been together?" Maggie asked.

Denise shrugged. "It seems like forever and not nearly long enough." DJ cast a level gaze upon Maggie. "Have you ever met somebody and known from that single moment alone that this person is the one you want to spend the rest of your life with? Just like that?" Denise looked back at Randa, watching her actions through the window. "Like you have found that missing piece in your life and suddenly you feel complete."

Maggie nodded. "I felt that the moment I met Simon."

Both women watched Randa working in the kitchen. DJ could see her pulling cups from the wall cupboard and she smiled.

"I used to watch her when she wasn't aware. Watch the way she would care for Sara. I couldn't have asked for anybody better. The warmth, compassion and love she showed Sara were such a comfort to her. To me it seemed like I fell in love with her again each new day. She made Sara's final days as comfortable as possible. I could never thank her enough for what she did but I plan to spend the rest of my life trying." Shaking her mind from wandering thoughts, Denise blinked and smiled shyly. "Sorry!"

"That's okay." Maggie placed an uneasy hand upon DJ's arm. "I understand what you mean. Simon was a counsellor at the school where I used to work. That is where I met him."

"You're a teacher?" Denise asked surprised.

"Yes for eight years now."

"Gosh!" DJ chuckled and shook her head.

"Anyway I met Simon at the school. He helped a student of mine who was going through a rough patch. Because of him many students got through tough times and the pressure of exams."

Denise studied her cousin's soft expression, realising she really did love this man. "He sounds like a good person."

"He is... and a good father."

"That's good. I think... no, I know, Sara would have been happy to know that."

Maggie's expression cooled. "Would she?"

Denise realised Maggie's internal feelings. Understanding her cousin needed answers; DJ placed her hand on Maggie's shoulder and inclined her head towards the house. Both women made their way down the long garden to the back door. Denise placed her hand upon the handle then froze.   Taking a deep breath she turned to Maggie.

"What I'm going to tell you will be as hard for me as it was for the person who relayed it to me. Everything I tell you I assure you is true. I found it hard to understand why Sara never told me about you either... but now I think I do. All she ever did was what she thought was right. For you... for me... and I realised she didn't love me any less... and she loved you just as much."

Denise didn't wait for Maggie's answer. Pushing the door open she stepped into the kitchen, closely followed by Maggie.   The redhead seemed hesitant to enter at first. Randa noticed this and did her best to welcome Maggie. Taking her grey suit jacket, the blonde led Maggie further into the kitchen. They had decided to stay there and talk at the table so DJ pulled out a chair for her cousin.

"So how was the traffic coming down, Maggie?" Randa inquired as she carried the teapot to the table. She placed a cup in front of Maggie.

"Busy.   I knew I might get caught in the traffic returning from work so I left home earlier to make sure I had enough time."   Maggie placed a single spoonful of sugar in her tea. "Do you have any...?"

"Cream," Randa said.

"Umm yes... how did you...?"

"A good guess," Denise answered, looking momentarily at Randa. She didn't want to tell Maggie that was another trait she shared with her mother. DJ didn't know how Maggie would welcome that information until she was sure she was more comfortable with them and the memory of Sara. They had much to discuss first.

Randa brought a pot of cream from the fridge and placed it by Maggie. "We did consider sitting out on the patio this evening but the wind picked up too much." Randa sat down at the kitchen table with DJ and Maggie on either side of her, facing each other.

An uncomfortable silence floated over the room only broken by the tinkling of a metal spoon against porcelain. Denise looked up from her cup, her eyes moving between Maggie and Randa. *God I have no idea how to start this.*

Drumming her fingertips upon the polished wood of the table DJ gazed anxiously at Randa. The tension in the room hung over the three women seated around the table. Denise suddenly found her drumming fingers captured by a warm hand. She smiled at Randa and threaded their fingers together.

Taking a deep breath, Denise turned back to Maggie. "If you have any questions I'll do my best to answer them. Otherwise I'll just try to tell you everything that I know."

Maggie removed a small silver spoon from her cup and placed it upon the saucer. She gazed at DJ cautiously. "I want to know everything. I think I am entitled to that. The complete and unvarnished truth though."

Brushing her tongue over her front teeth Denise nodded. "Okay." Squeezing Randa's hand a little tighter, Denise began Sara's story.

****

Except for the gentle tones of DJ's voice the room was relatively quiet. The poet sat holding Randa's hand as she told Maggie the story of her conception, Sara's pregnancy and her birth. Denise had thought long and hard about whether she should include the story of Sara's relationship with Diane. She had initially intended to leave that out but on Maggie's request for the 'unvarnished truth' Denise told her of Diane as well. She hoped in some way it would help Maggie understand Sara's feelings. Maggie sat quietly during DJ's account, not uttering a word or question as she listened. By the time Denise finished, three cups of cold tea sat untouched upon the kitchen table.

DJ gazed steadily into Maggie's watery eyes. "Giving you away was one of the hardest decisions Sara had ever made. She did it because she thought you deserved so much more than she could provide for you."

Maggie nodded silently. She looked down at her teacup and fingered the delicate pattern around its edge. The depictions of old English roses were finely hand painted on each cup. It was a matching set that had belonged to Sara. "Could I see a picture of her?"

204

Surprised by the question and the fact that she had forgotten to pull out the scarce amount of photographs they did own, DJ rose to her feet. "Sure... of course. Why don't we go into the sitting room?"

"Excellent idea," Randa echoed as the three women exited the kitchen and headed for the front room.

Earlier that day the poet had debated on whether to take down the painting of Sara and herself when they were younger. She hadn't been sure whether Maggie seeing such a thing at this delicate stage of their meeting would produce any form of resentment. After careful consideration Denise decided to leave it hanging. Not only was it a good likeness of Sara during her younger years but also the painting wasn't large or overbearing.

Taking the lead, followed by Maggie and then Randa, DJ led her cousin into the sitting room. The curtains were still open but dark storm clouds gathering overhead cast the room in an eerie gloom. DJ switched on the main light and walked directly towards the side, freestanding unit. Opening the middle drawer she rummaged around the piles of letters and documents. Though they never possessed a great amount of photographs, Denise was aware of shots that had been taken during Sara's early years, plus the ones they had taken at Christmas. As DJ searched the drawer she heard Maggie and Randa take their seat. *Where the bloody hell are they?*

"Denise?"

"Hmm?"

"If you're looking for the photographs they're in the cupboard below that drawer."

"Oh!" Denise grinned, wondering how it was possible that Randa knew the location of things better than she did herself. Pushing the drawer closed and bending down, DJ opened the lower cupboard. She spotted the small pile of prints and removed them from the top shelf. Turning back to Maggie and Randa, Denise said, "We don't have many pictures but everything we do have is right here."

Taking a seat beside Maggie, Denise sorted through the small stack of shots. She found a picture of Sara as a young woman. The shot was taken at the first primary school she had worked in. She was surrounded by several of her pupils.

"This was taken in Sara's first place of employment." DJ handed the photograph to Maggie. "I think that would have been around a year before you were born."

Maggie stared down at the picture. She smoothed her fingertips over the silky finished black and white print. "I see I didn't inherit the dark hair. I suppose that would have been my father's genes." Maggie smiled then as she said, "She was beautiful."

"Yes she was," DJ agreed. "You may not have her hair colour but you certainly have her eyes." The poet looked back at the photographs in her hands and sorted through them again. "This was taken at Christmas." She handed Maggie a picture of Sara and Randa. "She was quite ill at that point but she never lost her spirits. She was so brave… right up until the end."

Maggie turned from the photo to Denise. "I was wondering. How did Sara die? I've just realised I was never actually told that. Or maybe I was but at that point I was just too shocked to have taken anything else in."

"That's understandable," Randa said softly. "It was quite a surprise all round. We can understand how it must have been doubly so for you."

"Yes." Maggie turned away guiltily. "There are, however, certain parts of my behaviour that I am not so proud of. The way I contacted and verbally attacked you for one. I am so sorry for that. I suppose at the time there was just a lot I didn't understand."

Denise smiled reassuringly. "That's okay. Whatever may have happened in the past has brought us to this point. Right now is all that matters."

Nodding, Maggie looked back at the photograph of Sara and Randa. "Yes… I suppose so." She studied the frail woman sitting beside a crouching Randa. "How did she die?"

Denise suddenly found herself at a loss for words. Turning to Randa DJ looked to her for assistance. The nurse seemed to have a greater capability for understanding and communication with others. Much better than DJ believe her own skills to be. Talking about the disease that had killed Sara would possibly lead to explaining the hereditary aspects of ALS. Denise knew Randa would be much better able and qualified to explain the details to Maggie.

"Maybe you'd like to take this one."

Randa pursed her lips as she moved to sit closer to Maggie. "Sara died of a disease called ALS or Amyotrophic Lateral Sclerosis." Noticing Maggie's confused expression Randa knew she needed to elaborate further. "In this country it is more commonly known as Motor Neuron Disease."

Clarity shone in Maggie's eyes. "Oh of course. There was a case on the news not long ago about a woman with the same disease. I am aware how severe it is."

"It is," Randa continued. "And Sara had a more aggressive form of the disease. From the time of diagnosis to her death... only about six months had passed."

When a silence overtook the room, DJ turned to Maggie in question. The woman's face portrayed an expression of confusion. "Are you all right?"

Shaking her head Maggie shrugged. "I don't know. I just don't know how I feel about all of this." Maggie sighed. "She was my mother... I feel like I should be saddened or hurt after hearing of the way she died but I don't know how I feel. This is still so bewildering to me."

Denise rose and stood beside the fireplace as Randa took Maggie's hand. "You don't have to understand your feelings now, Maggie. That will come in time. What you need now is to know all the facts."

"All the facts?" Maggie asked Randa.

Standing at her place by the mantle, Denise pushed her hands into her pockets. She didn't know whether telling Maggie all the facts about Sara's disease was such a good idea at that moment but she also didn't want her cousin to feel that they were keeping important information from her.

"There are other facts about the disease that people are not always so well aware of," DJ said carefully. She looked again to Randa for guidance.

A deep frown creased Maggie's brow. "Like?"

"Like," Randa began cautiously. "Like the fact that if it is a particular variation of the disease that seems to be familial, there is a higher percentage chance of it passing genetically."

"And if it is this form of the disease, how high a percentage chance are we talking about here?"

"Half," Randa confessed.

Confused blue eyes moved around the room as Maggie tried to digest what she had just been told. "This Motor Neurons Disease," she began. "This is the one that slowly paralyses the body? Am I right in my understanding here?"

"That's right." Randa released Maggie's hand and folded her own together in thought. "It's a neuromuscular disease characterized by a progressive deterioration of motor nerve cells in the brain and spinal cord. When that happens and the motor neurons can no longer send impulses to the muscles, they become paralysed and begin to waste away. This leads to a complete paralysis of the body though the mind remains unaffected."

"And I may have this?"

Denise could clearly see the alarm growing in Maggie. "We just have to be aware of the possibility. A lot of the family died quite young so we don't know all our health history, but I am not ruling out the chance that I may also one day have this. I just think it is fair that you should be aware of that."

The expression of fear in Maggie's face heightened and Denise began to feel a little concerned. *Damn, I have to right this.* "Look, Maggie, this isn't…"

"Isn't what?" Maggie interrupted. "Isn't something to be concerned about? Isn't something serious?" The redheads voice grew higher. "Because if that is what you were about to say then you are wrong. You have just told me that there may be a chance that I might one day have this disease."

"A slight chance," Randa pushed.

"What does it matter?" Maggie rose to her feet and took a step closer to DJ. "This may not concern you so much but it does me." Denise attempted to speak but Maggie cut her off. "I am a mother... I have two children to think about... **and** a husband. How am I supposed to take this? How am I supposed to tell my husband?"

Denise felt her frustration level rise as she pulled her hands from her pockets and attempted to calm her cousin. "Maggie, listen. I do understand how you feel... honestly I do."

"How could you?" Maggie retorted. "You don't have a husband... children. You don't have family to consider like I do."

"I have Randa."

"That is not the same. You're... well you are both..." Maggie shook her head. "My god, I can't deal with this." Her eyes drifted around the room as her thoughts pondered on what she had been told. An irrational tone tinged her voice. "This is not what I came around to hear. I wanted to know about Sara and what do I find? That her legacy to me is a great possibility of a terrible disease... and if I do have it then what is the chance my children might as well?"

Randa placed a calming hand upon Maggie's arm. "Why don't we all sit down?"

"Sit down?" Maggie snorted, her expression loaded with anger induced by her fear. "I need to get out of here... I need to think"

Spinning around, the redhead fled from the room. DJ looked to Randa shocked as she heard the front door open and slam shut. Turning towards the fireplace she kicked the side of the mantle as she shouted, "Shagging hell!" A sharp pain shot through her toes but she ignored it. "This is **not** good."

"We have to go after her, Denise."

Randa turned to face the door but DJ stopped her. "Let me go... I want to talk to her."

Receiving a nod of agreement Denise squeezed Randa's arm gently before heading towards the front door. She pulled it open and saw a heavy downpour of rain. *When did this start?* Grabbing her jacket from the side coat hook Denise stepped outside relieved to see Maggie's car was still parked in front of the house. Her cousin had left her keys in the coat, which was still hanging beside Randa's on the coat hook.

With the car still being there, DJ knew Maggie had to have taken off on foot. Squinting through the downpour of rain and darkened evening, DJ ran out into the street. The road was blocked at one end so Denise knew Maggie could have only run one way.

Setting off down the street the dull pain in her toes didn't hinder her progress as she searched for her cousin. The rapid fall of rain pounded down upon her head and shoulders, quickly soaking her hair and clothes. The droplets blurred her vision as DJ reached the corner of her street and turned to the left. In the distance she could just identify Maggie's red hair as she ran further down the street.

"Hey! Maggie! Wait!" DJ shouted but her cousin didn't appear to hear. Cursing once again the poet followed her down the street. She was heading toward the town centre and in the distance DJ could see an increase of people milling around the remaining open shops and public houses.

"Why do I feel like I have just made a terrible mistake?" Pushing rain soaked strands of hair from her face Denise ran faster. The rain began falling harder, pounding upon the tarmac path and forming small puddles by the roadside. DJ reached the end of the road and found herself entering the town centre. A green double-decker bus passed her forcing a jet of cold rainwater to shoot up from the curbside. The sound of passing vehicles echoed around her. Further ahead Denise noticed Maggie stop by a pelican crossing.

"Maggie, please wait," Denise shouted. "This is silly. Come on, we need to talk." The poet almost growled as Maggie crossed the road. "I'm getting frigging soaked here!"

From the other side of the road Denise watched as Maggie stopped. She leaned against the supermarket's grey brick wall, her head falling into trembling hands. Seeing a chance to reach her, Denise stopped by the pelican crossing. Intent on speaking with her cousin and desperate to calm the upset woman she ran out into the road. The last thing DJ felt was the impact of a heavy vehicle as it collided with her body at high speed.

Chapter 17

Randa stood in the living room peering out the window at the increasing downpour. A quick flash of lightning coincided with a sudden jolt to her heart.

"Denise!" she wailed knowing for certain that something terrible had happened to her partner. She began to pace, torn between running out into the night to find DJ and knowing she needed to stay in case Maggie or Denise came back. Just when she was sure she was going to lose her mind with worry a police car pulled up in front of the house. Maggie and a police officer stepped out. The redhead ran up the walk, but Randa met her at the front door before she could knock.

"Denise…where is Denise?" the blonde yelled, grabbing Maggie's upper arms as if shaking her would get the story out quicker.

"She…Oh, Randa, it's my fault…she was coming after me…"

"Maggie! Stop it!" Randa interrupted. "What's happened to Denise?" Randa's voice was rising, bordering on hysteria. Maggie could only tremble and shake her head.

The police officer came up behind them and said in an official voice, "You are Miss Martin?" Randa nodded. "And Miss Jennings would be your…?"

"Partner," Randa supplied. "What is it? Where is she?"

"I'm afraid she's been taken to hospital, Miss. A vehicle crossing Dorset Road struck her.

"Is she...?" Randa breathed almost not wanting the answer.

"Alive when I saw her last, miss, but seriously injured." The nurse closed her eyes and took a steadying breath. She opened them at the officer's next question.

"I understand there are no close relatives?" Randa glanced at Maggie who avoided her gaze.

"None," Randa stated flatly. "Except me."

"Well then, if you would accompany me, Miss, I'll take you to St. Michael's Hospital. The Emergency Department staff will need information for her treatment and I'll need a statement for my report as well."

Randa quickly gathered up her purse, jacket and Denise's briefcase with her cell phone in it. As she moved to join the police officer, Maggie approached her and reached to touch the nurse's arm.

"Don't touch me!" Randa snapped as she whipped her arm away from the redhead. "If it wasn't for your childish letters and your jealous threats we wouldn't be here and Denise wouldn't be hurt! You badgered her for the unvarnished truth but when you got it, what did you do? You ran. You're a coward, Maggie. Too bad you didn't inherit a little of Sara's courage!" As the nurse's protective nature reared up and asserted itself, Maggie moved back unconsciously. In the face of Randa's rage even the police officer seemed stunned.

"Let me tell you something else, Maggie. You better pray Denise doesn't die because if she does there won't be a hole small enough in this country for you to crawl in to hide from me!"

Turning to the police officer she said simply, "Let's go."

****

Randa was sitting in the Emergency Department waiting room, head in her hands, when Diane appeared. The nurse silently thanked her foresight in bringing Denise's briefcase. In addition to Denise's insurance information she found Diane's number programmed into the

213

cell phone as well as Carl's. Each had assured her they would be there as soon as possible.

Randa had arrived with the police officer an hour earlier. After helping with the paperwork and providing the staff with needed medical information, she was relegated to the waiting area, assured she would be informed of any news when the staff had it. Randa was torn between the knowledge that she would be in the way as the team worked on Denise and an insane need to see and be with her lover.

You've got to be all right, Denise. Eternity will not be enough, remember?

Diane moved to Randa's side and slipped into the uncomfortable chair there. She put her arm around the nurse and Randa turned into the comfort of an old friend.

"How is she, Randa?" Diane asked.

The nurse absorbed the support and replied, "Not sure yet, they're still working on her."

"How did this happen?"

"We invited Maggie up here to get to know Denise and learn about Sara. It seemed everything was going as well as could be expected, and then we got to the part about how Sara died and what that might mean for Denise and Maggie. Maggie freaked out and ran off into the rainstorm. You know Denise, she would never let Maggie try to absorb that alone. She left to find her and the police said she was in a pedestrian crosswalk when a car hit her. They said the driver never saw her in the heavy downpour." Randa's voice shook after the last sentence. She sat back but held on to Diane's hand.

Through double doors a baby faced young man in scrubs and a long white lab coat emerged. *She's being taken care of by a teenager* Randa thought. Coming closer she could see now he was at least ten years older than he initially appeared to be and had an aura about him that gave her confidence.

"Miss Martin? I'm Dr. Merritt, I treated Miss Jennings." He reached out and shook her hand.

"This is Diane Barlow, doctor. We're Denise's family. What's happening with her?"

214

Dr. Merritt pulled a chair up in front of the two women. "It was fortunate Miss Jennings was brought here. We may be a small hospital but we have a first rate trauma team. First let me assure you straight away she is in no danger of dying." Randa felt an unmistakable medical "but" coming up and she cursed herself when her nursing intuition was correct.

"But," the doctor continued, "She does have very significant injuries. Both bones in her right forearm are broken and her right shoulder was dislocated. We've moved the shoulder back into the correct position, casted the lower arm and put the whole arm in an immobilizer. She had a large amount of bruising to the right side of her body where it impacted with the vehicle. Her blood counts and blood pressure were low so we inserted a needle in her abdomen to check for the presence of blood there."

"What did the tap show?" Randa asked.

"You have some medical background?" the doctor inquired.

"She's a Registered Nurse and a damned good one too," Diane said with a reassuring squeeze to Randa's hand.

The doctor nodded. "Well then, it will be easier for me to explain this information. The tap was positive for blood. We sent her for a stat CAT scan of the chest, abdomen and pelvis. What we found was a laceration to her liver which was bleeding into her abdomen."

Randa shook her head with concern. "Damn, you'll need to operate. When will she go in?"

Dr. Merritt smiled. "She went to the operating suite 15 minutes ago. Dr. Patel was finishing up an appendectomy and was already here. She was very confident based on the scans that the laceration could be repaired. As far as Dr. Patel could see on the scans the liver injury was Miss Jennings' only abdominal injury but she will of course do a visual inspection during the procedure."

Diane breathed a sigh of relief. "That doesn't sound so bad." Randa knew in her heart the bad news wasn't finished.

"What we are most worried about though is the fact that Miss Jennings was unresponsive at the scene and has yet to regain consciousness. A scan of the brain showed a small subdural hematoma on the right side. It appears stable and at this point our inclination is not to surgically remove it. We're hoping that her unresponsiveness is related to a severe concussion and therefore temporary, but this is something we will monitor closely after surgery. That's it. Do you have any questions for me?"

"When will I be able to see her?" Randa asked.

"Post-operatively we will be monitoring her in the Intensive Care Unit; you can see her then. There's a family room outside the unit where you can wait. I'll have the head sister let you know when Miss Jennings arrives there." Dr. Merritt directed them toward the ICU and then headed back to the Emergency Department.

Randa turned to Diane. "I'm staying until I know Denise is going to be all right, but I need you to do me a favor. Can you go back to our house and check on things? I'm pretty certain the lights are on and the door is unlocked and…"

"Randa, it's fine. I'll take care of everything. DJ is going to need you here, I know that." The older woman hugged the blonde close. "Sara said you were the best nurse she had ever met and a true match for DJ. You're going to need both of those qualities to help her recover from this. Promise you'll call me if there are any changes."

The nurse hugged Diane again. "I promise. Thank you, Diane. I can see why Sara loved you."

Diane laughed softly and patted Randa's hand before drawing away. "And because you know DJ, you know why I loved Sara. Two peas in a pod, that pair. Well, I'll be on my way now, but I'll be back in the morning." She left Randa in the family room, waiting alone for the poet.

****

Randa sat in the chair by Denise's bed watching other nurses moving around their patient in an efficient and orderly manner. *Amazing how little is different in what a nurse does in this country and in the U.S.* Randa surprised herself by referring to the States as the "U.S." and not "home".

Guess home is wherever Denise is she thought.

The poet had been moved into the Intensive Care Unit about three hours previously. Randa had been allowed to stay at Denise's side though it was a violation of the posted visiting rules. Randa stayed out of the way of the staff as they cared for the brunette and though she observed what was happening, she didn't want any part of the medical aspect of the poet's care. She just wanted to be there for Denise, to support and love her. When the staff wasn't in the room, Randa talked to Denise, feeling her partner would know she was there.

"Come on, Denise. It'll take more than a speeding car to stop you. The only thing it really did was give you a lovely new haircut." Randa referred to a patch of hair on the right side of Denise's head that had to be shaved to put staples into a scalp laceration.

"Diane was here earlier. She went back to the house so we don't have to worry about that. We're so lucky to have her; she's a good friend." Randa reached out to take Denise's hand, careful to not disturb the IV inserted into the poet's wrist. A squeeze to the hand did not elicit a similar response from the brunette.

Denise hadn't opened her eyes or spoken since her admission to the ICU and for a moment Randa was content to gaze at the poet's face and rub her thumb over her fingers. As she sat there, scenes of their life together played in her mind. She remembered how her heart nearly stopped the first time Denise opened the door of the house in Derbyshire, their first kiss just last New Year's Eve and the wonderful night they first made love.

They had been through some rough times as well. Randa's eyes misted as she thought of the night Sara passed away. Standing with the poet as a piece of their hearts went with Sara had been the most devastating moment of her life. They had only made it through with the help and support of one another.

Randa glanced at the hand making contact with Denise's larger one. The silver band on her ring finger gleamed though the light in the room was muted. The nurse returned her gaze to Denise's face, willing her to open her eyes.

"Denise, I need you to wake up. I need you to show me the doctors are guessing right about this being temporary. I want to start living our lives again. I want you to tease me and make love to me and argue about chocolate with me. I want to lie in our hammock and plan our future. I want to kiss you until you're breathless and let you know how very much I love you because I do, Miss Jennings. You're my life and nothing in my life will be right again until you wake up. I love you, Denise. I guess it's as plain and simple as that. Oh, and one more thing. When you're up and out of here, we're going to see your friend the jewelry maker and get a ring made for you too. You belong to me as much as I belong to you and we're going to spend the rest of our very long lives together. Please, love, please wake up!"

Randa had held her emotions together since the first moment she heard Denise had been hurt, but now she felt her tenuous hold on control slipping. She lowered her head as the tears she had held back for so many hours flowed unchecked down her cheeks.

"Juniper," a hoarse and cracked voice said.

Randa's head popped up and she found herself being regarded by two groggy but aware blue eyes.

"What did you say, Denise?" Randa said as she rose to move closer to the poet.

"Juniper..." Denise whispered through dry lips as she gave Randa a weak smile. "My middle name...it's Juniper."

Randa smiled as a fresh flow of tears started. "That's terrible, love," she said as she placed gentle kisses on Denise's cheeks and forehead. "That's just terrible."

The weak smile stayed on the poet's face as Denise closed her eyes again firmly entrenched in healing sleep.

Chapter 18

The feeling of a soft, caressing sensation travelling over her wrist pulled Denise from her sleep. Taking light breaths, the poet attempted to open her eyes for the second time. This time it felt easier. As dark eyelashes slowly parted the single hospital room was revealed to her. Blue eyes slid from left to right in a quest for visual information. DJ knew she was in a hospital; that much was apparent. She also knew why she was there but the poet had no conception of her injuries. All Denise knew was that her entire body ached and her head throbbed. Her newly opened eyes felt sensitive to the light but she managed to accustom them to the glare.

Becoming increasingly conscious of her surroundings, Denise once again became aware of the peculiar tickling sensation caressing her skin. The poet attempted to turn her head but the sheer stiffness her body felt caused her to remain still. Instead hazy blue eyes shifted to the left and gazed down. The sight of a crown of blonde hair beside her arm warmed her heart. Denise realized what she could feel was Randa as the nurse sat with her head resting upon the bed, sleeping. Her gentle somnolent breaths prickled DJ's skin.

Denise attempted to speak but the words got caught in her throat. A chain of dry throaty coughs followed, causing DJ's body to tense with increasing spasms of pain. Grimacing at the agonizing sensations, a sense of relief washed through her as Denise heard a welcome sound.

"Denise love, can you hear me?"

DJ lightly squeezed the hand that had wrapped itself around her own. She swallowed and groaned harshly, her

220

eyes once again tightly closed together.

"Denise, look at me?" Randa asked, accompanied by a soothing caress to her arm.

Feeling tears of frustration sting her eyes, Denise slowly looked towards Randa. The sight of loving green eyes caused further tears to slip down the side of her cheeks. She smiled, feeling tightness in her lower lip and realized the flesh must have split.

"Hi," Randa said and kissed DJ's uninjured hand.

"Need a drink," Denise whispered hoarsely.

The blonde shook her head. "You can't, love. Not yet anyway. Hold on." Randa disappeared momentarily from view only to return holding something cold against DJ's lips. "Here, take this."

Feeling the chilling sensation upon her flesh, Denise took the small chip of ice into her mouth. The cool ice instantly melted in the heat of her mouth causing a trickle of refreshing water to slip down her throat.

"Better?"

"Hmm."

"How do you feel?"

Licking her lips Denise said, "Like I was hit by a ton of bricks."

"Try an SUV!"

"Ugh." Releasing Randa's hand DJ lifted her own and gently prodded her lip, feeling the swelling. "What's the damage?"

"Well..." Regret shone in Randa's features as she listed DJ's injuries. "You've got two broken bones in your right arm. You dislocated the shoulder too, which had to be reset. You have major bruising down the right side of your body and your liver was lacerated and bleeding into your abdomen. They had to operate to repair it. You had a small bleed on the right side of your brain... but that was stable. The only major concern was the fact that you were taking so long to regain consciousness. Now that you have, I think you're going to be just fine."

Denise listened to Randa recount her injuries, feeling a sense of shock. When she finished the poet looked at her in disbelief as she gently fingered her brow. "And I am still in one piece?"

"Thankfully." Randa rose from her chair in which she had been keeping a constant vigil beside DJ's bed. She leaned forward and kissed Denise's brow, lightly running her fingers through her dark fringe. "I was so scared, Denise. When the police came to the door I just knew something terrible had happened. I felt like I couldn't breathe. I was so scared I would never see you again."

Taking Randa's hand, Denise placed it against the uninjured side of her face. She smiled as the last thought that occurred to her before she lost consciousness, entered her mind. "You know... the last thing I remember... before it went black was the fear that I was about to leave this world and I never gave into your quest to discover my middle name. Silly huh?"

"Your name?" Randa asked with a slight, withheld smile.

Denise smiled, feeling the tug once again on her lip. Grimacing, she closed her eyes. "It hurts to smile." Reopening blue orbs she regarded Randa clearly. "And you wonder why I was so reluctant in telling you. Don't think I don't remember you..." Denise took a light breath. "...Laughing. You called it terrible!"

Randa shrugged. "But anyway, I don't think it was silly to think that about your middle name. Maybe it shows you were thinking of me. Does that mean I was your last thought?"

"My first... my last... and all those in-between that are not occupied thinking about chocolate." Denise grimaced, as an intense feeling of pain ran through her.

The smile fell from Randa's lips. "What is it?"

"Starting to hurt more." The pain steadily grew causing DJ to groan out her discomfort.

"Hold on, love, I'll get the nurse." Randa reached out to a button by the side of the bed and pressed it twice. Within moments a West Indian nurse dressed in a light blue uniform came through the door.

"Her pain is coming back," Randa said. She didn't want it to appear like she was encroaching or trying to do the nurse's job, but she had to add, "She's going to need another shot of Morphine."

The tall nurse nodded. "I'll get it for her. Doctor Merritt was just about to..." She stopped as the man in question appeared behind her.

"Ah, I see the patient is awake again," he said to Denise as he entered the room. "How are you feeling, Miss Jennings?"

"Like crap."

Randa rolled her eyes. "Yes, ladies and gentleman it's the famed poet, renowned for her gift of words... D Jennings." Randa shook her head. "She needs another dose of Morphine."

Doctor Merritt nodded as he turned to the nurse. "Give her four milligrams of Morphine IV please. The nurse left to retrieve the strong painkiller. The physician pulled an ophthalmoscope from his pocket and began to examine DJ's eyes. "I'm relieved to see you conscious. We were a little concerned that it had taken longer than expected for you to come around. I presume Randa has filled you in with the state of your injuries?"

Denise nodded.

"Good and how are you feeling?"

"I hurt, I throb and I'm broken. Apart from that I suppose I should be glad I am still alive." Denise felt a responding squeeze from Randa at her words. The nurse returned at that point with a syringe and administered the medication through an access port near the site where the IV entered DJ's skin.

"And how does your head feel?" the doctor continued. "Any headaches... changes in your vision?"

DJ cast her eyes around the room. "I see fine."

"That's good. Well, being as though I know you are in capable hands with Randa here, I'll leave you two alone. I will be back later to talk to you again when I get the results from your latest scans."

When Doctor Merritt left the room Denise looked back at Randa. "He's okay." The poet took a shallow breath and sighed. "So, Nurse Randa, now that I am in your capable hands... what do you intend doing with me?"

"Feeling a little better?" Randa asked with a wry smile. "I think the Morphine must be taking affect."

Denise closed her eyes as her body sunk into a luxurious feeling of cocooned comfort and security. Her mind drifted, floating on a cloud of sleepiness as she slipped into a light but disturbed sleep.

****

Denise felt alone. She was cold, wet and afraid, surrounded by semi darkness. Devoid of energy, her legs felt weak and numb, yet she was running, feeling she was unable to stop. Ahead of her Denise could just see Randa but however hard she ran, she couldn't seemed to get any closer to her partner. Her legs ached and her chest stung with a need for breath. Suddenly Denise found herself running faster, rapidly getting closer to Randa, but out of nowhere bright lights blinded her eyes. The sound of screeching brakes echoed in her ears as she felt her body collide with a solid force and fly like a rag doll through the air.

"No!"

Denise opened her eyes in terror to find herself once again in the ICU room. Breathing harshly and her heart pounding rapidly within her chest she searched around the room frantically. Randa was nowhere to be seen. Closing her eyes, Denise tried to take calming breaths. *I can't believe this happened,* she thought. *Why did this happen?*

It was a fact of life, DJ acknowledged, that bad things happened when you least expected them to. Unlike in the movies where atmospheric music and cleverly manipulated tension can lead the viewer to suspect something was about to happen, in real life that was not so. The house fire and the death of her parents; the surprise reality of a terminal illness, they were all examples of how fate had played its part in DJ's life. *You never know just what is around the next corner in life,* Denise thought to herself. She felt angry, and frustrated that this had happened, just as things appeared to be going well for Randa and herself.

Lifting her one good arm, Denise lightly covered her eyes with a slightly bruised and grazed hand.

"Denise?"

The poet uncovered her eyes to find Randa re-entering her room. A profound feeling of relief flooded her senses.

"You're awake! Are you okay?"

DJ shook her head. "I had a bad dream. Left me feeling a little rattled." She held out her hand for Randa to take and the nurse accepted it gladly. Randa leaned forward and kissed DJ's fingers gently.

"Sorry I wasn't here when you woke up."

"Randa you don't have to be here all the time. I don't know how long I am going to have to stay here and you look like you haven't slept in days."

Randa smiled. "Is that your way of telling me I look like hell?"

"You always look good to me," Denise replied.

"Well that's good then because I'm not going anywhere. So how are you feeling?"

"I don't know. How am I supposed to feel? I feel okay I suppose." DJ took a short breath. "Could I have another one of those icy things?"

"Sure." Randa reached over to a fresh selection of ice chips. She lifted one from the glass container and held it towards DJ's lips. "I was out with Carl. He turned up about twenty minutes ago. He's out in the waiting room now. I must admit, it would have been better to finally meet him under different circumstances but he seems nice. Very worried about you though so naturally that boosted his stock with me a couple of notches!"

DJ readily accepted the refreshing chip of ice. "Is he allowed to come in?"

"For a couple of minutes. Visits to ICU's are usually kept minimal and short. Being as though you seem to be doing okay I'm pretty sure you'll be transferred to a regular room soon."

"Okay... can you bring him in?"

As Randa nodded and turned to leave, Denise called after her. The blonde turned back to DJ in question.

"Not that I want to appear vain," DJ said, "But how exactly do I look? I mean to an outside point of view. I don't want to scare anybody!" Denise watched Randa closely as her eyes swept over her prone form.

"Well most of your body is covered so a lot of your cuts and bruises aren't visible. The only things showing really are your arms and face. Your right arm is in a cast and an immobiliser and your left, like your face, is cut, scraped and bruised. Then you have a couple of staples on your head... your chin... your..."

"I get the point," Denise interrupted. "I look literally as bad as I feel!"

Randa stepped forward and leaned carefully over Denise's bed. She kissed her gently and DJ reveled in the soft lips upon her own. She closed her eyes, basking in the simple contact that was nothing more than a loving caress of reassurance.

"You may look a little more colourful than usual but you still look great."

Denise smiled slightly as she gazed into sea green eyes. "The heart can see what the eyes cannot."

"Pardon?" Randa asked.

"I mean that you look at me with your heart because you love me... there is a difference."

"Does that matter?"

DJ shook her head. "No, I like the way you look at me."

"Then that's okay." Placing one more kiss upon Denise's forehead Randa turned back towards the door. "I'll be back in a minute."

Denise watched Randa leave with a smile. As the door closed she looked around her room. There didn't seem to be much to it. She hoped when she was moved to a regular room she would at least have a television. That thought made Denise remember the interview that was to be broadcast the evening before. Denise made a mental note to try and remember to ask Carl how it turned out. She knew with absolute certainty Carl would have watched it.

Raising her arm, Denise studied her left limb and hand. Flesh that wasn't covered by a hospital gown was littered with abrasions and bruising. The reality of her condition sunk into her mind and a raw feeling of frustration warred within. The notion that she wouldn't be able to do a lot of things for herself became an increasingly exasperating thought. Although she knew Randa would be more than willing to help in anyway she could, the simple fact that she would temporarily lose a certain amount of her independence was highly worrisome. *Thank god I'm left handed,* Denise mumbled as Randa and Carl entered the room.

Denise watched Carl closely to gauge his reaction. The editor looked down at Denise, his eyes wide with shock.

"Jesus, DJ."

"I love you too, man."

"I can't believe it. How do you feel?"

"Why does everybody keep asking me that? How do you think I feel?" There was no resentment in DJ's voice as she responded to Carl. "I feel great! They got me on Morphine!" Denise winked conspiratorially. She was putting on a brave face and she knew it. Even with the Morphine, DJ was extremely uncomfortable.

Carl sat down on a chair on the opposite side of Randa. DJ felt Randa take her hand and a soothing thumb caress her skin.

"Well, you'll never guess what?"

"What's that?" Denise asked Carl.

"The press already knows about the accident. Apparently it didn't take long to find out whom it was. I got a telephone call just before I left from your local paper. They wanted direct information about what had happened. It seems your getting hurt on the night of your first screen interview is big news." Carl shook his head. "I won't be surprised if the local press don't then inform the nationals."

Denise rolled her eyes. "So how was the interview?"

"You're not worried about the other stuff?" Carl asked.

"Nothing I can do about it."

"I suppose." Carl shifted back into his chair. "The interview was great. You looked fantastic. I have to say I think you look good on the small screen. There was even a shot of Randa."

"There was?" the nurse asked.

"Uh huh. When DJ mentioned you there was a shot of you standing in the background watching."

"Wow, I might have to send a copy of that to my mom!"

"You taped it?"

Randa nodded as she said, "Yes."

Carl smirked. "So did I." Placing a hand upon the bed the editor turned a serious eye upon Denise. "Listen, I know I can't stay much longer but I want you to know that whatever you want is yours okay? Anything you need me to do, just say."

"Thanks, Carl. If you can just deal with any questions, that would be great."

The editor gave an affirmative nod. "What do you want me to say to the press?"

Denise thought momentarily. "Something honest but concise I think."

"Consider it done." Carl stood slowly. "I better get going then before one of those nurse's comes in here and tries to manhandle me." Carl paused, "Hmm, actually come to think of it..."

Randa chuckled as she rose to her feet. "Careful. I heard the sister doesn't take any crap!"

Carl pouted. "Aw, okay." He turned back to Denise. "Remember... anything you need, DJ, just let me know." With a wink to Denise and a smile and nod towards Randa, Carl exited the room.

Denise yawned.

"Are you tired?" Randa asked concerned.

"A little, that bad dream earlier woke me up with a start."

"What was it about?"

The poet shook her head. "It doesn't matter... it was nothing out of the ordinary... just your run of the mill bad dream." Though the dream had shaken Denise she didn't want to pin any importance on it or make it seem worse than she knew it was.

Thinking back to the accident, Denise remembered the reason she was out in the streets in the first place. "What happened to Maggie?" She noticed Randa's eyes glaze over with anger.

"I don't know where she is and to be honest I don't really care." The nurse folded her arms and looked away from DJ. "It's her fault you're here. You nearly died because of her."

"It wasn't her fault."

"The hell it wasn't," Randa said angrily.

"Hey!" Denise reached out, grabbing hold of Randa's tense hand. "It was an accident, all of it. Me running out into the road, even though I was at a crossing, and that person not seeing me. None of it could be helped. If anything, blame the stupid weather. Let's just be glad it wasn't any more serious and that nobody else got hurt. I know I am."

Randa sat down, still seemingly unconvinced so Denise decided to change the subject.

"Thank you for calling everyone, by the way." She frowned. "How did you get Carl's number?"

Randa shrugged. "I brought your briefcase with me. I knew it had your cell phone inside and that you had all your important numbers programmed into the memory."

"My briefcase?" Denise said surprised. There was a certain writing pad in her briefcase that she hadn't wanted Randa to see. She wondered whether the blonde had found the item in question. Denise had pondered for quite a while about when to show Randa what was written on the pad. It was a poem. She had written it for her, but was unsure when, where and how to give it to her. Deciding to find out whether in fact Randa had read the poem – and dreading the answer at the same time – DJ addressed Randa cautiously. "Did you look around the case?"

Randa shrugged. "Well I did... kind of. Just to occupy my mind."

"And you looked in my pad?"

The blonde blushed and hesitated before replying. "Okay I did... but I swear as soon as I read the title and saw my name and the notes around the side I shut it back up."

Randa fidgeted in her chair. "I was tempted to read further but I swear I didn't. I knew that if and when you wanted me to see it you would show me then. It was hard though," the nurse smiled.

Blue eyes regarded the ceiling in thought. *I could wait... but with all that has happened now might be as good a time as any!* That decision made, DJ said, "Where is my case now?"

Randa inclined her head toward the other side of the room. "In the corner, out of the way."

"Do you mind bringing it to me?"

"Of course not." Randa rose from her chair and crossed the room. She picked up DJ's case from the floor and carried it back over to her partner.

"Can you open it and take out the notepad?"

Nodding, Randa did as requested. She pulled the pad from inside the case and placed the carrier upon the floor. Handing the pad to Denise, Randa sat back down. Curiosity shone upon her features.

Lifting her notepad cover, Denise looked at the precise handwritten verses. Her heart hammered anxiously. She had envisioned a different scenario than this but the poet knew that she wanted and needed to do this now. Turning back to Randa, DJ held out the pad. "Will you read it out... please?"

"Um... sure." Licking her lips Randa cast her eyes down toward the notepad. Her voice quivered with anticipation as she began to read:

"If only I had the eloquence
To put in simple words
Just how your presence changed my life
And lightened up my world

If I only had the voice
Then for you I know I'd sing
A ballad of the greatest songs
A lover's harmony

But if you had the eyes

That could see inside my soul
A once and lonely heart you'd find
Because of you is whole

And if you were to touch me
I know you'd surely feel
My body tremble at your sweet caress
With you I'm healed

When we are together
The love I feel inside
Shows you are my destiny
From that I'll never hide

And, my heart, I know I love you
And I hope that you will see
That you and I were meant to be
So, my love, …"

Randa paused… her glazed eyes turning towards Denise in bewilderment as she continued with the last line, "… please marry me."

Silence filled the room and DJ bit her lip, her breathing tight and shallow. "Randa, I…" The poet stopped talking as Doctor Merritt entered the room.

"Hello, Denise." He sat down in Carl's recently vacated seat. "I have the results from your scans. I am pleased to tell you that your neuro status is okay and you are getting stronger. There is also no evidence of any further internal bleeding."

DJ briefly looked over to a quiet Randa. With regret she realised she would have to put off Randa's response to her poem. Already the anticipation was eating away at her insides. She turned to the doctor. "That's good then. Does it mean I can go to a regular room?" she asked and looked back at Randa. A hesitant expression appeared in the blonde's eyes causing a sudden feeling of nervousness in Denise.

Doctor Merritt continued. "We did however identify a problem. The kidney function tests on your chemistry panel are worrisome."

"How bad are they?" Randa asked instinctively.

"Bad enough that we'll start monitoring her BUN and creatinine twice a day until we see some improvement."

Denise frowned. "What is that?"

"Those are tests that monitor how good a job your kidneys are doing filtering the toxins out of your blood stream," Randa answered. "Her tests were normal before surgery?"

The doctor nodded to Randa's question then addressed DJ. "This means your kidneys have stopped functioning properly since your surgery. This may be due to the IV contrast dye used for your scans. Have you ever had any type of scan before using a contrast dye?"

"No," replied the poet. "I've been pretty healthy up until now."

"Well, it may be nothing to worry about. This could resolve spontaneously."

"And if it doesn't?" The poet asked nervously.

"If not it may mean you could go into kidney failure and need dialysis, either temporary or permanently."

"What's the worst-case scenario?" the poet asked.

Dr. Merritt looked uncomfortable. "You could progress to complete kidney failure and need a transplant."

The breath left DJ's lungs as the news registered in her mind. "A transplant?"

"That's worst case scenario," Doctor Merritt insisted. "Like I said this could resolve spontaneously."

"And it might not." Denise looked worriedly at Randa seeing the same highly distressed expression in her eyes that she was feeling within herself. Alarm filled her senses as the poet's mind naturally pondered the doctor's words.

Chapter 19

Dr. Merritt excused himself and left the room to continue on his rounds of his patients. Neither Randa nor Denise seemed to know what to say. The poet stared straight ahead apparently trying to come to terms with the information the doctor had given them. Randa looked at her lover and experienced a feeling of helplessness. It was a feeling she was having all too often lately.

Looking down, she saw the pad of writing paper she still had in her hand with Denise's eloquent and sweet proposal on it. Slowly she slipped the pad back into the poet's briefcase. *I'm not going to hold her to this proposal, not now when she has so many more important things to deal with. I do want to marry you, Denise but I'm not going to put any pressure on you right now. When you're past all this then we'll plan our future together. Until then I just want you to concentrate on getting better.*

Randa felt like she was doing the right thing for Denise, but another part of her wanted to take Denise into her arms and show her how ecstatic the proposal had made her. Moving to Denise's bedside, the blonde reached out and took her partner's hand.

"Are you okay, love?" Denise appeared anything but okay at the moment, but she squeezed Randa's hand.

"I will be. I'm just trying to understand what's happened. It seems that since I woke up it's been one thing after another trying to keep me off balance. I need a little time to sort out what all this means."

"Anything I can do?" Randa offered. She brought her hand up to move a dark lock of hair off DJ's forehead and she winced involuntarily when she spied the laceration and shaved area on Denise's head.

Denise was about to speak when she saw the direction of Randa's gaze. Reaching her left hand up she touched the area recently stapled closed. Eyes widened as she felt around the injury and she turned a questioning look up at the nurse.

" My hair?"

"I'm afraid so, love, they had to close up a nasty cut on your head," Randa said with sympathy. "It'll grow back in no time though."

Denise surprised her by giving her a wide smile. "I guess if you want to do something for me, you can bring me a pair of scissors. Maybe we can even things up a little bit. I had been thinking about getting it cut anyway. It looks like the decision has been made for me now."

Randa laughed and realized Denise had surprised her once again by her resilience. She leaned over and kissed the poet on the top of her head, moved down to her forehead then continued on to place a soft kiss on Denise's lips.

"I was so worried about you," Randa murmured against Denise's mouth. "If something had happened and you had been taken from me, I'm not sure I would have survived." Denise moved her uninjured arm up and around Randa's head to press the nurse closer but grimaced as the increased pressure caused pain to her split lip.

"Ouch!" she exclaimed and brought her fingers to her lip. "Remind me to kiss you passionately after I heal up a little, okay?"

"You can count on it," Randa agreed as she moved back from Denise. Neither said a word but only looked at the other as unspoken love and reassurances were exchanged.

"What's going to happen to me, Randa?" Denise asked, tension evident in her voice. The nurse looked at her partner and knew she couldn't look into those cerulean eyes and lie.

"We don't know, Denise. Maybe your kidneys will start working right on their own and everything will be fine. If they don't then we'll deal with that situation when it occurs and we'll deal with it together." Denise studied her for a few seconds then nodded.

"How long until we'll know?"

Tell her straight out. Randa. She needs to know you'll always tell her the truth. "It depends on your lab tests but I don't think it will be more than two or three days before we'll be certain."

Denise nodded and fell silent. Randa wished there was something more she could do for her partner but as she looked down at their rejoined hands, she couldn't think of a damn thing.

****

It was late in the afternoon by the time Randa stumbled into the house. The dark circles under her eyes were evidence of the emotional stress she was dealing with. A stumbling gait gave away her exhaustion and the persistent rumbling of her stomach reminded her she'd had nothing but tea and coffee in the hospital cafeteria since the previous evening.

Diane emerged from the living room and assessed Randa's condition immediately.

"I saw the taxi arrive. My goodness Randa, you're positively dead on your feet. Come into the kitchen dear and let's get some food into you. I made a nice roast beef, as I didn't know when you might be back. Let me heat some up for you and you can fill me in on how DJ is doing."

"She's not much different from when I called you earlier," Randa said as she followed the older woman into the kitchen. "Her lab tests were a little worse this afternoon as compared to this morning but not by much so we just have to wait and see about her kidney function. The physical therapist came in to work with her and then she is being transferred to a private room on a general surgical ward. I thought I would come home to get cleaned up and get a bite to eat. I'll head back to the hospital in a little while."

Diane looked up at the nurse as she removed a pan from the oven and began slicing two thick cuts of roast beef.

"You most certainly will not, young woman. First you will eat some supper, then you will march upstairs and take a long hot shower then you are going to lay down and get some sleep."

"Diane, I can't. Denise needs…"

"DJ needs you strong and healthy and to do that you need to eat and rest properly. She told me how you made her do the same thing when the both of you were taking care of Sara. I was told to remind you of that." Diane added roasted potatoes to the plate and a puffy golden brown object that looked like a pastry.

"You were told? You've talked to Denise?" the nurse asked.

"Not quite. Carl just called. Apparently he got back to the hospital just a few minutes after you left to get a taxi. DJ gave him these instructions to pass on to you so these are 'orders from headquarters'. He stepped out to use his mobile phone and call me here. You are threatened with a paddling from her good hand if she sees you anywhere near the hospital before morning." Diane set Randa's plate in front of her as the blonde took a seat at the kitchen table. The older woman turned to the refrigerator to retrieve a glass of milk to accompany the meal.

"That sounds like Denise. Actually, that sounds like me. I guess if the tables were turned. I'd be telling her the same thing."

"Of course you would and even though both of you would instinctively want to be there for each other, I would hope you as a nurse will know what's best."

"Boy, using my own profession against me? That is so not fair, but you are so right. I'm so tired I know I can't be thinking clearly and I don't want to miss anything or do anything wrong when it comes to taking care of that stubborn Jennings woman."

Diane chuckled and her eyes shone behind her small glasses. "Stubborn is exactly the word for the Jennings women. Medical science may work on the physical ills, but they'll never cure that stubborn streak."

Randa smiled and took a bite of the tender beef. "God, that's so nice. I'm sure my stomach thought my throat was

237

cut because it had been so long since I last ate." She savored the flavor then glanced back at Diane. "What's this?" she asked, indicating the golden brown object.

"You've never had a Yorkshire pudding? How can you eat roast beef without some?"

Randa looked at the object. "That's what a Yorkshire pudding looks like? That's nothing like what we would call a pudding in the States." She picked up the light crusty object and took a bite. "Not bad, a little plain but not bad."

"I hope the Prime Minister appreciates my efforts because I'm about to spread a little English culture," Diane teased as she brought forth a gravy bowl and showed Randa the proper way to eat a Yorkshire pudding. The blonde made short work of her supper and leaned back in satisfaction.

"I feel almost human again. Thank you, Diane, that was delicious."

"You're most welcome, my dear. Maybe you can repay me one day by making some of those enchiladas of yours that DJ is always raving about. They sound wonderful"

Randa was surprised. "She likes my enchiladas? She usually is teasing me that we Americans like our cheese way too much for it to be healthy. So she likes them, eh? Well she's going to have some the first thing we get her home and you are most definitely invited."

"I'd like that very much," commented Diane. The expression on her face became serious. "Randa, what will happen to DJ if her kidneys don't start functioning properly? She won't die, will she?"

The nurse was quick to reassure her friend. "No, she won't die. If her kidneys don't recover, she will need dialysis probably three days a week through a device they will implant in her vascular system. That means she would be hooked up to a machine to filter her blood and take fluid off her system for about 3 hours on each of those days. Her blood pressure might be affected and she would need to observe dietary restrictions. She's young and healthy though so if her kidneys do fail, she will probably be placed on the list to wait for a suitable kidney donor for a transplant. A transplant would mean more surgery of course followed by a lifetime of anti-rejection drugs. Anyway you look at it, it won't be fun."

Diane thought about this. "My kidneys aren't all that new but if DJ needed one, she could have one."

The nurse was touched by the offer. "That's so sweet of you to offer but the kidney should be as close a match to Denise's own tissue type as possible to lessen the chance of rejection. Let's hope that none of us need to get typed and that her kidneys start to work on their own.

"Yes," Diane said thoughtfully, "Let's hope they do." She was silent a moment then glanced at Randa. "Now then, girl, be off to the shower and bed. That woman in the hospital is going to need you tomorrow and she is going to need you well rested. I'll come by bright and early and take you to see her."

Randa rose and after placing her dishes in the sink, walked slowly with Diane out of the kitchen. "You're a godsend, Diane. Do you want me to walk you to your car?"

"No, I can manage. You just go on upstairs now. I'll turn off the lights and lock up on my way out."

Randa nodded and gave the older woman a hug. "I'll see you in the morning. Good night, Diane."

"Good night, dear." Diane watched as Randa made her way up the stairs and waited until she heard the bathroom door shut. She stood a minute with a thoughtful look on her face then nodded and walked into the living room. She rummaged through her purse until she came up with a half sheet of paper with a telephone number written on it.

Dialing the number, Diane waited as the line was picked up and the person she wanted to speak to answered.

"This is Diane Barlow, calling from Bakewell. I think we need to talk."

****

The chatter of multiple voices echoed down the hospital corridor. Denise turned her vision towards her private room's door to see whether Carl had returned. Her friend had left to make a phone call to Diane and had yet to return. She had sent him out with orders for Randa to get some rest. Denise was worried about her; the blonde had looked exhausted and DJ wanted her partner to get some much-needed sleep. With both Carl and Diane on her side Denise was sure that between them they could convince Randa to get some sleep.

Sitting in a semi upright position in her bed Denise looked down at the immobiliser holding her right arm. So much of her body hurt. The bruises that covered a large percentage of her frame were painfully making themselves known. Only once had Denise dared to take a look at the multicoloured contusions that adorned her. The sight was shocking and the poet was very glad they were temporary. However, the pain that wracked her battered body felt almost unbearable. DJ had to constantly remind herself that it wouldn't last forever.

Casting her eyes around the room DJ looked at the small combined television and video mounted high upon the wall. Though it was switched on the sound had been muted. Denise stared aimlessly at the evening soap opera having no idea what was happening or for that matter who the characters actually were. Denise's mind couldn't venture much further than the reality of her health. She still felt shocked and uncertain as to what the future held. If she was honest with herself, Denise could admit she was scared. Whether she spent her life on dialysis or was able to get a transplant, even then as Randa stated, there would be a lifetime of anti-rejection drugs for her. Neither prospect filled her with any degree of hope or encouragement. One fact began to dominate her mind – if the worst was to happen she didn't think it would be right to expect to hold Randa to her proposal. The fact that Randa hadn't even mentioned it led the poet to believe that maybe she didn't want to disappoint her with a negative answer after the news of her failing health. As the seconds past, DJ's mood grew increasingly somber.

"Rallying of the troops accomplished, Captain."

Denise turned to see Carl re-entering her room. He switched off his mobile and slipped it into the inside pocket of his jacket.

"You spoke to Di?"

The blonde man nodded. "Yes. She said she would make sure Randa got some rest and proper nourishment before she returned... in the morning!"

DJ nodded. "Good."

Carl sat down beside Denise's bed. He picked a grape from the bunch he had brought in earlier. Rolling the small green fruit around his fingers he studied DJ's tense expression. "You're worrying about this kidney problem, aren't you? Try not to dwell on it too much. I know you."

"It's not that," the poet dismissed.

"Then what is it? What's wrong?"

"Carl?" Denise gazed at the editor seriously. "If I tell you something, promise me it will go no further than these four walls."

Carl held up his right hand. "Soul of discretion. What's going on?"

"I um... I asked Randa to um... to marry me."

The editor paused halfway in his quest to pick another grape and looked at Denise through wide eyes. "Oh, wow!"

"Hmm!"

"What did she say?" The poet's expression confused Carl.

"Nothing," Denise said. "Straight after the doctor came in with the news and she didn't get a chance to respond. The trouble is that she still hasn't. Now I'm not sure whether I just made a terrible mistake."

"Hey, don't think like that." Carl took DJ's left hand. "You both had a lot to take in and now have a lot to think about. I'm still shook up myself. Randa probably needs thinking time."

Denise sighed, that was what she was afraid of. With all the thoughts that were bombarding her mind she was scared some of them may in fact be on the nurse's mind as well. "That's what is worrying me."

Carl frowned.

"This may sound a little backward but I'm kind of scared she's having the same thoughts as I."

"You're losing me now, my friend," Carl said in confusion. "What are you talking about?"

"I feel... with everything that has recently happened that holding her to that proposal would be wrong. I have no idea what the future holds for me or how things will turn out. I don't want to hold Randa down. I just feel like she is being pulled through the wringer and it's all because of me." Denise stared ahead to the muted television. "She can do without this stress, Carl. I don't want to be the cause of any anguish she may feel."

Carl looked steadily at Denise with astute vision. "Look, DJ, I may not know Randa all that well, but I see the way she looks at you... like you are the only person in the room! We all know you have a brooding streak a mile long. You just need to talk to her."

"I'm not sure I can at the moment. Not about this. I don't want to put any pressure on her." Disengaging from Carl's hand, Denise lifted the small glass of water from her unit and took a sip. She was very glad she was able to drink fluids again. "I love Randa," she said seriously. "I love her with a depth I never thought possible, but I don't want anything short of the best for her and I don't feel that in me... not like this. I no longer feel like a complete person." Denise turned away from Carl with misty eyes. She had always felt that loving Randa had made her feel complete but now she felt less than what she wanted for **her**. DJ feared she could no longer be everything she had been and her uncertainty fuelled that inner doubt.

"Listen," Carl looked at Denise seriously. "I don't want you to say anything else like this and I don't want you to think it. What I want is for you to do is to talk to Randa. That is the only thing that will ease all these thoughts." Carl decided to attempt a little pulling of his own rank. "Now as your editor... I demand that you take heed of my words!"

A small smile tugged the corners of Denise's lips. This was typical 'Carl' behaviour. "It's like that, is it?"

The man turned very serious. "I know that woman loves you. Hell I love you, my friend, and I disagree with you totally on this. I know she will too. I understand that you can't help feeling this way at the moment. I can't begin to understand completely what you must be going through but don't doubt Randa." Carl smiled. "I've seen the feistiness in her eyes." He paused… "Do you trust her?"

"With all my body and soul," Denise said with conviction.

"Then have faith in that, my friend." Carl said simply.

****

Sitting upon the edge of her bed Denise looked down at her feet. That morning the nurse had told her that she should try walking, but rather than wait for somebody else to be around, she was already attempting to stand for the first time since the accident. With her right arm held against her body, Denise balanced herself using her left hand as she rose to her feet. Her head slightly spun and her vision darkened momentarily as a bout of dizziness overcame her.

Regaining her bearings, Denise opened her eyes and took a breath. She looked down at the hospital issued gown and hoped Randa would remember to bring her something a little more decent to wear! Taking her hand from the side unit DJ stood on steady legs. "Well that's not so bad," she muttered. The poet was eternally thankful that her legs hadn't been injured in the accident. Apart from scattered scrapes and bruising, her lower limbs were fine.

Taking a step, Denise jumped and fell back into a sitting position upon the bed as a voice startled her.

"What are you doing?"

"Ouch… damn it." Denise winced as the sudden pressure jarred her bruises.

Randa stepped into the room. "Oh, Denise, I'm sorry, but what were you doing? You really should have somebody with you, just in case you feel a little weakness or dizziness."

"I was fine." Denise gripped the bed sheets as the throbbing receded.

"Stubborn, stubborn, stubborn!" Randa cupped DJ's cheeks and redirected her gaze.

243

Looking into sea green eyes Denise saw the concerning shining through. She was right though and DJ knew it – she was stubborn. If she was to attempt walking she didn't want her hand held like a child.

"How are you today?"

Taking Randa's hand with hers, Denise held it against her cheek. "It's on my mind constantly. Pain is a good reminder, you know. It's always there... a throbbing reminder that I could be looking at a lifetime of this. Drugs... hospitals..."

"Oh, sweetheart." Randa kissed DJ gently.

Denise smiled. "Hmm, now I feel better. Do that again." She closed her eyes as Randa's lips caressed her own softly. "I dreamed about you last night." The words were muttered quietly against Randa's lips.

"And?"

DJ grinned crookedly. "Let's just say it gave me a few ideas."

"You're not telling me?" Randa kissed DJ again, running her tongue along her top lip. Her actions proved to sway the brunette.

"Well let's just say it involved you and me. Add a bottle of something chocolaty and take away our clothes!"

"Maybe I should quietly leave and pretend I didn't just hear that!"

Both women turned to see Diane standing in the doorway. Within her arms she held a small bunch of flowers.

"Should I have taken longer getting these?" she asked, indicating the flowers.

"Di!" DJ grinned, pleased to see the older woman. "I forgot Randa told me you were coming in today."

"Evidently." Diane walked further into the room and placed the flowers upon the bottom end of the bed. Randa backed away from DJ as Diane placed one arm carefully around the poet and hugged her cautiously. "How are you feeling, honey?"

"Okay."

Randa walked over to the door and picked up the overnight bag she had placed there. She set it upon the bed and slid open the zip.

Still sitting upon the side of her bed Denise peeped inside the bag. "What have you got there? Any presents?" She wiggled her eyebrows hopefully.

"Maybe." Randa dipped her hands into the holdall. First she pulled out some clothing. "Some sweat pants… so you don't have to wear just that thing anymore!" Randa placed the garment on the bed and dove back into the bag. She took out a long box. "Sara's hair scissors. I didn't think I could trust myself cutting your hair so Diane said she would neaten it for you. She took a professional course!" Randa said impressed.

DJ frowned as she turned back to the older woman. "You used to cut men's hair!"

Diane rolled her eyes. "Don't worry, honey. I'll stay away from crew cuts. I'm not planning anything drastic. I'll just neaten it up. I do know how to style hair. How about a 'shortish' Meg Ryan style?"

"As long as you're not thinking of a Yul Brenner style, I think I'll consider it!"

"Right." Randa's hands disappeared inside the bag once again. "Most importantly I thought that because you had your own room with that TV/VCR combo, I would bring in something for us to watch." Randa held up a single black cassette tape. "It's the recording of your interview on 'The Open Book'."

"Great!" Denise smiled at Randa.

Looking between the women, Diane crossed the room, deciding to give them a few extra moments of privacy. She picked up the flowers and headed towards the door. "I'm going to get a vase and put these in some water."

"Thank you, Di." DJ looked at the floral assortment. "They are lovely."

The older woman smiled and left the room.

Alone once again Denise looked silently at Randa. The blonde nurse was looking down at the red and blue sweatpants that she was refolding neatly. DJ's concerns of the day before returned to mind and an air of nervousness fluttered around her.

DJ didn't know whether she wanted Randa to mention her proposal or not. It certainly hadn't turned out the way she had planned. The quiet evening with a picnic under the stars was very different from lying injured in a hospital bed. She was pretty sure that if Sara knew of her plans she would have given Denise her usual speech on the forgotten art of chivalry. Deciding she needed to talk with her lover, Denise rose slowly to her feet.

"Hey, are you okay? Randa asked as she stepped around the bed.

"Uh huh. The nurse told me today I should try walking. I'm glad to get out of bed." Denise walked slowly towards Randa, feeling her abused and stiff body protest the movements. "Randa?"

"Hmm?"

The poet took a breath of courage. "About... I was... well I..." she sighed and realised she was unable to broach the subject. The words refused to come. Whether it was nervousness or outright fear, Denise found she couldn't discuss her proposal. *Maybe I just need to concentrate on my health,* she thought.

Randa frowned and asked, "What is it?"

DJ decided to change the subject. "I just wanted to tell you that I've missed you. It's not much fun in here... especially at night."

"Tell me about it."

With a small nod Denise looked down at her feet. "I'm scared," she whispered.

"Pardon?" Randa stepped closer.

"I said I'm scared." Denise looked up at Randa. In her partner's eyes she saw only love and understanding. "I feel like parts of myself are rebelling against me and I have no control over my own body. I don't know what is going to happen to me. That feeling of the unknown... it's scaring the hell out of me, Randa." A lump rose in DJ's throat as tears clouded her eyes. She had tried so hard to keep calm and confident but the actuality of her possible future hung before her like an unwanted destiny. "I don't think I can cope."

"You can." Randa wrapped her arm around the uninjured side of Denise. "I'm here. Whatever happens we will face it together, Denise." She wiped a tear from DJ's cheek.

Denise sniffed and sighed. Her eyes shone with tears. "I feel so helpless." She looked down into misty green. Unable to speak, Denise pulled Randa closer and placed her cheek upon Randa's head.

"I love you," she heard Randa whisper.

Touching the blonde, feeling her body against her own made Denise feel calm. The poet closed her eyes with a feeling that her physical contact with Randa was like touching her very own anchor. She realised again how much she not only loved but needed Randa. The thought did scare her. Without the acknowledgement of her proposal from Randa, DJ was uncertain of where she stood. It was not that she doubted Randa's love for that was unquestioned. What bothered her was the simple fact that Randa had made no mention of what she felt was greatly important to her and she was scared of the reason why.

Feeling another tear escape her eye, DJ prayed for the strength she would need to face her uncertainty. She remembered Carl's words and reminded herself to have faith in her love and trust of Randa. That alone would pull her through.

247

Chapter 20

Randa woke with a start, her heart beating fast and an uneasy feeling in her stomach. She cut her eyes to the illuminated alarm clock and was dismayed to see it was only five thirty in the morning. She peered around in confusion, unable to determine what had woken her up. She didn't think she'd had a nightmare or that there was a problem in the house.

What the hell is going on with me? She thought as she flipped the covers back in disgust. Pushing her hair back from her forehead, she ambled over to the window where the eastern horizon was just starting to add lighter hues to the night sky. *Unless I'm up working I don't even want to see this time of morning.* She couldn't shake the feeling that something was wrong.

This was the third morning following Denise's accident. She'd made a lot of progress and her diet had been advanced to soft foods. Randa had walked with Denise in the hall and convinced the brunette to take a little more pain medicine to make movement more comfortable. Finally the poet's IV had been discontinued leaving only a capped needle in her arm for the still needed antibiotics. Randa talked the staff into letting her give Denise her sponge bath and provided the poet enough attention that she was purring in relaxation when it was finished.

In the afternoon Dr. Merritt had visited and said one way or another they would have some idea what Denise's kidney status would be in twenty-four hours. The previous day's lab tests were progressively worse and the doctor had a specialist on call to implant a temporary dialysis catheter in the poet's chest if the need arose. He had stressed that he was giving Denise's kidneys another day to kick in but after that they wouldn't have any choice but to start the dialysis. Denise had been unusually quiet the rest of the day and it was with reluctance that Randa left the hospital that evening when visiting hours were over.

Thinking about the visit yesterday made Randa realize what it was that had been bothering her this morning. *Denise! Denise needs me.* It was suddenly crystal clear to her and she hurried to the bathroom to splash water on her face and brush her teeth. More awake now she returned to the bedroom and threw on clean Levi's and a light cotton shirt. She went downstairs and phoned for a taxi as she scribbled a note for Diane. She knew she couldn't wait for Diane to give her a ride to the hospital on this morning.

In the few minutes she knew she would have before the taxi's arrival, she made herself a quick cup of tea and reached into the refrigerator and pulled out a little of the leftovers from last night's hastily thrown together supper. *Night worker...any food, any time.* She silently thanked her durable stomach for putting up with the abuse she had been heaping on it in the last day or so. Finishing her tea she went to the front door and attached the note for Diane. She locked the door and stood on the front steps, willing the taxi to hurry along.

****

Randa entered the hospital through the main entrance. It was much quieter than the entrance to the Emergency Room that she had entered through just two evenings before. Walking up to the main desk she told the security person she was there to see Denise Jennings and gave her room number.

"It's well before visiting hours, miss," the guard informed her. He looked annoyed at the interruption of his enjoyment of a cup of tea and a newspaper open to coverage of English rugby.

"I understand that but if you could just call the floor she's on, I mean ward," Randa instructed, remembering her British terminology, "I'm sure the nurse will let me see her."

The guard stared at her for a minute then realizing he wouldn't be getting rid of her so easily, picked up the phone and tapped in four numbers. "Ward Sister, please," he requested. Randa felt impatience rising but was determined to stay civil to the man.

"Is that the Ward Sister?" the guard was saying in an official tone. "There is a visitor here for a Denise Jennings. I've told her visiting hours are…" He stopped abruptly and listened. Looking up at the blonde he asked, "Would you be Miranda Martin?"

"Yes, that's me."

The guard spoke in a hushed tone into the telephone then hung up. "You can go right up, Miss. Take the elevators over there to the third floor and go left to the nurse's station."

"Thank you," Randa said and moved toward the bank of elevators the guard had indicated. She had been ready to try and find a way to sneak in to see Denise and was surprised at the fact that she was being allowed in without a problem.

The elevator doors opened on the third floor and a sign directed her to the nurse's station where a matronly woman with gray hair met her.

"I'm the Assistant Ward Sister, Miss Martin. Miss Jennings' room is straight down this corridor, the fourth door on the right." Randa thanked the older woman and started down the corridor, but stopped after a step. Turning back she approached the nurse.

"Uhm, Sister?" she said attracting the older woman's attention from the chart she had opened. Friendly hazel eyes looked up at her in question. "Can I ask you something? Why did you let me come up here early? I know it's way before visiting hours so why did you make an exception for me?"

"I'm not sure I know what you mean. Miss Jennings told us you were her family and she needs her family right now. She also told us you were a nurse so I'm sure you know what bending the rules means."

Randa nodded thoughtfully remembering the many times she had bent the rules for family, friends and lovers. She had even allowed one man to sneak a beloved pet ferret into his wife's hospital room. She smiled at her British counterpart. "Yeah, I guess I do know about that."

Randa moved back down the hall and toward Denise's room. As she was entering, a phlebotomist who was leaving the room gently tipping a green-topped lab tube back and forth in her hand met her. Randa watched the tube be slipped into a wire cage holder as the blood drawer moved on to the next room. The nurse couldn't help but think that so much information about the future that she and Denise were going to have was held in that seven-milliliter container.

Pulling her eyes away from the retreating form of the phlebotomist, Randa entered the room. Her partner was sitting up in a recliner facing the window, a pensive look on her face. Her new haircut beautifully framed her features but the calm façade couldn't hide the fact that Denise was brooding. The face she knew and loved so well didn't hide many secrets from her now. Randa's heart ached for her partner.

You want answers, don't you? The blood they just drew might give us some answers but what if they aren't the ones you want? Randa stopped in her tracks, her jaw dropping. *You idiot! Answers! Denise wants answers! Could you have messed this up any more than you have?* The blonde smacked her hand to her forehead in irritation at herself. DJ turned at the sound, bringing those intense blue eyes to bear on the nurse.

"Randa, what are you doing here at this time?" Denise asked rising slowly and awkwardly from the chair.

"Don't be coy with me, Denise Jennings. You knew I'd be here. Isn't that why you gave my name to the Ward Sister?"

Denise grinned. "I suppose I hoped you'd get here early. I miss having breakfast with you especially now that I can have breakfast again." She dropped a quick kiss onto the nurse's lips. "We have a little while before the trays are due to arrive. Sit with me?"

"Of course," Randa replied. They moved to the bed and sat together watching the sun slowly start to peep over the hills surrounding the town. Randa reached over and took Denise's hand in hers, lacing their fingers together. They watched the scene unfold through the window for a moment, neither feeling the need to speak. Randa screwed up her courage and turned a little on the bed until she was looking directly at her partner but keeping the poet's hand firmly in her own.

"Denise, I think I owe you an apology. I've been awfully rude to you."

The poet's brows knit together in confusion. "You've been rude?"

"Yep, my mother always taught me that if you're asked a question, it's rude not to answer. The other day you, in your own most beautiful way, asked me a question."

Denise looked down and said, "Randa, you don't have to..."

"Yes, I do," the nurse interrupted. "Look at me, Denise." She waited until the poet raised her eyes. "I thought by not answering your question I was keeping you from having to deal with even more than you already were going through. I thought I was protecting you, but I thought wrong. I want there to be no doubt between us, now or ever, so if you will allow me, I'd like to do it right this time. Will you ask me again, please?"

Denise looked into sincere green eyes and saw the love shining there. It was love that would see them through any problems they would have. "Randa Martin," the poet whispered, "will you marry me?"

Randa smiled at her partner. "Denise, before I met you I had no idea how much was missing from my life. From the moment I read your work to the moment we spoke online to the moment we met face to face to the moment we first made love I found out what those missing things were. You have made me feel happy, safe and loved. I love you, Denise Jennings, and it would be the greatest joy in my life to marry you and spend the rest of our lives together."

Denise looked as if she wanted to say something but instead she leaned forward and shared a deep kiss of commitment with the nurse. When the kiss ended Randa moved closer and held the poet in a comforting embrace.

"Denise?"

"Hmm?" the poet replied, relishing the feel of the blonde's arms.

"I know you wanted to ask, but you didn't so I'll just tell you. Yes, I'll marry you no matter what we find out today. We're in this together, always."

Denise had no reply to that, only nodding and squeezing her good arm around Randa a little tighter.

****

Several hours later Randa and Denise were watching "Antiques Roadshow" on the BBC. As the show ended Denise turned to her partner.

"Did you see that little porcelain figurine of a Japanese woman with an umbrella they said was worth two thousand pounds?" At Randa's nod, the poet continued, "Well, there was one just like it in Sara's bits and bobs box."

Randa thought for a second, and then said, "You're right! What do you know about that? I guess we'll have to get the box back out of the attic now. Two thousand pounds, that's about thirty five hundred dollars. That's a tidy sum."

"You know, I'm not that fond of little porcelain figurines. What would you think if I sold that piece and maybe match whatever it would get with my money to create a fund for ALS research and treatment in Sara's name?"

Randa nodded. "I think Sara would be very proud to have that done in her name and I'm very proud of you for thinking of it."

"I had been thinking about doing some kind of funding or donation for a while but I'd put it off when all the controversy around Sara cropped up. I didn't want any negative publicity to offset the good it will do, but I think maybe now it's time to get things started. I also thought maybe I could donate my profit from Sara's book to the fund as well."

Randa was set to reply but the door to the room opened and Dr, Merritt walked into the room with Denise's chart in his hand. Both women tensed visibly as he opened the chart and made a brief note before looking up.

"How would you like to go home tomorrow?" he said with a smile. "I think if your lab tests tonight and tomorrow morning continue to show the kind of improvement that they showed this morning, it should be fine for you to be discharged."

Randa let out a whoop and jumped from the chair to hug Denise who didn't say much except a whispered "Thank God." Randa moved to hug the doctor who blushed deeply at the gesture.

"I'm very happy to bring this kind of news to my patients. My congratulations to you both."

Denise did speak then. "Speaking of congratulations doctor, how would you like to come to a wedding?"

****

It was the early evening. Visiting hours were just about to begin. Denise stood at the entrance to her room peeking out of a gap in the door. Blue eyes scanned the corridor as keen ears listened carefully. With a furrowed brow DJ turned to Randa who was sitting on the bed shaking her head.

"No sign yet," the poet said. She looked back through the gap in the door. "She always comes down at this time to be ready for the evening visitors. I saw her yesterday and I'll be dammed if I'm going to miss her today."

Hearing the bed creak DJ turned to see Randa approach her. The nurse arched her eyebrows, still shaking her head as she chuckled. "You are just too much. I didn't realise I was committing my life to a stalker."

DJ rolled her eyes as she whispered, "I'm not stalking. I'm just waiting with enthusiasm."

Peering over Denise's shoulder Randa looked out towards the corridor. The first couple of visitors were beginning to migrate onto the floor.

"Damn it," DJ cursed. "Now the vultures are beginning to arrive." She turned around to Randa and addressed her seriously. "Okay this is the plan." Denise handed the contents of her left hand to Randa. "You will have to do this as you're more mobile than I am."

"Plus I have two good elbows for nudging!" Randa joked.

Denise grinned. "Exactly... but let's hope it will not come to that."

"You're serious, aren't you?"

"Too right I am." Denise heard the tell tale sounds of squeaking wheels and looked once again out into the corridor. "Okay I heard that she only carries one or two of them but they do go quickly so you will have to make haste." Denise pulled the door fully open.

With a salute Randa headed out into the corridor and disappeared around a corner leaving only the sound of retreating chuckles as she embarked upon her mission.

Finding herself alone Denise walked over to the window and looked out across the main entrance of the hospital. She watched with interest as an ambulance pulled rapidly in front of the emergency doors. Its siren died as two paramedics dressed in green overalls jumped out of the vehicle. A doctor dressed in a white overcoat walked out as the paramedics wheeled a patient out of the ambulance. *That was probably me*, DJ thought, realising she was witnessing a similar scene to how she was probably brought to the hospital. A shiver passed through her at the notion and Denise realised how lucky she and been. So many road accidents ended in death each year and if the driver of the car that hit her was going any faster she was sure she would have been part of that statistic. *I could have missed out on so much*, she thought. *I could have left behind so much.* Staring aimlessly out of the window Denise trembled as the shock chilled her.

Minutes later familiar footsteps walked into the room. "Well, guess what?" Randa said. When no response was forthcoming the nurse placed down the contents of the small plastic bag in her right hand and walked towards Denise.

"Hey?"

The poet was pulled from her daze by a gentle hand upon her shoulder. Shaking her head from morbid thoughts, Denise turned to Randa. Her expression held startled confusion.

"Denise?"

"I did come close, didn't I?"

"Close?"

"To missing out on life with you." DJ took Randa's hand. "It's a terrifying thought, Randa. I don't want to miss out on one second with you."

"You won't," Randa assured her.

"I don't plan to." Looking down at the ring upon Randa's finger, Denise twisted the silver band around her slender digit. "You know, things could have been so much worse. I feel so lucky that I've had this second chance with you. I'm not going to waste a moment of it. That's why I've had an idea."

"Really?"

Nodding her head affirmatively, Denise smiled. "But it's a surprise. I'm not telling you yet."

Randa poked out her bottom lip. She fluttered her eyebrows in hope but DJ shook her head.

"No clues?"

"Not yet."

With a sigh Randa wrapped her free arm around Denise. "Lucky I'm patient **and** I trust you!" Reaching up onto her toes, Randa kissed DJ softly. "So... guess what I got?"

Blue eyes lit up immediately. "Oh don't tease me."

Randa grinned as she disengaged from Denise and walked back over to the poet's bed. She lifted the plastic bag and turned back to DJ. "You were right; she only had one." Randa dipped her hand inside the red bag. "So..." her hand rose slowly out of the carrier. "The only dark chocolate, mint crisp bar of chocolate, ma'am." Randa presented the chocolate bar to Denise.

"Oh yes!" With a rakish grin Denise said, "I knew if we got there first we would get it." She attempted to take the chocolate from Randa but the blonde pulled her hand away.

"Oh no!" Using her index finger Randa pushed Denise back to sit upon her bed. Sliding the shiny wrapped chocolate from its paper wrapper, Randa began to peel off the green foil wrapping. "Surely you're not going to deny me the enjoyment of this..." Breaking one square off the bar Randa held it against DJ's lips.

"Hmm!" Denise accepted the chocolate blissfully. "Mint chocolate... my favourite." She took Randa's fingers and sucked the melted substance from her warm digits.

Skin flushing, Randa broke a second piece and held it out to Denise. "Want more?"

"Oh yes."

Randa waved the chocolate back and forth before she swept her tongue over the warm candy. "Tell me your surprise."

"Man, that is below the belt," Denise said in shock. Taking the blonde's hand swiftly she pulled the warm chocolate toward her lips. With a hidden smile she bypassed the chocolate and planted her lips upon the inside of Randa's wrist. Kissing the soft skin Denise mumbled, "Besides there's so much more tastier delights to me than chocolate."

Randa whimpered as soft lips travelled up the inside of her arm. "It really isn't a good idea to start this now," she warned.

"I didn't start it... you did." Denise moved her lips to Randa's neck where she planted a trail of moist, soft kisses upon heated skin. The kisses stopped abruptly as a knock sounded upon the door. DJ groaned and pulled away as Randa moved to pull open the door. From behind the blonde DJ was unable to see who it was, but Randa's surprised remark gave her a pretty good idea.

"You've got some nerve!"

Getting up from the bed, Denise looked beyond Randa to see Maggie standing awkwardly by the entrance. Genuine surprise filled her. She had constantly wondered if and when she would see her cousin again but never considered the possibility that Maggie may turn up at the hospital... and she wondered why now. Of course it was

257

possible but she thought there would have been some warning before hand.

DJ hadn't spoken to Randa about the nurse's feeling towards Maggie. Seeing how much Randa blamed Maggie for her accident, the poet hadn't wanted to broach the subject until the situation had calmed somewhat. Being as though Doctor Merritt was very confident in her full recovery, Denise saw this as the perfect time to hopefully strengthen some fragile family ties. She hoped the fact that Maggie showed up was a sign that her cousin wanted the same reunion.

Placing her hand upon Randa's shoulder Denise felt the tense muscles underneath her palm. She squeezed her partner's shoulder gently before addressing her cousin.

"Maggie, this is a surprise." DJ smiled cautiously. "I... we weren't expecting you."

Nervous eyes wandered around the room before Maggie looked back at Denise. The poet noticed her cousin had yet to make real eye contact with fuming green. "May I come in?"

Denise looked down at Randa who portrayed a typical defiant posture. Her arms were folded and she stood directly in front of her lover in a protective manner. Wrapping her arm around Randa, Denise took a gentle hold of Randa's hand and held the blonde against her body as she moved backwards. "Of course you can."

Randa said nothing but her posture remained tense as Maggie stepped into the room. She closed the door behind her and looked back at the two women cautiously.

"I'm sorry," she said quietly.

"Sorry?" Randa repeated.

"Yes... I'm sorry. I never ... would ever want anything like this to happen." Tears filled Maggie's blue eyes. "It's all my fault."

"You've got that right." Randa stared furiously at the redhead.

"Okay... that's it." Denise stood between her partner and her cousin. "It was nobody's fault. It was an accident."

Randa's eyes blazed with anger. "You nearly died, Denise. All because she overreacted."

258

"I didn't overreact," Maggie stated fiercely. "I was shocked and scared. How was I supposed to feel about the information you had just given me?"

"Like an adult perhaps!"

Denise sat down feeling tired and exasperated. Looking between the two women she said, "Alright, that's enough now." She sighed. "All this anger and hate. It's all down to fear. Fear of what may have happened and of what may happen. Fear of what we may lose and what could be lost. If we had any real choice over all this then life would be a lot different and easier... but we don't. Things happen... beyond our control... it was an accident." DJ looked towards Randa and held out a hand that was immediately taken by her partner. Denise looked beseechingly into deep green eyes. "Let's not let negativity win. Please?"

Closing her eyes Randa sighed. She cupped DJ's face with both hands and looked back at her saying, "You're right. I was so scared that I might have lost you that I couldn't see past that fear where Maggie was concerned." An emotional battle seemed to war within the blonde's eyes before Randa kissed Denise softly and turned to face Maggie. Still holding DJ's hand, Randa spoke to Maggie. "I'm sorry for the way I spoke to you, Maggie. The thought of losing Denise was just... it was too much for me to deal with."

Maggie nodded. "I do understand. I'm sure I would have reacted the same way if I were in your shoes. But I really do regret the way I behaved. I suppose I just needed time to think."

"And you've had that time now?" DJ asked.

"Sort of." Maggie walked over to one of the comfortable chairs beside DJ's bed and sat down. "Actually I received a telephone call from Diane Barlow."

"You did?" DJ and Randa asked in unison.

The redhead smiled and then nodded. "We had a long talk and she made me see things a lot clearer."

"She did?" they said together again.

Maggie fiddled nervously with the edge of her suit jacket. "She um... she also told me about your kidneys failing and I want you to know that I'm here if you need a donor. No matter the circumstances, we are family and I'd like to help you in any way I can." Maggie paused to study DJ's stunned features before saying, "I had a long talk with Simon. He believes that if I feel it is the right thing to do then I am here to help... if our types match that is. There should be a greater possibility of a match because we're related, right?"

Denise looked up into Randa's smiling eyes briefly before looking back to Maggie. "That is wonderful of you to offer Maggie and I thank you so much but it really isn't necessary anymore." With the redhead's confused expression DJ elaborated further. "We got some good news today; my kidneys are functioning again and I'm going to be fine."

"You are?" Maggie rose from her chair. "Why that's wonderful news."

DJ nodded with a wide smile. "Basically it means I get to leave here tomorrow and go home." The thought of returning to her comfort and privacy with Randa filled Denise with much joy. Ever since Doctor Merritt had informed them both of the news she couldn't wait for the time to arrive. During the short time she had known the doctor both she and Randa had grown to like him immensely. They got on very well together and she was very pleased that he had accepted her invitation but one thought did occur to her, *I really should find out his first name!*

Coming out of her thoughts Denise watched Randa sit down beside her. Their hands laced together as Denise addressed Maggie. "So is the air cleared?"

"Almost," Maggie replied. "There is something else I would like to discuss first."

Randa squeezed DJ's hand as she said, "The ALS."

Maggie nodded. "I was wrong to feel like I should lay the blame upon Sara... my biological mother. I do realise that now."

Running a hand through her shorter styled hair, the poet looked out beyond the window. She saw a flock of birds fly swiftly by. "It's hard. I understand how you feel because I feel it too. That doubt lingering in the back of your mind. What if? If only. Why? The desire for things to be so much different; yet at the same time, not wanting to change a moment of it."

Looking away Maggie said, "I didn't know how I could ever deal with such a notion and then I realised... with a little help from Diane. I just have to accept this. It's not an inevitable certainty. There is nothing I can do or say that will change what is meant to be. And I am not the only one in this position."

Denise wrapped her one good arm around Randa's shoulders. "The lucky thing for both of us is that we don't have to face this possibility alone. Whether this were to happen or not, Simon will always be there for you... right?"

Maggie nodded.

"And I'll **always** be here for you," Randa said. She laid her head upon DJ's shoulder.

Turning, Denise kissed blonde locks. "I'd say we were both pretty lucky. I think together... as a family we can deal with anything." The prospect of gaining more family members filled the poet with hope and happiness. She suddenly felt like their lives were falling into place. Although there would always be the possibility that either she or Maggie could one day also develop ALS, DJ knew that was something they couldn't let dominate their lives. If they did there would be no living.

"So," DJ rose slowly and faced Maggie who did the same. "No regrets; no more apologies. A fresh start?"

The request was accepted with a relieved smile. "I suppose there is nothing left to say but welcome to the family!"

Beaming, DJ put her arm around her cousin who mirrored the gesture. "Ditto." She heard Randa rise behind her and moved away from Maggie. Denise watched both women study each other cautiously before a smile broke out on both faces. They moved to shake hands, but thought better of it as both women hugged much to DJ's relief.

Withdrawing first, Randa addressed Maggie happily. "I guess because Denise got the honour the first time I'd like to be the one to invite you and your family to a marriage... a joining ceremony!"

Maggie's eyes switched between the two women. "You mean...?"

Denise grinned.

"Goodness gracious. This is a surprise." Maggie hugged her cousin again. "That would be wonderful. Thank you, and congratulations." Pulling back, Maggie asked, "So who did the proposing?"

"That would be me..."

"In her own unique way," Randa added.

DJ shrugged. "Why be traditional or predictably boring, right?"

Maggie laughed at that. "I say exactly the same thing when my husband makes comments about the fact that I seem to dress after I open the bedroom curtains. Or I'm embarrassed to say when I eat certain foods with my fingers!"

"My god!" Randa exclaimed. "You two really are related. If there was ever any doubt that just confirms it." The nurse inclined her head towards DJ. "She does exactly the same thing."

"Great minds think alike," DJ said to Maggie.

"Precisely."

With a faux expression of alarm Randa said, "What have I let myself in for?"

Denise wrapped her arm around Randa's waist. "Too late now, honey, I've got you!"

"Wouldn't have it any other way," the nurse replied.

"Me either."

No matter what the future may hold, Denise knew with Randa she would look forward to it with nothing short of excitement. For a long time the poet never thought her life would be anything to look forward to. That wasn't to say that she was unhappy, she was just content in the life of anonymity that she lived. From the moment she met Randa, DJ felt life blossom within her and she wanted to experience

262

the world. To sample the delights she had only written about and stretch her vitality to its ultimate endurance. To Denise – Randa simply was life.

****

The next day DJ sat patiently upon her bed. Dressed in her everyday clothes she was perched upon the side of the bed beside her packed overnight bag. Today was the day she would be able to return home and the poet had awoken early in anticipation. She had dressed and packed her bag knowing Randa and Diane would arrive to pick her up by eleven o'clock. It was half past ten but DJ's impatient nature and excitement had taken over.

A knock captured Denise's attention. She turned to see the smiling face of Doctor Merritt peeking through the doorway.

"Somebody looks eager to go! Why is it that all my patients are so quick to want to leave me? Is it my bedside manner?"

"Your bedside manner is fine," Denise replied. "I would just rather be the recipient of a certain other person's bedside manner. No offence."

Doctor Merritt laughed as he entered her room. "None taken." Under his arm he held a dark blue, plastic clipboard and he held it out in front of him. "I have a couple of forms for you to sign before you leave." He handed the clipboard to Denise who placed it upon the bed. "Just sign the bottom of both forms." He gave DJ his pen and watched as she signed the first sheet of paper. Then he lifted the top form so she could sign the bottom. "Good job you are left handed!"

"You're telling me!" Completing her second signature Denise held the pen out to the doctor. "Is that all?"

"Well…" the man hesitated as he moved his hand to his back pocket. "Almost."

Denise watched in amusement as Doctor Merritt pulled a book from his back pocket. She instantly recognised it as one of her own.

"My mother's a fan! I know it was unprofessional of me to ask when you were under my care but now... well I was wondering whether you would sign this for her. It will be a surprise."

"Of course." Denise chuckled as the doctor placed down the book and held it steady with the front page open. With only one arm DJ would be limited in movement for quite some time. "I was wondering anyway... what is your first name?"

"It's Ezekiel."

"Pardon?"

He smiled. "Most people call me Zeke."

"I think I'll be one of those people as well!" Denise signed the book for Zeke's mother and handed the pen back to the doctor. "You'll have to come around for dinner some time. I'm pretty sure between Randa and myself we can cook up something edible. Failing that we can always order takeout."

"Oh!" Zeke's face brightened. "I'm quite partial to Mexican."

The poet rolled her eyes. "I see you and Randa will get on like a house on fire."

"Ah and speaking of the blonde blushing bride... have you set a date yet?"

"Not yet." DJ frowned in thought. Not only did they have the date to set but she also had to make plans for Randa's surprise. She wanted to take the nurse on surprise holiday for their honeymoon. "I think we are kind of planning something in the autumn. We could do it around my birthday or the day we met. It's something we can discuss when Randa and I get home."

"What are we discussing when we get home?" Randa asked as she entered DJ's room.

The poet's face lit up as she took her partner's hand. "How much you love me."

"Like there's any question." Randa kissed Denise. "So are you ready to go? Diane is waiting in the car."

"I think she went to bed dressed and ready to leave last night," said Zeke.

Denise chuckled as she addressed the doctor. "Is there anything else?"

"Nope." Doctor Merritt tucked the clipboard back under his arm. "Just be careful and take care of yourself. I am sure Randa will do a fine job of that. In the mean time... I suppose I shall see you both soon. Have a safe journey home."

"Oh we will." Denise followed Randa to the door happily. After so much upheaval she was glad to be going home. *I wonder how much fooling around one can do with only one good arm,* DJ thought lasciviously as she and Randa left the hospital.

Chapter 21

"Don't cry," Randa pleaded. "There's nothing to cry about."

"I'm your mother, it's your wedding and I'll cry if I want to. It's a mother's prerogative," Janice Martin sniffed. "You look beautiful, Miranda."

Randa felt beautiful in her dress of sea foam green that reached to just above her knees. The color complimented her eyes and the style flattered her figure. She looked in the mirror of the upstairs bedroom with a degree of satisfaction. *Heh! The cleavage on this thing ought to cause Denise's eyes to pop right out of her head.*

Denise. Randa sourly thought about her fiancée and the issue of clothing. In the two months they had been planning the wedding as Denise recuperated from her injuries, it had been the only bone of contention between them. The poet had steadfastly refused to wear a dress, opting instead for either an elegant tuxedo or a simple black pantsuit with a frilly white shirt. No amount of pleading or persuasion had been able to change her mind.

"The last time I wore a dress was exactly that, the last time I wore a dress. Randa, be reasonable, I want to be comfortable when I marry you. I'll be nervous enough with our family and friends here all watching us. At least you can let me wear what I want," Denise had begged. The plaintive look in those blue eyes was enough to make Randa give in but she wasn't happy about it.

That one detail won't spoil this day though, the nurse thought. *Nothing can spoil it.* The mid-September day was warm and clear and they had been able to stick with their first plan, which was to be married by Sara's rose garden. The summer had lengthened and the roses seemingly were giving the pair a last flash of brilliant color as a wedding gift. Chairs were already set up for the guests and a small canopy was set up for the couple and Father Brian, the priest from St, Bartholomew's, the church Sara had attended. Randa liked the vicar and it showed because they were having him hold their rings. She wouldn't trust them to just anyone. The couple had visited the jeweller Denise had used previously and they now had matching silver and Blue John rings. Randa touched the empty ring finger on her left hand. *It'll never be off again after today.*

"Randa? Randa, it's almost time." Janice Martin's words roused her daughter from her thoughts. The nurse turned to smile at her mother.

"I'm so glad you're here, Mom. It wouldn't be the same without you or Derek with me."

"Like I had a choice. DJ sends two first class tickets to England and has a limo drive us from the airport. She's a hard person to say 'no' to, even if I had wanted to which I didn't. I wouldn't have missed this for all the world." Janice's voice took on a wistful tone. "I only wish your dad could have been here." Randa's father had passed away almost three years earlier.

"Do you think he would have been happy about this? I hadn't been dating women very long before he died to really know what he thought about it."

Janice placed her hands on Randa's shoulders and looked directly into her eyes. "Your father loved you very much and I think he would have admired DJ and respected your choice. I suppose what I'm saying is that if you're happy, he would have been happy. Happy and proud, just like me." Randa's eyes misted as she reached forward and hugged her mother fiercely.

"Hey now, don't get that gorgeous dress all wrinkled. And don't cry. You know a wise young woman once said there's nothing to cry about." Randa gave a small laugh and craned her neck to see the watch on her mother's wrist.

Go ahead and go downstairs, Mom. We only have a few minutes and I just need one or two alone to get myself together."

"Okay, I guess it won't do for the mother of the…of **one** of the brides," Janice corrected, "to be late." With a last quick hug, Janice headed for the door. Reaching for the knob, she turned back one last time.

"I love you, Randa. Be happy."

"I am, Mom," the nurse assured her. "See you downstairs."

Janice left the room and Randa turned to the mirror. A calm, happy and confident woman looked back at her, but that exterior hid about a million butterflies in her stomach. *I wonder how Denise is holding up?*

****

Denise was downstairs in Sara's old room speaking into the telephone. Last minute confirmations for flights and accommodations had to be made. The surprises needed the finishing touches and the poet's concentration was broken only when a special knock was tapped out on the door.

"Michele!" Denise exclaimed as she threw open the door. "You made it!"

"The entire British Navy couldn't keep me away from this little party. It's not everyday you see your best childhood friend get married." Michelle had been Denise's friend since she came with Sara to live in Bakewell. Neither of them had known of the feelings between Michelle's mother, Diane, and Sara until much later.

"I can't believe you still remember our secret knock. How long is your leave?" DJ asked. Michelle had enlisted in the Navy just over six years before and was very happy with her choice of profession.

"Forty-eight hours. Just enough time to get here, watch a miracle occur and get back to the ship."

"A miracle? That's a bit strong don't you think?" the poet said, mock annoyance in her voice.

"DJ, you never had any inclination to settle down with anybody. I always pictured you being the reclusive poet, mysterious and solitary with your work being your one true

268

love."

Denise laughed at that. "Things change I suppose. A year ago I couldn't have predicted this, couldn't have predicted Randa."

"You're sure of this then? You're really in the 'forever and ever' kind of love?"

DJ's eyes were shining with certainty. "Completely and utterly."

Michelle smiled at her friend. "I knew it the moment I saw you, I just wanted to make you say it before I gave up my revered status as best friend."

"Give it up? Michelle, I…"

"Don't need to say another word," Michelle interrupted, raising her hands to her friend. "You love her and she's your best friend now. That's just as it should be. I wouldn't step aside for anything less for you. I hope she knows what a great bargain she's getting in you."

"I tell her all the time," Denise said.

It was Michelle's turn to laugh. "I better get outside. My friend is getting married soon you know. Uhm, DJ, you aren't planning to get married in that are you?" She pointed to the jeans and tee shirt Denise was still dressed in.

The poet looked down. "Bloody hell! I've got to hurry. Get out of here now and I'll talk to you later."

Michelle left the room laughing as Denise realized frantically how little time she was going to have to get ready. Moving to the bed she reached underneath a pulled out a large white box and set it on top. Looking at the box, she seemed to come to a decision, nodded and removed the lid.

****

Randa watched from the upstairs bedroom window. The gathering of family and close friends was modest as the guests assembled at the entrance to the rose garden. Janice Martin settled into a chair near Diane and the two started chatting quietly. Maggie and Simon arrived with their two children, Roman and Kelsey. Greeting them were Carl and Chris. The nurse saw Michelle walk up to her mother and give her a quick hug over the shoulders before taking a chair behind her.

Derek stood behind the seated guests conversing with Zeke Merritt. The nurse noted how they laughed, smiled and leaned into each other. *So that's the way the wind blows? You go, Derek.* Randa saw Father Brian move to the canopied area and that was her cue to head downstairs. She would leave the house by way of the front door, go around and meet Denise who would come out of the back door and together they would walk to the rose garden. The blonde thought it was quaint that Denise insisted they not see each other before the wedding.

"Seeing one bride before the wedding is bad enough. Can you imagine the amount of bad luck we would have if we saw **two** brides?" Denise asked. Randa laughed but humoured her partner. She didn't laugh during the night though when she tossed and turned, missing the warmth and comfort of the poet's body next to her.

Randa pinned a small corsage of joined red and white roses to her dress. Denise would wear one exactly like it. *To pin to her suit or tuxedo or whatever she finally decided on* the nurse thought as she moved out of the bedroom, across the landing and down the stairs. *Well at least she's finally out of that cast.* She went to the door of Sara's room and knocked softly.

"Denise? It's time," she said in a soft voice.

"I'll be there in two minutes," came the slightly muffled voice behind the door. Sounds of activity made Randa smile. *I'd be willing to bet she got sidetracked and is just now getting dressed.* It was her wedding day though and she wouldn't tease the poet about it. Instead she knocked softly again.

"Denise? I just wanted to say in my last moments as a single woman that I love you very much and I'm so glad to be marrying you today."

Activity ceased behind the door and poet replied, "I love you too, Randa, more than I could ever say. I'll meet you outside."

Randa smiled at the words and walked to the front door. Strange she thought, now that I'm actually doing this

I'm not nervous anymore. This is my destiny and I'm ready for it. Exiting the house, Randa felt her heart soar a little higher with every step.

Taking enough time to make sure Denise could get to the back door, Randa came around the house to see the guests waiting. Smiles were everywhere and the nurse could almost feel the love and support flowing from them. A movement from the house caught her eye and the back door opened slowly as she approached.

Denise stepped out and down to the ground to meet her partner, but Randa had stopped dead in her tracks. The nurse's mouth dropped open a little as she saw the poet emerge in a dress similar in style to her own and in a color the closest to the lovely blue of her eyes as man could devise. As beautiful as Randa had always found her, there was no comparison to today. Denise was radiant. Her dark hair, now grown to the nape of her neck, was shining in the autumn sunlight. The guests seemed to be as surprised and impressed as she was.

She wore a dress Randa realized. *She did it for me.* It was only then the nurse noticed Denise's hand extended to her. Shaking herself, she walked to the poet and took the offered hand.

"You are stunning, love," Randa murmured. "Thank you for doing this. Was this the surprise you were hiding from me?"

Denise bestowed a loving smile on the blonde. "I just thought the pictures might look a little better this way. Shall we?" she asked nodding toward the canopy and Father Brian.

"Oh, yeah," Randa replied and together they walked to the front of the small gathering of well-wishers. Father Brian stood facing the guests while Randa and Denise faced each other. He addressed the company.

"This past January, two or three days after the New Year, I was visiting a wonderful woman in her home. She was desperately ill but had maintained a faithful heart and courageous outlook. On this particular day Sara Jennings wore that mischievous smile on her face that I knew meant she was about to tell me something that she thought would

271

interest or possibly shock me. She enjoyed doing it," he smiled. "That day she asked me to preside at this occasion."

Randa and Denise were incredulous. Two or three days after the New Year meant they had only recently shared their first kiss.

"Sara knew even then," Father Brian said, answering their unspoken question, "that these two were destined to be together and would be here pledging themselves to one another one day. Sara was a very clever woman." The gathering chuckled.

"Now if this was my usual service and the usual circumstances, I would begin by saying 'Dearly beloved, we are gathered here today'. Of course that's where the similarity to my usual service ends. What I would like to say is this: these two remarkable young women are here today to be joined in a union every bit as strong, loving and binding as that of your more garden variety marriage. They are joining together and creating a family by both love," he said as he indicated the guests, "as well as by blood. These family connections will serve to support them, encourage them, occasionally vex them and of course to love them."

"As members of that family, I would like you to listen with love in your hearts to Randa and Denise as they exchange their own vows." Father Brian looked to Randa and said, "Will you now speak your vow and give a symbol of your love?"

Randa smiled shyly at the vicar then turned to Denise. The love on the face of her partner was breathtaking and the nurse felt at that moment that there was no one else but the poet and herself in the whole world. Green eyes locked onto blue as Randa began to speak.

"Denise, I wanted to go first because I know my words aren't going to be able to match yours. Your words are what first captivated me and for a while I wondered if it was the magic of those words that I loved. Now I know that what I love is the heart and the beauty that showed through those words. The world will get to read the novels and poetry of D Jennings, but I will get to hold Denise in my arms, to love and be loved by her. You are my life, Denise, and I give you my promise to love you for the rest of our lives. As a symbol of that promise I give you this ring." Randa took the ring being held for them by Father Brian and slipped it on the ring finger of the poet's left hand.

"No matter what happens in our lives, no matter what hardships come our way, I will be with you and love you, always." Randa saw the misting of Denise's eyes and knew her words had been heard and understood.

Father Brian looked to the brunette. "Denise, will you now speak your vow and give a symbol of your love?"

"Randa, before I met you I didn't know what it was like to see the sunrise in another's eyes. To feel my day was complete simply because I saw your smile. Before I met you I never felt whole. My heart lacked a lover's beat and my spirit existed in shadows. You gave me love; you showed me life. You proved there was a reason to greet each new day with a smile and I want every deed I accomplish to only make you happy. I could never place a price upon the utter joy you have blessed upon me. So I offer you this, my promise and this ring." Denise placed the other silver ring on Randa's finger, kissing the hand briefly as she did so.

"You captured me... mind, body, and soul and I pledge here today that I willingly dedicate my life to loving you alone. You have left your mark upon my heart and forever and to eternity I belong to only you."

Randa wasn't sure she could hear anymore without bursting into tears of joy. She was relieved when Father Brian placed one hand lightly on each of their shoulders and said. "By the grace of a good and loving God, I pronounce these two as joined partners. Let us all wish them every happiness as they seal this union with a kiss."

Denise smiled down at Randa. "Our first as a married couple," she said as she lowered her head.

"There will never be a last." Randa vowed as their lips met. Neither could recall a sweeter kiss shared by them in the entire time they had been together. Denise's arms came around Randa and the nurse willingly melted into them. It was several moments before the cheers and applause of the small gathering invaded their senses and they broke apart reluctantly. The group was descending on them rapidly with tears and smiles showing in equal measure.

Denise looked deeply into Randa's eyes. "Promise me we'll continue this later?"

Randa smiled at the brilliant blue eyes of her spouse. "I suppose one more promise today won't hurt me. I'll be there with bells on."

"And nothing else I hope," the poet whispered then turned to accept the congratulations of their family and friends.

Life with her is never going to be predictable a delightfully shocked Randa thought. She brought her arm around Denise's waist and held on tight as the ride began.

Epilogue

The tranquil sounds of gentle waves lapping upon a shore accompanied an assortment of tropical birds soaring happily in the deep blue sky. Subtle scents of a sun-drenched beach permeated the salty air. Upon the stretch of vacant beach a large hammock hung between tall palm trees. The hum of two muttering voices drifted across the still.

Eyes closed against the gleaming sun, Denise lay with her arm wrapped around her partner. A blonde head rested snugly upon her shoulder. "So you really want to give up working on the Brightwood site?"

Randa nodded. "Yes. Just to explore my options a little more. I mean, I will always be a nurse... it's second nature to me; it's who I am. I just need to take time out for a while."

"You know..." Denise started. "I did speak to Carl about my little proposition. If you still wanted you could consider being my editor. This doesn't have to be a final decision on your part but I know you would be great at it. That is one door open to you if you wish to take it."

"I could give it a try."

DJ smiled. "And if I was to ever write a novel based in a hospital I would have the best adviser one could possibly find!"

"That you would!" Randa said with a laugh and Denise chuckled, wrapping her arms tighter around her lover.

Silence stretched between the women as minds wandered. With a deep sigh of contentment, DJ kissed

Randa's forehead and smiled to herself. "Randa?"

"Hmm?" Came the languid response.

"You know all that marriage stuff… the traditions about love, honour and obey, etcetera?"

"Mm-hmm?"

The poet grinned evilly to herself. "Well go get your woman a drink, wench!" DJ chuckled as she waited for Randa's response. She was surprised when the felt the hammock sway as Randa climbed out of the recliner. Opening her eyes she peeked through heavy lids.

"Back in a moment," Randa said as she trotted off towards their small rented beach house.

Lifting her head, Denise watched Randa in surprise and confusion. Her eyes drifted down to the nurse's bikini clad behind as she disappeared inside the wooden beach house. *I was only joking,* she thought wryly.

Hearing a peculiar sound Denise turned her head towards what she presumed was another unusual bird. The bright glare of the sun stung her eyes and she closed them again, letting her head fall back into the hammock.

It was their second day on the Caribbean Island. Denise had rented a small stretch of beach for her and Randa to enjoy for two blissful and undisturbed weeks. The exotic atmosphere and intense heat was more than she had ever experienced but the poet was adapting proficiently. Wearing little more than clothing that resembled skimpy underwear, DJ was basking in the dry heat.

Lacing her fingers through her hair, DJ's head lulled to the side sleepily. The ocean's soothing sounds relaxed her tranquil mind. From the distance she heard the crunch of footsteps making their way toward her through warm sand. Turning back to the sound, DJ was about to speak. The words died upon her lips only to be replaced by shocked spluttering.

As cold water dripped down her face, Denise rose to her elbows and looked up at Randa. "Hey!"

A wide grin and twinkling green eyes greeted her. "Wench?" Randa asked simply.

"I was joking," Denise chuckled. She wiped a hand over her face.

"I'll give you joking!" Randa brought the half full glass of water from behind her back and aimed it towards DJ.

The poet rolled out of their hammock on the opposite side of Randa. She faced her partner and held up her hands. "Don't do anything you may regret," she warned.

Randa's eyes sparkled with mirth as she flipped her wrist sending the remaining contents of the glass hurtling towards DJ. Denise gasped as cold water splashed against her body. Shaking wet hair out of her face she glared at Randa. "Oh you are in so much trouble!"

"Come and get me," Randa taunted with a smug grin as she dropped the glass to the sand.

Denise laughed. "Oh, you'll get it alright." Dancing blue eyes watched Randa take off towards the ocean. After giving her enough of a head start, DJ followed behind in hot pursuit. Long legs ate up the gap between them as Denise closed their distance. She watched Randa head into the water and followed her rapidly. "Ready or not," DJ shouted as she swept Randa off her feet and they tumbled into the surf laughing. Denise rolled over, trapping Randa underneath her long body. The lapping waves washed around them as DJ held Randa's arms over her body. "You get me wet... I'll get you wet!"

"I can think of more pleasurable ways you can get me wet!" Bucking her pelvis Randa rolled Denise onto her back. "Or vice versa." Randa reversed their positions as she pulled DJ's hands above her own head. "Who's the wench now, hmm?"

"I'll be anything you want!" Denise wiggled her eyebrows suggestively. The seawater soaked her skin as sand slipped between their bodies.

Holding herself carefully over Denise's body, Randa grinned down into cerulean eyes. "I don't know... I'm kind of happy with you being my 'wife'!" She released DJ's hands and moved back as Denise rose to a sitting position.

"I am too." Running her fingers through the damp tresses at the back of Randa's neck, Denise pulled soft lips towards her own. They kissed passionately under the

277

tropical sun as roaming hands mapped large expanses of naked flesh.

Pulling back, DJ gazed into desire filled eyes. "So… before I get sand into places that I allow only you to venture," she grinned, "Want to go and get in the shower? However much I want to run my tongue over every inch of your body, I don't want any crunchy grains getting in between my teeth!"

"Oh you can be so romantic!"

"I do my best."

Randa rose to her feet, pulling Denise with her. "Okay then… lets get in the shower, Casanova."

DJ smiled secretly as an idea formed within her mind. Earlier that day she had been on an early morning amble around the small island and found a secluded spot in the centre of the isle. The beauty of the area instantly captured her attention and she had wanted Randa to experience that too. Now she had another idea in which she and Randa could take advantage of the sights.

"What's going on in that brain of yours?"

Taking Randa's sand speckled hand DJ pulled her towards the palm trees.

"Where are we going?" the nurse asked.

"You'll see."

Venturing into the shade of the trees Denise guided Randa through the tropical foliage. The sight of fresh fruit growing on a variety of trees amazed the poet. Growing up in England she had only ever seen apples and plums. She remembered during the summer when she was a lot younger how she and Michelle would go scrumping in the neighbour's gardens for their fruit. DJ could recall many a time being chased down the street by an angry property owner.

"Where are you taking me?" Randa inquired. "I thought you wanted to get in the shower?"

"I did… but now I have other plans." Spying a familiar overgrowth of shrubbery DJ swept it to the side and led Randa into a hidden cove. The beautiful sight of ancient rocks housing a crystal clear waterfall greeted them. The echo of tumbling water falling into the pool below accompanied the exotic sounds of nature. A spectacular rainbow arched over the waterfall as the hot sun refracted the mist of moist droplets.

"What do you think?"

Randa turned as she captured the sights around her. Looking back at DJ, a wide smile lit up the nurse's face. "It's beautiful!"

"Second only to you," Denise said as she pulled Randa closer, and then with her into the pool. Its rippling surface engulfed their lower bodies as Denise pulled a willing Randa towards the waterfall. Within moments the sound of bubbling water was accompanied by heated moans of pleasure as they began a sensual exploration of one another.

Gathering the blonde within her arms Denise kissed Randa with an increasing hunger. Her hands roamed with purpose down the lithe body as she searched out the material of Randa's bikini. Gathering the white cotton within her hands she slowly and intentionally began lowering them down Randa's legs.

"Have I told you how very much I love you today?" Denise whispered hotly.

"How about you show me?"

"Oh yes…" The poet complied willingly. "Every day for the rest of our lives."

Randa held DJ close against her body. "I love you, Denise Juniper Jennings."

The poet smiled as her lips searched every inched of Randa's flesh. "Are you going to constantly tease me about that?" she mumbled good-naturedly.

"Every day for the rest of our lives," Randa replied as her body surrendered to an overflow of breathtaking pleasure.

The End

Val Brown and M J Walker

About the Authors

Val Brown is a healthcare professional with many years in Nursing. Her current job takes her to all parts of the United States.

Writing was only just a fantasy until she met a certain British poet online and started a writing partnership and friendship that has led to the publishing of this first novel.

Though she enjoys exploring and traveling, family and friends will always be her main interest.

MJ Walker lives in a small, rural village in England.

She was first published as a poet at age seventeen in the United States followed by her inclusion in many anthologies in her native country. Through her offerings on the web, MJ met and teamed up with Val Brown, an American nurse.

She is a part-time numismatist and currently studying Journalism.

Limitless D2D	Order Form	
The Amazon Queen By L M Townsend	20.00	
Define Destiny By J M Dragon	20.00	
Desert Hawk, revised By Katherine E. Standell	18.00	
Golden Gate By Erin Jennifer Mar	18.00	
The Brass Ring By Mavis Applewater	18.00	
Paradise Found By Cruise and Stoley	20.00	
Spirit Harvest By Trish Shields	15.00	
Omega's Folly By Carla Osborne	12.00	
Up The River-out of print ...While supplies last... By Sam Ruskin	15.00	
Memories Kill By S. B. Zarben	20.00	
Connecting Hearts By Val Brown and M. J. Walker	18.00	
	Total	

South Carolina residents add 5% sales tax.
Domestic shipping is $3.50 per book
Visit our website at: <u>http://limitlessd2d.net</u>
Please mail your orders with a check or money order to:

**Limitless, Dare 2 Dream Publishing
100 Pin Oak Ct.
Lexington, SC 29073**

Please make checks or money orders payable to:
Limitless Corporation

Limitless D2D	Order Form	
Shattering Rainbows By Ocean	18.00	
Kara: Lady Rogue By j. taylor Anderson	18.00	
Mysti: Mistress of Dreams By Sam Ruskin	18.00	
Indiscretions By Cruise	18.00	
A Thousand Shades of Feeling By Carolyn McBride	16.00	
The Amazon Nation **By Carla Osborne**	20.00	
Poetry from the Featherbed By pinfeather	18.00	
Encounters, Book I By Anne Azel	22.00	
Encounters, Book II By Anne Azel	25.00	
The Fellowship By K. Darblyne	18.00	
Deadly Rumors By Jeanne Foguth	20.00	
	Total	

South Carolina residents add 5% sales tax.
Domestic shipping is $3.50 per book
Visit our website at: http://limitlessd2d.net
Please mail your orders with a check or money order to:

Limitless, Dare 2 Dream Publishing
100 Pin Oak Ct.
Lexington, SC 29073

Please make checks or money orders payable to:
Limitless Corporation

Limitless D2D		Order Form	
Cat on the Couch By Cathy L. Parker	16.00		
Commitments By Cruise	18.00		
Up The River, Revised By Sam Ruskin	18.00		
Return of the Warrior By Katherine E. Standell	18.00		
Haunting Shadows By J M Dragon	18.00		
A Saving Solace By D S Bauden	18.00		
Passion's Phrases By Charlsie Todd	15.00		
Perhaps by Chance By K. Stoley	18.00		
Port of Call By K. Stoley	18.00		
PWP: Plot, What Plot? By Mavis Applewater	18.00		
Queen's Lane By I. Christie/J A Bard	18.00		
	Total		

South Carolina residents add 5% sales tax.
Domestic shipping is $3.50 per book
Visit our website at: http://limitlessd2d.net
Please mail your orders with a check or money order to:

Limitless, Dare 2 Dream Publishing
100 Pin Oak Ct.
Lexington, SC 29073

Please make checks or money orders payable to:
Limitless Corporation